Praise for

The Hatbox Letters

"One of the most appealing novels to be published in Canada in the last
decade. . . . Beautifully written and emotionally wise, this is a debut novel
with a difference. Its melding of past and present in the life of its protago-
nist is so well woven it will prove a boon to readers with a taste for fiction
and non-fiction alike. . . . Rich, elegiac and full of resonance, [Powning's]
novel is more than impressive. It is a winner."
—*The London Free Press*

"Blessed with a fabulous eye for detail. . . [Powning] makes Kate's garden
a visual treat. . . . The imagery is evocative and clear, and the feelings of
love and loss are transmitted effectively and elegantly. *The Hatbox Letters*
conveys a sense of wonder and wisdom."
—*The Vancouver Sun*

"Powning has an unerring sense of pacing and balance. . . . She can wrest
mesmerizing passages from scenes other writers might gloss over."
—*Edmonton Journal*

"*The Hatbox Letters* will appeal to anyone who enjoyed the charming
correspondence in Richard B. Wright's recent literary bestseller *Clara
Callan*. . . . The narrative of *The Hatbox Letters* is as warm and vivid as
actually sitting next to the wood stove of Kate's Maritime kitchen.
Powning also has a knack for imagery that drops the reader firmly into
the musty comfort of a Connecticut summer home in the early part of
the twentieth century. Other authors bring us close to historical periods;
Powning puts us there."
—*Winnipeg Free Press*

"Filled with beautiful descriptions of the natural world, the seasons and
the journey towards acceptance and a certain peace of mind, Powning's
book is a fascinating trip through generations of a family."
—*The Toronto Sun*

BETH POWNING

The Hatbox Letters

A NOVEL

VINTAGE CANADA

VINTAGE CANADA EDITION, 2005

Copyright © 2004 Powning Designs Ltd.

Published in Canada by Vintage Canada, a division of Random House of Canada Limited, Toronto. Originally published in hardcover in Canada by Alfred A. Knopf Canada, a division of Random House of Canada Limited, Toronto, in 2004. Distributed by Random House of Canada Limited, Toronto.

Vintage Canada and colophon are registered trademarks of Random House of Canada Limited.

www.randomhouse.ca

Library and Archives Canada Cataloguing in Publication

Powning, Beth
The hatbox letters / Beth Powning.

ISBN 0-676-97640-9

I. Title.

PS8631.O86H38 2005   C813'.6   C2004-906977-2

Text design: CS Richardson

Printed and bound in Canada

4 6 8 9 7 5 3

To

my grandparents,

Roger Wolcott Davis (1890–1959)
and
Helen Merriam Davis (1885–1969)

and to Peter

with love

Though lovers be lost love shall not;
And death shall have no dominion.

Dylan Thomas

Contents

PART ONE   1. Kate   1
2. Sandpipers   13
3. Rain   30

PART TWO   4. Asters and Woodsmoke   53
5. Measles   89
6. Harvest   101

PART THREE   7. Love Letters   117
8. The Blizzard   140
9. Muskrat Trail   176
10. The Isolation Ward   190
11. Broken Glass   207
12. Elizabeth Park   215
13. A Windfall Apple   233

PART FOUR   14. Black Ice   255
15. Sally's Café   271
16. Tulips   284
17. Quaco Head   301
18. Dovetail Joints   315

PART FIVE   19. Barberry Pie   325
20. Summer Wind   340

Part One

1. Kate

KATE LEANS IN THE DOORWAY OF THE LIVING ROOM, arms crossed, the sleeves of a cotton sweater shoved to her elbows. Her forearms are sinewy—brown, dry-skinned, thorn-scratched. She wears two silver bracelets and a thick gold wedding band. Some women, she realizes, remove their rings.

In the corner is a stack of nine antique hatboxes. She has not touched them since they were set down a week ago, delivered by her sister, who drove them up from Hartford. They are oval or round, some tied with string, some decorated with maroon-and-silver stripes, others printed with gothic landscapes—willows, mountains, ruined castles. Their smell has begun to permeate the room even though the windows are open. It is the smell of her grandparents' attic, a smell she has not forgotten but thought had vanished, like the past itself. That it has not and is still here, this aroma of horsehair and leather, of apples and musty quilts, of old dresses and satin ribbons—that this smell still exists here in this Canadian river valley, six hundred miles north of her grandparents' house, is disquieting. It awakens a feeling in Kate that she remembers from childhood, composed of odd emotional strands: love, sorrow, pain, contentment.

The arrival of the hatboxes is untimely, since disposses-sion, like grief, is an act of which Kate has had her fill since Tom's death a year and three months ago, from a heart attack at age fifty-two. She's hauled garbage bags of clothes, like lumpy corpses, down to the washing machine, unable to give away anything that might bear his painty, sawdusty smell. Sorting through the clothes, she was relieved whenever she came across T-shirts like Swiss cheese or underpants held by threads to waistbands no longer elastic. Choices made easy: *Okay, throw this away.* No one in her family has wanted to face making such decisions about the papers in these hatboxes. They have been lugged from place to place, from barn to base-ment to closet, ever since the big house in whose attic they'd accumulated for five generations was sold.

She goes into the living room and squats by the boxes. Their papered cardboard is dry as old plaster. How strange, she thinks, that they are here, now. And she finds herself wishing they could have remained forever under the attic's cobwebbed window, their contents spilled, letters stuffed by children's hands back into envelopes embroidered by the teeth of mice. Like leaves in a mulch pile. Forgotten, skeletal, slowly reverting to dirt. So it might have been if the house had not been sold, if time had not stalked on relentless legs, like a heron, and bent its long neck.

She slides her fingers over a lid, remembering the excite-ment she and her cousins had felt about these boxes and the disappointment of finding only papers whose half-read sen-tences were like windborne music or distant surf, faint hints of a larger sound. The box is so desiccated that its lid is loose and lifts easily, releasing the concentrated mustiness within, so familiar that tears spring to Kate's eyes. It takes her to the closets, bedrooms, pantries and cupboards of her grandparents' enormous, white-clapboarded house on the tree-lined street of the village where Kate grew up. She and her sister could leave their own home, walk past the tiny general store, with its wooden porch and post office, past the library and the church, and be on Shepton's lawn in ten minutes. Shepton House had been named by her great-grandmother for the English town where some branch of the family originated. *Shepton,* they called the place after a while, dropping the pretentious "House." The word, spoken and accompanied by memory, is what a spell might be to a shaman: an evocation, a tumult of associations. She stirs the papers. Like the snow-flattened leaves of early spring, they are brown and soft, overlapping, their corners fanned. Some are in bundles, tied with faded cotton string. Most lie in a dismaying confusion. Kate pauses, looks out the window. River light quivers in trees at the bottom of her lawn. She is still squatting, irresolute. *Why did I agree to take on this responsibility? Now—of all times.*

She slips into a sitting position, crosses her legs. The house is so quiet. No one will be coming to visit until Thanksgiving. Her daughter, Christy, is in Halifax, her son, Liam, in Ireland. She listens to the sound of an empty house, thinking, *Am I still a wife?* She sees her future not the way it is now but the way it was supposed to be; this, unlike the bald fact of Tom's death, is a loss she can't share, a grief she can't reveal. She is allowed to mourn the past, Tom as he was, the sound of his voice, the body that once cradled hers; but the future that was theirs—its loss has become like a new death, the death of someone no one else knows. A hidden corpse. It ebbs away, her memory of how it felt to slide her hand into the back pocket of Tom's shorts, to relate a rambling dream and not care whether he listened, to casually wipe mustard from his chin. This loss of intimacy is the hardest, for with it goes her sense of self. She cannot bear to be with long-married couples: she's watched a husband lift a strand of windblown hair from his wife's mouth, has seen a wife peel a hard-boiled egg and hand it to her husband. It is dangerous, as well, to be in places—dinner parties, picnics—where conversational lures may attract memories, or feelings. She feels stripped of some sleek texture, as if she has lost her favourite silk scarf, orange-pink and luminous as sun-filled tulips, that carried in its folds the wife she once was, the wife she would still be.

She leans forward and rummages in the hatbox, knowing that she is being hooked by its sweet smell. She tips reading glasses from her head, settles them on her nose, unfolds a paper and presses it to her face. She breathes deeply. *What is it?* Lately she finds herself in a peculiar state, slowed, as if float-ing without impulsion, in which she examines her own feel-ings. There's a familiar, disturbing stab in her heart that she remembers from when, as a child, she laid her head on Shepton's prickly pillows, or lifted the lids of stoneware crocks or opened the games cupboard under the stairs. It's a small ache, a presage of grief, evoked by the distilled smell of age. It's a reminder, she thinks, of joy's sorrow-edge. Of how every moment tilts on the brink of its own decline. There's some-thing else, though. Responsibility to the past. And flight from its demands. The feelings she's come to recognize, holding in her hand, say, a small pin that Tom was once given at a cere-mony in Ottawa "for service to the arts." How, she chastises herself, during her process of dispossession, could she think of parting with this piece of silver? Doesn't she have the respon-sibility of memorializing Tom?

Digging through the soft papers, her fingers encounter something thick, stiff, unyielding. She feels the thrill of discovery, slides it loose. It's a large black-and-white studio portrait of a family. She sits back, touched. People, with their expressive eyes—it's as if she's rescued them. She turns the picture over. On the back, someone has written, in pencil:

"On the occasion of Ellen's eighth birthday." She pushes her-self to her feet, lifts the hatbox and sets it on Tom's drawing table. She puts the photograph on the table and studies it. Father, mother and four children. The oldest child is a girl. There are two boys in knickerbockers, and on the mother's lap sits a younger child with corkscrew curls. She passes her hand over the portrait the way she has caressed, with a finger, Tom's handwriting. Her grandfather must be the older of the two boys. *This is my grandfather. Here are his parents, his brother and sisters.*

She slides into the chair at the oak table, which is pushed against a window overlooking the porch and the river. In its sliding drawer are Tom's Conté crayons, charcoals, oil sticks. Next to the table, on the lower shelves of a built-in bookcase, are Tom's working journals, which Kate has not touched since the day of his death. She has not sat at this table, either. This was Tom's place, and she has kept it dusted but uncluttered, like a shrine. Yet here she sits. It is the first thing she has done since his death that seems more than a divestment. It is a willed action that blunders clumsily but definitely against the obdurate past. She lays her hands on the light-paled wood and spreads her fingers, thinking that she does not inhabit Tom's spirit as she sits in his chair, nor does her mind glance towards his reaction. He did not know of the existence of these papers, never saw these hatboxes. Perusing her family's past, she is leaning towards a future he will not share.

She scoops a handful of papers from the box and shuffles through them, peering at the headings of bills and receipts. They are dated 1902, and are addressed to Mr. Charles Thomas, Roselawn Street, Hartford, Connecticut. *Charles Thomas. Must be Grampa Giles' father. My great-grandfather.* They must have been comfortably well off, she thinks. Here are receipts from a livery stable, indicating that they didn't own a horse and carriage, yet she finds receipts for dancing and music lessons, for the Philharmonic and *Harper's Magazine,* for Italian sherry, French brandy, ale, rum, rye, for white roses and chrysanthemums bought by the dozen. The faded handwriting is elaborate, written with broad-nibbed ink pens. The invoices are decorated with etchings: a cow in grass beneath the heading "C.J. Anderson, Pure Milk," and beside "Brown, Thompson and Co., Dry Goods," a brick building towering over tiny trolley cars and women in long skirts. There are receipts for a Barzoni violin (twenty-five dollars); for portrait photographs, with a list of names.

She looks from the list to the photograph, matching names to faces. *Charles and Lilian, the parents. Children: Katherine, the oldest daughter, with hair piled like a Gibson girl; Giles (my grandfather) behind his father's chair; Daniel, the younger son, one hand on his little sister's shoulder; and Ellen, the birthday child, in a middy blouse, on her mother's lap.*

Her fingers tiptoe through the papers, seeking more photographs. She pauses over a small brown pamphlet—"Intermedial penmanship, Giles Thomas." *This was Grampa Giles!* Eight lines per page, written in a ten-year-old's careful cursive, with blotches: "Two tarts too sweet to eat"; "Join the joiner's plane"; "Some swans new moon." She digs deeper, caught by a peculiar heading, scraps of paper with pencilled scrawls, one-cent postcards. *Ah.* She lifts out another photograph. Her great-grandparents—Charles and Lilian. She places this picture next to the other. They are older. The man's face is marked by disappointment. His eyes, Kate thinks, stare out at a bleak prospect. Lilian is not so much despairing as resigned. Kate studies the collar of her great-grandmother's dress. It is made of lace, is as wide as her shoulders and extends to her ample bosom, framing a locket that lies at the precise centre of her chest. Kate touches it, wondering whose picture it contains.

She half-turns on her chair and looks at the hatboxes in the corner. Maybe, she thinks, this is not a bad time for them to have arrived in her life. *I could easily spend the entire day rummaging through them.*

No, remember what you decided.

Lying in bed this morning, watching sunlight travel over the plaster walls, hearing the garbling honk of south-bound geese, she'd decided to go down to the Bay of Fundy. Her friend Caroline had invited her to go with a group of friends, and she had said no. This morning, though, she'd determined to go anyway, by herself, and not to the beach where her friends would be gathering. She's been reminding herself that she has to make an effort to get out of her house, exercise, go places. She often finds herself sitting with a book in her lap, staring out the window, lost in memory. Aloneness has become a place of safety and confinement, like a windowless room that is both sanctuary and cell. She's aware of its attraction but knows that it gives her no nourishment.

She turns back to the desk, puts the photograph of her great-grandparents back into the hatbox, props the portrait of the family against the lamp. She stands, stretches and goes into the kitchen. Its ceiling is embossed tin, cream-coloured. The north window overlooks the river, and next to it is a screen door that opens onto the porch. There's a wood stove, and the floor is covered with black and red linoleum tiles, some of them buckled and cracked. There's an unfinished wood table with spool legs, a rocking chair, wooden cupboards painted green. Kate uses the wood stove even though there is a small electric range in the corner by the sink; she keeps the windows open until frost, loving the way wind moves through the room, stirring the pull chain of the overhead light, sighing through the screen door.

She should get ready to go. *Leave now, or later?* Nothing is imperative. Time is flaccid. *Tea, a Thermos of tea. Sandwich. Binoculars, all that beach stuff.*

She plugs in the kettle, takes a metal tea caddy from the cupboard. It was her granny's. At fifty-one, Kate is pleased to see that she is beginning to resemble her grandmother, whose thinness, narrow nose and anxious eyebrows she has inherited, although Kate is neither humble nor tiny. Rather, she is tall, and her pleasant expression has become strained, her direct gaze intimidating. In groups, she's silent, diffident when probed for opinions. Her smile is tentative, fleeting.

One side of the tea caddy is dented, and the lid, as a consequence, has to be pried. Kate feels defensive as she wrenches it open and then realizes that Tom's irritation about this caddy still lingers and affects the way she takes it down, the way she half-turns as if shielding herself and it from criticism. She wonders if relinquishing this sense of Tom's watching—it has to happen—will bring her freedom or emptiness. Lately, the two seem the same.

From the gauze bags rises the dark spice of tannin and tea dust. Memory rises . . . *mulch pile, bone-dry folded flags, beehive, wood crumble.* . . . She lifts a teabag to her nose, watching a wasp trailing a broken wing, and realizes suddenly that this cluster of memories has been drifting in her mind ever since she awakened, and is the remnant of a dream. She stares sightlessly out the kitchen window at the glinting river water, trying to remember it. *Oh yes.* Shepton had become a house with two sides. One was filled with clear light. But the other was dark and abandoned, enormous, with room upon room the colour of dust, wallpaper curling from plaster, stairs fragile as papier mâché.

She has been dreaming of her grandparents' house ever since the arrival of the hatboxes, whose odour must be rising up the stairwell, creeping into her bedroom. This is one of those dreams, she thinks, that snags in the mind and becomes as real as memory, so that eventually you're not sure whether it really happened. She runs it by again, trying to dispel its effect, yet she feels as if she's incurred a loss. She feels the unspecific longing of—*what does it remind me of?* Adolescence. When nothing seems to have been lost, and yet one is filled with grief. When one has no idea that one is in mourning for childhood itself.

She pours water into a teapot, stirs the teabags, lifts a Thermos down from the cupboard. She's imagining the village street of her childhood. She sees a child's view of houses, large as ocean liners, tipping back against the wondrous sky. Shepton was one of them. It had a porch all along the front and a row of trees so enormous she didn't even notice the second storey. Windows, curtains, seen through leaves. Stone steps, so wide she took three or four steps to cross each one, her shoes slippery. Someone's hand, someone high over- head. Step up. Step up. Grampa Giles' hands. If she reached both of hers up at the same time, her dress rose. Sunday, and the church bell was ringing. There they were, walking across the lawn going to church. Grass like green threads sprouted in the damp soil beneath the forsythia bushes. They passed the steps of the chapel where Kate would go to kindergarten and during naptime lie on her back under the piano and pretend she was the person who had carved its legs. And the church bent back against the sky, white clapboards and clear win- dowpanes. Steeple, a white cloud passing behind it. Now it was Granny's hand that held hers. Granny wore red shoes. Kate leaned to touch one with her finger, and Granny stopped walking and peered down too, pivoting her toes so they were lined up like two red plums.

Kate wants to tell these memories to Tom. Her heart feels swollen with the number of things stored up to tell him. On mornings like this, pinioned between late summer and early fall, the air tinged with coolness, they would sit on the porch in wooden rocking chairs wearing baggy sweaters or fleece vests. Kate with one knee bent, heel propped on the chair's rung. Maybe writing a letter to her parents, her pen moving rapidly, sporadically. Tom drawing in his sketchbook with the black, pebbly cover. Short sideways strokes of his pencil. Emphatic, then pausing, considering, like the lingering stillness after a question. Unlike the dream, which she has deliberately summoned, this vision of a late summer's morning in the cool of the front porch—goldenrod, fresh-cut grass—flashes baldly, like lightning, and makes her heart twist. How can it be gone? How can this life possibly be gone? The past stands so close, beckoning her, luring her with its shallow beauty, and she feels both tempted and enraged. She hears the thrum of a motorboat. She sees bits of it through the trees, white, black, a flag, as it powers downriver. She hears the expiring slap of its wash. *He's gone.* She makes herself think this, as she does many times every day. *Here you are, Kate, a widow.* An eddy of air comes over the grass, stirs the light chain, carries the sharp scent of chrysanthemums. She listens to the crickets, thinks how they make two sounds at once, a long shrilling from which break separate voices that rise and fall in a pulse both irregular and rhythmic. Summer's requiem.

Decisions have become more difficult to make since she's been alone. She needs to be firm with herself. *I'm going to go to Mary's Point, see if the sandpipers are still there. I need to hear the sound of waves. Stare into a boundless shining sky. No, I don't want to go with anyone else.* She answers another voice in her head that queries her choice. *Because I'm going to visit Tom's cliff, sit with my back pressed against it. See if he's there. Pick out a gull and pretend it's him, as I did when the kids and I flung his ashes off the cliff.* She remembers how a gull swooped near, dipped its wing into the air's muscle, reached through Tom's glittering dust and carried him out to sea.

She goes upstairs, makes her bed, collects a wool sweater, wool socks, the bird book from the back of the toilet. As she comes back down the stairs, she stops and looks at the hatboxes piled between the couch and the fireplace. She thinks again about what it is that worries her about exploring their contents. The letters and papers might, her parents told her, go back as far as 1797, when her great-great-great-grandmother arrived at the newly built house with her husband, carrying garden seeds in twists of paper. If she learns the real history of Shepton, will her memory of it be warped, her own place in its history diminished, her love for it compromised?

In the kitchen, she opens the refrigerator, takes out cheese and mustard, makes a sandwich. "Okay," she murmurs. "Do I have—book, binoculars, Thermos?" She stands, considering, the strap of a backpack slung over one shoulder. No one could ever tell her what colour her eyes were. "Hazel," her grampa would say. "Like mine." Neither green nor grey nor blue, their colour is nondescript, like the mouse-brown hair of her childhood that would neither curl nor hold barrettes. Her skin is weathered, and tiny stiff brooms etch the corners of her eyes. A couple of months after Tom's death, on the day of her fiftieth birthday, spent alone, she cut her hair. It's like a cap, hangs straight across her forehead, cups the back of her head. Her pianist fingers are strong, long—slightly longer than Tom's—with baggy knuckles.

She goes to the back door. The garden is shining. Every leaf holds a spear or prism or cup of light. Shadows double the petals of giant zinnias. Yellow leaves spiral down from the apple tree, twirling on the air like tiny coracles. There is a sense of repose in the persistence of flowers that continue to form buds, to hold soft blooms up to the ripening sun:

coneflowers, phlox, shrub roses. She steps onto the porch, turns the key in the lock. The air smells of woodsmoke and ripe apples. She walks down the path, remembering the chaos of beach trips with children. *Christy, not now, come on honey. Liam, did you remember the kite?* And she is thinking how odd it is that in her waking mind the one place in her life that seemed perfect, Shepton, stays that way; yet in her sleep it has two sides, one bright, one dark—one perfect, one imperfect. And in her dream it is the dark side, the place she never knew, that she longs to visit.

2. Sandpipers

THE ROAD TO MARY'S POINT RUNS THROUGH RAGGED coastal country. Kate catches glimpses of the sea, but for the most part she passes spindly spruce trees and abandoned farms whose pastures sprout goldenrod and juniper. The fireweed has begun to lose its lower petals; the season advances up the tall stalks, and the pointed pink tips are no longer part of a luxuriance but seem forlorn reminders, like crumbs on a cake plate. The light, however, is rich. Shadows are intense, and bungalows, barns, marsh grasses, asters seem sharp, significant, like objects seen through binoculars.

It's early afternoon by the time Kate arrives. She pulls her car into dusty grass at the side of the dirt road. She shoulders her backpack, strides past other parked cars and turns up a gravelled walk, past a small interpretive centre that has appeared since she and Tom first learned about the annual migration. She follows a narrow path that winds beneath alders, stepping aside for strangers who acknowledge her with brief smiles, trailing past with their smells of aftershave, deodorant, perfume, sunscreen; she remembers how she and Tom had to remind themselves that they, too, were trespassers in the birds' world, even though they'd discovered this event when there was no path here and hardly anyone but themselves sat on the beach, elbows bracing binoculars.

She comes out from the damp coolness of the alder canopy. She stands on the sand, absorbing the sensation of being in this beloved place without Tom. She wants to call his attention to the delightful feeling of slippery sand beneath her hiking boots; point out the fact that the tide has just turned and is on its way out; observe to him how, far off, to the left and right of the wide bay, red cliffs flash as if sending messages over the light-sheened sea.

She walks slowly towards a row of driftwood logs lined with birdwatchers, binoculars pressed to their eyes. The annual sandpiper migration has become as much a part of New Brunswick's summer ritual as strawberry suppers, Canada Day fireworks. Three posts hold small signs: "Do not advance beyond this point." Just beyond are the semi-palmated sandpipers, so close that Kate can see the knobby hinges of their frail legs, their splayed claws, the gleam of their eyes. There are perhaps fifty thousand of them, massed for safety. They roost on one leg, heads tucked over shoulders. Later, when the tide is out, they will disperse across the vast flats, stabbing the mud with their long beaks, fattening on Fundy mud shrimp, preparing for their journey to Suriname. At first it is not apparent that there are thousands of individual birds. It is like the pictures Kate has seen of worshippers bent to prayer before the Kaaba in the court of the Great Mosque at Mecca. The birds, like the men, are without distinction, fitting as smoothly as cobblestones into a pattern.

She finds a space on a sun-warmed and splintery log. People shift to accommodate her. She glances sideways, hoping she won't know anyone. Wind scuds across the bay, sighs in the spruce boughs, lifts tiny feathers on the birds' heads. Sand furls along the rim of a dune. She can hear the steady running of a freshwater creek that winds from a salt marsh, cutting a channel that makes the birds' roosting ground a promontory. Dogs pant patiently, restrained on leashes, curled close to their owners. She notices a familiar-looking man in a canvas hat whose hand rests on the binoculars that hang around his neck but who seems to have lost interest in the birds, although his eyes follow them. Down the beach, well away from the signs, sea grass is bright green against the slick, red mud, and two little girls turn cartwheels.

A shadow passes. Binoculars swoop upwards, someone points. The birds rise with a muted thunder, their wings serrate the light. For an instant, a peregrine falcon zigzags through the flock. Then it drops from the belly of the rising bird-cloud. In its talons is a sandpiper, crumpled like a ball of paper. People stand, point. Cry out. It is hard to decide which drama to observe, the escape of the falcon with its prey or the flock's display as the birds rush seaward like a single entity, a ballooning flame that rises and falls, expands and implodes, one instant silver and the next black. The flock speeds back towards the beach, passes close to the watchers, makes a dazzling turn, fast as thought. Then, with a diminishing roar, the birds waver, their legs drop, stretch. They touch down. They fluff their feathers. Kate, watching through her binoculars, observes that they pluck at their breasts the way humans pull coats up around necks after a shock. *Trying to put ourselves back as we were.*

After a while Kate stands slowly, trying not to make a sound. She withdraws into herself as she walks past the birds so she will not startle them. She passes the cartwheeling little girls, who look at her blankly without registering her presence. "Watch, Megan!" the red-haired one says, spreading her arms and beginning to run, her knees lifting high. She tilts towards the sand, palms outward. Barrettes are slipping, ponytails come loose. Kate slides her eyes at the girls, pinching her lips in a rueful smile. She herself was a champion cartwheeler, exasperating her sister. She is remembering what it was like to live inside a body and be unaware of its presence. She remembers the lovely stretch from arm to belly when she hung from the maple tree in their front yard, the unforgiving scrape of bark across palm, the stemmy earth smell of leaf piles. Falling, rolling, kicking. She thinks of belly-sleeping. Of waking from night's deep oblivion as if having been tossed in surf and finding oneself on warm sand. Now, in middle age, she begins to feel stiff, although once stretched, which she does frequently and unselfconsciously, like a ritual—clasping her hands, palms outward, swinging her arms over her head—she walks athletically, long-legged.

She passes the cliffs that the kids referred to as "Dad's." As she stops and tips her head, gazing up, she realizes that her world is strewn with objects that are Tom's; she trips over them, as if they're out of place. They're things that delighted, bemused, outraged him. A particular group of trees on a hillside, just past the abandoned cheese factory: serviceberry, cherry and wild apple. In May they seemed to float amidst the spruces, pink-veined petals dancing. Or the old barn in Millstream with two doors side by side, one blue, one red, the colours barely visible, soft as lichen. Permanent wooden signs on the mowed lawns of white houses with no flower gardens: Christ Died for Your Sins. The bank that one day had been denuded of its violets and forget-me-nots, "decorated" (said Tom, fingers poised) with grey gravel and three statuary deer. He would study them, eyes narrowed as if gauging life's ironies. The golden-grassed, red-bushed marsh in October. The cliffs. The streak of sliding water over planes of red rock. These rocks seemed like beings, he would say, geomorphic embodiments of time, tablets inscribed by the earth's ancient shudder. Here they were, these things, without him. Forty feet up, the cliffs jut outward, their slabs sharp-edged, slanting fissures tinted by tiny blue asters. Here, on the beach, the rocks are wave-scoured, and she runs her hand along an arch smooth as a dog's brow. The sun is not yet low enough to form the profound shadows that Tom loved.

She finds a sun-baked hollow. She sits, slides off her backpack, bends to unlace her boots. Suddenly a feeling sweeps over her; she leaves her boot half-laced and sits upright with a sharp breath. Her heart, for an instant, is dragged downwards, blood thickens. Memories surface so unexpectedly. She recalls that the day before Tom died, they'd gone down to Cape Enrage so he could photograph sea cliffs. It was low tide, and they had walked on the water-firmed sand beneath the cliffs, where eons were tipped sideways; where time was buckled, fluted, compressed. "Look at this, *look* at this," he had said, gripping the air with both hands, holding his passion like something slippery. That was the day they'd challenged each other to find one perfect stone. Hers sits on her bedside table. It's shaped like a goose egg, veined with blood-red lines like Tibetan prayer flags. And then they had sat on the cape's grassy promontory, gazing across the bay at the bulk of Nova Scotia. The wind had been so strong she had burrowed against him, and he had been pleased and thrown an arm around her shoulders, squeezed.

How amazing, she thinks, that this memory should return only now. She has been inhabiting a mental landscape where every image, like a road cursed with evil charms, leads her not outward into possibility but always back to a single day: to all the minutes of that morning just before Tom thought to drop his cigarette into the ashtray even as he bent forward with an expression of frantic shock. She finds herself reliving the sound of his breathing on that morning, since she was the first to wake. And hearing the blue jays, urgent, as if spearing summer with their cries. Over and over again, she sees him stooping, opening the screen door for the marmalade cat and leaning to scratch its head. She remembers the note he was scrawling as he drank his coffee: "Call Christy re books." She sees herself picking it up when she returned from the hospital, staring at it uncomprehendingly. What books?

They were such pals, Tom and his daughter. Christy was studying physiotherapy and encouraged him to take up running so she could practise plantar fascia taping. "Nope, no running for me," he said, patting his cigarettes in the pocket of his denim shirt and looking out at the river with an insulated expression. His eyebrows were black, his eyes deep-set, monkey-brown. He was a few inches shorter than Kate, heavy-jawed and restless. "I canoe, sweetie," he told Christy. "My shoulders will go before long. You can work on them." He'd leant over his match and come up grinning.

Kate frowns, staring out to sea. The back of her hand is pressed to her forehead, fingers limp.

"I love you, Daddy," Christy had said just before she went out the door, the last time she saw her father. She'd sounded patient, making this sentence so simple that its poignancy was evident. A red scarf held back her curly hair, she wore a backpack on her shoulders, had freckles like those Kate had had as a girl. And Tom, who could never say "I love you," had caught her to him in a hug.

Liam? When was Tom's last conversation with his son? Liam, two years older than Christy, had quit art school in the fall of that year and flown to Ireland, where he'd found work as a labourer on a construction crew. What would Tom and Liam have talked of? Money and responsibility, Kate imagines, underscored by Tom's mounting irritation over what he perceived as his son's inability to stay focused. *Not love.*

Stop it. He's not here. Look at what's around you.

The receding tide makes a soft wash. A rising slur, a sigh. A few sandpipers have strayed. She takes a deep breath, drops her hand from her brow and stares at them. The falcon, presumably, still hunts. The little birds take a few running steps and then stop to plunge their long beaks into the mud. Kate lifts her binoculars and watches one bird until she feels the pull of the south, sees only wind sweeping the grasses forward and the spark of light on pebble. She takes another breath and resumes unlacing her boot. Bare feet, toes gripping sand.

And last night's dream about Shepton, which she will never tell to her husband, returns.

She leans against rock, crosses her legs at the ankles. She sees again the decaying side of her grandparents' house; how in the dream it was actually attached to the real house but was far larger. *Why,* her dream self had wondered, *did I never explore this part of the house?* She tastes the dream's mixture of illumination and despair. Finding something when it is too late. The dream is displaced by the real memory of her grandparents' apple-scented home, and she realizes she is smiling. She wonders what her face looks like. Is it gentle, sad, loving? No one will lean forward and ask her what she is thinking. She pulls sand with her fingertips as if massaging a scalp. Her eyes become vacant, sightless, as she attempts to recover this feeling of her childhood. Instead, she is gripped by its opposite: a sense of isolation heightened by anger. *Why am I alone on this beach at the age of fifty-one, for God's sake?* She has no place of refuge. She can drive home to her kitchen, her rocking chair and red porcelain teacup, the white goose-down quilt on her four-poster bed and the sound of water slapping in the reeds, but she will not be gathered by the house, she will not be snug within it. She will sense, rather, its skeleton, the shape of a place without illusion, like November trees.

Those hatboxes. They are making me dream of Shepton.

Thoughts of Tom are overlaid by an image of her grandparents, Grampa Giles lowering himself next to Granny on
the porch. There they sit, so quietly, as the sun sets. And the
house behind them. Kate lifts her binoculars. The rock is
warm against her back, but cool wind sifts through the waf-
fled weave of her cotton sweater, and she knows that soon she
will have to resume walking. She pauses before pressing her
eyes to the binoculars. *World upon world.* The receding tide
reveals periwinkle colonies, tiny snails lining rock crevasses;
she could lift bladderwrack from its holdfast and find, in the
damp darkness, a world of barnacles, dog whelks, Irish moss.
The water of tide pools, cupped in red rock, shimmers with
reflected clouds. Later she will crouch, as she and Tom
crouched, and will be plagued by observations she cannot
share. *Look, this barnacle is sending out its feathers. See the red
starfish?* But now she lifts the binoculars and follows one of
the strayed sandpipers. It sprints forward in sudden running
starts, as if windblown. It bends its head, makes quick stabs
at the mud. Its feet leave a trail of linked stars. She aches for
its self-absorption, its seeming carelessness, its solitary excur-
sion on the shining mud flat, even as its flock—she swings
her binoculars upwards—rises; she can hear the wing-
thunder from here.

Scanning the sky, she tries to think of a time and place
since Tom's death when she felt freed from the bony angularity
of her solitude. As if scrabbling through a box of photographs, she deliberately conjures images of her present life:
the porch at sunset, poplar leaves like silver coins; the clanking moorings of river boats; a drift of apple blossom over
dew-darkened violet leaves; her daughter's voice on the
telephone, too warm, hiding unhappiness; a friend's living
room, where anxious faces seek her eyes; January branches
seen through the kitchen window, feathered with sun-struck

frost rime. Their bed. Her mind betrays her. Their bed. Not yet *her* bed. She and Tom, snug in bed within the house that bears their history.

She does not want this vision but can't resist it. It sweeps over her. It is of both of them beneath their summer quilt, listening to the wide-throated roar of river rain; it is also of evening in a New England village, when she gets up from the porch where she's sitting with her grandparents and pushes open the warped screen door, goes into the vestibule, where a leather quiver hangs, filled with arrows whose feathers are half gone, and steps into the living room. It is the same sensation as when, seeking sugar cookies—large, vanilla-flavoured, toasty-brown—she steps into a house that to a child is a place with neither precedent nor foreboding, whose horsehair couch and mahogany sideboard, whose ticking clocks and narrow hallways, whose smell of dry wood and old quilts is so much a part of the present, of the night of throbbing frogs, that walking in its rooms is as simple as crouching within the grasses of a hayfield. On the porch, Granny and Grampa Giles wait for her. Granny's knitting is in its basket, her hands are folded in her lap. Grampa Giles sits upright, one arm along the back of the swinging couch. Kate knows, somehow, that there is nothing in their minds but her return.

She leans forward and laces her boots. It's time to move. The sun slides over the zenith. She has her food and Thermos of tea, but will walk for a while and seek a more sheltered spot. It is as much her mind she wishes to leave as this warm rock and this particular view. Tom, sliding into the realm occupied by her grandparents, makes her feel like the sandpipers that have strayed. Besides, the man wearing the canvas hat has appeared around a point of rock, and she wishes to escape his attention.

Kate drives slowly to the dead end of her street, where the pavement devolves into a gravelly turnaround next to the old carriage shed that is her garage. She is always pleased to see their beloved house, set so far back from the street that only intriguing bits of it are visible through the leaves of giant maples. It's a Victorian house, grey with red trim, the corners of its porches overhung by century-old lilacs, the shingles on its upper storey shaped like fish scales. It faces the river, and from the rooms of her house, Kate can hear boat traffic: the slap of sails, the throaty chugging of motorboats.

She left the garage doors open, and she drives in, turns off the engine, gathers her possessions. She hears the drone of a lawnmower, a sound that she loves and Tom hated. *Corey's here.* She opens the gate of a vine-covered pergola and steps onto a stone path. The path leads past an apple tree and winds across the lawn, heading towards the side porch. To her left, a terraced lawn rises from the back of the house, each side bordered by wide, curving beds of old-fashioned perennials—iris, campanula, peonies, foxgloves. A dense hedge of lilacs conceals a secret garden, where tulips, in spring, float like miniature balloons anchored over a sea of forget-me-nots. Stone steps lead to a vegetable garden at the top, cloistered within a fence of woven willow saplings. Up there, too, is Tom's studio.

She stops beside the apple tree. She can't see the boy; he must have gone around to the far side of the house, where a strip of lawn is shadowed by woods that run down a hillside into a lazy, mud-banked creek. The house bulks comfortably against the sky with its shoals of pink clouds; scarlet runner beans on the trellis flash like tropical birds. Her eyes follow the long, gentle slope of lawn that runs from the porch down to where the land flattens into black river soil. Ferns sway in shadow-swept beds around the trunks of silver maples, willows, poplars. Through the shifting leaves, she can glimpse red light glancing from wavelets that seem to move forward yet stay always in the same place.

She looks up through the branches of the tree. In spring, the smell of its blossoms fills her kitchen. *This is where we began.* Here was the garden's genesis, as if the tree were a gentle spirit. Beneath it, a wooden bench angles so both the back garden and the river are visible; here, Christy dressed and undressed her Barbie doll, tiptoed the doll's pointy feet on make-believe paths between white-veined hostas. The leathery leaves lift and fall; one flashes gold while the next stays dusty green.

What is going to happen to me? Tom's death is like a rent flag; she lives surrounded with edges too roughly torn to repair and that do nothing but flap idly, fraying and becoming daily more transparent. The gardens—like the swing that hangs crookedly from a maple tree (one rope rotten); like the flagpole with no flag and the overturned canoe on the rafters in the garage and the path to its jetty in the creek, which Kate has not gone down once this summer; like the wooden lawn chairs side by side and the forget-me-nots that creep beneath the lilac hedge and the gutter that hangs from the front porch whose run-off has dug a deep rivulet through the phlox and leopard lilies—the gardens seem poised at the beginning of devolution. The only constant in a garden is change, and Kate wishes only to keep them as they were; she can't bear to imagine them as they might have become: Tom, swinging a grandchild round and round, the child's teeth perfect as corn kernels. He would, of course, have repaired the swing, built a sandbox under the maple. To this end, she does nothing but weed, knowing that the place broods, waiting for an animating vision that now can come only from her.

She goes on down the path, climbs the back steps, fishes out her key. She stands on the porch for a moment before opening the door, looking up at the shadow-striped gardens, the lawn with its clots of wet grass. *How few couples garden together.* Often one or the other is the gardener, usually the woman. But she and Tom gardened the same way they canoed: together they planned the route, envisioned its general shape. Each one grubbed, or paddled, pursuing the course—and one person's energy bloomed when the other's flagged. This year there was plenty of heat and rain, and the delphiniums grew to almost six feet and then bent after the last storm since Kate did not stake them. She hasn't edged any of the beds, so they begin to seem unkempt, ill-defined; the boy runs his machine as close to the gardens as he dares, but still leaves a green fringe along their edges, untidy as a hanging hem. The perennials she did not divide last fall— the baby foxgloves and rose campion she did not dig from their haphazard seeding, the invasive gypsophila and sun-drops, which should have been restrained—have spread, wandered, the pools of colour break down, odd clumps stand alone and seem diminished. Nor did she prune the raspberry patch, since it was Tom's love and chore. The canes are leggy, bent at the tips, and the patch is choked by last summer's dead stems.

She steps into the kitchen. Now it is the living room that burns with sultry light and the kitchen that's falling into dusk. Oblique rays bend across the floor, illuminate cupboard hinges, a cotton scarf hung on a chair back. She sets down Thermos and binoculars, stoops to unlace her sandy hiking boots and puts them away beneath the coats hanging by the back door.

The house is just as she left it this morning. In the living room, she can see the hatbox, still sitting on Tom's table, the photograph propped against the lamp. She feels a searing stab of anticipated happiness, so unaccustomed that it surprises her. Tonight she'll delve deeper into the hatbox. She hopes for diaries, letters. More photographs.

She should start supper. She should go out and see how the boy is coming with the lawn.

Instead, she pivots the rocking chair to face the window overlooking the porch and the river, sits with her sock feet on the windowsill. She thinks not of the day just past, but rather, with the yearning that has become like chronic pain, of how she and Tom would have spent such a lovely Saturday. Working in the gardens, of course, all day—edging, clipping, dead-heading, weeding—and then, in late afternoon, they would have washed their hands, gotten cold beer from the fridge, gone out on the veranda. They would have watched the river-light glancing through the trees; discussed, perhaps, whether to go canoeing now or later, in the cool of evening.

She places her memory during the first summer that the two children were both away from home. The rooms of their house had felt larger, and in the mornings, when Tom had gone across the lawn to his studio under the maple tree, she had noticed how bands of sunshine, as if made bold by quiet, lingered on the living room's varnished oak floor, bent at the wall and then travelled up over the wallpaper and the maple wainscot, trembling with leaf-shadow. And she had listened to the house's quiet, with the teenagers gone, and after a while it felt, not empty, but like the momentous space between an orchestra's tuning and the conductor's emergence.

She remembers a particular afternoon when they sat sprawled in rocking chairs, leaning forward to squint through binoculars. Tom's hair was grey at the temples. He was wearing shorts and a black T-shirt, crusty with acrylic paint: The Guggenheim, it said, in white letters. She imagines his hands as they held the moisture-beaded beer glass. They were small hands, sun-browned, strong. She remembers thinking how the public, seeing those hands in documentaries or television specials, would never imagine the places his fingers had drifted on her body the night before. The high-ceilinged bedroom overlooks the side lawn and the river; from its window they could see the moonlight stretching and folding, revealing how the river was never entirely motionless, even in the dead of night. In the empty house they had been free to utter their cries of rapture and had rolled apart, afterwards, with arms outflung, laughing at the shadowed ceiling. Their bodies had been slippery with sweat, and they'd taken cool showers and come down in their bathrobes—his was a heavy silk one she'd bought in a second-hand store on Queen Street in Toronto—and they'd leaned over the porch railing to gaze up at the dusty streak of the Milky Way. A green light on the bridge had winked as the poplars bent in a warm breeze. They'd heard the rising sigh of leaves and the hollow pull and slap of water against mud. "Listen," she'd whispered. She'd sat on the railing with her arm around a post. She felt young because she wore no underpants, and she'd shrugged back her bathrobe to show Tom how her breasts were like silver spoon backs. Her hair, still shoulder-length, brushed her skin like spiders traversing the back of her neck. "Otter," Tom had said, cupping one hand to his good ear. An otter, or a muskrat, splashing into the creek. And then came the portentous four-note hoot of an owl.

His public, she thinks, crossing her ankles on the windowsill, never saw his tenderness, but instead were seduced by the sharp outlines of his public image, heard his forthright comments, which were frequently solicited by the press and were accompanied by photographs of him taken within the landscapes he painted: cliffs, skies, marshlands. He was hawk-eyed, craggy, and they marvelled at his small man's energy and the luminous power of his paintings. After Tom's funeral, the dealers came and went and will come again. There will be loose ends for Kate as long as she lives. Retrospectives, requests for slides, curators calling to ask for Tom's unpublished statements; an artist's work endures. Without Tom, the paintings are only more valuable.

She smells the sweet, drenched scent of cut grass. The engine of a powerboat slows to a low throb as it approaches the bridge.

The porch door is open, and she hears the savage *chereek* of the osprey. She picks up the book she was reading this morning: *Out of Africa* by Isak Dinesen. Lately, Kate has been reading memoirs of place. She seeks evocations of places that are so deeply experienced that every part—trees, wind, mountains, sky—becomes vivid, distinct, imbued with a sense of eternity. It has different names and is unnameable, the thing Kate has lost and that once made the moments of her life seem filled with potential and poignant radiance: stones, tide-swept grasses, the rusty stillness of autumn.

She hears steps on the porch, a knock rattling the screen door in its frame. It's the boy. He's thirteen. He's peroxided his hair and has two earrings in his left ear. His hands hang from his wrists like mismatched socks he's been told to put away.

"Mrs. Harding? I'm done."

She tents her book on the table. "Oh, hi, Corey." She gestures vaguely, impatiently—*why doesn't he come in?*—but he only sidles halfway through the door as if afraid of being caught. She unfolds herself from the rocking chair, rummages in her wallet, hands him a ten-dollar bill and a two-dollar coin that he doesn't look at but stuffs in his pocket. She glances out the window. "Well, it looks great as usual. Thanks a lot."

"Well. Bye, then," he says.

She steps out onto the porch to wave. He walks down the path with shoulders slouched, studying the river with a sideways glance, bouncing on the balls of his feet.

He walks as if happy to be gone. Or is it she who wishes to be thirteen, walking away from the peculiar, reserved lady who is sitting all alone in a darkening kitchen, reading a book? She leans over the railing. The red-painted floor casts a rosy glow onto the white ceiling. She looks down at a sun-baked rivulet where the broken gutter pipe has sent torrents of water into the garden. Nothing has any connection to anything else. The canoe has no relationship to the broken swing. The kitchen seems unconnected to the living room, save as a passage. Tom's studio, locked, is an enigma, something found that she dare not investigate. Everyone—Tom, Christy, Liam—has abandoned this once-beloved home, and she is left with what feels like a collection of objects at a yard sale. Among the belongings left in Liam and Christy's bedrooms are a glass horse, tiny Dungeons and Dragons trolls, high-school yearbooks, colour prints of forgotten junior-high friends, a ripped snowboarding poster, a stuffed monkey. She knows they would not mind if she gave some of these things away, packed others in boxes. She and Tom were going to redecorate those rooms: strip the wallpaper, paint the walls colours they'd never used before (*Ochre? With dusty blue? Here, look at this straw yellow, or what about this moss green—what do you mean, yuck!?*); pull up the carpets, either paint the floors (*Ivory? Blue? Like the floors at King's Landing Historical Settlement?*) or sand them back to the colour of raw wood, make them glossy with varnish. They were, during the months before he died, talking about how they were finding themselves, with amazement, at another beginning.

She goes into the kitchen. She takes a beer from the refrigerator, sits back in the rocking chair. She opens the book, finds herself in Kenya. She reads of its mountain air; how in its "blue vigour" Isak Dinesen felt a lightness of heart and would awaken on her coffee farm thinking, *Here I am, where I ought to be.*

Here I am, Kate broods, pinching her lips between her fingers and staring through the window at willows that are not restless but stir with ceaseless motion. *Here I am,* she thinks, wishing it were true, *where I ought to be.*

3. Rain

In the dying days of summer, thunderclouds pile over the river valley, and hayfields the colour of newly woven baskets are bordered with goldenrod, aster and cattails. Birds bead the phone lines like black pearls, so numerous the wires sag. School hasn't started, but there's a sense of anticipation. When Kate goes grocery shopping, she sees mothers pushing shopping carts piled with loose-leaf binders, pencils, packaged paper. Lawns are mown meticulously, as if for the last time. Gardens are bright with late annuals: marigolds, snapdragons, cosmos. The wind is stronger and smells of apples; in Kate's garden, the pink lavatera have unfolded their final blossoms.

Kate is lonely, but not alone. At the library, where she's begun to work part-time, there's a party to celebrate the end of the summer reading club. Her phone rings frequently. Parents begin to contact her, signing up their children for the piano lessons she's given for years. She receives frequent calls, too, from family members who are aware of Kate's impending second winter of widowhood. Christy phones from Halifax, Liam from Ireland, her in-laws, Tom's parents, from Victoria. Her own parents phone every Sunday morning from the retirement community in Florida, where they've recently moved. She pictures them as they talk: her mother, Alice, tall, spare, brisk, a linen blouse accentuating the darkness of her creased, age-spotted skin; Sam, her small, lawyer father, still handsome and clear-eyed, although increasingly confused. Her parents ask her if she is getting along, pulling together. Her sister, Ruth, eight years older, who has always treated Kate with an air of bemused off-handedness, now speaks to Kate cautiously, uncertain of who she has become.

It begins to rain. It rains for days, a good rain, generous, the drops large and warm. Slugs make holes in the tomatoes. Last week's cold mornings, the twist of autumn, seem anomalous. Kate sleeps with her window wide open. The river is quiet beneath the stroking rain, bowed, lulled, like a horse in a pasture. Rivulets run down the banks; birds rise heavily, making single cries, and the ferns tremble.

After breakfast, Kate sits on the porch. Her bracelets jingle as she shoves the sleeves of her sweatshirt up over her arms. She lays her hands on the broad armrests of her rocking chair; through the trees, she can see how the surface of the river is dimpled by raindrops. Everywhere, stillness is shattered, and then resumes. Kate hears a splash that is small and distinct and comes only once, unlike the pattering rain. An osprey rises from the river. She sees a flash of silver. Fish in its talons. Its cry—*kyew kyew kyew kyew*—is savage and yet sweet, like the memory of consolation. The sound trails away, and Kate sits forward on the edge of her chair, chin on fists. She watches the place in the river where raindrops mouth and soothe the spreading disturbance.

It is unsettling the way places remain and people vanish. The place of her childhood is still there on a Connecticut hilltop, more or less unchanged. Just as this porch, where she and Tom rocked, drank beer, laughed with friends, is still here;

there's the railing that Tom leaned his elbows on, propping binoculars, watching the dive of a fish hawk. There's his rocking chair. And here she is, inhabiting, with pain, a vacancy. Moving through places where Tom should be standing. Passing through the place his arms might be, extending to embrace her. Ever since the dream of Shepton, she has felt as if she's searching in the dark for something essential. Blindly patting familiar places. Seeking a key, a match. For some reason, it is not Tom who has bidden this bewildered and urgent search, but her grandparents.

All those houses, clustered at that end of the village street, just before the hill plunges down into the valley. There was Shepton, Granny and Grampa Giles' big house. And just next to it was Uncle Oliver's house—Sunny Hill, they called it. The driveway in between the two houses. Its asphalt cracked. Anthills in the fissures. The windmill over the barn, the tennis court covered with apple leaves. Then Great-aunt Phoebe's house, the old Chelsea Inn, just across the street. Phoebe never used it; it listed like a ship, settling ever deeper into the soil, its windows blinded by brown paper shades, backyard overgrown with American bamboo. Nor did Uncle Oliver use his house, other than on the Fourth of July and a few weekends. But Granny and Grampa Giles stayed at Shepton all summer and only went back to their city house when the goldenrod burst into seed, when the birds flocked and flew in dark ballooning clouds, when the ditches were filled with wild asters and Concord grapes.

How can this memory seem so real? As if she is actually there on that childhood porch, at the same time that she is here on this one.

Shepton's front lawn sloped down to the street. A long side lawn stretched from the house to the church's chapel. Between these lawns was a row of seven old maple trees and a stone wall. There was a third, terraced lawn, higher up. She feels herself on a summer's evening, walking beneath the maples. The lower lawns were in shadow, but along the edge of the upper lawn hollyhocks shone in the setting sun, and on Grampa Giles' grape arbour, green grape clusters were edged with shadow. Her feet made no sound on the cushiony grass. Grampa Giles offered a penny a twig to anyone who wanted to gather them. Tree frogs began their evening song, a dark, throbbing *chee chee chee chee*. And Granny was sitting by herself on the south veranda, knitting. She wore a grey skirt and a white blouse pinned at the collar with a brooch of tiny porcelain flowers. She sat with her ankles crossed. She needed no light to knit, even though she watched her moving fingers with her head tipped to one side. Up over the hayfield, the sky was spread with tissues of pink cloud. In the myrtle bed that spread out from the veranda to the stone wall, the star-shaped flowers were pale blue and the roses on the trellis, to Granny's right, had become luminous. Over Granny, angles of roof either held the cidery light or cast blue-black shadows; there were dormers, ells, gables, porches, sheds. Leaves layered the gullies between roof pitches. Now Kate could hear the sound of Granny's rockers, going back and forth over the grey-painted porch boards. Grampa Giles came around the corner of the house. He had a big belly and moon-silver hair. Kate's presence lit his face; his mouth lifted in a gentle, sober smile. Granny, too, looked up. Her hands fell to her lap and her face relaxed from its customary sadness, and she, too, smiled as if she'd been waiting for a grand-daughter to step from the gathering dusk.

Kate slid onto the couch that was suspended from the piazza ceiling by chains. And she was in the warm heart of family. There she sat with her grandparents, freed from the bossiness of an older sister, returned to herself. Granny loved everything about her: her freckles, her ten-year-old tummy, the red plastic hairband holding back her straight brown hair. Grampa Giles was interested in the scabs on her knee, and if she told him about her bicycle crash he did not quiz her but half-closed his eyes and nodded sympathetically. And the night rose. Down the street, lights came on behind the small-paned windows and flickered as breezes lifted the leaves of bridal wreath and mock orange bushes. Up in the hayfield fireflies blinked like loose Christmas tree bulbs, and the rusty chains of the swinging couch creaked as Grampa Giles pushed the floor with his dubbined leather boot. Then Granny whispered, "There are sugar cookies in the kitchen," and Kate got up and went inside. The rooms were lit only by the afterglow of sunset, and she could see the white throats and collars and wrists of the family portraits.

This house was both theirs and hers. These things were both theirs and hers: brass samovar and cut-glass cruet; wing chairs and piecrust tables. Badminton racquets in the closet under the stairs, birdies with cracked rubber tips, the catcher's mitt and golf bag, the folded reams of bunting, the tennis trophy cups. Upstairs in the bedrooms, theirs and hers: the monogrammed hairbrushes, chests filled with quilts and pillowcases. Rush-woven footstools, tiny rimless spectacles. Taffeta dresses, thunder jugs, decaying parasols.

As she walked through the darkening house, she could hear both the solemn, mortal ticking of the grandfather clock and the monotonous teeming of insects, and the house seemed weightless, without substance, submitting to the summer night that rose around it and within, like a tide. She found the cookies on a plate in Granny's little kitchen, the one room in the house that felt modern, with its new gas range, its new cupboards. It was like the bridge of a ship, its navigational instruments keeping a boat's old timbers and wave-worn prow on its course. She walked back through the quiet rooms. She could see the backs of her grandparents' heads through the long windows of the parlour. Grampa Giles adjusted a sweater over Granny's shoulders. The cool was rising at last from the roots of the earth.

Kate sits with her fingers intertwined, clasping the back of her head. Her elbows frame her face, shelter her like a wimple. She stares at the white-painted boards of the porch ceiling, seeing the frayed webs of departed spiders.

Kate has lunch with Caroline before her afternoon shift at the library. They sit at the oak table in Caroline's kitchen. The room has not changed since the 1970s. On the counter are wide-mouthed glass jars with cork stoppers. They hold dried beans, granola, rice, their contents labelled in faded calligraphy. Over the sink, the window is propped open, its screen beaded with raindrops. The sill is jumbled with handleless mugs, broken pottery bowls and tiny earthenware planters filled with cactuses. Kate glances into the living room. The small house is in transition. The girls have left, but some of their possessions remain—a guitar with embroidered strap, stacks of sheet music on the floor next to an upright piano— and Caroline and Brian have painted the walls a warm brick red and bought a leather couch with matching chair.

"Nice!" Kate says, nodding at a new pine desk in the corner of the living room, where she glimpses a computer, printer, textbooks. Caroline has begun taking courses at the university in Saint John. She's short, even-tempered, her freckled cheeks marked with smile lines. Her hair is neither gingery red nor grey, but bears strands of both in equal parts; she carries her bellied softness like a dancer. Brian teaches at the high school, has one more year until retirement.

Caroline tips a big spoonful of tabouli salad onto Kate's plate. "What's new?"

She asks it bravely, Kate realizes. Or provocatively. But this time, since Kate does have something to tell, she feels a quickening of spirit, as if she joins, just for an instant, a more vigorous rhythm.

"Do you remember Gregory Stiller?"

Caroline slides into her chair, picks up her fork. She loves to cook, and eats with unabashed pleasure. She takes a mouthful, rolls her eyes and chews, smiling. "Cilantro," she murmurs. Then her eyes narrow; she thinks for a minute. "Oh, my *God!* Gregory Stiller. Married to Karen. Their son. Oh, that terrible tragedy. What was his name?"

"Jerome."

"That's right. And they had a younger daughter, Jane."

"I saw him at Mary's Point," Kate says. She sets down her fork, lifts her mug and cradles it with both hands. "We were walking on the beach. He recognized me immediately. I wasn't sure who he was at first. I tried to avoid him, but he came up to me and said 'Kate?' Remember how we spent a lot of time together when the kids were little? Then they moved to Fredericton when their children were about ten or twelve. We've been completely out of touch ever since. I saw him at Jerome's funeral, but of course he wouldn't remember."

"When was that?"

"The funeral? About nine years ago. Jerome was twenty."

"God."

"We sat on the rocks and talked for an hour."

Kate senses that Caroline feels as much curiosity about her as she does about Gregory Stiller. It is a familiar dynamic, Kate realizes. When she talks, her friends are suddenly attentive, as if they are trying to imagine where she is inside herself but don't dare ask, and hope she will say something to help them understand. As she felt, she suddenly realizes, about Gregory, as she listened to his unbearable, unthinkable story.

She lays her hands on either side of her plate and looks at Caroline, who pauses with a forkful of tabouli halfway to her mouth, surprised by Kate's intensity. "Jerome dropped out of university and went out west. He was living in Banff with a bunch of guys. Karen and Gregory had a really hard time staying in touch with him. Then in late October they got—" She takes a breath. "Oh God. That phone call." The Mounties, she says, had wanted to know if Karen and Gregory had heard from him. His roommates had reported that both he and his climbing gear had been missing for several days. Immediately, a search-and-rescue operation was started, but by then it had begun to snow. Eventually, they found his climbing gear on a ledge in the mountains. It was in a neat pile. Organized. The rope coiled. Sling, carabiners, arranged. There was a sheer fall—hundreds of feet—from the ledge. Because of the storm they couldn't get down to the place where he would have landed if he'd jumped or fallen. They had to abandon the search. "It was too close to winter. They told Karen and Gregory it was conceivable, but highly unlikely, that he would have been able to walk out in those weather conditions."

Kate looks out the west window. She can see the river at the end of the street. Grey beneath the rain-bearing clouds, it slides past weeping willows, rippling steadily forward as it did even at the moment of Tom's death. "They told Gregory his son was probably dead, and that it might have been a suicide, but they couldn't know that for sure, either."

Caroline presses her fingers against her lips.

"So Karen and Gregory went an entire winter not knowing. *Not knowing*. Contacting every missing persons bureau in North America."

Caroline closes her eyes.

"You wouldn't dare to hope," Kate says. "And you wouldn't dare not to hope." Her voice hardens. "They found his body in the spring. The coroner called it a suicide. They didn't have his funeral till May."

"How could you bear it?" Caroline says. "How could you live?"

Kate considers the question. If it had been Christy, or Liam, rather than Tom? Every grief, she supposes, is as distinct as the person you mourn. You bear it. You never know how.

After work, Kate walks home through the rain. She sets her umbrella on the porch; raindrops bead its fan-shaped pleats. She stands on the porch, working the key in the back door, while all around her the world teems: leaves are battered, rain splashes from gutter pipes, she feels dampness on the backs of her hands. The house is dark, silent. She hangs her raincoat in the closet, heels off her rubber boots, tosses the mail on the kitchen table. Flyers, promotions, trial subscriptions still arrive in her mailbox addressed to "Tom Harding." She takes her running shoes from a canvas carry bag, sits on a wooden chair, leans forward to fasten the laces. The kitchen smells of tea and damp newspapers. Through the screen door to the porch she can see how the flowers of scarlet runner beans, on the trellis, are occasionally struck by raindrops; how they tremble and seem entirely unharmed. The kettle is always ready, on the counter, and she plugs it in. It begins its sighing rattle.

She thinks of Christy and Liam. *When did I last call them? Only a few days ago; it's too soon to call again. No, really, I shouldn't call them. I have to think of their needs too.* She's reacting like a wife: as if Tom shrugs, sweeps a page of today's paper, calmly tells her to do whatever she wants. But would he have? Would he have urged her to call? She feels a prick of irritation. That, too, is like phantom pain, for it takes nothing whatsoever to provoke it. Her vision of Tom is like all the other things in this house that she can't give away. It's forlorn, hopeless. Yet less forlorn than how she fears she'll feel without it. Tonight, Kate has no meeting to attend, no planned visit. The idea of curling up in an armchair with a book is not comforting. She has no interest in fiction. She dares not drink. She has no desire to start working on the kids' rooms. She will not impose herself on anyone. And here, in her own home, she faces something else that she cannot name. Or will naming it make it less real? Abyss, void, silence, the face of pointlessness.

She stands abruptly. *Stop that.* Food. She will cook. She'll make some sort of supper for herself and then will bake. She'll fill the house with the smell of melting chocolate and hot sugar, or cinnamon and apples. She will listen to the rain, as night encloses the house like dark petals. She'll observe how light from her windows fans across the wet grass in cornucopias of spinning raindrops. She'll make a few phone calls. She'll rummage in the hatboxes. She'll take the clothes from the dryer and fold them. She may reach bedtime without hearing the house's true silence.

The phone rings.

"Hello?"

A man's voice. Light, hesitant. "Yes, hello. May I speak to Kate Harding?"

She pauses, for an instant. Like a startled cat. "This is Kate."

"This is Gregory Stiller."

"Oh, hi! How are you?" She pictures him, squatting on toe and heel, spilling pebbles from one hand to the other. At first they had stared at one another, amazed. He had looked intensely into her face and seemed, oddly, to be seeing someone else. Her younger self, perhaps. Then they had begun a rush of reminiscences. How they had had such a good couple friendship, she and Karen, he and Tom; how their kids had been of similar ages; how they had camped and canoed, cooked in each other's backyards.

He says, "I was so amazed to run into you."

He hesitates, and she recognizes the cadence of need. In the silence as he frames his next sentence she remembers how, on the beach, he had stared out over the receding tide and asked a few careful questions of her. He had bowed his head, listening to her answers. He seemed less interested than patient, biding his time, buying credit. Tom's death, he indicated by his polite silence, left him surprised but untouched. Yet he had neither pitied her nor treated her like a widow. She had felt the lowering sun burnish her face, and leaning against the red rocks with her feet crossed at the ankles she had felt relaxed, pleasantly careless. Then he had begun to tell his story. He had talked steadily, the pebbles making small, dry rattlings as he passed them back and forth.

She unplugs the kettle. Steam rises, but it falls silent. "Where are you calling from?"

"Actually, I'm in town. I mean I'm here. At the gas station. I wondered if I could stop by."

Oh God. Such revelations as he made to me should be like a feather studied, carried in one's hand for an afternoon, then cast back to the sands. He can't expect what occurred because of context and circumstance—our surprised recognition of one another like wine within the glass of the afternoon's driftwood, pink-flowered sea rocket, plover cry and sea wind—to be repeated in my kitchen with its fly-specked Audubon calendar and the sad smell of tea.

"I won't," he adds, "stay long. I have to be in Saint John by seven. For dinner."

"Yes, of course, Gregory. Do you remember where the house is?" And as she says this she remembers how in such a circumstance Tom would stand in the doorway between the kitchen and living room, mouthing at her "Who is it?" and she would raise her hand as if to catch his curiosity and throw it back, humorously.

He sits in the rocking chair by the porch door, and to Kate's surprise the sound of rain maintains the sense of separation and inclusion they felt on the beach, when each one was diminished by wind and sky, yet relieved by the sense of scale. Here in the kitchen they still feel close to water, the river's leaden twist, the sky's dissolution; they hear steady splashing coming from the broken gutter pipe and breathe the end-of-summer scent of drenched marigolds, damp porch furniture, sodden roses. They drink Earl Grey tea. She puts a plate of maple leaf cookies on the table, and he takes one but bites off only one lobe. His hand, she notices, shakes.

Although she has not seen him for years, she can still see his young face. It hovers, for a while, like evening light, until she realizes she's become accustomed to his face as it is now. She remembers him as a young father. His wife was short-haired, athletic; they had two blond children, a boy and a girl; he was a freelance writer working as a stringer for a national magazine. He wrote book reviews for the local paper. She remembers how the smile lines at the corners of his eyes were strongly defined and made his face friendly. He loved inconsequential stories of small-town life; he leaned forward when you told him something, face alive with expectation. He grinned, frequently, a good grin revealing short, perfect teeth. When he laughed, he threw his head back and his eyes almost closed, became a blue glint behind a slash of white-blond eyelashes. He and his wife shared Kate and Tom's love of nature. Together, they pored over survey maps, planned weekend trips, discussed sightings of owls, fireflies, otters. When the children were little, they made frequent expeditions along the Fundy coast: backpacked to remote beaches, set their tents on sandy knolls, cooked over driftwood fires, watched with benign pleasure as their sweatered, fat-handed children patted cold sand, snapped red-speckled legs from dead crabs.

Now his hairline has receded. His fair skin is no longer suntanned and wind-flushed, but is pale beneath its freckles. There are permanent red blotches on his cheekbones. Smile lines still fan from his eyes, but they are mere presences, reminders, like haggard dogs in a famine. He's not fat, but has thickened; he sits in the rocking chair as if his body is an unwanted weight that accompanies him. She has a vague sense of his success in Toronto. He's reached a level of prominence on one of the big newspapers, Kate's not sure which.

"That beach where we met each other," he says, setting down his mug, "was one of the places Jerome and I used to go to climb." His eyes narrow in a smile that she does not return. She thinks of how people circle around Tom's name, warily, sparing themselves the sight of her pain.

"I remember that," Kate says. She is surprised at how the memory returns, like fog lifting and revealing a forgotten landscape. "Yes, I can see Jerome. Going up that chimney place, where you had to brace with your legs."

Gregory's eyes leap to her face. *He's actually seeing me, just for an instant. Not grateful, but curious at my tone.*

"I went there because it was his birthday."

"You didn't tell me," she says. Her voice is reproachful, almost tender.

He nods, a bow to her ignorance, acknowledging his part in it. "Didn't I? Well, he would have been twenty-nine."

The rain seethes on the river, and on the bridge the whine of tires becomes a rhythmic rush. Leaves hang, unresisting. Moist air rises through the screen door, touches their ankles. Raindrops on the porch roof are not evenly spaced—some are louder than others, then there are pauses. Kate thinks that each tap is like an unanswered question. She sits in her characteristic sprawl, long legs outstretched, arms crossed over her chest. A manly pose, Tom told her. She has not yet stopped collecting questions for Tom. Now she is wishing to mull over their times with Gregory and Karen. And she remembers, as she does many times every day, that she has only one mind now; only one set of memories.

"I always celebrate his birthday. That was one thing Karen and I agreed on. We would mark the day he was born rather than the day he died."

Does he talk to other people like this? His back is to the open door. He stares at the floor, unaware of how he sits within a landscape of red flowers, glistening porch railings, misty trees.

"It was a depression," he says. "Although he had never suffered from depression before, at least not that we were aware of. One day he phoned and told us how he despised the young men he was living with. We told him to move. He said he couldn't afford to. We offered to send money. He was offended. He said he would deal with it, he wasn't going to tell us his troubles if all we could do was treat him like a child. I often think of that day he set out with his gear. I try to imagine his state of mind. He must have hitchhiked up there. What did he tell the person who gave him a ride? It drives me crazy to think that there's someone out there who was the last person to talk to Jerome. The police tried to find whoever picked him up. Never did. What if I'd called him that morning? We even talked of flying out for a long weekend. Instead, Karen and I decided to send him a parcel of new winter clothes. Flannel shirts, good socks. About three weeks after he went missing, the parcel was returned to us. I'll never forget the smell of . . ." He grips his face.

Kate knows. To ask. "Of what?"

"The clothes," he manages. "The new clothes. Karen— the love. The hope we sent with them."

He slides a thumb under his left eye. He makes a vague gesture with his right hand. He's staring intently at nothing. "That question, you know. Did he jump or did he fall? I'll take that to my deathbed. I picture him going up to the edge, looking over. Somehow slipping. But Jerome was a climber. I taught him. You saw us; you remember. He climbed like a squirrel. Karen and I thought of drugs. Could he have been in some kind of altered state? Lacking judgment, perception? I spent months, as I told you, tracking down those other boys he was living with. I called the landlord. I talked to the town cops. Yes, there were drugs. To what extent was Jerome involved?" He shrugs. "No one could say."

Of all the ways Jerome could have died, Kate realizes, death by climbing accident would be the cruellest blow to his father.

"There was no note. No letter to us. Nothing in his room or possessions that would indicate any kind of premeditation. No reason. Nine years later I still lie awake at night. I haven't found an answer that makes any sense to me. I'm still raging at him. I'm furious with him for doing this to himself. To us. Or else I'm arguing with him. Persuading him. I can't tell you how many times I've made that phone call in my head. The one on that morning. Or I'm just holding him. Well. You must have seen it on the news."

He looks at her. His face is haggard. She gazes at him assessingly, fingers pinching her lips. She takes a deep breath. "Tom heard it on the radio. Back in October, when the search and rescue started. He left the studio and came down to the house. I was right here, at this table. We sat down and talked about you. You and Karen and Janie. We remembered Jerome and Liam trudging along with their little backpacks."

Gregory's eyes swim with tears. Tears leap to Kate's as well.

"We—" She takes another steadying breath. "We talked about how we wished we could help. How we wished we knew how to pray, or believed prayer would help."

"I left the church over this," Gregory says. "Karen, however, became more devout. It was the beginning of our drawing apart."

He takes a slow breath through his nose and stares out the window. He's looking at the runner bean flowers but doesn't see them; he has ceased to see the world as it is. Kate remembers how, at the beach, when he'd told her of his divorce, he'd been gazing at the sandpipers without seeing them. Instead, he'd been watching the past turning in his mind like a movie that's playing whenever you turn on the television. *This part. Here's the telephone call. RCMP locate the body. Circumstances point to suicide.*

"Were you with Tom when he died?" he asks.

She opens her mouth but can't make herself say the words: *We were both sitting right here.* Instead, she points to the chair across from her. Gregory's eyes clear. Kate sees him seeing her. She feels as if it is the first time someone has looked at her since Tom died and not seen Tom as well.

"I haven't stopped wondering where Tom is," she says. "At first, I'd hear his feet on the stairs. I'd sit up in bed with my heart pounding. I'd even get up and go look. Then I'd expect him to be home when I came back from somewhere. I'd push the door open very slowly." She takes a sudden breath. "I might walk into a lingering smell. Cigarettes, acrylics. He has to *be*. I feel that he and Jerome must—" She glances at him, sees how his head is bent, staring at his hands, which hang between his knees; he is unaware of how the light coming through the door behind him lies on the folds of his shirt, the curve of his cheek. "Or rather, can't *not* be, in some form."

The moment, like a gate, stands open, but neither Kate nor Gregory speaks. Her words make a meaningless patter like the raindrops and expose their mutual loneliness.

"Were you and Tom good friends when he died?" His voice is harsh, so she realizes that this is not what he really wants to talk about.

She nods.

"You would think," he says, staring at the backs of his hands, "that a couple would be each other's solace. But this is not what happens. One day she would believe he was alive, the next day she would be sure he was dead. If I was making phone calls to Child Find on the day she believed in his death, she would rage at me for raising false hopes. Tell me I was in denial. She went into counselling, as did Janie. I assumed that she blamed me for teaching Jerome to climb, for pushing him, for never giving him enough credit. Sometimes she would admit that she did feel such blame. At other times my guilt would infuriate her. 'This is not just about your failure as a parent,' she would say. She'd accuse me of being possessive, even of grief. We began an elaborate dance of recrimination. We were parents who had failed their essential mission of keeping their child alive. I became obsessed with control. I spent the winter phoning, making lists, keeping folders, organizing, trying to find anyone who might have clues. Trying to make myself believe that Jerome had walked out of those mountains and was living another life somewhere. She pointed out that I could not control the most basic of things, why should I try to make up for it? We would say unspeakable things to each other. We would hold each other and weep. I began drinking heavily. Janie. Poor Janie. After the news that Jerome had disappeared, she spent a week at home with us, then she had to go back to Halifax, where she was at Dalhousie. At first, Karen and I went over there every weekend, until we realized she didn't want us. It was, well—"

They sit listening to the rain.

He glances at his watch. "Oh, my God."

He gets to his feet abruptly, a man late for his next appointment. They move towards the door, slicing bits of information into the air as they go: her work at the library, which he just now remembers to ask her about, his conference. She turns to scribble his phone number. They stand on the porch and evaluate the rain, laughing as they might in public, shedding intimacy like shaking off raindrops. A handshake pulls into a quick hug, and he goes down the path past snapdragons that float soft as moths in the leaching light.

The rain intensifies and shrouds the sky, making darkness come early. She stands at the porch railing, looking out over the lawn and through the trees to the river. Crickets trill with a ratcheting pulse, like cogs slipping into place. Rain splatters steadily; the air carries the smell of sodden ferns. She watches the slick leaves of the Solomon's seal below the railing nodding, bouncing, and thinks of the resiliency of plants—how they do not resist being struck and so are unharmed. Raindrops do not burst against leaves but slide, tenderly. Above Kate's head raindrops cling, elongating, to the soffits. They are cloud grey, do not sparkle yet are light-filled. She feels gentled, wants to weep but knows she won't. It's a different anguish from the grief she has become accustomed to. It is a feeling both familiar and troubling, like music one loves, yet can't identify. She's surprised to realize she welcomes it.

She goes back into the kitchen, peels an onion, then finds herself in the pantry staring at a shelf and wondering distractedly why she is there—*oh yes, olive oil.* Standing over the frying pan, she realizes that this anguish is about some sort of loss and beginning at the same time; in this case, how Gregory Stiller knew almost nothing of Tom's career or their children and met her not as a stranger but without reference to anything that might define who she had been or become. And it makes her both angry and hesitant. She takes her anger like a page of writing and examines it. She still wants to be Tom's wife. Married, she had been more than herself. She carried her husband with her, in her walk, her attentive listening, her advice and withheld opinions, her laugh. Her life with Tom was implicit as power, allowed her to be gracious, made a sheen around her like silk. Now she wonders who it is that Gregory Stiller thought about as he drove away from Mary's Point a few days ago, presumably pondering their encounter. *Who do you think I am?* And she realizes that, although she is angry that he does not see Tom's presence in her, she is also frightened, or startled. She veers, as if the rooms of her self have been rearranged and she no longer knows where anything is.

She lights the half-burned candle on the kitchen table, sets down a placemat, silverware, a cloth napkin. On the classical music station a string quartet plays Beethoven. Spoon clinks against china as she ladles potatoes onto a plate. It is the worst of sounds, the clinking of silver against porcelain in a room where one eats alone. She sets her plate on the table and pulls out her chair, then sits facing the window that overlooks the river. *This is the most unnatural of acts. Even cows graze in groups; ravens, apparently, alert their kind to carcasses, you always see at least two on a roadkill.* After Tom's death, her heart was so heavy in her chest that it seemed to pull her forward over the table. Lifting fork to mouth, she thought of herself as a monstrous infant, taking nourishment without knowing why; obeying instinct when her will told her not to. Now she has enforced rituals. *Music. Don't read, look at your food. Use fresh herbs, make your own curry with cardamom seeds and anise. Eat yams, make orange sauce for your beets.* But still it is an act to be endured and is, of all the lost intimacies, the most forlorn.

She finishes eating, washes the dishes and turns off the sink light. A street lamp half-hidden by the trees winks as the leaves that fracture its light lift and fall in the rain. She has no dread of the next moment, but feels as if her body is lighter, without the burden of impulsion. For an instant, she senses the freedom of presence. She is watching the rain. She is, like the spinning drops, falling through the night.

She goes into the living room and pulls the chain of the lamp on Tom's desk. The windows are open, and she can hear the splash of rainwater. Its sound is careless, domestic, like a forgotten faucet. She settles her reading glasses on her nose, reaches into the hatbox and lifts out a bundle of letters. She angles them randomly to read their addresses. She returns to the one on top of the pile. Printed on the front in elaborate typescript, it reads: Burial Certificate from the Massachusetts Cremation Society, Boston, Mass. Running along the top in small letters are the words "This certificate should accompany the ashes to their destination." She turns the envelope sideways. Someone has handwritten a name in ink: Ellen Pierpont Thomas. The envelope has never been opened.

Gingerly, feeling the peculiar guilt of opening a letter not addressed to oneself, no matter how old, she slips her finger under the seal, tearing the paper very slightly. Inside is a single small sheet of paper. She unfolds it as carefully as she might spread the wings of a dead butterfly. It is a standard undertaker's burial certificate, with the details filled in by hand. It states that Ellen Pierpont Thomas died in Hartford, Connecticut, from measles pyemia, on the 16th day of April, 1906, at the age of eight years and four months.

Kate sits with her elbows on the table, fingers pressed to her cheekbones. The document, she surmises, was sealed because no one could bear to open it. Perhaps it had been slid into a desk drawer along with the year's receipts.

She studies, again, the photograph of her grandfather's family propped against the lamp. The family is content, as yet unravaged. She gazes into the child's calm eyes. She reaches forward and touches her great-grandmother's proud face. She slides her fingertip to Ellen's cheek. This little girl, Kate thinks, with the pity of omniscience, has only four more months to live.

Part Two

4. Asters and Woodsmoke

ONE SATURDAY MORNING, AS SHE OFTEN DOES, KATE goes with her friend May to the farmer's market. The market is held in the parking lot of the old IGA grocery store, which is now empty, its plate glass windows covered with plywood, a realtor's sign on the door. It is September twentieth, and the air bears a knife-edge. This is the last market of the year.

Kate stands in the sun-flooded kitchen, shrugging into a jacket. She wears jeans and heavy wool socks—grey with blue toes and heels—and old leather sandals. "Were these Tom's?" she wondered when she buckled them. She hadn't given away some of his socks and sandals since their feet were the same size.

She slings her leather handbag over her shoulder, glances into the dusty slumbrousness of the living room. She is struck by the earnestness of human beings, by the patient accumulation of things meant to shape a life: a "living" room, with its empty chairs, empty couch, its books and magazines, its piano and stack of hatboxes.

There's a knock at the kitchen door. "Are you ready, Katie?"

May is eighty years old but looks seventy. The collar of a white polo shirt accentuates the deep tan of her skin, whose wrinkles are pale, like parched gullies. Her hair is caught back in a short ponytail; her blue eyes are amused and sad. One hand is raised, fisted, ready to knock again.

"Ready!"

They walk down Kate's path, let themselves out the gate. The air smells of frost and cold mud. They walk along the street beneath the maples, and their feet scuff leaves, gravel, twigs. May is a birder and amateur botanist, belongs to the Kennebecasis Valley Naturalists Club. She's been a widow for twenty years. She points out the spiderwebs that litter the lawns like dropped handkerchiefs. They are like fist-sized tents, silvered with dew. "Look, look there," May says, excitedly. A fly blunders into a web, the spider darts from its hiding place.

Kate watches May's still-supple crouch. She finds herself tucking away a fact, like dropping a pebble into her pocket. It is her habit of hoarding things to tell Tom. *She takes yoga classes. She's quite amazing.* Yet even as she remembers this, she feels herself resisting this world of widows who have reshaped their aloneness, who have ceased mourning the future. They seem to her brave and resilient, tough, busy. There seems to be much they could say, but do not.

"I find," Kate says, as May rises, "that this is a season when I remember my childhood."

"Which season do you mean?" May says matter-of-factly, brushing her knees. She's aware that Kate seldom, lately, initiates conversations. "Late summer or fall?"

"This time when there begin to be heavy frosts and you can smell winter on the air. When I was growing up, the sight of frost on yellow leaves made me feel both frightened and excited. Something to do with school starting. New pencil boxes. The smell of new binders."

"Did you have to wear petticoats? Those scratchy ones?"

"Yes, I wore them. Only to church, though." Kate remembers that May would have dressed her own little girls in those years. "But I think I felt that something had truly ended, even as something else was beginning. The end of a childhood summer. When, oh, you know, you could *read*." (*You could read . . .* Tom would have known exactly what she meant . . . *that kind of reading . . . that loose-limbed, free-falling entry into a book's world . . . unfettered, unbounded*.) "You could lie on your stomach," she says to May. The words she selects make a simple melody; harmony unfurls in her mind. "Reading a library book with your chin cupped in your hands. (*The pages dog-eared, their edges soft as blankets*.) Or you'd go swimming and stay in the water until your fingers were white and wrinkly. (*Time had no dimension, went all ways at once, perhaps was vertical? Layered, or like, oh, falling asleep in the afternoon and waking up at bedtime . . . it didn't seem to exist. Somehow that sense of ending sharpened my memory*.) Now, every year at this time, I feel a kind of homesickness. When I smell asters and woodsmoke."

"Chrysanthemums? Cider?"

"Yes, and when I see the spiders, black and yellow, and thistles in the pastures. I'm there, back again, in the place of my childhood, as if it was still going on. When wild grapes stood in baskets on every porch. And my Granny . . ." Tears thicken her voice, and she clears her throat. May nods comfortably and says nothing.

They reach the end of the street and turn up the hill towards the town's unfocused centre. Across from a gas station is the town hall and a brick fire station. The street is lined with large Victorian houses with turrets and cupolas. One is a bed and breakfast, "Riverside Manor." A Canadian flag hangs over its grey steps. Next to it is a hardware store and the old IGA. Around the edge of the parking lot are tables covered with pumpkins and squash, preserves, freshly baked bread, honey, sausages, hand-knit sweaters, crocheted slippers. They are shaded with yellow awnings. Kate and May, walking on the sidewalk, discuss each other's children, May's grown grand-children. Kate imagines herself as a raven, flying over the river-side town, tipping her glossy eye to watch two grey-haired women walking briskly, their hands caressing the air, describ-ing to one another roles they once played, lives they now view from a distance.

When Kate arrives home, bearing homemade bread and farm eggs, she dresses in gardening clothes: rubber boots, baggy track pants, a hooded sweatshirt and a canvas vest she and Tom shared indiscriminately, each claiming ownership. Only yester-day had she thought to buy bulbs: hybrid tulips, ordinary cro-cuses—purple and egg-yolk yellow—and a few woody, turnip-shaped narcissus bulbs. She carries the white plastic bag as she lets herself out the back door. It is nothing like the large canvas carry-alls she and Tom once took to the gardens, filled with heirloom daffodils, their names marked on small paper bags: 'Hoop-Petticoat,' 'Campernelle,' 'Swansdown,' 'Beersheba,' 'Dreamlight,' 'Eggs and Bacon,' 'Colleen Brawn,' 'Old Pheasant's Eye.' They'd pored over bulb catalogues, sitting at the kitchen table, perhaps during a March blizzard. They'd sharpened pencils. Read out loud to one another, Tom laugh-ing: "Like all poets, grows well in damp conditions."

She stands on the stone path next to the apple tree. Her day is foreshortened. She has only until early afternoon, for she's agreed to go visit Gregory Stiller in his new house in Saint John. The conference he had alluded to had in truth been a visit to finalize a job offer. He's now the publisher of the province's largest daily newspaper. Not only has he moved down from Ontario, but his house is furnished and he's been at work for a week. It's as if he wants to present her with a life equal to her own: house, job, friends.

On the phone, she had heard the warmth in his voice, remembered the boyish enthusiasm that she and Tom found so appealing. He had even suggested a marvellous little restaurant where they could have an early supper. Kate had listened, let him think the restaurant was his discovery, didn't tell him that it was her and Tom's favourite place to eat. Yes, I'd love to come, she'd said; what else could she say?

She pulls on gloves whose leather fingers are board-stiff. After Tom's death she dreaded being alone. Then she dreaded intimacy. Now she has begun to fear the proportions of her own dread. It no longer seems that she is acting from her own clear desire when she declines a dinner invitation, says no when a friend asks her to a concert, tells May she doesn't want to join the yoga class. Fear stalks her like a cougar, has its claws hooked into her softest flesh. So she told Gregory Stiller yes, she would come. Now, anticipating the visit, her heart rate accelerates, her brow is furrowed. She walks down the path towards the tool shed that's attached to the garage. *Don't think about it. Don't think about it.*

Caroline's car slides to a stop at the street's dead end. She opens her window, leans out. "Hey! Don't you look attractive!"

Kate steps through the pergola. The clematis vine hangs limply, its dead leaves softening the stone path.

"What's wrong?" Caroline adds. "You look distressed."

"Oh . . ." Kate lifts her shoulders, thinks she will shrug the question away. Then she remembers. Yes, she told Caroline about Gregory. "I'm going to have supper with Gregory Stiller tonight."

"Oh, Kate! That's so—"

"But it makes me feel sick."

"Why?" The car is still running, but Caroline flicks off the radio. "Isn't he a perfectly nice man? Old friend? Lots to reminisce about?"

Kate studies her friend. Weighing how much to tell, to accept, to forgive. Caroline is not a widow. Not yet a widow. "It's not Gregory I'm worried about. It's me. How I'll be so—" *No, I can't tell her, because I've never described to her, or to anyone, how I feel skinless, coiled inside my cocoon, unready to hatch.* "Oh, I'll be fine."

"Of course you will." Caroline is still watching Kate keenly. "Well. I'm off to Saint John, wondered if you wanted me to pick up coffee for you at the market."

"No, I'm—well, come to think of it, yes. Please. Thanks so much! The usual."

"Okey-doke." Caroline trails her hand from the window as she looks over the back seat, reversing. Kate stands in the street, waving. *Life for Caroline is still blossoming, she has fertile soil with which to nourish kindness.*

As she gets the wheelbarrow from the shed and fills it with tools—bamboo rake, leaf-shaped Korean cultivator, square-ended spade, bulb trowel, watering can—she turns her mind deliberately away from tonight's engagement and begins pondering, instead, a photograph she found last night. It was a picture of Giles' mother, her own great-grandmother, Lilian Thomas. In the black-and-white photo, Lilian stood by the Shepton rose trellis that Kate remembers. How strange it is, Kate thinks, dropping the bag of bulbs into the wheelbarrow, to see pictures of long-dead people in places one knows well; it makes them seem like materialized ghosts. She grips the wheelbarrow's handles, pushes it over the path. It jounces, springy on its fat tire.

The day seems large—a New Brunswick expression that delighted Kate when she first heard it: *a large day*—but rather than the expansive joy intended by the phrase, she feels that the clearing sky exaggerates her sense of aloneness. Two ducks fly over the river. She smells the earthy scent of wind-stirred

water. She turns past the porch, passes one of their own trellises, the one she and Tom built for the virgin's bower clematis.
This side of the house catches the morning's first warmth, and
Kate recalls how the photograph of her great-grandmother cap-
tures a summer's fragment when the Shepton roses, on a similar
trellis, were blooming. She has been drawn to the family papers
every evening with the same preoccupied intensity that she once
took to her piano, feeling in her fingers the sonata she might be
working on. The papers exert a similar pull. In the written
word, the past is ongoing, unfinished, and her heart yearns
towards the hopeful tenderness of certain phrases, feels the
poignancy of what was never intended to endure.

She stops, looks at the curled clematis vines on the trellis
and remembers a morning when Christy, eleven years old,
leaned out the window. "Look, Daddy," she'd called. Kate and
Tom came from their various squatting endeavours in the gardens. Stood looking up, hands shading eyes. She was striking
a pose, and Christy's child-face is so vivid in Kate's mind that
she can't believe she won't reach out and find Tom at her side,
grinning upwards. It's the same sense of pity, of sorrow, as
when she looks at any photograph of her beloved granny, or
her father as a sweet-faced child, or the doomed Ellen. It is not
a longing for time past, but rather an ache for the past's innocence, for the time stretching between this moment and that,
which is for these people as yet unlived. An ache for the brave,
hopeful faces they turn to the future, with all its unfolding
perils that she, the onlooker, now knows.

She heads up over the lawn with her wheelbarrow, thinking of Granny, whose name was Hetty. In the photograph of
the rose trellis, Hetty stood facing her mother-in-law with
her back to a wicker baby carriage, as if she hid or protected
the baby it contained. She wore a dress whose soft folds
draped down her arms and across her breast, accentuating

her submissive stance. She held her arms at her sides, her hands behind her, gripping the carriage's bamboo handle. And Lilian, her mother-in-law, came advancing towards her like an ocean liner in full bore. One foot was lifted, one hand raised as if to emphasize a point. She seemed a different species, so much larger than Hetty, big-bosomed, her skirt trailing on the grass.

Kate pauses, then drops the handles of the wheelbarrow. She stands by a bed of perennials with her hands on her hips. She's not seeing the shredded chrysanthemums or the browning gypsophila blossoms but rather how her grandmother stood so meekly, feet close as if to take up as little space as possible. How worried Granny seemed, raising timid or beseeching eyes to her mother-in-law. And Kate, stepping forward on one foot to uproot a clump of vagrant daisies, realizes how little she knows of this imperious great-grandmother; how few stories have been told about Lilian; and how, in the Thomas family, unpleasant things are never discussed.

Unsure of how to tackle this mess of a flowerbed, she pushes the wheelbarrow to the centre of the back lawn, where she can see the perennial gardens ribboning upwards to right and left, the stone steps leading to the upper terrace, the opening in the lilac hedge leading to the secret garden. The house rises behind her. Sun strikes its upper storey and releases the smell of damp shingles. The sky is watery blue, veiled by cobwebs of cloud; the sun's rays are shattered by the trees on the east slope. Shadows spread like a palm, fingers of darkness separated by light. Last year she might have turned unthinkingly to look for Tom's face in an upstairs window. Today she does not, yet still grief impedes momentum, like exhaustion. At every moment she thinks of life as it was: Tom, trowel in hand, striding up the stone steps, passing through the damp shadows, pointing, calling to her, the black soil, the mysteriously desiccated bulbs, here they envision poet's narcissus, there a mass of daffodils with ivory trumpets rising over a sea of succulent snow drops; and then the bitter blade of reason makes a swift cut and the vision falls. In its place is emptiness. No one walks up the steps. She looks at the small bag of bulbs. She will plant them, haphazardly. She does one thing, and then another, but really she is waiting. She is waiting to truly understand that Tom is gone; for some conclusive moment when agony will break over her like a massive wave and she will find herself staggered but standing.

Simple tidying needs neither enthusiasm nor imagination, only organization. So she sets her tools where she will need them and begins raking the lawn. Yesterday's gale has torn seed heads from stalks, stalks from roots; the lawn is strewn with dead branches, rotten apples, wet leaves. She trundles the wheelbarrow down a path between wispy grasses to the mulch pile beyond the raspberry patch. It's a place enclosed by three wooden fences where she throws organic wastes. There's a scurf of coffee grinds, the rotting fabric of a teabag, a banana peel, all half-obscured by last week's load of leaves that have turned the colour of creek water, tannic brown. Kate upturns the wheelbarrow, feeling a despairing sense of her own slipshod habits. Well, but this was Tom's, this place with its sweet-rot smell. It was never a mulch pile, but a compost heap. Tom was the compost maker, just as Kate was the baker. There were many other equivalents: she paid the bills; he fixed engines. He hectored the bank manager; she bought the groceries. Now she has lost the habit of separating grass clippings from twigs, of organizing materials into separate piles for Tom to incorporate into his lovely layerings. Like a cake, he'd say, pausing to light a cigarette, enjoying the sight of fresh horse manure emptied from bags and spread over a thick layer of grass, leaves, garbage, old hay. He'd slide his shovel into a bag of lime. Or he'd turn the pile. On a wet autumn morning. Steam, rising. The trees golden in morning's haze. And always, when she needed it, there was the crumbly black soil. Marriage is an organism, Kate thinks—alive because all the parts are functioning. Now, without a compost pile, without a mechanic, without a carpenter, without an aggressive bargainer, Kate feels that her world, like the day, is too large, pulling apart, disconnecting.

She trudges back along the narrow path. The raspberry leaves are dark purple. The canes sweep low, unpruned. Did Lilian feel like this—as if her world had no centre? Kate wonders. She was a woman who had lost both a child and then, ten years later, a husband. He was not much older than Tom when he died, and none of his grandchildren knew him. She stops, suddenly, struck as if for the first time by this fact: *As none of my grandchildren will know Tom.* She leans forward to negotiate the slight rise up onto the lawn. *Now I know why I'm so curious about Lilian.* She wonders what she might learn from this great-grandmother who suffered as perhaps no one else did in that placid family. But she doesn't look, Kate ponders, scratching her rake over leathery round apple leaves, stooping to pick up worm-streaked windfalls, like a woman who has lost both a child and a husband. Well, how *would* you expect such a woman to look? she asks herself, tossing an apple into the wheelbarrow. Hesitant, she muses. Silent, thin. Perhaps broken, emotionally fragile; certainly not large, imperious and demanding. But loss, on the other hand, might engender command, worn as a mask or a shield from intimacy; Lilian may have forced people to do her bidding, trying to control a treacherous world. *After all, this was my own father's grandmother, and he never speaks of her with tender longing, the way I speak of Granny, who stands there so quietly in the photograph as if it is she, rather than Lilian, who is the broken soul.* But Granny, in Kate's mind, was the most contented human being in the world, and a person so gentle that no one could ever dream of saying a harsh word to her. What could Lilian possibly be saying, her hand flung forbiddingly? Did she think of little Hetty as the usurper of her son's affections? For by the time this picture was taken, judging by the baby in the carriage (Kate has begun to collate dates in a notebook), Lilian would have suffered both losses.

Am I becoming like her? Retreating behind my own shield, fearing intimacy, becoming cold, reserved?

Kate stops to pull twigs from between the rake's bamboo tines. Suddenly she's surrounded by tiny blue-winged insects. *Snow flies,* the children called them. Just as snow fleas springing from melting snow indicate the advent of spring, so these aimless haphazard flies, whirling in sunlight like dandelion seeds, mean that winter is close at hand. *Oh look, snow flies!* It's like tripping; she looks to see who noticed. Everything of grace and beauty, of oddness or humour, makes her glance sideways, eagerly. *Do you see what I see?*

The morning's sharp coolness evaporated with the dew. Now the air is hazy, sunflowers and cosmos shed yellow pollen, the aerobatic insects drift and spin. *Who cares if I tidy up these bushes, rake the lawn? It's quite possible that not a single person will see this garden before the snow comes, or if they do, they will see it as it is (messy) and not as it might, or should be.* Nonetheless, she rakes, just the way she tidies her great-grandparents' papers. *Who will ever care?* She thought this even as she spread receipts over her living-room floor, one pile on the seat of a chair, several on the couch, many on the carpet; here the receipts from the shoe store, here the ones from the silversmiths, the ice cream purveyor, the dry goods store, the apothecary, the brewery, the livery stable, the stone masons; here tax bills, school bills, dentist's and doctors' bills.

Who will care? But she squared the pages, the papers sliding past her parallel palms, their edges as perfectly matched as their age would allow. She pushed plastic-coated paper clips onto their corners. She found pictures of Charles and Lilian; of their surviving children, Daniel, Giles and Katherine. She found frames for them; placed them on her desk.

She put every receipt that might refer to Ellen in a box decorated with painted wildflowers that she found in her own daughter's bedroom. So far, Kate has found little in the hat-boxes that refers to Ellen; no pictures, and only a few receipts wedged in the long list of dry goods: a doll, hair ribbons, child's shoes. She found a dressmaker's receipt for a child's coat. A trip to the dentist for teeth cleaning. And the death certificate that did not, apparently, "accompany the ashes to their destination."

Kate has found only one picture of the family that includes Ellen, and none of the child by herself, although there are numerous receipts from a photographer's studio for portraits of all the children. How lightly, she thinks, raking poplar leaves that have gathered beneath the cinnamon rose, a small girl drifts. How faint her footprints.

Several nights ago, she found a small catalogue for Larkin Soap. Prizes were given for ten-dollar combinations; if you bought tar, sulphur and oatmeal soap, they'd send you elaborate rewards, such as a "Zimmerman autoharp" or a set of silver flatware or a ribbonless typewriter with felt rollers. Kate had held the little catalogue, mesmerized, turning it over and upside down and sideways. All the pictures had been inexpertly cut away, as if by a child's hand.

Kneeling, prying up weeds with the point of her cultivator, snipping soft stems with secateurs, Kate imagines the city house where her grandfather and his brother and sisters grew up. It would have been newly built, like all the other houses along the broad, unpaved street. They'd have been large, these houses, wood-shingled, three-storeyed, with turrets, gables and carriage sheds. They'd have been filled with children, servants, dogs, lawn games, mahogany furniture, musical instruments. Striped canvas awnings overhanging porches, casting scalloped shadows on their painted floors. Cool shade spreading from rhododendrons, purple blossoms dangling from wisteria arbours. American flags hanging from gables and white-painted poles; servant girls setting pitchers of lemonade on wicker tables. Steam rising from the street's watered soil, and women drifting like feathers down the sidewalks, skirts gathering hot dust, sunshades against their shoulders. Meticulously raked gravel paths, lilac hedges, flowering vines on pergolas and trellises. In summer, the houses would have settled into anonymity behind a froth of petals.

Theodore Roosevelt was the president, and Ellen, like every other little girl, must have longed for a teddy bear. The cook—whose half-monthly wages Kate had found, signed by a "Mary Heaney"—was Irish. She pictures her as small and wiry, grim-mouthed and kind-hearted. Kate imagines Ellen sitting at the kitchen table. Mrs. Heaney made ginger snaps while Ellen snipped those pictures from the soap catalogue: desks and Morris chairs and blue-flame oil cookstoves, just the size for her paper dolls. And then what? Her mother, Lilian, swept down the stairs pulling on kid gloves with pearl buttons. Ellen ran into the front hall, where a wash of sunlight cast the shadows of potted palms over a Turkish reclining couch; she stood under the hat rack, shining blond curls reflected in the enormous gilt-framed mirrors; she put her hand up to her mother's, and they went out the front door and walked to a trolley stand at the end of the street. She wore a dress with sewn pleats down the bodice, as she's wearing in the one existing photograph; she was serious, wore short bangs across a broad forehead that accentuated her round, wide eyes. She caught her lower lip in seed-pearl teeth. What if (Kate kneels, reaches into the branches of a rose bush with clippers) they were going to a birthday party, where Ellen would catch the measles?

She lays the rake tines-up, scoops stems and weeds onto it. She carries the slippery load to the wheelbarrow and dumps it. Then she sits on the stone steps and listens to the Saturday sounds of a small town: the passive drone of lawnmowers, the sharp thuds of car doors slamming, the pocking of a basket-ball. A sailboat passes slowly, sail furled, outboard motor thrumming. She leans back on her hands and watches river water crease black, velvety, before the boat's bow. A short while ago, here they had been, Tom and Kate Harding, living in their place, its character formed by things they'd collected—hawk feathers on windowsills, small oil paintings hung in unexpected places, beach stones in baskets—or bought at auctions: beds with painted headboards, oak tables, stoneware crocks. By choices they'd made, seemingly long ago. Curtains chosen, rooms painted, holidays taken. Whispers in the dead of night. *Shall we make a baby? Do you love me?* She thinks of nights spent at the bedsides of feverish children. Anger. Her back to Tom, staring out a window at the river. The long untangling that is a marriage, tugging persistently at loops of desire and fear, of privacy, of disunited paths, of opposing decisions. How alone they'd felt, how singular. And how particular their own creation—this home, these children. Themselves. So distinct. Tom. And Kate. And now she senses that she may be less alone than she feels. Who she is, she thinks, is not only the result of her own choices but of her family's. Unknown people. Their choices, their circumstances. Making character, layer upon layer. This fact folds around her, just as, in the mulch pile, rose petals are absorbed by maple leaves cupped within slabs of hay. Lilian's needs and demands pressed against Kate's grandparents, whose personalities, in turn, folded round Kate's father. And then, she muses, herself. Malleable, shaped.

The gardens on the lawn's west side bask in full sun. She feels heat burning between her shoulders as she gathers broken stalks of hollyhock and monkshood, then squats to pull up limp nasturtiums, to tug at black-leaved marigolds and rubbery snapdragons whose tenacious roots cling to the soil. She is thinking about the brash and ignorant quality of hope. Over and over again, she has sifted through the week preceding Tom's death, seeking the small memories that surface continuously, like mussel shells in mulch. She asked him never to smoke in the car again. They made love once, but not the day before he died. He'd cut his finger, and she made him change the bandage, which was encrusted with dirt and paint. They quarrelled and laughed, went to Canadian Tire and pored over paint samples. Expended their vitality on a spirited discussion of whether to paint the wainscot in a contrasting colour, and if so, dark or light.

Kate closes her eyes, breathes deeply through her nose. There was one argument that kept flaring up, like a fire whose source you cannot find. About Liam. Who is like Tom in appearance (wiry, black-haired, brown eyes with a guarded expression) and like Kate in temperament: reserved, yet tolerant; easy with people, but not a leader; no overriding passion and a capacity for aimlessness. She remembers one argument in particular, when both children were still in high school and Liam, in his final year, hadn't yet gotten around to applying to art school.

It makes no difference that Tom is dead. The argument still has not been put to rest.

"I'll do it for him," he'd said, forearms squared as he pulled a T-shirt over his head. They were undressing after a party. Wine-blurred. The children were not in the house.

"Right," she'd said. Mocking, disgusted. Sitting on the side of the bed, working at the clasp of a bracelet.

"He has more talent for drawing than I have." Rabbits, dogs, faces. Copied from *National Geographic* and subtly transformed, so they were distinctly Liam's. He's done this since childhood, randomly, easily. Like a hunger that he knows how to satisfy.

"If he misses the deadline, he misses the deadline." Kate had shrugged, annoyed. "He wants to take a year off."

"You think we should support that?"

And it was not Liam, Kate thinks, that they were discussing. *It was me, it was our differences. It was his incomprehension that I could let my piano playing slide. Not practise except for my own pleasure. Be content to teach children. Turn down offers to accompany. And what right does he have—did he have—to push Liam, to push me? As if he owned our talent? As if he had some right to shape our lives?*

There were some things they were learning to leave unsaid. On this night, she had been unwise. "Sometimes, Tom, you are so—"

He turned to face her. Eyes boring into eyes, like gravel in flesh.

"Like a pompous old rooster. With this family your little flock."

Oh, Tom, I'm sorry. Such wasted opportunities. *If we had known how little time we had left.*

She stands, pushes the wheelbarrow to the pile of stalks and vines, gathers them from the lawn. Did Lilian ponder, with agony, Kate wonders as she drops armloads of dead flowers into the wheelbarrow, the weeks and days that preceded

Ellen's death? Did she regret moments of heedless busyness, unexpressed affection, a cross word; did she endlessly relive the very day, the very moment that her child caught the measles? Did she blame herself, think that she should not have allowed Ellen to attend the party? But there would have been no more reason to do so than there would have been to keep her home from school.

Kate kneels at another perennial bed. She imagines how they would have left the house, filled with the decorous excitement of a mother-daughter outing. She pictures Ellen, kneeling on the wooden seat of the red-and-yellow streetcar, gripping the sill, watching the world slide past like a patterned ribbon. Beneath the awnings of butchers' shops, men hauled blocks of ice with giant tongs. Horses stood patiently, hitched to covered wooden wagons. There were barbers' poles, boys in cloth caps carrying newspaper bags. Gasoline-powered cars, shining with brass, roared down the streets, terrifying horses, causing fascinated pedestrians to cluster and point. It was April, the buds of young lindens were fatly pink, the light would have been sharp. Ellen slid down from the window and snuggled close to her mother, placing her boots, which did not touch the floor, side by side, peering to see if toe and heel were aligned. Kate imagines the corsets that pinched Lilian's waist. Lilian couldn't turn her head easily, but had to bob like a bird, as a starched white collar held her head straight beneath a deep-brimmed hat surmounted with a fan of stiffened lawn. She stared out the window with her round, wide eyes, her expression surprised, affronted, as if by the fact that she did not always receive what she expected. Did she wonder about her husband's diffidence, his cordial formality (as he appears in every photograph)? She was, after all, his second wife. He'd been married to Lucy Smith when Lilian was only seventeen, but Lucy had died of yellow fever.

Kate wipes nasturtium slime from her hands onto the seat of her track pants, wondering if Charles had married Lilian out of expediency or as a solace from stupefying grief. How long might it have taken him to learn to love again? (If he ever did.) Did Lilian hide the suspicion, even from herself, that she might love him more than he loved her? And Kate makes a portrait in her mind of this never-known great-grandmother who sits beside her little girl; even in the streetcar, Kate imagines, Lilian—who grew up at Shepton, spoiled and pampered by adoring parents and four older brothers—might feel the tenuousness of a world that had previously seemed her due. Something might be missing at its heart, a blind, binding absolute like the love that she feels for this little girl and feels, in no similar degree, elsewhere. The last child, the sweetest, the easiest, the closest to her heart. So, for example, she took the streetcar because Ellen loved it, when Lilian herself would have preferred the comfort of a carriage. But she knew that in the evening, when the family gathered before dinner and Charles had been lulled and made passive by his whiskey and soda, Ellen, sitting on a hassock, her eyes wide, making sweeping gestures, would be able to entrance them with tales of the streetcar, a motorized bicycle, a white dog, the fruit bouquet on a lady's hat; and of the party, Madeline Parker's teddy bears and the raspberry icing on the immense birthday cake.

Kate throws off her vest, pulls her sweatshirt over her head. She looks at her watch. It's eleven-thirty, and she has finished cleaning up the garden, more or less. The bright green lawn appears brushed from her raking, like the hair of a wet dog. The perennial beds seem tamed, their wild disarray vanished. Now she stretches with her palms clasping her waist and feels despair like a raven clutching her shoulder. To continue, now, is to begin the process of choice. Which perennials shall be divided, which spring bed dug up, which root-bound bulbs pried apart?

Which day lilies laboriously shovelled and ripped from the soil, their root blocks sawn? Where, in August, was there no colour? Which plants invaded their neighbours? It is a kingdom over which she has dominion, begun when she and Tom were— *what? My God, only a bit older than Liam and Christy are now, with a hip-held baby and a towheaded toddler*—and she is over-whelmed by the sheer scale of this by-now storied heritage garden. It is included in the town's garden tours, the only time Tom was happy to be invaded by the public; its textures and patterns have been transmuted by Tom into chalk and oils.

No, she's done enough for now, and so she gathers her cast-off clothing and walks across the lawn towards the house. *Coffee, leftover rice and beans, an apple.*

She listens to the phone ringing, pictures Christy's apartment; *probably not too invasive to call Christy at lunchtime on a Saturday.*

"Hi, Christy."

"Hi, Mum! What are you doing?"

"We had a storm yesterday. Made a mess of the garden. Just cleaning, raking. Having a lunch break because I've gotten to the hard part."

"Oh."

I don't need to say it. She hears. She remembers. Glancing from her window, playing with a friend. There were her parents, out in their beloved garden. Like moles. Bent-backed, wind-whipped. Probably the garden was less an entity than part of us, like the sound of our voices, the texture of our skin, the expression of our eyes. Such a sudden, desolate sound in Christy's voice. Thinks she should help me. Or talk about Dad. We both feel that we fail because we can't heal each other.

"I'm going to have supper with Gregory Stiller tonight. I told you about meeting him on the beach, didn't I? How well do you remember Jerome and Janie?"

"I remember Janie. Jerome, well, he was Liam's friend."

"Gregory is divorced. Did I tell you that?"

"Mum."

"Yes?"

"It's totally okay for you to go out to supper with him. It's great, in fact. I'm glad you're going out. You *should*. You should do more things with your friends. You're going to get . . ."

What. She can't finish the sentence. Neither can I. We don't know how it ends.

"I can't wait for you to come for Thanksgiving, honey."

"Love you, Mum."

She realizes that she can't contemplate the garden as a whole but must start in one place. One thing, she knows, will lead to another; just as the garden itself, in the beginning, started indiscriminately, without plan, and grew. She steps to the back of a wide border, carefully placing her boots between a clump of Siberian iris and the leggy grey stalks of rose campion. She begins pruning a Hansa rose. The wet leaves of a peony brush the backs of her thighs. By early afternoon, the day has become gentle, the soil steams, there's a smell of sun-warmed apples; spent leaves separate suddenly, spin through the mazy air. Kate clips the rosebush, removing its twiggy core.

When the garden began, Tom was teaching at the high school. They had very little money and, of course, then there were no nurseries, no garden centres. This Hansa rose: yes, they were driving in their green pickup truck, Liam asleep in the car seat, it was early July when the haying was just beginning. They drove up a valley where wind-sleeked timothy rippled in white waves; an abandoned farmhouse stood in a hayfield, uncut grass restless around it. Its wood shingles were silvery grey, its black windowpanes glittered. It did not have the rank desolation of decay, for it was surrounded with rosebushes bearing dark pink blossoms. They imagined the ghost of a woman, discussed how her spirit might visit the vagrant roses, the only remnants of her garden. They returned in the fall and dug up two bushes, planted them in what was still their grassy backyard, liking the way these found plants were haunted by the poignancy of hope, or choice. Someone had brought a piece of one place to another, perpetuated a link to a grandmother, or Scotland, or a beloved homestead.

So Kate, finishing pruning the rosebush, feels enormous obligation. Some of these plants must be divided or else, root-bound, they will gradually die. From some she should have collected seeds. Others need mulching, fertilizing, pruning. There are already signs of decrepitude, of neglect. Stalky stems. Disappearances. As she gathers the snippets of the rosebush—they snag on the rake's tines—she feels a creeping pall of inertia, the impulse to do nothing. Choices, so difficult, even the simple ones. Every day she must summon grim anger in order to throw back her blankets; to leave the hot shower and step out into the chill air; to stand up from the rocking chair once she's seated cross-legged with book and tea. She tries to recall, rolling the wheelbarrow once again to the mulch pile, what it was that gave her such energy, the unflagging impetus to work at creating an imagined future. *All I seem to want to do is wait, wait for something to happen that I can't imagine or create.* Is the garden possible? Is such a beautiful thing self-sustaining? Can she be its guardian without energy? She could let it go. She flips the wheelbarrow upside down. Let the garden go. Phone collectors, let people come and dig up whatever they want, save only the parts of the garden that she and Tom collected from the wild. Jack-in-the-pulpit, dug from the shaded hollow by the creek. Wild violets, forget-me-nots, blue flag iris, mead-owsweet, trillium, the mass of trout lilies by the swing. Plants without a breeding history. Plants unshaped by human dreams. Wordless plants, unstoried, never passed from hand to hand.

Gathering her tools, she feels the frustration of knocking at the door of a room that is empty. That no one opens it infuriates her. She's enraged that Tom does not come, smiling, to ask her what she wants. *What do you want, Kate?* he should be saying in his tender voice, the voice heard only by her and the children. *I want to confer!* her mind shouts. *I don't know what you planned to do. Where were you going to put that* bloody *mass of iris? Those lilies were yours. Did you know the pink delphiniums disappeared? I don't know why. I mulched that bed.*

The garden has reached a certain point, its heart generously filled with soft pink roses and spires of foxglove, with monkshood, sweet william, harebells and lavender-grey mounds of velvet-leaved artemisia; and so they had planned to let the colour drift into cool shadowy greens, spill like water into the margins of the woods. There was to have been a trellis. They had found a barn foundation, had begun negotiations with the owner for the square-cut stones. Under the trellis would have been opposing seats and a stone floor; then wide stone steps winding down into the trees, bordered by shade-loving plants. In the house are notebooks filled with drawings, descriptions. Tom's watercolour wrinkles the last page of his journal.

Looking at the garden, Kate can see only what should have been.

He meets her at the door. She's wearing a leather jacket and a brown scarf with metallic cross-threads that shimmer gold in certain lights. He's wearing jeans, a baggy sweater and slippers.

He ushers her from the vestibule into a living room. The floors are newly varnished. He offers her house slippers. He's looking at the shiny floors with pride. He's had them sanded down to the fibre, removed their history. "Someone walked all over this house in spiked heels," he says. There may have been, she thinks, water stains, places where kindling was dropped, a toy thrown, the Christmas tree dragged. But now this house gleams. It is narrow, only one room wide.

"You'll find it," he'd said in the jocular tones of new ownership when she called to recheck directions. "It's the narrowest house on the street." The street is broad, tree-lined, and runs downhill so steeply that it appears to end in the oily waters of the east harbour.

She does not take off her leather jacket. "I'm a bit chilly actually."

"Yes, it was a cool day, wasn't it?"

"Well, it wasn't bad for working in the garden."

"Oh, yes, your garden. You're famous for that garden, did you know that?"

Ah, he's been discussing me. "It was Tom who made the garden famous." She notices the dryness of her tone and ameliorates it. "If it is," she laughs, "which it really isn't."

They're standing in the front room. Net curtains are drawn across a bay window, obscuring the street. Kate checks her impulse to open them in order to see the sky and the opposing houses; she loves how windows frame views and so separate them from their contexts, like photographs. The days are drawing in. It's four o'clock, and in the sun's molten generosity the city smoulders, its colours rich: brick walls, the shadows of flagpoles and steeples, autumn decorations on stoops—pumpkins, yellow and russet chrysanthemums.

Gregory turns away from the window, walking with the slipper-shuffle that reminds Kate of Badger in *The Wind in the*

Willows. The stereo is turned low, as if he's made sure to match its volume to the muted light; Ella Fitzgerald sings "I'm Putting All My Eggs in One Basket." Kate walks behind him, feeling dutiful and somewhat dispirited, as if following a docent or a guide; pain needles her heart. It's the displaced feeling of childhood, a kind of homesickness that strikes anywhere. She is not riding the edge of Tom's wave. He would have walked close at Gregory's side, leaning slightly forward in his eagerness to inspect, to critique, to offer expansive suggestions. She'd have been free to watch, amused, exasperated, familiar with the ensuing ruffled feelings, or aroused defensiveness, or sycophantic agreement. But now Gregory goes ahead of her, talking. The house is so narrow she walks directly behind him as they thread their way through the living room, past a leather couch and a wrought-iron table, on it a vase of yellow roses and periodicals neatly aligned with titles showing: *The New Yorker, Guardian Weekly, Canadian Geographic.* " . . . So lucky, it hadn't gone on the market yet . . ."

He precedes her into the dining room. He looks at her, expectantly. There's a magnificent, glass-topped table. A sideboard, brand new but made of worm-riddled pine with crude wrought-iron handles. Hand-blown goblets behind its glass windows. A carpet on the floor from some Central American country, its colours vivid, saturated, like the feathers of tropical birds: red, yellow, turquoise, ochre.

"Lovely," Kate says, relaxing in spite of a stab of envy. For it's a peaceful room, despite its lack of history. He shows her the kitchen. He's installed new cupboards, green Formica, a dishwasher.

They return to the living room, troop up the stairs. In the front bedroom is his office. He hasn't finished unpacking; the grey carpet is strewn with cardboard boxes, only a few books lean haphazardly on shelves. The desk is veneered maple.

There sit his anonymous grey plastic tools: computer, printer, fax machine, telephone. But on a shelf at face level are two colour photographs in gold frames: Jerome, grinning, deeply tanned, ski goggles on his forehead; and a studio portrait of Jane, looking startlingly like Gregory's wife at the same age, short blond hair around a face flushed from sun and wind, smile slightly remote, eyes both friendly and quizzical. He dismisses the room as of little interest, although it is the place she finds most intriguing. She tips her head slightly to read the spines of books, notices photo albums, a manila envelope from which protrude black-and-white photographs, a box with its lid half off filled with newspaper clippings. But he is proceeding down the carpeted hall. He opens the door to a masculine bathroom—maroon towels, black shower curtain with cream-coloured liner, a framed print of a Japanese brush painting. Everything appears to be new. Down the hall is his bedroom. He opens the door in a token gesture, and she peers in with the masked courteousness such a glimpse requires.

Then he says: "But now this, Kate, *this* is why I bought the house!" She laughs, pleased by his enthusiasm. "Come," he beckons. They go down a narrow, windowless hall. At the end, three steep steps lead to a platform and a door. In the door is a round double-glazed porthole. "You see," he says, sniffing it. "It's real. It's really from a boat. I swear you can still smell the salt. I'll never wash this window. Leave it weather-stained." She stands next to him on the platform. Their shoulders touch, and she smells pine-scented soap, the clean threads of his sweater. His eyes squinch as he grins, the friendly lines fan from their corners, the white-blond lashes come together. If she hadn't known him when he was twenty-five she would not be shocked by change but would see only an attractive middle-aged man, fair-haired, fair-skinned, smile lines drawn beside a sensitive mouth, his freckled face mapped by weather-wrinkles and an expression, which she notices for the first time, of sweet sadness that is restful, inviting. He pushes open the door with one hand, rests the other hand on her back, lightly, and she steps outside. "At night," he's saying, as he turns to close the door, "this is extraordinary." It's a small second-storey deck lined with wooden benches with sloped backs; it feels like a sailboat's cockpit, snug and contained even while surrounded by space.

On the other side of the harbour the oil refinery claims the sky. "It's beautiful, isn't it?" Kate exclaims. "Like the Emerald City." Needle-sharp spires glitter, white steam unfurls against coppery clouds. The refinery is incomprehensibly complex, a maze of pipes, cylinders, spires filigreed with cat-walks, storage tanks, ranks of bent metal tubes like giant sink elbows. Cars and trucks ripple across a causeway. A tugboat passing beneath the prow of a tanker catches the sun on its cabin window with a flash of light. Below them, the slanted planes of rooftops are softened by yellow-leafed maples. She hears the mewing cry of gulls, smells the sea. It is a view and a vision of this city she has never seen before. Her face relaxes, her smile is delighted. Gregory, noticing, stands slightly closer to her, puts one foot on the deck seat, rests his elbow on his knee. She folds her arms across her chest and her leather jack-et creaks. Wind lifts the end of her scarf. She narrows her eyes, nods as if to herself, letting the sea carry her eyes to its van-ishing point.

"At night," Gregory says, "you can see only the lights and the white steam. It becomes absolutely gorgeous, magical."

"Disembodied," says Kate. "No structure; only the thrum-ming beast and its many eyes." He looks at her, startled, begins to speak, then says nothing. She realizes that he feels ownership of this vision and so she walks to the end of the deck, peers over. "Do you have a yard?"

He laughs. "Kate, if you can believe it, I do not own one square foot of dirt." She thinks of window boxes, of a deck garden, but only nods, wondering if he had a garden, or a yard, in Ontario. Below is a paved driveway bordered on one side by the neighbour's white-shingled wall and on the other by Gregory's barn-like garage, its foundation slightly off-true, like many of the hillside buildings. "I could put an apartment in the second storey of that barn," he says. "If I needed to. Rent it."

"It could be very nice," she says. She imagines, again, window boxes filled with geraniums and blue lobelia. They contemplate the clapboards, white as gulls' wings in the clear sea light. Gregory leans his elbows on the railing, props his chin on his thumbs. Kate returns to the harbour view. On the wind is the din of traffic, a boat's horn, the peculiar meshed roar of the refinery.

"Well," he says, straightening. "That's it. That's the tour. Shall we have a glass of wine before venturing forth?"

She feels herself tighten; her heart skips a beat. Just then a seagull slants down the sky riding a current of air, sweeps so close to them that they can see its startled yellow eye. It opens its beak, makes a harsh cry and abruptly veers away as if appalled, gathering the air beneath its wings.

Kate laughs, and then relaxes. "Yes, sure," she says, and follows Gregory to the little door, feeling as if something inside her has been erased, but not quite able to figure out what it is that's missing.

She sits on the leather couch; he faces her in a pine rocking chair. The wine is golden, the colour of Kate's great maples before they were storm-stripped. She lifts the glass to eye level, tips her head slightly to see the room's colours and shapes stretched within the goblet. Notices how Gregory wonders what she is doing. (Tom would have lifted his own glass, also observing the room's distortion, spun the stem, saying, "Look at the colours in the bookshelf, now that is terrific.") She takes a sip. It is a complex wine, soft, crisp, surprising.

"What a lovely wine, Gregory," she says. She asks about his recent past. He tells her about the small house he bought in Toronto five years ago, the parts of his life he's happy to remember: a trip to China, the people he will miss from his last job, how he was flattered to be recruited for his current position. She sits in the couch's embrace, thinking that she may have misjudged this man. The conversation will tip her way soon. He interrupts himself to say, "But what about you?" and she smiles. "No, no, finish telling me about—" And he is pleased, and she is pleased. He turns on a table lamp; now it is Vivaldi whose music surges like a quiet sea. Kate's jacket hangs on a peg beneath stained-glass tulips in the vestibule's window.

The phone rings.

"Excuse me," he says. "Ordinarily, I'd let it go to my voice mail, but I haven't gotten around to setting it up yet."

"No, no, that's—" Her fingers rise and fall like a fan, folding.

He doesn't pick up the phone on the table beneath the stairs, but goes all the way back to the kitchen, leaving her with Vivaldi, and dusk.

"Hello? Janie!"

Kate sits forward on the edge of the couch and sets her wine glass on the table. Her face assumes the guarded alertness of an unwilling witness. She hears the scrape of chair legs, then an eloquent silence. It stretches, becomes increasingly taut. She looks at her leather jacket. It hangs next to Gregory's raincoat, a Tilley. Tom had such a raincoat that they found on a rack at a second-hand clothing store while waiting for the ferry to Grand Manan. It cost ten dollars and was several sizes too large. Tom cut the sleeves off and wore it as a painting smock. They talked of framing it. Under Gregory's raincoat Kate sees, with dismay (for she and Tom used to joke about them), a pair of toe rubbers. The CD comes to an end, and the silence in the house is like the silence of Kate's own house when she returns to it and must set in motion the illusions that make it bearable—lights, radio, sautéed garlic. Sitting in this man's house, she can do nothing but reach for her glass of wine. What did he tell her? He had not heard from Janie in over a year? And before that, after the divorce, there were years when she refused to speak to him and he only heard about her from his ex-wife.

"I understand," he says. His voice rings with compassion. "No." Suddenly he is on the defensive. "No, really, Jane, I do." He sighs. She hears the rapid tapping of a closed pen against wood. He speaks forcibly, as if interrupting. "Look. It doesn't matter where I live. Where I go. What I do. Your mother is a self-sufficient woman. There was no reason I should tell her." Silence. "The way. Oh, from the paper. Perhaps she didn't have time to listen to her voice mail. Look, Jane, she's never home, I was never home, I left her a message. All right. All right. Well, now I'm here, and you both know it. Why the Maritimes?" A sharp sigh. Kate feels her own heart racing. He speaks, then, as if to an unreasonable child but adds an edge of irony. Kate imagines herself as a young reporter. "It is a paper that needs a total overhaul. Design, personnel, marketing strategy. Really, no, truthfully I *don't* understand. It never crossed my mind either you or Karen would care if I came down—No, I'm not subconsciously—What? Well, yes, as a matter of fact I did. I did go down there on his birthday. What did *you* do on his birthday? Of course I care. Of course I care what you did. You didn't want me to. No, just a minute.

Remember the time you returned the presents I sent? When were you ever not screening your calls on your birthday? I got the message."

Kate stands, walks to the window and pulls back the curtain. Across the street two little girls sit on a front step. One looks up the street, the other looks down. They wear brightly coloured windbreakers. Darkness collects in the angles beneath the steps, a plastic bag blows past. "Janie, I'm here for myself. For my career. What I do. What I'm good at. What? Well, that's your mother's perspective. And that's between us, not between you and me. Look, Jane, I have to—" Kate drops the curtain, walks to a CD rack, inspects the cases. The pool of light thrown by the table lamp does not adequately light the shelf, and she looks for a wall switch. "Yes, actually I do. No, just an acquaintance who stopped by, but I should go. Thank you. Honey, you don't have to. I said I understand. I think I do. What do you think was the first thing I unpacked? Oh, I did? Well, but it's true. On my desk, looking at me every day. Look, there's a foldout couch in the living room." Kate glances at the leather couch. This can't be true. "I would love to have you come visit. I'm glad you called." Kate pictures him leaning to put the phone in its cradle, preparing to say goodbye. She stands in the middle of the living room. "Oh, honey. Please don't—Of course I can say it. I love you. I love you more than words can say. I miss you, too." Scrape of chair legs, again. She pictures him leaning over the table, head on hand. "What? Who? Oh my God, Janie. I'm so sorry. Your friend? Oh my God. Who found her? Of course it wasn't your fault. Why would you ever think—But you couldn't have known that. You couldn't have."

Kate steps to the vestibule. Takes her coat from its hook. She doesn't put it on but turns the doorknob, opens the door, slips out. She closes the door without a sound, stands on the doorstep and pulls on her jacket. One of the little girls waves. She waves back. Both little girls wave and then bury their faces in their knees, giggling. Someone opens the door behind them. Kate sees the edge of a mother; an essence, like a bird's profile. Hand, reaching down. Light falling on curved cheek, arm, glancing eye. The little girls, like ducklings. Arms up, questions: *What is for us? What is for us?*

Kate sits on the doorstep, wraps her scarf around her mouth. Eventually she drops her head onto her knees. She wishes to leave and yet cannot bring herself to do so.

She's watching the lights of the refinery glittering through the branches at the bottom of the hill when he opens the door and finds her on the step. He ushers her inside with one hand on the small of her back, just as he had ushered her onto the deck, earlier, but now she resists and he insists. "No, no, no," he says impatiently, before she can speak. Shuts the door, flicks on the light in the vestibule. The splotchy red patches on his cheeks have spread. His eyes are opened unnaturally wide. He glances at her only once as he takes a jacket from the coat hooks, then does not look at her again. "My daughter. You didn't need to leave." Is he irritated? At her? At her delicacy, her considera-tion? Shocked, Kate feels her own cheeks flush. He presses his fingers against his forehead, one arm in the jacket. She thinks he may be going to faint. "Her friend. Overdosed on every pill in her cabinet. Survived, but just barely." His eyes narrow, he thrusts his arms into the jacket, shrugs into the shoulders, pats the pockets for keys.

She leaves first and stands on the sidewalk while he locks the door and goes along the alley to the garage. Up and down the street, windows glow, railings are edged with light, dry leaves crab along the pavement as if pulled by invisible strings. She herself is also made helpless by the impulses that draw her forward: pity, fear, obligation. Tom would have slashed them free. But Gregory's car pulls up, and he leans over to open the passenger door.

As they drive to the restaurant, Gregory is still flushed and attempts to hide his agitation by expounding on the city's points of interest. He drives erratically, pointing out a carved stone archway or the corner tower of a house ("A classic example of the Queen Anne period"). The car drifts, and he adjusts it with a sudden sharp jerk of the steering wheel. Kate makes a fist and presses it against her knee. He drives up a steep winding road to Fort Howe, a reconstructed blockhouse whose cannons point over the city. They get out and stand beneath its flagpoles. Plumes of steam and smoke rise from mills, factories, the refinery, and although Kate can see the ocean's glint she cannot imagine this place as the wilderness it was when Samuel de Champlain sailed past a forested point and found a Maliseet settlement by the Reversing Falls, a seething turmoil of grey water spanned now by a bridge and on whose steep banks perch narrow houses painted blue and mint green, a massive pulp mill, a paintbrush factory and the sun-burnished windows of an abandoned mental health institution. He is playing the role that he may remember she and Tom encouraged: the native New Brunswicker educating Kate (American) and Tom (Upper Canadian.) She has lived here now longer than Gregory, and has made it her home in ways he has not. He will never understand this, she realizes, sliding back into the car, as he makes no rejoinder to her observations but instead calls her attention to things he can name or explain: the hand-carved spires of St. John's church, "completed in, oh, I think it was around 1826," or the proliferation of mansard roofs and iron frames after the fire of 1877.

The restaurant is Guatemalan, has rust orange walls and a pink ceiling. Embroidered red shawls are pinned, fan-shaped, over wooden macaws on stands and the window is filled with cactuses and jade plants. Through a door at the end of the bar, Kate glimpses a child kneeling on a chair at the table where his mother chops onions. He drives a toy truck past her flashing blade. The mother laughs, speaks Spanish to a tall, slow-moving man who wipes his hands on his apron and contemplates his grill. Year-round Christmas lights loop the window. Pink, green, dark blue. A CD plays, a woman sings plaintively and there is a smell of garlic and cilantro. The table for two, against the wall, seems tiny; apologizing as their knees collide, Kate shifts her chair back. Red wine—they lift their glasses, but hesitate and do not touch the rims together. Their eyes slide to the other diners as they sip, unfold napkins, lean forward on elbows.

He takes three swallows of wine and sets down his glass. His heightened mood has subsided.

"I feel as if I'm inside an orange or a peach in this restaurant," she says and is swept with sorrow. *Oh Tom, Tom. We spoke a language all our own; no wonder I stay at home.*

"Hmmm?" He leans back. His eyes glance from table to table, yet he sees nothing. His thumb runs up and down the stem of his goblet. Suddenly, as if he's alone, he closes his eyes and takes a deep breath through his nose. His chest expands slowly. He slides the fingers of one hand up hard between his eyebrows. He seems to have forgotten she is there. He is reliving his conversation with Jane. He shakes his head slightly; his mouth twists. He passes his hand over his face.

He's looking into her eyes as if he's just woken up. Seems surprised, bewildered. She reaches her hand across the table, and he takes it. Her grip is stronger than his. Her eyes are steadier. His eyes slide away, and he withdraws his hand. He shakes his head. He picks up his menu, stares at it and abruptly puts it down. "She wasn't a close friend of Jane's," he says.

"A friend, nonetheless."

"No, but I mean it isn't as if Jane was deeply involved with this girl. It is more that it brought back, you know, feelings."

He lifts his wine glass. His hand shakes, and he sips, looking away. "Jane was a quiet, stubborn, determined girl," he says. "Always. She knew exactly what she wanted. She succeeded at anything she put her mind to. She didn't need help, she didn't need direction, she didn't want advice. She took up Scottish dancing when she was four. Her idea. Won the Selection Meet Competition for New Brunswick when she was ten. Went on to the nationals. *You* remember."

"I remember."

"And so on, and so on. Piano. Debating championships. Scholarships. She was like an icebreaker. Straight ahead. Resistance crumples. So when Jerome died—she was eighteen—well, there was a pattern established. She was never one to show her needs, or ever seem to need anything—advice, or encouragement. We gave her praise, of course. She was so self-reliant. Whereas, Jerome—I worried. I worried so about him. He was unmotivated. He seemed to have no driving interests. Didn't do particularly well in school, although clearly he could have. Janie went into counselling during that terrible winter. She's been in therapy on and off ever since. So has her mother. Karen tells me that one of Janie's feelings is that it should have been she who died. Since we clearly cared more for her brother than for her." He makes a slight grimace, closes one eye and touches its corner with his finger. "Maybe I did show more, oh, not love, but care for Jerome. Concern. I spent more time with him because I was trying so hard to get him involved, to get him to see that he could be good at something. Outdoor education, I thought that might be his métier. He was a beautiful climber. He had natural strength and agility and courage."

He takes a large sip of wine. "Janie told me, years after we lost Jerome, that I made it clear by my actions that without him I wasn't a father any more."

Kate leans back in her chair, arms folded across her chest, feet crossed at the ankles. She knows without looking at the menu what she's going to order. She doesn't toy with her napkin or her wine glass. She remembers how Tom always told her that in this restaurant her skin absorbed the walls' colours; she feels her cheeks glowing both from the wine and from having spent the day outside. She realizes that Gregory is talking more to himself than to her, although he thinks otherwise. It is a habit of aloneness that she dreads developing. She narrows her eyes, watching him; within the fine folds that fan from her eyes is skin the colour of cream.

"I never knew," he continues, "the degree to which people are terrified by suicide. There's a stigma. People will say how sorry they were to hear of Jerome's death, but then—" He picks up his menu. "They leave it at that."

"It's not quite the same for me, but similar. Just after Tom died, no one wanted to make me cry. What they didn't understand was that I was always crying. Inside. I needed to cry. I wanted only to hear Tom's name in someone else's mouth. I still do. To prove that he really existed."

Gregory glances at her, nods. He seems, occasionally, to forget that she, too, has suffered a grievous loss. And more recently.

Now their reflections bend in the restaurant window, and after taking their order, the waiter lights a candle at their table. Gregory orders more wine, but Kate covers her glass with her hand. And he continues to talk about Jerome. Wine-loosened, he returns to the years when he and Kate knew one another. He loves remembering Jerome as a child. All he has told Kate about Janie is that she is twenty-seven, unmarried, lives in

Toronto and has a responsible job at the Toronto-Dominion Bank. What does she do, Kate wonders, on her weekends? Is her hair thick and blond, does she still look like a Scandinavian princess? Have her eyes darkened—stained by grief and longing? How long will she wait for her father? He slides the shuttle of his sentences, weaving the memory of his son. It is Janie, however, whose absence Kate feels.

And she thinks that he is like a man who dances with darkness and expects an empty floor on which to execute his arabesques. Is this true? Or is it simply that Janie's friend's suicide attempt has shaken him? He asks her nothing about herself, yet after the meal, while they wait for coffee, he reaches across the table. She readily slides her hand forward between the empty glasses, the crumpled napkins, thinking how he seems not to care how she sees him, what she thinks, how she might respond, but is grateful for her warm, steady clasp.

Kate walks up the path. She's left lights on in the kitchen, the living room, the upstairs bedroom. It's eight o'clock, and over the river the sky is pale enough that she can see a bird passing swiftly, as if hunted by darkness. The night air holds the river-damp, and she slips her hands into her pockets. How many times has she said to herself, *I have never felt this lonely.*

She presses her forehead against the door as she turns the key.

She stands in the kitchen, where a table lamp by the window casts enough light to make shadows loop like shawls. Through the window she can see the green light on the bridge, trees barely distinguishable against the darkening sky. She sits in her rocking chair without taking off her jacket.

She rocks. Tom is somehow present in this house, and she is comforted.

5. Measles

SHE TAKES OFF HER JACKET, HANGS IT BY THE DOOR. A red light on her phone blinks; she picks up the receiver, listens to a message from Caroline: "Yes, Kate, hi. I got your coffee, sorry I didn't bring it over. I'll stop in tomorrow."

She dials her parents. "Hi, Mom. I just called to say good night."

"Oh, sweetie! Wait till I get Dad."

"Katie?"

"Hi, Dad. I just called to say good night."

They do, in fact, sound drowsy. They've been sitting on their patio playing Scrabble. She pictures their tiny apartment, bland as a hotel suite.

Her house feels emptier when she hangs up. She's tired, but feels too edgy to go to bed. She decides to change into more comfortable clothes. She goes upstairs, passes the doors of Christy's room, Liam's room, a guest room. Spare rooms. *Like me. Spare. Marginal, not needed. Empty.* As she walks down the hall, she listens, thinking that emptiness is less the absence of sound than it is the absence of the possibility of sound. The air is filled with what is, rather than what might be. No one will cough, or rustle paper or open a closet door.

Only the house itself makes its peculiar sighings and ticks. Settling timbers. A mouse in the attic.

It strikes her most often across the chest. Loneliness. Longing. A slow tightening, making her aware of the weight of her heart.

She changes into black leggings that have lost their elasticity. A long-sleeved T-shirt. The disputed canvas vest, whose whereabouts depended on who shelved the laundry. She runs her hand down its front, seeks the pocket as though she might find something there of Tom's. It's still Tom's vest. *It was Tom's, I would never admit it, but really I always knew.* She steps to the open window. The night air is sharp, smells of mud, wet iris blades, dried ferns. She can see the river, a metallic gleam through the trees. Soon she'll see more of it, when the trees lose their leaves. She puts her hands on the windowsill and presses her forehead against the glass. This is a posture she recognizes in herself, the way she turns her back on the house and its demands.

Back downstairs, she goes to the living room, where Tom's drawing table is in the process of becoming hers. It is covered with stacks of letters, sorted and secured with rubber bands. Photographs, piled on edge in a box. Receipts, paper-clipped. A hatbox on the floor, its oval top slid sideways. She sits at the table, turns on a lamp. Here, too, the windows are propped open. She hears leaves rustle as the trees sway in a night breeze. A few crickets splinter the quiet with feeble chirps. She settles her chin in her hand. She thinks how Gregory Stiller makes her feel disarranged, unsettled. She wonders if it is because of the way, after his second glass of wine, he reminisced about their joint family adventures. He set his words down definitely, like bricks, and she did not dare join with her own memories, or contradict his. It would be, she sensed, his version or none.

She leans sideways, rummages in the hatbox, removes a packet of what seem to be postcards and unties the string wrapped round them. "Received with thanks from Mrs. Charles Thomas." Kate turns them over, one by one. They are receipts for membership dues, all for the year directly after Ellen died, 1907–08. The Board of the Orphan's Asylum, the Town and Country Club, the Altar Guild of the Cathedral, the Horticultural Society, the Society of Colonial Dames, the Women's Aid Society of Hartford, the Hartford School of Housekeeping, the Musical Club of Hartford, the Law and Order League, the Society of Mayflower Descendants, the McKinley Club, the Connecticut Indian Association. Kate imagines the great emptiness that Lilian filled with a clamour of women's voices, extolling righteousness, patriotism, duty, order, culture. She guesses that no one could bear to speak of Ellen.

Where do they go, the recently dead? At the beginning, they seem close. It's—*what is it?* Kate closes her eyes, retrieves the months immediately after Tom died. Yes, a sense of closeness: rooms seem smaller, their space filled, an excessive weight to every object, both solid and ephemeral—chairs, saucepans, sunlight—as if the material world is intensely present. Perhaps Giles sensed this, and felt that his little sister was hidden, here and there. His brother's Barzoni violin, that Ellen loved to touch and longed to play, was pushed onto a high shelf. No longer used. Lilian probably emptied Ellen's room. Where did she put everything? Could she have borne to give these things away, or did she hide them in the attic? Will Kate someday find a box filled with pinafores and hats, paint-boxes and crayons and porcelain dolls, a Peter Rabbit book? Did Giles haunt the rooms of the house, seeking these things? His remaining sister, Katherine, would have returned to college. Only Giles and his younger brother would have been at home. The house itself must have seemed dead, its rooms silent, love contracted into the most restrained of gestures.

Kate picks up a photograph of her grandfather. He's about sixteen, wearing knickerbockers and ribbed knee socks. He's a handsome boy with a high, broad forehead and a sensitive mouth that lifts at the corners in a half-smile. His eyebrows sweep low, like a hand shading his eyes from sunlight, making him appear wary, prescient, calm. Kate realizes, suddenly, that she can't remember the sound of her grandfather's laugh, nor of her grandmother's. She remembers only Grampa Giles' calm, gravelly voice, speaking of lettuce or rain. She studies the photograph, imagines him as a teenager, looking out the window of the big Hartford house. Was that when he became a gardener? Had his own father lost the heart to care for the extensive grounds? Giles would have seen dark-leaved peonies, perhaps, sprawling their ant-infested pink flowers over a brick path. Or lemon lilies, their flowers like duck's beaks, gawky on long stems. Untended: no neatly trowelled soil, no space unclogged by weeds, no sliced sod dividing lawn and garden. Did he try to galvanize his father, rashly digging, hoping to provoke a response? As Christy has tried to motivate Kate: *I'll come home, Mum; we can do the pruning together.*

Kate picks up one of the piles of paper-clipped receipts. Bills for Giles' father's physical training lessons—they cease after April 1907. She reaches into a box by the light where she puts photographs as she finds them: walks her fingers through their soft edges as if she's going through a card catalogue. There. She pulls out a studio photograph of Giles' father, Charles. White hair, parted in the middle. One eye is stern, the other is frightened. Heavy moustache, drawing his lips downward. A sad face, a hopeless face. She imagines this man, her great-grandfather, falling into a depression after Ellen's death, cancelling appointments, sitting in the library with an unlit pipe in his hand, newspapers fanned on the floor around his chair. Did Giles think that someday the parents he once knew would finish their mourning and that the father who planted onions, lifted dumbbells, raked the driveway until it looked like a Japanese garden would return? That the mother who sang, who browsed in her rose bushes on summer mornings, wielding clippers, who presented Mrs. Heaney with recipes for snow pudding and charlotte russe would come back? But they do not appear to be a family that would have wept publicly or known how to mourn privately. *Keeping up. Holding up.* They would have pretended to accept, and to move on. Such families, Kate thinks, may never finish mourning, since they never dare to begin. Ellen, perhaps, was like something fallen overboard—they reached, desperate, but once she could not be retrieved they turned their faces away.

Is this how Christy sees me? Is this why Liam stays in Ireland? Am I like an uninhabited shell? Have they lost me as well as Tom?

Kate keeps papers pertaining to Ellen in a small cedar box, its lid weighted with a purple-grey stone. She opens the box, removes a brown envelope and slides out the two pieces of paper it contains. One is from the Massachusetts Cremation Society; the other is from the Office of Registrar of Vital Statistics. "I have viewed the body and made personal enquiry into the cause of death of Ellen Pierpont Thomas." Measles pyemia. Death from *measles.* These are the saddest documents Kate has ever seen. The words bring tears to her eyes every time she reads them, and yet she returns to the documents again and again. She unfolds them, stares at their statistical reduction of a child's life. Underneath Ellen's name is a number: 2174.

Kate closes her eyes. All those things in Shepton—spinning wheels, hand-stitched quilts, creaky four-poster beds, beaver hats, flatirons used as doorstops—those things that had seemed to be hers, inhabiting her time and space naturally, like leaves pattering down on October mornings, had really belonged to other people: the pale-eyed people of daguerreotypes. Those things with their closety, old-wool smell had made her feel not the truth of the past but its anchoring power, evidence that places endured. Proof that it was possible to build a sanctuary into which time could not trespass. But this document, like Kate's dream of Shepton's unvisited rooms, makes Kate feel as she does when she sees the Milky Way on a winter's night and realizes that the universe is real. *They were alive, those vanished people.*

She unfolds another document she discovered several days ago. It is an ordinary receipt, written on cream-coloured paper in a spidery scrawl. She reads it. "To Everett J. McKnight, M.D. For professional services rendered to date (April 11th to April 16th). For 2–1/2 hours surgery, Mrs. Biddeford (assistant), chloroform, laudanum, misc. $41, less credit."

She tips from the bookshelf a heavy textbook that Christy bought for a first-year course: *Major Human Diseases Past and Present.*

Measles, often accompanied by an infection of the middle ear called mastoiditis.

And Kate imagines how, on the morning after the birthday party, Ellen woke with a fever and chills. Lilian called Dr. McKnight on the telephone, and he came by in the afternoon. "Measles," Lilian told Mrs. Heaney after he left. "Holy Mary, Mother of God," Mrs. Heaney, who had seen death, whispered. Red, swollen skin around Ellen's left ear. Ellen held her hand over it and screamed. They pried the hand away to apply cold compresses. Her eyes glistened with fever, her lips were swollen and parched. Lilian did not go to bed. She fell asleep on the couch, or in armchairs or in the rocking chair by Ellen's bed. The cry rose. "Mama, Mama." Lilian lifted Ellen's head, pulled the hair from her neck. Tendrils peeled from the skin like the thready veins of a Christmas orange. The sheets were soaked. "There, my darling, there, now," Lilian crooned, dipping a cloth in warm water, passing it over forehead and shoulder, thigh and anklebone. Pulling down the nightgown. Tucking up a sheet. A blanket. Smooth, cool, peaceful. "Shush my darling. Shush, it is gone." Fingers brushing temple, displacing pain.

An abscess in the mastoid could cause pus, which enters the bloodstream, causing pyemia, a form of septicemia (blood poisoning).

Dr. McKnight. A smell of pipe tobacco and starch. Moustache the colour of scorched linen. He lifted Ellen's wrist, pressed his warm thumb against her vein. Lilian was silenced by the doctor's presence. Otherwise, she would have whispered to her child, "Spring is coming. Soon you'll be running on green grass. It will pass, my darling. This will pass." The doctor leaned forward, spoke distinctly. "How does your ear feel today, Ellen?" No, Lilian thought. Don't speak of it; the pain is gone. Ellen's hand clutched her ear. Evidently, the pain had returned. Glided, twisted, snakelike. Loop on loop. No end to its coming. She began to rock to the mad rhythm of pain. The thin cry poured from her mouth. Lilian's hands went to her temples; she pressed the skin of her face until her own eyes became mad. Now Charles was in the doorway. They clustered together.

To relieve the abscess necessitates surgery, which in the days before antibiotics held the risk of further infection.

The doctor murmured. Would they please prepare a table in the kitchen, with lights and clean sheets to wrap around the patient. Could he use the telephone to call his assistant? Charles preceded the doctor down the stairs. Lilian watched them for an instant, hand pressed to her heart. Ellen's little voice rose in a long quavering wail. "I'm coming, my darling," Lilian called, her voice loamy with fear. She hurried into Ellen's room. The child lay on her side, hands clasped to her head. She rocked like something once swinging wildly that has almost come to a stop, her hand clamped so tightly over her ear that the tips of her fingers were white. Lilian knelt by the bed, laid her cheek on the pillow. The child opened her eyes. Like a question. Look at me, my darling, Lilian beseeched wordlessly. See my love. But between mother and child was the featureless landscape of pain.

Folding the ear forward, drilling into the mastoid with a small hand drill . . . The wound would be left open so the pus could drain.

Charles carried Ellen into the kitchen. The doctor was washing his hands in the sink. Mrs. Biddeford, the assistant, a spare, grey-haired woman. Sorting things, lifting and replacing shiny objects, like Mrs. Heaney polishing silverware. Charles lowered Ellen to the table, held her shoulders. Her sister, Katherine, swaddled her in a sheet. Now Lilian stepped forward and cupped the little girl's head in her hands, making tiny circling motions with her fingertips. She laid her cheek on Ellen's hot face. Ellen tried to reach for her, but her arms were bound. Her eyes widened in terror. "Darling, the doctor is going to make you go to sleep, and then he's going to take away the pain." A terrible smell filled the room. The woman stepped forward with her hands spread and hidden beneath a cloth. Her face was stern, she showed compassion by swiftness. "Careful, now, Mrs. Thomas," she said. "Hold her head still." If she can keep her voice in the child's mind. Something she loves. "Lullaby, and good night," she sang. The cloth lowered over Ellen's face. The child's face turned, turned. Tears lodged in the corners of Lilian's mouth. She tasted them as she whispered the song. "Lullaby, and good night." "One," the woman counted. "Two, three, four." Ellen's body went still. Dr. McKnight glanced sharply at Charles. Charles wheeled, took Lilian's arm. She let herself be led from the kitchen, looking back to see the oak cabinets, the black coal range, the oatmeal-coloured mixing bowls, the red and blue windowpanes. On the table, the misplaced image of a shrouded child in the place where Mrs. Heaney kneaded bread.

Once in the bloodstream . . . high temperature and rigours, spiking fever, coma.

That night, Ellen became rigid, shook in violent spasms. The bed's headboard clattered against the wall. Lilian, kneeling, bathed the child in cool water. Mrs. Heaney, Katherine, Charles. All running. Down the stairs to fetch towels. Back again with a tray of tea. Pouring water into a glass. Now a stream of words poured from Ellen's mouth. She was at the party where she contracted the measles. She spoke with the flat, terrible brightness of delirium. "Madeleine's teddies, one named Charley. Charley, Matthew, Christopher. Funny names, aren't they? Haven't they had their cake? Mama? The teddies haven't had their cake. The icing is pink. The girls. On their teeth. Pink teeth, their teeth are—No, a kitten. No. No. Take it out. Take it out of there. Get the kitten. Get the kitten."

Lilian felt that if she responded steadily, her voice would override Ellen's delirious talk, and she might restore normalcy.

She took everything the child said and twisted it back into sense. But now Ellen tried to sit bolt upright. She was screaming, eyes wide open. They forced her down. Another spiking fever seized her. Lilian was emptied of emotion and yet filled as if with a surfeit of life. She bore this child over again. She would give her life, once again. She was focused with the violence of a woman in labour. It was two a.m. No one thought of going to bed. Giles and Daniel tiptoed to the doorway and then went back to the third-floor staircase, where they sat, shuddering like wet dogs, arms clasping their legs.

Charles telephoned for Dr. McKnight. It was pouring rain, and the stable lantern that hung from the porch illuminated the glistening branches of rose bushes. Slugs of rain twisted down the windowpanes. When Ellen lapsed into silence, there was whispering. The steady drumming of rain. Then the sudden clatter of horse hooves. Dr. McKnight had arrived. Charles hurried downstairs. In the light of the street lamp, he could see the horse's white-rimmed eye, its slick neck curving to tightened reins. The doctor stepped out, his top hat and leather bag sleek as sealskin, streaming with rain. Lilian heard only the cessation of horse hooves and then low urgent voices in the hall. Steps hurrying up the stairs. A sense that, now, all would be over, better, with the arrival of authority. She sat back on her heels, felt her hands tremble as she pushed back her hair. Ellen lay on her back, her eyes closed, her face pinched by a turban of white linen. She was no longer crying. Her voice rose in an unending monologue, the words clear and perfectly enunciated. The doctor stepped over the threshold. She opened her eyes and stared straight at him. "A big lion watching with the mice and the grass I did put the scissors I told her she took my kitten no there no over there it's coming this way no don't, don't, don't—" Dr. McKnight stopped, shaken. His eyes darted to Lilian, but she did not see his expression. She rose from her knees, reached for Ellen, her hands spread as if she cradled a bowl, or a baby. All night long the fever spiked and fell. The little girl either burned or shook with cold. By early morning, when the room was greying with a sunless dawn, she had fallen into a coma. At ten o'clock on April 16 she drew a faint breath. The next breath never came.

After death, the body will be covered with tiny abscesses, the fingernails streaked with splinter hemorrhages.

Giles had fallen asleep on the stairs with his head on his knees. He woke to the sound of his mother's thick cry. *Ellen. Ellen.* Like a rope twisted, released, twisted. Katherine appeared at the foot of the stairs. The brothers and sister stared at one another. Then Katherine put her hands over her face and turned away. The boys stumbled after her, stiff-kneed. In Ellen's room, there was Father in his shirtsleeves, his hands gripping the bed's footboard. His eyes so wide it seemed that his face had shrunk. Mother. Kneeling at the bedside, face pressed against the blankets, arms outstretched as if holding the hands of someone who'd pulled away. The doctor eased shut the clasp of his bag, seemed not to want to leave the room. There was Ellen's small face, eyes closed, lips parted as if in mid-word, her serious, innocent, happy world lingering and yet fading even as they watched.

No one made a sound after Mother's long wail. Katherine, Giles and Daniel went to their rooms and sobbed into their pillows. Charles sat in the library with the curtains drawn, gripping his face. Lilian cried steadily all day long. She and Mrs. Heaney washed Ellen and changed her clothes. Giles carried tea into the room. He saw Ellen's white skin peppered with abscesses, saw the tiny red streaks beneath her fingernails.

They handled her tenderly, as if she were sleeping. Brushed her hair, bound it with a pink satin ribbon. Late that evening the undertaker came. A heavy, balding young man wearing spectacles. Hairless cheeks, pink and pendulous as a pig's rump. He wrapped the child in a white flannel blanket, leaving her face and the hair ribbon exposed. Bent, lifted the small, stiff bundle from the bed. Lilian reached forward. Charles restrained her. She turned, and they clasped each other, eyes closed, Lilian's face pressed into Charles' shoulder. The family followed the undertaker down the stairs. Watched from the porch as the young man continued down the stone path, walking away into a wet April evening, carrying Ellen in his arms.

An aggrieved meow comes from just beyond the kitchen door. Kate stands, dazed. Oh, yes, Mr. Winkles. She goes to the kitchen, opens the back door. The cat shoots past her ankles. She steps onto the porch and stands with her hands on the railing, listening to leaf-rustle, smelling not winter but summer's close, the smell of dried sunshine, of crumpled heat.

She is imagining Tom slumped over the kitchen table with one hand flung outward. It is the image she dreams of, over and over again; she wakes from the dream and sits up in bed, palms outward, as if she's entangled in spiderwebs. The worst thing: that he was leaving her and she could not call him back. *Tom. Tom. Tom.* She crouched, arms around his shoulders, lips to his ear. *Tom!* Shouting. And he did not answer. She sees Gregory's face as he envisions Jerome's fall. *Oh, Lilian,* she thinks, as if her great-grandmother is listening. *We try to call them. Tom. Ellen. Jerome. And they are too far away.*

6. Harvest

KATE FINDS HER GRANDFATHER'S DIARIES TUMBLED
loosely in one of the hatboxes. The books are bound in soft,
scarred leather. They fit in the palm of her hand, and she picks
them up, one after the other, and scans the dates. They are
five-year diaries, starting in 1911 and petering out in the blank
pages of 1934. She arranges the little books in chronological
sequence on her table and then opens the first one only long
enough to read his name—Giles Wolcott Thomas—written
on the flyleaf in the handwriting she remembers, only it is the
more careful script of a younger man.

For several days she keeps this first diary, unopened, in the
middle of Tom's drawing table. She knows that once she
begins reading it, Grampa Giles will become a different person. She lays her hand on it and looks out the window at the
trees, which, in the first week of October, are at the height of
their colour. The season is in full flight, like the birds. Wind
devils branches, leaves rush down the sky, the river's choppy
light is oblique. Kate's house is like a ship; outside its windows
nothing is still, and like waves at sunset, colour dips and glides
beneath the sky.

One day she opens the diary and begins to read.

July 7, 1911—Note from Cousin Lyman today. Sends congratulations on Yale graduation. Also letter from Knox, Judson, Anderson and Marshall. I shall start work at the firm on September 5. Mother much improved, due to all papers being signed. Relieved, no doubt, to be at last the sole owner of Shepton. I am glad the uncles had no use for the place. Father and I are drawing plans for the expanded orchard. Will plant more Gravensteins and new improved varieties. Mother wants a rose trellis by the hatchway. Spoke to Mr. Emmet about addition of bathrooms and dining room. Will begin terracing new lawns next week.

July 10, 1911—Continued fine weather. Reuben Pearl's team of Belgians mowing upper field. Shot a woodchuck from the bedroom window. Pleasant working outside all day.

July 17, 1911—Grange picnic at Bigelow Hollow. Thunderstorms. Daniel here for the weekend. Lawn torn up by tip bucket. I worked with Tom Riley and co. most of week. West slope is dug and smoothed.

Every word falls into her mind the way leaves fall from the trees, revealing the strong grey forms that have been hidden all summer. Her grandfather's young heart lodges in Kate's, and she carries it with her all day, a peculiar excitement, like the lopsided chaos of love, even though she allows herself to read only a page or two of his diary each day, wanting it to last.

Christy is coming home for Thanksgiving, which is on the second Monday of October. Liam, in Ireland, will not remember the day. Kate and Christy share their certainty of this, and laugh. Christy has begun speaking of her father as if she's decided, or someone has counselled her, to weave his character into her life's texture. *Dad hated turnips. Let's make Dad's pie. No, Mum, don't you remember? Apple with crumble crust, the crumble was important.* They piece together the man they both knew. Christy's Tom is different from Kate's. Kate listens, wondering, amazed at the wrongness of her assumptions, discovering the tenderness and strength of this relationship between father and daughter. So Christy did not mind Tom's acerbity. Pitied and understood his frustrations, saw how he projected them, saw the loneliness this caused him. And was not afraid of his stubborn disparity—Tom, sitting by the window, striking chalk on paper, one strong line, another strong line, the repellent tightness of his mouth, cigarette smoke riding vagrant eddies; Christy would not hesitate to throw an arm over his shoulder, tighten it when she felt his resistance, gaze not at her father but at his drawing until his edges softened. He looked up, squinting, saw the fly-specked lampshade, his own charcoal-blackened hands, and reached up to pat her cheek.

The day before Christy is due home, Kate's house is filled with clear autumn light. Cool air fills the kitchen when she opens the porch door for Mr. Winkles. It is invigorating, evokes both endings and new starts, sharp with the tang of bruised leaves and a bite of woodsmoke borne on the north wind.

She calls her parents. "The air today reminds me of Shepton. Of Thanksgiving at Shepton."

"We have the air-conditioning on," her mother says. "I think it's about ninety-five here."

"Do you remember Granny's pies, Dad?"

"The pies? Oh, yes. Pumpkin."

"Granny said *punkin*," her mother says.

"What was Grampa Giles' favourite?"

"Apple," says her father, who cannot remember if they dined at home or in a restaurant the night before. "Apple," he says briskly. "Made of Gravensteins."

When she hangs up, a wistful smile touches her mouth, lights her eyes. She was able to alleviate their worry over her with a scrap of happy news. Christy. Coming home tomorrow. And how she is going to a farm stand this morning to buy apples. And how she will be making pies, like her Granny's, this afternoon.

As Kate drives slowly upriver, her window open, Grampa Giles, in her imagination, sits mute, restfully, beside her. She goes so far as to put her hand out, smiling; shakes her head at herself. But she would tell a friend, if asked, that indeed she feels his presence. It is because of her mission, perhaps, and the cold, astringent air. Apples. She's going to buy apples and cider. Christy has been specific: Be sure, she warned, to get Gravensteins. When Kate, with amusement, asked why, she answered, "Because we *always* have Gravensteins, Mum, they're a good pie apple." And Christy does not realize that these are her great-grandfather's words, that she has been hearing his voice in Kate's, who grew up with apples.

The farm stand overlooks a marsh where the river winds in lazy oxbows. At this time of year the marsh spreads like a weathered carpet, light-burnished, pooled with red-leaved low-bush blueberries and golden bracken, with bursting cattails and the shiny, dangling buds of alders. Sun is both mellow and harsh, slices and settles.

There are several cars parked on this Thursday morning. Bushel baskets of apples are set outside on wooden stands. The apples reflect shining squares of sunlight. Labels on sticks lean from the baskets: Melba, Cortland, Gravenstein, Jonagold.

There are apples in white paper bags with heavy paper handles; applesauce in glass jars; chrysanthemums—yellow, apricot, blood red. And there are piles of turbaned buttercup squash and pumpkins, jars of creamed honey, bunches of dried strawflower and Indian corn. Kate climbs out of her car. She takes a deep breath of the crisp air and does not go into the dark interior of the shed, where she can hear laughter, the clattering slide of a credit card processor, the snapping rustle of plastic bags. Ducks explode from shallow water across the road; their wings raise a froth, they paddle half-airborne and then lift, wings rising and falling as they dwindle into the distant whiteness between sky and water.

Everywhere in her grandparents' houses was the smell of apples. Their tang hung on the trapped air inside the green Chevrolet beach wagon; mingled with axle grease on Grampa Giles' wool jacket; drifted with dust motes in the barn by the tennis court or brightened the cold air in the entry hall of their winter house. The smell lingered long after the apples were gone, and so was poignant, ghostly, permeated the houses with a sense of nostalgia, the sharp prick of loss.

Kate ambles past the baskets of apples. She walks with the tall woman's slouch that made her height match Tom's. She wears her scarred hiking boots; she's wound a long red-and-orange scarf around her neck, wears a faded denim jacket whose white threads soften its texture, like the grey stems of steeplebush in the marsh or the silver sheen of her short brown hair. She stands before a basket of yellow apples whose skin is streaked with red, making a blush, like a bird's breast feathers.

Did the village children raid her grandfather's orchard, she wonders? If so, Grampa Giles didn't complain. He grew the apples, after all, to give away. And Kate's current lightness of heart, caused by the anticipation of her daughter's visit, is a distant echo of the intense excitement of childhood, when the entire family, all Granny and Grampa Giles' offspring, gathered at Shepton over two consecutive weekends in October to harvest the apples. Her grandparents did not change, during these gatherings, but rather their characters intensified. Grampa Giles became not stern but grave, his lawyer's voice less patient than measured. And Granny's eyebrows raised, making lines like ice fractures in her forehead. She tied on her bib apron as soon as she'd hung up her city coat in the hall beneath the stairs. Cartons and cartons of food came in, carried by aunts and uncles and cousins. Yellow pine needles were slippery on the driveway's cracked asphalt as they stepped out of the cars carrying pies, baskets, suitcases. Roar of wind in the maples. Drifts of leaves, fetched up like flotsam against stone walls. The scratching scuff of footsteps going along the leaf-strewn flagstone path. And Granny at the back door, taking, taking. Smiling, worried. Pies from hands, coats from children's shoulders, jars of pickles, roasts. Up by the barn, the gargling rattle of the tractor. Whiff of exhaust. The wind, snatching phrases: "—Baskets? More in the—"

Kate and her sister walked down from their own house, where, unlike their grandparents, they lived year round. They carried small suitcases and wore trousers and penny loafers. The recent war ebbed at the shores of consciousness, although the children did not realize this. Their father's navy uniform still hung in a closet. Kate, encountering it, was frightened, as if she'd found an intruder, hiding. They slept with their girl cousins in an unheated room over the ell, once a maids' dormitory. There were three or four iron bedsteads with china chamber pots beneath them, made up with coarse cotton sheets and threadbare blankets. Dead flies crunched underfoot on the unpainted floor, and from three low, dusty small-paned windows tucked under the eaves they could look directly down at people passing on the flagstone path. Paintings in scrolled frames were stacked, turned to the walls. The girls sat on the beds, showed each other their new sweaters or necklaces, talked about boys and teachers, acted out their own importance with insouciant shrugs. Later, they ran together like a flock of birds, six girls and two boys; scrambled onto the wagon. Grampa Giles sat on the tractor, straight-backed, wearing a khaki shirt, trousers, a wool jacket and the pith helmet that was as much a part of him as his pocket watch. He smiled, turning to check on them before engaging the clutch. The wagon tongue clanked against its hitch; the children braced themselves with flat palms or reached for the bushel baskets. They lurched up over the lane. On the left, a hayfield stretched away to distant trees and roofs the size of playing cards. Beyond a stone wall were Grampa Giles' beehives, at their entrances the tiny, teeming diamond-flash of bees' wings. On the right, with its summer house, was the clay tennis court surrounded by a tall chicken-wire fence laced with red-leaved poison ivy. Tennis balls, testaments to its inadequacy, lay in nests of dried grass beneath the apple trees. Grampa Giles' trees were pruned into the shape of squat, tidy hens; there was not a dead branch to be seen, they were jewelled with apples. Remnants of an earlier orchard stood along the north wall, tall ancient Russetts and Baldwins shaped like elms, sparse, scarcely fruited, planted by a great-great-grandfather. The family spread its tools. The children carried baskets from the wagon, Uncle Oliver spread a plaid blanket over the prickly grass for Granny, two fathers poked ladders through the branches.

Kate, lifting a basket of Gravensteins and gathering it in the crook of her arm, remembers a morning last spring when she watched cedar waxwings stripping a serviceberry tree of its blossoms and was reminded then, too, of the apple-picking of her childhood, how the family, swarming over trees and grass beneath the cloud-streaked sky, was like a flock, as purposeful, as joined. She stands on the packed earth of the farm stand's driveway and watches two women bending to help children into a car. It occurs to her that she is long past this stage of her life and is surprised by her own sense of disorientation—*No, wait, I've been married, I've had my tiny children, my husband has already finished his journey*—as if some part of her has forgotten who she has become and is still waiting for life to unfold. A wind passes over the marsh; the reeds flash like a sword-brandishing army, and Kate hears the searing cry of a blue jay. Across the road a field slopes to the sedgy marsh; windborne thistle seeds glisten, shiny as the wings of small birds.

Kate and Tom decided that this was their favourite season, since nature, by October, had spun herself time to rest, and the dying leaves floated into an oncoming peace. It is this sense, Kate muses, hugging the basket, that Tom's death has shattered. It is the sense of things happening when they should, as one might expect, harvesting at the time of culmination, skin-bursting apples plucked from trees and a family held within this grace, like seeds snagged by goldenrod. Instead, Kate is assaulted by longing. She tries to keep herself from the futility of wishing for Tom's return; surrounding her like skin is her desire to know where he has gone. His absence gapes, an opening leading nowhere.

She picks up a gallon of cider and goes into the shed to pay. On the counter are pumpkins, posters, lottery tickets, a cardboard carton of straws; cars pull in, a radio plays country music. There's a freezer with a clear plastic lid. She peers in, sees pink bubblegum and green pistachio ice cream. The young woman at the counter went to school with Christy. As she pays for the apples and cider, Kate hears in the young woman's polite questions that she, Kate, is blank as the sky, only Christy's mother, whose future is predictable and of no interest.

She tries to wedge herself back into her lighthearted mood. *Christy is coming home. I'm going to make pie, cook a turkey.* She puts her apples on the back seat, sets the cider on the floor, slides into the car and turns the key. She tries to remember when these words—pie, silverware, wine, asters— were like invocations; tries to recall the feeling of anticipation that lifted her heart as she drove up the valley. But like mist, these feelings cloak ordinary things and make them mysterious, then dissipate. She swings the car onto the road. The feeling has gone because she is compelled, lately—*a new stage of grief?*—to shoulder aside the present moment in favour of images that return her to times when she felt like a firefly at dusk, a minnow in shadows, a child beneath blankets. Small, safe, included.

As she drives downriver, she thinks of the little chestnut-brown diary sitting on her writing desk. It seems to be the only thing in her life that compels her, makes her feel both tender and anxious. The diary has become numinous; she imbues it with qualities beyond the evident. She finds it difficult to maintain her self-imposed rule of restricting her reading to only a few pages at a time. What she feared is indeed happening; Grampa Giles is changing, becoming someone she never knew, yet she can't resist seeing it happen. It is like hearing an artist describe the ideas that motivated a painting and the techniques that produced it, then standing, once again, before the picture. His secrets lie on the page, and she reads them, intrigued, dismayed, then tiptoes, wondering, back to her own memory-grandfather. What could he have meant, for example, by "August 5, 1911—F. did not come. Can't be easy for her. I spoke to Mrs. Heaney." Or "August 12, 1911—Had to change plans yet again. Mr. Emmet won't continue. I drove down there, tried to smooth feathers. Sometimes I wish they would speak their minds. I can't cross-examine my own father."

As she drives slowly with her window open and her cotton scarf double-wrapped around her neck, she wonders if anyone, any more, makes cider like Grampa Giles. The cider she bought today is pasteurized: it will not begin to work if she leaves it too long; she won't be able to peer through the cloudy glass of its jug to see a teeming scum on its surface; its cork will not pop, nor a froth of sticky foam creep onto the floor.

They made cider at the end of the apple-picking weekends. Kate, driving with her elbow on her open window, watches the winding road with a half-smile and cat's eyes that see what is before them through some other, secret, image, remembering how, on the second Sunday, they would have woken to a day of sunlight tarnished as old gold by the wind-flayed leaves. There were enough beds in the house for the entire family, four couples and six children. The beds were named for vanished people or events—Delia's bed, the Lincoln bed, Katherine's bed—the bedrooms called by name: the East Bedroom, the Blue Room, the Bee Room. Two bathrooms, converted from small bedrooms, were slotted into awkward places. The only access to the attic was in the corner of the Men's Bathroom, where three steps led up to a door. The Women's Bathroom was on two levels, the claw-footed tub on the lower level, and then a step up leading to sink and toilet. The toilet perched beneath a sloped plaster ceiling; a tiny skylight slanted over it, like a stamp. Spigots hissed air, there were round, hand-knit facecloths made of string, and dust-smelling towels.

After a breakfast of oatmeal and applesauce, percolated coffee in teacups, hand-squeezed orange juice thick with pulp, they walked across the lawn to the church, where hymns from the pipe organ spilled like broken beads from the open doors. The family filled two pews. The girls wore white gloves; the women's faces were veiled with stiff netting freckled with black silk dots. Later, purified, the children sprawled on the sun-warmed floorboards of the side porch playing Parcheesi, while the women cooked and the men, trapped in their Sunday clothes, wandered restlessly between the kitchen and the wicker chairs on the front porch. The family ate Sunday dinner—lamb, succotash, mashed potatoes, apple pie with chunks of cheese—and then tramped upstairs to change their clothes. In the kitchen, the women took turns at the sink, scouring the enamelware roasting pan and butter-blackened pie tins, wrists braceleted with iridescent suds. The girls whisked thin wet dishtowels over china plates. Meanwhile, Grampa Giles and his three sons and the boy cousins dragged the cider press onto the driveway. Over the barn roof, the windmill's vane swung to the northwest; its wooden blades began their ponderous revolutions. Grampa Giles tipped bushels of apples into the iron hopper. They bounced like rubber balls; some spat out, while others, caught by the fly-wheel, cracked wetly. Dishevelled yellow jackets appeared like a bell-called congregation, wings splayed as if flung in rapture, legs dangling. They teetered on the edge of the press, crept sluggish along the spout. Cider welled, trembled, poured down a syrup of summer, as much the distillation of time as juice of apples.

Kate drives down the hill. The church spire rises above the Victorian roofs of her riverside town, but she is seeing her memory-grandparents: on the day of cider-making, Granny wears a soft grey sweater, and she's brought a nail box filled with juice glasses out to the driveway. All weekend she's been working, concentrating her love for this family like dough in her hands. She mixes, stirs, kneads, shapes, bakes, cleans. She holds her eyebrows raised, making worry wrinkles on her fore-head. She is lame, limps. She wears leather shoes specially made so one heel is higher. Even so, her steps are uneven and she *tap*taps all day long, never laughing, hardly speaking. Her smile, however, bursts forth. "Look, Granny!" A sparrow's nest, found in the barberry bushes, windlestraw as brown as old silk, woven round and round. Granny stops, touches the nest, but it is the child she finds wondrous and at whom she gazes. When the cider swells in the spigot, Grampa Giles straightens with his hand at the small of his back and catches Granny's eye. She smiles at him. At that instant, there is no longer a next moment. This is the time. They have reached it. Granny hands glasses to the children. Grampa Giles walks towards her, watching her face as she gazes at the children, who cluster at the iron spout, kneeling to tip juice glasses flecked with blue and red stars into the warm cider. He puts his arm around her, and they stand back a little, watching their family. Grampa Giles: big belly, steady eyes under slant-ed, judicial eyebrows. Granny, weightless as a sparrow. To the children they are the sun and the moon, or the maple trees, or the house with its many beds. Shapes in the October air, their hair holding light. Smiling.

Kate turns onto her own street, thinking how harvest, and its celebration, was more important to her grandparents than Christmas. *Harvest.* She whispers the word. It begins as a hard sound, trails off. She imagines the harvest moon, swollen, the red of a hand held before light. Orange-coated hunters, boots on frozen earth. A time of pickling, canning, curing. Trees blazing with the peculiar glory of culmination. *We gather together, to ask the Lord's blessing.* One table, chairs wedged close, hands passing butter and relish; sharing, feasting, mak-ing a bulwark against loss and oncoming winter.

Kate reaches the turnabout at the end of the street. She steps out to haul open the garage doors, gets back in the car and eases it into the garage. Turns it off. Sits listening to the ticking of its cooling engine. She thinks of untimely death.

Unexpected endings. For the first time, Kate's longing for her childhood warps, like familiar music abruptly stopped. In her mind she's watching darkness fall as her grandparents leave behind the great sheltering house of all of their childhoods; she hears how their voices drift off, sees how they sit in silence as they return to the city, the car ringing with a one-note tinkle as the glass cider jugs jiggle in their cartons. The lights of the city flash past their windows. They think, perhaps— Kate leans over the back seat for the cider and the basket of Gravensteins—of how they harvested every apple, broke no branch, guarded every bud; how they gathered every fallen leaf for the mulch pile, let no lettuce go to waste, treasured every child's drawing. As if they could bear no more untimely harvests and so scoured the orchard, saved the summer, captured whatever they could.

It is early afternoon, and the stalks of delphinium and foxglove are half-buried in browning leaves. The windows flash, the mown grass is bright green. Kate feels her hiking boots tip over the uneven stones in the path to her house, and her heart lifts. She hears in her mind the words that were once like a charm. *Apple pie.* Yes, its power has returned. She feels a blessed clarity, like clouds breaking, sun shafting a brown pasture, making a pool of light. One simple thing. *Apple pie, because my Christy is coming home....*

Part Three

7. Love Letters

THEY SPEND THANKSGIVING MORNING COOKING. KATE rolls pastry while Christy sits at the kitchen table, one leg folded beneath her, peeling apples. Christy is filmed with sadness, Kate thinks, as she slides the pastry into the pie plate. *Funny how our children begin to seem patient, wise. How we begin to ask them for answers.*

Later, they sit on the porch, sipping wine in the afternoon sunshine. Leaves scratch along the floorboards. The smell of turkey makes the house seem potent, alive, a place of potential.

"He loved you so much, Mum. He was gentler to you than to anyone else."

"He adored you."

"I know." Christy's eyes fill with tears, but she smiles. "I miss him. I'm always coming up with questions, and I automatically think, 'Oh, Dad will tell me.' Then I remember."

Kate puts her hand on Christy's knee. She and Tom were reserved with their affection towards each other, towards the kids, but Christy picks up her mother's hand and kisses the palm. *Where did she get her generosity, her physicality, her openness?*

The next morning, Kate puts Christy on the bus. She stands, waving, as the bus pulls away from the gas station, passes the red brick courthouse, turns up the street that leads to the highway. It is easier, this time, to say goodbye. Walking home, she realizes that other things have changed. Over the weekend, they spoke to each other slowly, as if removing their clothes layer by layer, pausing for courage. They gave each other memories, small gifts offered hesitantly. Here was a father. Now you take a husband. So they tasted each other's loss and saw one another with new eyes. Less a child, less a mother; more a woman, more a friend. Tears glistened, and they laughed easily.

The week after Thanksgiving, as always, the wind rises and the trees lose their leaves. Nothing is hidden or protected. Kate's footsteps are hollow on the porch floor when she crosses it to take down the wind chimes. Beneath a lemon yellow sun, the river is metallic; ice crinkles the black soil along its shores, creeps into the reeds.

As the afternoons shorten, she walks home from the library in cold dusk, her breath smoking, gloved hands in the pockets of a long wool coat. She wears a toque with a tasselled tail. Its colours are Scandinavian: strong blues and reds, with white stars around the brim. Sunset stains the river as she strides beneath pools of street lights with her scarf around her mouth.

Soon the sky slides with its first snow. Kate's phone rings frequently. May tells her again it would be good for her to take up yoga. Caroline, more circumspect, suggests they set up a time for an outing of some sort every week, an offer that Kate accepts only as a good idea. She declines with mild irritation yet another volunteer job. *Oh yes, we widowed women need something to occupy our time.* Last winter, her first winter without Tom, she accepted many such offers with a sense of relief; now she recognizes that although she is less disoriented, she feels a new degree of aloneness. People are friendly, but treat her without last year's effusive warmth and concern. Already, they have forgotten the blood-warm waves of shock Tom's death inspired, how fear swept them close to Kate's pain. They see her steady, dry smile; notice, perhaps, the glaze of aloofness that sharpens her. She sweeps her scarves around her neck as if life has not ceased its billowing delight. But it has, of course.

She sits long at the breakfast table on the days she doesn't have a morning shift at the library. She finds herself not reading, not listening to music, not talking on the phone; rather, she sits over her mug of tea with ankles crossed, casting in her mind's darkness, hooking whispery voices saying words she can't understand. She listens, straining to hear, knowing that her subconscious mind is picking at the knot of her own past, untangling the person she may find herself to be. On the evening after the day of first snow, she cleans the kitchen, stokes the kitchen stove, shuts down the dampers, opens the oven door. The fire sighs and clicks. Logs crumble, sap turns to steam, makes wheezing whistles. She shoves the kettle to the back of the stove. There's an oil furnace in the cellar, but the wood stove is like another heartbeat in the house, so she uses both, sometimes simultaneously. She puts on the classical music station, takes a pot of tea to the living room. This room begins to seem inhabited; she is drawn to it. The piles of old gardening catalogues on the table by Tom's chair are untouched, but every other table and even the floor is covered with the results of her diggings through the hatboxes. They are here, oddly, the people of her family. Here (she lifts it with reverence) is Grampa Giles' diary. Here, discovered in one of the hatboxes, is a small hinged box with a wooden lid. She opens it. Someone's paintbox. She touches the crumpled tubes of paints, the wood-handled brushes, the worn sticks of chalk in tender colours—salmon pink, lemon, morning-sky blue.

She curls up in Tom's armchair with one leg bent. The kitchen fire hisses. She tips her reading glasses from her head, settles them on her nose, and unties the faded blue string securing a bundle of letters. The envelopes crackle as she shuffles through them. They are a correspondence between Giles Thomas and Jonnie Baker. His letters are postmarked Hartford. Hers are from Boston. Jonnie, she thinks, must have been Grampa Giles' special name for Granny, and these (her heart lifts) must be her grandparents' love letters. She organizes them as best she can by their franked dates. Then she slides the first letter from its envelope.

September 14, 1913
Grundmann Studios, Boston, Mass.

Dearest Giles,

Here is a picture of Edith wearing a red hat. Also a drawing of a funny stray cat we find sleeping on the windowsill every morning. See his bony ribcage and tattered ears? Today it was hot, and after our painting class, Edith and I burst from the studio and took the streetcar to the Boston Common. We fed the swans; they are as silly as our carp. Will you ever forget? "Do you like carp, Mr. Thomas?" I said, and you said you didn't know as you'd ever tasted it. I began to explain how I meant they were so funny with their fat, whiskery lips, and then I wondered if you were the sort of man who said funny things. Afterwards, I realized your lips were quivering ever so slightly at the corners! Can you believe that was only this past June? How things have changed. Last fall, before I knew you existed, I was reconciled to my fate (school-teaching like my sisters), until my darling father noticed my despair and packed me off to the Museum School. Now here I am—already my second year! Although now I have to temper my excitement with missing you.

Anyway, today it was SO hot, but even so, Edith and I had Turkish coffee and discussed our courses, which are wonderful, as usual. It is so marvellous to have my own place after having lived with the family of one of Father's parishioners last year. We are real bachelor girls. Our room has a sloping ceiling with a skylight. We have two beds, a table, a sink. Even a fireplace! There's a Persian carpet on the table. I wouldn't want your mother to see it. It's completely covered with drawing tablets, pens, chalks in boxes, playbills, novels. We put potted ferns and ivies on the skylight's ledge. Last night I stood beneath it and saw black birds falling like cinders against a crimson sky. I thought of you, thought of your wonderful country home that someday I would love to see. Please give my best regards to your family.

Yours faithfully, Jonnie

September 17, 1913
Roselawn Street, Hartford, Connecticut

Dear Jonnie,
I received yours with the greatest pleasure. We are all well here, although Father has a touch of his sciatica. We spent the weekend at Shepton harvesting apples. It was a fine crop, and we set aside many bushels of drops for cider. I am glad you are enjoying school, and I see by the drawings and miniature painting that you have not lost your abilities over the long summer of lazy days. I visited your mother and father, and your sisters, Hetty and Alma . . .

Kate lifts her eyes from the page, removes her glasses. Granny's name was Hetty. This is Granny's *sister* to whom Grampa Giles is writing. *Her sister.*

. . . and found them to be thriving, although missing you. I had dinner with them. My work is satisfying if exacting. I am currently involved in a real estate appraisal. By the way, I do remember the carp at Elizabeth Park. Do you remember how you instructed me with their Latin name, which I will now never forget (Cyprinus carpio), and the particularly apt lesson their name brought to your mind? Carpe diem, you said. I have placed your lovely lady in the red hat on my desk here in my boyhood bedroom, where I sit looking down on the porch awning. It remains terribly hot.

Yours, Giles

September 26, 1913
Grundmann Studios, Boston

Dear Giles,
I keep meeting interesting women. Yesterday a Judith Cotwell invited me to her studio apartment. You can picture us sweeping down the Boston streets, heads together, talking of such enlightened topics as women's suffrage, literature and the pros and cons of all-women exhibitions. Judith has eyelashes the colour of marmalade. She wears an enormous brown hat with a brim and a long, hooded green coat. One day I will paint her in this outfit. When we arrived at her place, we went up a set of steep stairs, and there on the landing was a stack of paintings. "Oh," she said casually (but not without pride!), "from my trip last summer." She went to France and Spain. I turned them over, entranced, as you can imagine. Tall poplars in a southern light, red tiled roofs. The titles themselves excited me. "Pont Aven from the Bois d'Amour." My favourite, though, was on her bureau in her bedroom. A charcoal of a serious young girl wearing a hat decorated with cherries. Her bodice faded into an

empty space. There's the merest suggestion of folded hands. It
reminds me of my sweet, darling sisters, whom I miss so much.
They are, like this painting, so patient, humble. They don't
want anything for themselves. Or rather, they seem content.
I wonder if they mind staying home. Neither has ever had a
beau; I don't know why. They go off to teach school as if it's no
more trouble than baking a pie. I sent a drawing of a lily to
Hetty. The day I cried in front of my father (did I tell you?),
Hetty retrieved a crumpled drawing of tiger lilies from under
the bed, where I'd thrown it in a pique. She told me I could be
an artist. No, she told me I was an artist.

Kate puts the letter down. She pictures the Bakers' house.
It was probably a wood-shingled, two-storey house, painted
grey, with a porch. A picket fence with a gate enclosed a small
front lawn. Arching over the dirt street were elm trees; behind
each modest house were vegetable gardens and piles of curing
stovewood. Kate imagines that it was a hot afternoon in late
summer. The air smelled of fresh horse manure and coal
smoke, and Jonnie sat at a small table in her bedroom,
thinking that she should go downstairs and help her mother
and sisters, who had been gutting and plucking chickens. She
heard the thud-chock of a boy splitting wood in the backyard, and down the hall the murmuring of voices as her
father, a teacher at the Hartford Theological Seminary, counselled a student in his office. On her table were two tiger lilies
in a vase, a dusting of black freckles on their arched orange
petals. They were fierce, brazen. She held her pencil like a
bow, little finger raised; she scritched tentatively and then
considered the drawing. She heard the door to her father's
study open; footsteps crossed the hall, went down the stairs.
She leaned forward over her table to peer out the window,
saw the young man's straw hat, his hand reaching for the gate.

She rose abruptly and stepped into the hall. Dr. Baker was closing his office door, rubbing a finger over his lower lip. He was a short, spare man with a sandy-brown tonsure like a hat brim around his bald head. He walked down the hall, one hand trailing the banister, the other patting his breast pocket, affirming the presence of a corncob pipe. "I can't draw," Jonnie said, her eyes brimming with tears. He stopped, startled. His eyes were sweet, quizzical. She invited him into her room with a sweep of her hand. "See?" Dr. Baker fumbled his spectacles from his jacket. He leaned forward, adjusting the rimless frame. Together they studied the drawing. Tears spilled, and she wiped her cheeks. "I'm frightened." Her lips trembled, she covered her mouth with her hand and spoke with her eyes closed. "All I can see is the schoolroom where I'm going to teach. Little faces. Rows and rows of little faces, expecting me to know how to teach them arithmetic."

When Jonnie came into the kitchen, her father was with her, one arm around her waist. He beckoned to Mrs. Baker, who glanced at Jonnie with alarm and dropped her blackened potholder onto the table. All three girls bent to their tasks. They could hear their parents' voices, murmuring in the parlour. Neither sister, Alma nor Hetty, mentioned Jonnie's tear-stained face.

I know they love it, Giles, when you visit. They never fail to mention it in their letters to me.

Kate thinks of the stereoscope she and her cousins found in the attic. She imagines Alma and Hetty sitting in the parlour on Saturday nights, after a day spent dusting rubber plants or standing on stepladders to scrub the embossed tin ceilings. The gaslights hiss, heavy *portières* are drawn, segmenting the room into two. The room is warm, crowded with furniture, pictures are hung high on walls papered with dark red rosettes. The girls are calm, competent. They read aloud, or play the piano, or gaze in fascination at places they will never visit, stereo views that they select from a basket: deserts with camel trains, palm trees, mosques, mountainscapes. On the round table is a Bible and a red-plush photograph album with fancy nickel work and metal clasps.

No one, Kate imagines, sat in the parlour on that summer night when Jonnie's parents decided to send her to art school, for it was too hot. Dr. and Mrs. Baker sat on the front porch, the broad armrests of their wicker chairs touching. Insects teemed, their clicks and trillings quilting the darkness. Jonnie and Hetty kissed their parents and sister and went upstairs to their shared bedroom. They lit a kerosene lamp; shadows swelled and subsided over the brown-flowered wallpaper. Jonnie sat on her bed with her back against the wall, sweat pocketing the backs of her knees. She ran her fingertips over the satin rosettes on the yoke of her nightgown. They were slippery, comforting, like pearls. Hetty turned her back as she pulled her slip over her head, and Jonnie saw how her spine was like a supple stem, bearing petals of blue shadow. Hetty raised her arms; her nightgown slid down. She sat on the side of the bed, drew her hair forward over her shoulder and separated it into strands. It was finer than Jonnie's, and there was less of it. It was not black, but the brown of winter grass. In all ways there seemed less of Hetty. She was tiny, smaller than their father. Her hands were deft, in contrast to her hesitant, whispery voice. Flick, flick, and then she wound the braid and pinned it on the back of her head. "You know, Jonnie," she offered, not being accustomed to contradiction, "You are an artist." She slid off the bed, crawled under the table. She pulled out the wicker wastepaper basket. It was filled with balled or ripped drawings. She retrieved a balled paper, spread it on her knee. "If only," she said, "I could hope to draw like you do." Jonnie tiptoed over and sat by her sister. Together they gazed at the tiger lilies. Pale, like suggestions, they were caged behind dark, frustrated scribbles.

You realize, of course, that my sisters intend to fatten you up. Here is a drawing of three green lizards (me, Hetty and Alma in another incarnation) riding on a winged orange beneath the harvest moon.

Your Jonnie

Kate folds each letter after she's finished reading and slides it back into its envelope. She puts this letter back on the pile. She opens another one.

September 28, 1913
Grundmann Studios

Dear Giles,
If only you were here to walk these streets with me on these delicious autumn mornings. I feel as if you were with me. Funny, isn't it? How we're with each other always. I forget you're not really walking next to me. I almost think other people must see you. When I step out onto the street, I always stand and take deep breaths of air. Sea air! The air smells of salty rope and fish. I can hear the crying of gulls, horse hooves on cobblestones, trolley bells. I hear the cries of people selling their wares. Every day on my way to the streetcar, I elbow my way through a river of vendors. I'm bumped by the edges of baskets. People shout at me and shove things into my face. There, just under my nose, is such a visual feast, which I take in my mind's eye to the studio—oysters, striped suspenders, pretzels, ground horseradish—and

there, too, are the brick walls, flushed with the lovely early light, sun shafts in steaming manure, carriage spokes flashing. Oh, how I love this city. Then the studio is so peaceful. My first class is below ground level. I see the yellow willow leaves piled against the narrow windows. Yesterday we had a male model dressed (don't worry!) in a loincloth. Professor Tarbell paces between our easels with his arms folded. He speaks quietly, always notices the thing that snags in my own heart as being not quite right. We wear white smocks and head scarves. We work so hard, with such concentration. So when we get to the school lunch club, we become very voluble. Do you know how many of these women have no intention of marrying or raising families? Never fear, it won't rub off on me. By the way, Edith and I found a little wooden box in an alley. I cleaned it and painted it blue, with gold hearts and children's faces. I am keeping your letters in it. I miss you so much. I can close my eyes and see exactly the colour of yours. Hazel—what is that? A pine forest in October, filled with hazy light. That little line beside your mouth that someday will be deep, after a lifetime of smiles . . .

Forever yours, Jonnie

Kate puts the pile of letters on her lap, draws up her other leg so she's sitting cross-legged, with her head against the back of Tom's chair. What can have happened? *Forever yours.* She is still absorbing the fact that Jonnie is not her grandmother, but her grandmother's sister. Kate turns her head into the chair's fabric, smells the faint sour smell of cigarette smoke. *I forget you're not really walking next to me.* So keen she is, this Jonnie. So sweeping, elastic, honest. Kate pictures her, jostled by street vendors, a young woman with black hair wisping from hairpins and curling around her face; eyes that see acutely even as they skim, dance, sweep past images, like birds riding wind.

Why did they call her Jonnie? She must be both soft and
angular, a girl with a boy's name; someone who doesn't quite
fit in the place she's supposed to go.

Somewhere in this house are the letters Kate and Tom
wrote to one another during the first summer after they had
fallen in love. *Where are they, those letters Tom and I wrote? I'm
sure we kept them, even knowing they'd be an embarrassment.*
They had been attracted by each other's passion for the physical world, for ways in which it might be described and
abstracted: Kate's love of reading and music, Tom's compul-
sion to draw and paint. When Tom returned to Ontario that
summer, they had written to one another of their respective
worlds. There had been pages, Kate remembers, of lavish
description: she wrote of the lush flowering shrubs and sultry
heat of Connecticut; he told her of the cliffs and wind-
tortured trees of Georgian Bay, where he spent that summer as
a camp counsellor. And they had reminisced of the winter just
past. Now she imagines someone in the future reading them—
Christy, or Christy's daughter. Kate feels the odd sense of a
familiar concept bending, losing shape. Time, collapsing.
Whose love is she reading about? Tears prick her eyes. Whose
love will that unknown granddaughter be reading about?
Here, in these letters on Kate's lap, a vanished girl still longs to
trace the line of a young man's cheek, still reaches her hand
into the dusty light of a Boston apartment, still closes her eyes
while her yearning mind thinks, "Oh, there he is." Kate, now,
lifts her own hand slightly above the chair's arm, over the place
where Tom's hand rested night after night. Her fingertips ache
with the sense of his knuckles and the three grooves in-
between. Bones like a fan. The hinged wrist.

She lifts another letter. She is hungry not for the past's
facts but for its heart.

October 1, 1913
Grundmann Studios

Dear Giles,
   I miss you, although I have much to keep my mind filled.
Such taskmasters are our teachers! I redid and redid a painting
last week—three women in a vestibule lit by late-afternoon
sun—I could not (but finally did, I think) make the rich
colours of the women's hats. We have recently discovered some
interesting fellow studio residents. There is a man in 54B who
specializes in illustrations of spiders. Also, there's a woman who
travels regularly to the Bronx Zoo. She sits on a stool by the cages
and models bison and jaguars in clay. We have become good
friends with both of these rather peculiar people. Gradually, I'm
sure, we'll discover other equally eccentric residents who live
below this long roof. I woke, this morning, from a dream that
surely came from last summer's horseback ride in Keaney Park.
Hetty and I, in the dream, were desperately going through my
bureau drawers looking for a riding costume, and Hetty kept
putting layer upon layer of clothing upon me so I could hardly
move . . .

   Jonnie and Hetty's house trembles in Kate's mind like a
projected slide, quivering with light. A veranda, vine-hung.
A dirt path, leading round to a fenced backyard garden.
Sweet peas and pink lupins against the weathered palings.
Mrs. Baker stood by a side door shaking crumbs from her
apron. The wine-glass elms made the street a shady tunnel.
It was a hot August day, and Hetty and Jonnie were scraping
through their bureau drawers trying to put together jacket,
blouse, scarf and shoes to match the gabardine jodhpurs bor-
rowed from Giles' sister, Katherine. Hetty stooped to peer
out the window. "Here he comes, Jonnie!" she said. Giles

approached the house. The entire family had fallen in love with him. He sat in the kitchen and sliced apples or carved eyes from potatoes with his sharp pocket knife. He taught Dr. Baker how to tie flies, he took Jonnie's easel back to his own father's woodworking room and brought it back perfectly repaired. He responded gallantly to the girls' affectionate teasing, never refusing a second helping of the apple pie they'd discovered was his favourite.

On this August afternoon, the city house was like an oven. The bedroom baked in the heat, smelled of oilcloth, of dry wallpaper. Air stirred the curtains, brought the scent of cut grass and wilted phlox and carried the throb of cicadas and the long rustle of leaves. Giles wore a straw boater. He walked from dappled light into shade. If he looked up, he would see two faces behind the screen, phantom girls. Jonnie whirled away, scooping up a blouse, but Hetty remained a minute longer, gazing at Giles. She was mesmerized by him; he was like music that touched her soul and made her feel utterly peaceful. She told Jonnie this, without an apparent shred of jealousy or desire. She straightened and gathered the shoulders of the blouse; Jonnie turned her back to her older sister, bending her knees so Hetty could reach, and Hetty drew the starched cotton up over Jonnie's shoulders and smoothed the back as if the cloth were on an ironing board.

. . . but I woke thinking not of the dream but of the real time. It was truly the beginning, I think. Wasn't it? How fortunate that my horse began to limp. Remember how you helped me slide down? We were in the heart of the forest, by a little brook. You had, as always, your pocket knife. I held the reins of both horses, and there was a thrush singing. All those green-gold ferns rustling, making a dance of shadow and light. The

*trickling brook. No wonder I return to that moment in my
dreams. Do you, my dear Mr. Thomas? I need not be asleep.
I sit here in the evening light listening to the city's distant
clamour, but I'm not really here, I'm handing you your reins
and your hand is slowly closing over mine.*

*October 7, 1913
Roselawn Street*

*Dear Jonnie,
    Thank you for decorating the schematic of the arbour.
I keep it here on my desk, imagining the day when it will really
be as you have painted it. I will plant the grapes next spring
and hope for the best. Some good cow manure will help. Work is
going well, although I am learning the necessity of diplomacy.
Now I am involved in reconciling neighbours over the matter of
an extended driveway, due to one party's purchase of a larger
automobile. You asked after my parents. Father never seems
entirely well. Mother worries about him. She feels that if he
could spend more time in the good air of Shepton he would
improve. He has dropped off more of his clubs and activities.
This, too, worries her, as I think she feels that a busy mind dispels despair. Her own formula seems to be perpetual planning
for the future. Just now, as cold weather makes the necessity for
shutting up Shepton an inevitable task, she is drawing up plans
for an extension to the dining room and a new upstairs bedroom. Her hope is that Katherine and her husband will spend
their summers there . . .*

October 14, 1913
Grundmann Studios

Dear Giles,

*I miss you so much. I miss your smile, your steady steps.
I miss the way you glance up from your absorption in self-
appointed tasks of unremitting kindness. I miss how you notice
small discomforts on behalf of other people. "Mrs. Baker, can
I get you a pillow for your back?" I see you shaking your head as
you read this, as if to dislodge a fly. Never mind. It's true.
I think about your mother. I remember the second time we went
to the park (yes, it was the second—I kept track until I lost
count at around eleven), and you told me of your little sister. We
spoke of her only that once, but I have never forgotten. Someday
I will paint a picture of her, if you will find me a photograph.
I think it is so sad that your mother and father don't speak of
her. I felt your deep and abiding sorrow that day . . .*

Kate pictures Elizabeth Park, where her parents took her
as a child to see the famed rose gardens. Jonnie and Giles, in
Kate's mind, walked through air hazy with pollen and the
supper-hour's coal smoke. Minnows of light trembled on the
shoulders of Giles' jacket, Jonnie's grey skirt swept over rose
petals on the path. "Do you have brothers and sisters, Mr.
Thomas?" she asked. Well, there's Daniel, he told her, who's in
the navy, presently stationed in the South China Sea. And
Katherine, married to a shy young scion of a wealthy family.
And then Jonnie said, "Just Daniel and Katherine?" And he
told her of his little sister Ellen. He did not describe her curls
or small pink fingers or paper dolls or sweet smile. He stated
the facts. Eight years old, measles, mastoiditis. Sick for a mere
week. A sudden death. "Oh, how terrible. How terrible," said
Jonnie. She stopped, stricken. She had no sense, on the rest of
the walk, of the park that surrounded them, with its white-

painted benches, latticed gazebos and raked lawns; no sense of the other couples who strolled arm in arm wearing white, men in flannel trousers, women in cool cotton, their skirts swinging. She saw only the translucent petals that faded into the dirt path like broken butterflies and Giles' face, turned down to her whenever she looked up. They came upon a narrow arched bridge with bamboo railings. Giles offered his arm. She slid her hand beneath his forearm, rested her fingers on his wrist. They stopped in the middle of the bridge, arm in arm. Below them, on a bench, sat Hetty, Alma and one of Giles' friends. Jonnie began to withdraw her hand, but Giles pressed his elbow to his side, capturing her arm, and then Jonnie's fingers spread across his coat sleeve.

October 21, 1913
Roselawn Street

My dear Jonnie,

Thank you so very much for the pebble. It is indeed exactly the size of my fingernail. I looked up, also, the Emily Dickinson poem. "If you were coming in the fall, I'd brush the summer by—" I read it aloud to Mother and Father after dinner on Sunday. Father was a great out-loud reader, once. I try to keep Mother down and get Father up. She is unremittingly busy with her clubs and committees. He, on the other hand, is increasingly retiring.

I visited your home last Sunday afternoon. I wonder if the day will ever come when I walk into your home without being swept with the memory of my first visit. Did I tell you that Our Mutual Friend (bless him for introducing us) characterized you and your sisters thusly: Hetty, the little one who loves birds; Alma, the oldest, with the crown of braids; Jonnie (real name Margaret), the painter who studies in Boston. That memorable afternoon I felt as though I'd stepped into the pages of a Charles Dickens novel. The house was like a ship, and your parents— captain and first mate—presided over that house filled with seminarians, children and the smell of hot gingerbread. Last Sunday I helped your father oil the chains of the swinging couch. Its creaking threatened to drown the voices of the singing brethren. We limbed the pear as well. Hetty is knitting Christmas surprises and particularly asked me to tell you that she misses her room companion. Mrs. Peacham, who was visiting, also sends regards.

Kate takes a sip of tea. A log collapses in the kitchen stove with a crumbling rush, knocks the side of the firebox. The radio is turned low; Vivaldi's *Gloria* ripples, two soprano voices blending and parting like a freshet. She imagines Jonnie's house on this particular evening of her young grand-father's memory; how the dark, high-ceilinged rooms were saved from gloom by the smell of molasses bread, ginger cookies, apple pie. How there was a sultry breeze, thunder brewing over the Connecticut River. And Giles, whose own house was so empty, so formal, wondered who all these people were who crowded the small rooms. Young men from the seminary, he gradually realized, who sat at the upright piano playing *Für Elise* and *Traümerei* or smoked pipes while sitting on the porch swing. And the families of other teachers or ministers. Giles was sent by friendly prompting to the kitchen door. He peered in and saw Jonnie's mother—thin, like Granny, with glasses on her nose and a bun like a dinner roll—bending over the firebox, shaking coal from a shovel. A cat meowed outside the screen door. One of the visitor's daughters—a small girl wearing a pink sash—jigged on her toes, begging for a plate of cookies to hand round. Seeing Giles, Mrs. Baker hastened to the sink to wash her hands. He noticed that her fingers were warped by arthritis; that her eyes were kind but distant, a minister's wife accustomed to brief but cordial attachments.

Jonnie rushed into the room. She clapped her hand to her mouth and stopped, seeing Giles, for it was only the day before that they'd made each other's acquaintance at the park. She swept a steam-moistened towel dramatically from hot gingerbread. "You cut it," she announced, handing him a knife. Their fingers touched. She carried a plate of the steaming gingery cake down the hall, and Giles, following, found himself in the front parlour, where young people were singing. Hetty, the sister who loved birds, the little one, bent over her father, who sat in a rocking chair, his feet rising from the floor at every tilt. There was Alma, braids wound round her head, sad eyes with dark pouches. The sisters gathered around the piano. Jonnie stopped by Giles. "Do you sing, Mr. Thomas?" No, no, he protested. Really, no! He lowered himself to a horsehair couch, holding a piece of gingerbread. Alma played the piano, sang in a low, steady contralto. Hetty warbled nervously. Jonnie drooped soft-shouldered over a mandolin. Later, Giles stood on the porch, hat in hand. "Come again, we'll try you with our butterscotch custard next week," and Jonnie hung behind her sisters, hands clasped at her waist, one hand squeezing the other as if to keep it from reaching forward.

Kate looks at her grandfather's diary. 1913. There.

June 24, 1913—Went to Elizabeth Park, met the Baker sisters. Alma, Hetty, Jonnie. Roses at peak.

Oh, but surely. *Surely* he must have walked home in a daze, thinking of how Jonnie had tried to describe her delight. Her hands would have made expansive stroking gestures, as if the air were a cat's back. Whole *beds* of roses, she'd have exclaimed.

June 25, 1913—Met the Baker family. The girls entertained us with singing. Thunder, heavy rain walking home.

Kate closes the diary over one finger, leans her head against the chair back. *Walking home.* He turned from the Bakers' porch. He smelled the earthy scent of approaching rain, saw that leaves were white and motionless as if turned upside down. He took the trolley and all the way to his stop saw not the rain nor the glistening beetled roofs of automobiles nor slick-backed horses nor shop signs nor telegraph poles with their rain-heavy wires but only the moment when, just before stepping from the porch, he looked up to see Jonnie's eyes staring into his. He walked with his resolute stride down the wet sidewalk of Roselawn Street. The fat raindrops of a tropical downpour made hollow patterings on his hat. He let himself into the vestibule. The mirrors sheened with dull light; he hung his drenched hat on the rack. In the parlour, his father had fallen asleep over his whiskey. Giles stood at the bottom of the stairs with one hand on the newel post. He stared at a silver bowl of peonies. White petals circled the floor, making the table seem to be itself a flower, floating on the summer dusk.

Kate realizes with a jolt that it is not summer, here, but the beginning of another Canadian winter. Outside, the frozen ground lies beneath a thin blanket of snow, and there are no crickets, no birdsong or sigh of leaves, only the rattle of bare branches. She smiles, looks down at the little book she holds in her hand. So then, she muses, he went upstairs, sat at his desk, drew this very book towards himself. He opened the soft leather cover. He drew his pen from the stand. His hand hovered. And all he could summon was "Met the Baker family." She pictures him. Broad, open forehead, eyebrows slashed low over his eyes, making him seem secretly amused, as if he knew more than he would ever reveal. Tenderness in his lips. She remembers how Grampa Giles seemed to be always straightening things: how he tried to keep everything tidy, kempt. How he could not bear an unweeded garden, or unharvested apples, or unresolved controversy. So here he was, she thinks, on this summer when he was only twenty-two, taking care of his parents. Staying with his father so that his mother, who needed the refreshing solace of her childhood home, could go to Shepton. Mrs. Heaney accompanied her. Cora, a freckle-faced Irish girl with a harelip, came in by day to clean and to make breakfast and dinner for Giles and his father. At the evening meal, his father sat with knife and fork suspended over his plate. His hands trembled slightly. His moustache lifted up and down as he chewed. The white moustache made his face dogmatic and stubborn, accentuated the shadows beneath his eyes and the droop of his eyelids. Up until now, Giles had spent most evenings sitting on the porch with a leather-bound copy of *Bleak House,* listening to the Delta Kappa Epsilon summer students singing on their porch down the street. Occasionally, his father joined him. Then Giles put one finger in the book's spine and held it closed, in case his father might have something to say.

Yet, surely, Kate thinks, leaning over his diary, after Giles wrote "Met the Baker family," he must have paused, shocked by change, absorbing his fearful confusion. Kate herself pauses. One hand rests on the letters in her lap. She clutches the diary in the other. In her memory, Grampa Giles is lodged like the words of a sacred text, a sacrament always available in times of need. How much change can she stand? Even Christy, over Thanksgiving, with her revelations about her father, made Tom, in Kate's mind, shift. The past, Kate muses, opens in increments, and the bits reveal themselves to be connected to a picture that becomes, finally, whole.

Even her vision of herself. Her own past, her own memories of Tom. Even their first love. *How seldom I think of it, how dismissively I shrug when Christy asks me, What was it like? How did you meet?* Why, she wonders is she reluctant to tell her? Because, she decides, the more often the story is told, the less of its feeling remains. Its quicksilver essence is lost, it becomes like a pressed rose, pale, with only the faintest scent. And it evolves, as stories do, with every telling. It becomes not memory but history. The storyteller's state of mind affects the way the story is told. So that now, when she opens that door again on the moment of meeting Tom in a Rhode Island bar, the picture is altered by the fact of his death. There he is, the handsome Canadian art student shrugged over a Narragansett beer; she's standing next to him, her heart failing, then surging as his eyes meet hers. And now she pities those young people, she can't see them without the future's shadow. The past, like the present, is fluid. Its truth changes as it is housed within its future. *Everything warps, even my dearest memories.*

Kate's hand falls loose on the letters. She sits cross-legged in Tom's chair. She closes her eyes, listens to the silence of a November night. She hears only the hissing snap of the kitchen stove and the rumble of the oil furnace. She feels her mind loosening, like an expired leaf. Where will it fall? What wind will take it?

There is no one to tell. Only Tom. Only in his presence could she press her hands to her chest, lean over her aloneness, cry to him: *Never, never, never again will your arms hold me. How can I bear it? How will I bear it?* It is all that is left, all that is real. Her heart, burdened with love.

Kate stands, hands shaking. She puts the diary and the letters on Tom's drawing table. She turns off the light. Grief wakens, blinding as love. She turns off the standing lamp.

The hatboxes become a pyramid of darkness, the street light falls on the carpet. She goes into the kitchen, lifts the lid of the kitchen stove and stirs the coals with the poker. The molten wood twists, fluid and without shape, beyond her tears.

8. The Blizzard

THE PHONE RINGS AT EIGHT O'CLOCK IN THE MORNING.
The house is filled with grey light. When the wind subsides,
Kate can see the snowflakes separate, drift; then the wind
whirls back and twists them into sheets of white flame.

The voice on the line is cheerful, relieved. "All schools in
the district are closed. I'm not going to open today, Kate, so
don't venture out. Curl up and read."

Kate lightens her own voice, feigning pleasure. Oh, the
delight of another day spent entirely alone! "All right, Mary!
Enjoy the storm."

All night it had poured. Water and wind roared like an
opened sluice. Every wire and branch was soaked. Then, in the
hour after daybreak, the temperature had plunged. The
weather office predicts that by midafternoon the wind chill
will be minus thirty. Power outages are feared. The radio
announcer advises people to fill tubs and set out candles. She
walks to the window overlooking the porch and the river. The
wind roams, makes a thundering thrum spiralled with whistles. The house shakes. Her afternoon shift, today, would have
made the morning precious by its brevity. Now the hours
sprawl and spill, losing value. She has filled her tub. She

should find candles, but hasn't. She stands listening to the wind, thinking it is the sound of emptiness.

How soon people let you go. How easily. Or did the Kate that was part of Tom-and-Kate die with Tom? Did she refuse requests and invitations last fall because she herself had lost the Kate that was? By now, mid-January, Kate has learned the price of her deliberate withdrawal. She feels not shunned but respected and gradually forgotten. "This is what she wants, she needs her time to adjust." As she gnaws at her aloneness, she senses that what she may gain from her brooding isolation may not be enough to make up for the friendships that are sliding away. Grief, though, has its demands. For a while she is seized with a panicked fear that she may forget Tom's face, and she sets photographs all around the house. She finds herself no longer raging at what has happened but questioning its truth. Sometimes she does not believe he is gone. She might not see her son for a year or more, but she knows where he is; she can imagine him walking the streets of Dublin, whistling. She can't imagine Tom's nothingness.

She turns from the window. There he is, on the kitchen counter. He's in his twenties, with shoulder-length black hair. She considers the photograph, feels outraged disbelief begin its slow clutch. He's not looking at her. He's frozen, time-mired. He grins ironically at the span of life; he wears tattered sneakers, bell-bottomed jeans, and there beneath the patched fabric are his thighs, with their spade-shaped muscles. In the pine woods, she unzips his jeans, slides them down. Her hands on the silky flesh, kneading his buttocks, soft beneath her palms. "Flex," she whispers and laughs. Hard as iron. They tumble to the needles, his mouth on her breast. The sky is sliced, they fall and fly in the blood-roaring moments, following, rising, breaking. They're on their way north to Tom's country, leaving behind the city where they met and a land at war.

Kate wears jeans and a grey sweater with a rolled collar. She wears heavy wool socks and Tom's slippers. She lifts the photograph from the counter, holds it with one hand, while the other hand steadies her elbow. Cold becomes apparent even though the furnace rumbles. She'll have to light a fire in the kitchen stove. The light casts pale shadows, so indistinct they are blue-grey. Upstairs, moon-parings of light will outline Christy's china horses, will pool the lips of Liam's imported beer bottles. Any door she opens will reveal only the light to be moving.

She stares at the photograph. Perhaps it was a mistake to have brought down these pictures. They remind her of what will never be again, of what will never come to be. Between these two poles of longing there is no present. She is the Kate who has ceased to exist. She presses the photograph to her breast and closes her eyes, remembering Granny after Grampa Giles died. They were going to church. The whole family was clustered at the door, starting out, but Granny was not there. Kate went to find her. She was in the front parlour, carefully lifting a large black-and-white photograph from the side-board. Granny smiled, not in the least disconcerted. "Let's kiss Grampa's picture," she whispered. Kate assumed this was a secret she must never tell anyone. They kissed the glass, first Kate, then Granny. Granny gazed at the picture, wiped the glass with the cuff of her sweater. Set it back beside some other old-fashioned, wide-eyed people.

Well. She has all day. *What shall I do?* She sets the picture of Tom back on the kitchen counter as gently as Granny set back her husband. Panic nudges her. It is the coldest touch. Fright bursts upwards in her heart like hawk-scattered birds. She leans into the vacant hours and senses free fall. Emptiness drains her. This winter she has realized to what extent the chaos of family—cigarette smoke, dirty socks spilling from

Liam's door, an argument at the breakfast table, the peace of the kids' departure, Tom ambling through the garden on his way up to his studio—was like a fire by which she was not consumed but refined. Now she is consumed by freedom.

There is, at least, the cat. Mr. Winkles. She hears him meowing. She cracks the door, and the cat bounds in, ears flattened, each whisker outlined in snow. Kate scoops him up. "Poor Mr. Winkles." But he wants food, not cuddling, and struggles from her arms. As she crumples newspaper, slides the dampers open, sets match to paper, she hears the dry scraping of cat food in the bowl as the cat eats. She stands before the kitchen woodstove, holding a cast-iron lid on its lifter. She stares into the firebox, where a feeble flame is caught by the draught and rushes upwards. The dry wood crackles, heat flushes her face. The refrigerator clicks on, makes its familiar hum. Wind pounces at the house; already a drift has formed along the porch railing. Snow streams from its lip, gradually forms a delicate, curling cornice.

She lets her mental picture of the day spin away. She waits for the fire to take hold so she can work a log onto it. *How we'd feel so safe. Cozy and absolved. The human world shut down and we'd wait out the wild, jumping up to inspect the state of the snowdrifts. I'd notice a flock of snow buntings riding the wind.* The fear-birds flutter in her heart, disturbed from momentary peace. Tom no longer feels close to her. *Some things have changed.* When did it happen? It's as if he's been walking away from her, turning to smile and exchange words. They wave, they call. He continues without a pause. He strides freely and turns less frequently. There's a moment when he sees something ahead that she can't see. *Tom? What do you see?* He hears her voice but not what she calls. He turns, even so, and gives her a great grin. In this grin is the smell of ferns and river water, every instant of comprehended pain and joy, arms around waists, ear on belly, face in shoulder. Then he turns and dwindles, vanishing into the blue-silver distance.

She turns and leans back against the stove, ankles crossed. She closes her eyes, presses her hand hard against her mouth. Tears roll, leaving salt trails, working their way down over the fine wind-wrinkles of her cheeks to gather in the corners of her mouth.

Grief. How strange it is, Kate thinks, wiping her face with her sleeve, staring out the window, where even the nearest bushes are the merest pencil scratchings. The wind has increased and the snow falls in every direction, as if dull sky-giants are emptying barrels of snow into the wind, not realizing what will come of their efforts. *Grief.* It's the reverse of what one would expect. It does not come like intense pain and then gradually ebb away to nothing. No, it is like some bizarre plant that does not seem to be growing until it unexpectedly sends forth a flower. The flower swells, erupts violently through the smooth stem. Its petals are succulent, blood red, gash the light, arresting as an open wound. Gradually, it withers, but the plant is filled with such flowers, curled, hidden, biding their time.

So he leaves me again and goes farther away.

She looks across the room. Every curve and plane—a leaf of geranium, the rocking chair's scrolled back, a red corduroy cushion—is brushed by the white light. It's a stilling weight-lessness. It drains things of colour, of impetus. Time seems suspended, and space recedes. She is looking at the picture of Tom, over there on the counter, angled towards the window; even from this distance she feels its peculiar arrogance. Why did she never see how he's looking through her, she who held the camera in the needled light? He's looking just as he looked in Kate's vision, when he grinned and walked on. What he sees, she cannot. He seems not to care.

Maybe they are right, those women, Kate thinks, who give their husband's possessions to the Salvation Army and sell their houses. In this house, she has to watch an epoch fade. The dents in the bottom panel of the cellar door made by Tom's morning kick: there they are. Leather gloves, bent in the gnarl of his fingers. How many times can she slide her hands into them and sense his return? The notebooks she has refused, so far, to donate to the universities who request them. Let them stay on their shelves until she can no longer remember the rustle as he turns their pages, the sound of his pencil as he sketches.

With no warning, the power fails. The refrigerator ceases to hum. The minute hand of the electric clock stops. In the basement, the furnace falls silent. The digital time on the microwave vanishes. The house is filled with absence and the presence of cold. Outside and inside are no longer separate. Kate stands listening to the roar of wind in the river poplars, the cracking groan of the heavy-limbed maples. Spindrift flicks against the kitchen window, icy crystals tap and slide like restless fingertips. Far off, the wind rolls in the interval trees, makes a wide-mouthed rush over the frozen river. The floor grilles breathe only cold air. The insides of the windows will be encrusted with frost by nightfall.

What is refuge, she thinks, making no move to put on more clothes, to fetch water from the tub or close the upstairs doors; what is refuge but hiding? Hoping not to be found, the child's truth-teaching game, turning the terror of predator and prey into delicious excitement? Coming home to this house on a winter's night, walking up the path together, the lighted windows, hot shower, standing in the upstairs hall humming provocatively, arms raised, the creamy stretch of lifted breasts revealing their silvery crescents, Tom making a tiger crouch at the bottom of the stairs, prowling upwards snarling, Kate shrieking, both of them lying beneath the swirl of duvet, warmth and darkness. *Was this refuge? This place, when all its elements were intact, connected?* "Don't," Kate whispers out loud. The birds in her breast have begun to spin upwards, whirling, going nowhere. "Stop it," she says.

The cat pauses on its way across the floor. Looks up, tail twitching.

"It's all right, Mr. Winkles." She squats. Pats him. Pats and pats him, until her eyes fill with tears and she feels the cold on the backs of her hands. She whispers. "Good kitty, good kitty." He closes his eyes, ecstatic. She scratches the furry wedge of his jawbone, knuckles between his ears.

She's aware of her own peril. It is one thing to discuss—as she and Tom did while canoeing before breakfast in the thin light of dawn—the concept of death-in-life, nature's cyclical cradling, every ending an implicit beginning; but then she was behind her husband's broad back, she had a belly full of coffee, and they drifted on the black water, postponing the day's routine. It is another thing to be afraid of oneself, alone in an unheated house. Sensing, in the emptiness, a desperate imbalance—less life than death, more death than life.

She begins to tell herself, calmly, out loud, the steps she should take to pull herself together, but the sound of her voice undoes her.

She goes to the phone, lifts the receiver. It is still alive. She touches her parents' number on the keypad, closes her eyes with relief as the connection is made. Her father has just come in from the swimming pool, where he spends hours sitting beneath a yellow umbrella watching chips of light dance in the blue-green water. As they talk, she pictures the enormous concrete pillars at the end of the curving drive, the golf course across the street, the palm trees lining Calle Grande, the white stucco clubhouse where in a minute her mother will go to her bridge club. She pulls their voices around her shoulders with relief, like a thin blanket.

Then she phones her daughter.

"Hello?"

"Oh, *Christy.* It's Mum."

She describes her situation: no power, the library is closed, the province is shut down. "How is it in Halifax? Only rain? Hard to believe! Well, I'm going to keep the fire going. I filled the tub, thank goodness. I think I'll spend the day going through the family papers. Yes, I'm making some headway, but I'm still stuck at the turn of the century. I'll set up in here by the stove so my hands won't freeze."

Cold is spreading swiftly. She jogs upstairs and puts on a heavier sweater, wraps a scarf around her neck, fills plastic cider jugs with water from the bathtub. She goes down to the cellar and gathers an armload of wood. Lets the logs roll from her arms into the woodbox behind the stove, lifts the stove lid and works chunks of wood over the coals. She kneels on the red and black linoleum tiles, scrabbles in the back of a mouse-smelling drawer, unwraps crackly cellophane from candles. The kettle begins a slow wheeze. The house shudders like a horse. She pulls the rocking chair close to the stove, adjusts the damper and goes into the icy living room for Grampa Giles' diary and the letters. She sets them on the table. Then she stands for a minute, arms crossed. *Here I am. Kate Harding. Snowbound in the Maritime provinces of Canada's east coast. Here are my ancestor's papers, which have been saved, handled over and over again, shifted from drawer to box, from attic to barn. Which have ridden from house to house in all manner of vehicles: Franklin touring car, Chevrolet beach wagon, pickup truck, finally coming up the Maine highway in the back of an SUV. Here they are, strewn on my table next to bread crumbs and candle wax, like—what? Like letters sent to me, from them.*

She scans the last ones she read—*where are we?*—oh, yes.
Jonnie went back to Boston in the fall of 1913—after the summer that she and Giles fell in love. She's been sending him
things. A pebble, a painting of Giles' proposed grape arbour,
miniature paintings and drawings. *If only they had survived.*
She unfolds a letter.

> *January 2, 1914*
> *Roselawn Street*

My dear Jonnie,
    *How I miss you after the Christmas vacation. I was so glad
that your father and sister asked me to accompany them to meet
your train. Did I look any different to you? You (I think I told
you) looked smaller. And more beautiful. But you know I don't
have much of an imagination, so parting is doubly sorrowful for
me. And encounters especially delightful. Mother and Father tell
me to send their best regards and to say how very much they
enjoyed our times together . . .*

> *January 6, 1914*
> *Grundmann Studios*

Dearest Giles,
    *You ask if you looked any different to me. No, you foolish
boy. I can remember every fleck of colour in your eyes, every
twitch of your so-subtle lips. I was so excited to see you that
I thought I might fall from the train. And, of course, the trolley.
Shall I remind you of what I said, or will you be able to
remember that forever? It is so cold today that I am wearing
gloves as I write. The skylight is covered with snow, so our little
room is dim and we feel like polar bears. I'm so enjoying the
Willa Cather novel you gave me for Christmas.*

Kate cross-references with the diary.

December 21, 1913—Went with Dr. Baker and Hetty to
meet Jonnie at train. Snowing. Hetty and Jonnie talking a
blue streak. Took the trolley to the Baker's house. Jonnie
looks well and happy.

Kate imagines Giles, Dr. Baker and Hetty blanketed in
wool coats and scarves. They'd have stood close together, feeling both the frigid wind coming from the opening at the end
of the platform and the hot, stale air of the station's domed
waiting room. Jonnie's train would have clanked and hissed to
a standstill. And then there she was, emerging from the train's
lighted interior. It's startling when a long-imagined person
appears. Giles would have been stunned by her vibrancy, felt
as if the imagined place he'd been inhabiting—Jonnie lodged
like a star in the darkness of his brain—had been ripped away.
She put a gloved hand on the side of the door. She was smaller
than Giles remembered her, never having seen her in winter
clothes. She was engulfed in a sack-like green wool coat with
a thrown-back hood, her throat wrapped in a black scarf. She
searched the faces below until she saw her family and Giles.
Giles worried that she might miss the step, for she let go of the
door, waved frantically until she had to reach back and press
her wool cap more firmly on her hair. She came down the
steps, one, two, jump. She ran first to her father, and reached
for Hetty at the same time. Her scarf flew back, a leather suitcase tumbled from her reaching arms. Giles picked it up. She
turned to him with her hands poised as if to catch a ball. He
set down her suitcase. Their eyes embraced, shy and delighted.
They took each other's hands, stood like people about to
dance who cannot hear the music for their joy. "Hello, Giles,"
she said, stilled. She forgot herself, her father and sister, the

train with its hurrying porters, the Christmas homecomings erupting around them—small groups of people who hugged, laughed, picked up bags and departed excitedly, arm in arm. She was without words or movement. She stood holding Giles' hands, her arms outstretched. Her eyes travelled over his forehead, his cheeks, his lips, returned to his eyes with increased wonder. "Hello, Jonnie," Giles said. Perhaps he'd feared that she might glance askance, lower her eyes politely. But it was as if she'd been waiting since September for this moment. As he had. They stood in air gritty with cinder dust, sharp with the smell of wool and cigars, and sensed the months of moments they had not shared. He felt the small bones of her hands through her gloves. He felt larger, expanded by experience; she appeared to him altered in a similar fashion—quicker, more animated.

They walked through the waiting room and stepped out into the night. It was snowing. The flakes fell through the dark invisibly, brushing their cheeks with cold paws. The streets were made fantastic by fans and oblongs of spinning light as the snow was illuminated in shafts of street lamps, in tubes of headlights, the splay of shop windows. The sky was a purple haze. Salvation Army soldiers stood at every street corner swinging handbells, and Dr. Baker dropped coins in a pot as they stood waiting for the trolley that snaked round a corner, its lights spoking the darkness like glittering wands. Behind them was a shop window filled with baskets of nuts and oranges. Candy canes hung from looped twine. Suspended Christmas tree ornaments turned slowly, sparkling with sequined landscapes.

The street was a confusion of cabs, cars, horses and wagons. Horns tooted, people shouted and jostled. Hetty and Jonnie chattered eagerly, but Giles could not answer sensibly if questioned. He carried Jonnie's suitcase, watching the streetcar as it twisted towards them, electricity sparking from its pantograph.

Jonnie beckoned to Giles. She stood on tiptoe and whispered in his ear. "I fell in love with you on a trolley, you know. After I met you in the park."

Then she turned and followed Hetty into the trolley. She glanced back at him; her cheeks were red and taut, fresh with cold. Snowflakes glistened on her black hat, and her hair, wisped round its brim, seemed alive. Giles stepped up after her, thinking of the desk in his room on Roselawn Street. The stamp-sized drawings. The packages with postage stamps that he couldn't throw away because of their water-coloured decorations: peaches, stars, lizards. The pottery bowl in which he had placed the pebble. She cast these things, he thought, into his hands as easily as she drew him into her world. It was a world in which things became displaced, spun like snow, touched, stretched, trembled. Reflections in the trolley windows were no longer doubled images, but became instead another dimension. He himself became dislodged on this very night as he rode through the streets of Hartford. After a while she leaned so their shoulders touched, and he picked up her hand like a bird he wished not to frighten.

January 10, 1914
Roselawn Street

Dear Jonnie,
I hope this finds you well. I am in good health. I've resumed going to the Y after the excesses of Christmas. Mother and Mrs. Heaney have only yesterday removed the holly ropes from the banisters, and the white lilies have been put to pasture. I miss

them, even in their decrepitude. I went to visit your family on Sunday, and the fir tree was stuck in a snowbank. Hetty was busily attaching suet bags to its denuded branches . . .

January 15, 1914
Grundmann Studios

Dearest Giles,

We can't seem to stop reminiscing, but I guess it's because it was truly the best Christmas ever. I can just picture the bedraggled tree, but soon it will be alive with little birds, as pretty as the decorations we made. Wasn't that a nice afternoon when we made the cardboard stars? You painted in the backgrounds so carefully. Well, I think it's a good thing you're going to the Y because then you can continue to gamely accept second helpings urged upon you by my mother and sisters. Remember the mince pie? And Father calling you a "good trencherman"? . . .

Kate turns the small, soft pages of the diary.

Christmas Day, 1913—Breakfast and dinner here with
Mother, Father, Katherine and Richard.

Kate pauses. Oh, yes. Katherine, his sister. Married to the wealthy Richard Goodale.

Went to tea and supper at the Baker's. Mistletoe, mince
pie. Many guests. Starry skies.

Kate pours tea into a mug. She cradles it in both hands. One side of her face is flushed from the stove's heat, and she gazes at the north window, whose glaze of frost obscures the porch railings. Snow slashes the east window, sand-like. The wind mutters, whistles, moans, rolls away and pounces back.

The Christmas of 1913 must have been, she thinks, unlike any other that Giles had experienced. Both Giles' and Jonnie's houses would have been festive in their own ways. Giles' parents probably entertained lavishly now that their daughter Katherine had married into the Goodale family. In the front hall, vases of white lilies and pots of poinsettias graced polished tables or were massed before mirrors; the stair's banister was looped with ropes of hemlock and holly; there was a silver salver filled with calling cards, mirror-doubled. Lilian and Charles swept through the front hall, exuding fragrances. Mrs. Heaney and Cora made meringues and custards, clove-studded hams, Parker House rolls, cinnamon snails.

The Baker's house, too, was filled with the rich aromas of baking ham, turkey, mince pies. There was a wispy fir tree next to the piano. Jonnie decorated it with cardboard stars painted with landscapes of pointed firs and crescent moons, foxes in snowy fields, polar bears in red snowsuits, Father Christmas entertaining tassel-hatted elves. Alma and Hetty hung mistletoe in unavoidable places. They appeared with flour-dusted cheeks, bearing plates of hot anise cookies. Giles spent Christmas morning with his own family but arrived at the Baker's house in time for afternoon tea. Jonnie was wearing an apricot-coloured blouse with filmy sleeves. The house was filled with guests: young men from the midwest, an elderly neighbour man, a widowed cousin. There was a pale sun, but the weather had no bearing on the day, since the house's heart was in the kitchen, where the coal stove radiated heat.

Jonnie made Giles sit in the cream-coloured rocking chair next to the steps to the back stairs, beneath next year's calendar. "No, Mother," she insisted. "This is the best place to be, closest to food." She brought him a cup and saucer of tea, a plate of cookies and a present wrapped in shiny paper. It was Edith Wharton's book *Ethan Frome*. She sat on the steps, and they turned the pages, looked at every illustration. A tortoise-shell cat jumped into Jonnie's arms; Jonnie bowed her head, crooning softly, and scratched the white fur under its chin. Hetty drew back the curtains and gazed out the window, her face flushed by the setting sun. The birds, she saw, were enjoy-ing the treats she'd given them: suet balls, bread crumbs. Sunset made the kitchen seem warmer, as if fire-lit. In the parlour, someone began to play "Angels We Have Heard on High," and Mrs. Baker stooped to open the oven and prick potatoes with a fork. Jonnie, crouched on the steps next to Giles' rocking chair, unfolded the wrapping on the gift he'd handed her. He, too, had given her a book, *O Pioneers!* by Willa Cather. One of the seminarians came into the kitchen; he snatched mistletoe from the doorway and held it over their heads. Hetty covered her mouth with her hands. Giles flushed. Jonnie leaned forward to bring her cheek within easy reach.

Kate sets down her mug and resumes shuffling through the letters. None, apparently, were saved for the rest of the winter. There are no more, in fact, until Jonnie returns to school again in the fall of 1914. She feels a pang. All those months without Jonnie's voice. At least there is the diary. Kate moves the rocking chair so it faces the stove. She opens the oven door, props it on a log. She puts potholders on the black-ened and bent oven rack, sits in the chair with her sock feet on the potholders. Her toes begin to burn, and she rubs her feet one over the other, absently, like an otter washing its paws, as she reabsorbs herself in her grandfather's world.

June 7, 1914—J. and I decided to announce our engage-ment as soon as she's home.

June 14, 1914—Both families concur with decision to wait a year. Then J. will be finished with school. Wedding planned for July 1915.

June 16, 1914—Working on another trust property. A Gillies family, Vernon Street.

June 20, 1914—Jonnie wearing ring. Looks lovely. Thinking of buying a small house next winter.

June 22, 1914—Went on river cruise tonight. Hetty and Alma came with us. Cool on water after extreme heat. Good rains, though. Gardens at Shepton doing famously.

June 26, 1914—Spent weekend at Shepton. Dug postholes for arbour. Grapes doing well in the seed bed; will transplant when arbour is finished. Father came, seems better. Mother in throes of planning more additions, picture window in west wall, another bathroom, etc.

July 10, 1914—Saw J's paintings of Elizabeth Park tonight. She brought them here to show Father, who was much impressed.

It would have been, Kate thinks, one of those lovely Connecticut river-valley summers. The fragrant, sweet-grass breezes of June were followed by weeks of shimmering heat and succulent rain. Raspberries were plump, fat-lobed. Beefsteak tomatoes grew so large they cracked, their juices oozing. Jonnie gathered her sisters into her courtship the way, after she was married, she would include them in her home. She was both agitated and dreamy; she sighed and smiled at the same time. Her love was like a feast she couldn't imagine not sharing. She kneaded bread vigorously with her sleeves rolled up, she spread lard with her bare fingers into the corners of bent-sided bread pans and then fell still, gazing, transfixed, at morning glories twined on strings, their edges translucent. Her sister Alma calmly took the pan from her hand, shooed her from the kitchen. Jonnie stood in the open door wearing a white skirt and a white blouse stained with strawberry juice. Her hair was in a loose bun, wisped around a high, satin-banded collar. She stood on tiptoe and plucked a blue flower. She stroked her cheek with it, brushed it across her lips. Hetty and Alma, watching, glanced at each other humorously. It was a summer of lemon tarts, raspberry sherbet, cherry pies, strawberry shortcake. Every morning the sisters washed and sorted fruit, sifted flour and sugar, softened butter. They made iced tea, cranberry crush. They sat in rocking chairs on the kitchen porch, overlooking their backyard with its lilac hedge, its staked tomatoes, raspberry canes and zinnias; took turns cranking the wooden handle of the ice cream churn.

Giles' responsibilities at the office increased as he proved himself to be thorough and persistent. He negotiated the appraisal of a trust property to its lowest possible value to satisfy the tax commissioner; then began the exercise of bettering the value as he tried to sell it. Afternoons, Jonnie took the trolley to Elizabeth Park, where she set up her easel and a folding canvas chair. She painted rose beds, grass, the winding paths and blossom-shrouded gazebos. She painted children in straw hats, women's graceful backs, sunshades held negligently. The landscape was never the same: roses bloomed and faded; grass was parched or rain-freshened; there were picnicking families or strolling couples; the ripening light softened or shimmered beneath grey storm skies or the white press of humidity or July's luminescent blue.

Jonnie and Giles discussed the war, whose unfolding horrors headlined every newspaper. They worried about his brother, Daniel, now a naval officer. But war was remote, would never cross the Atlantic. Their talk slid from the general to the personal. By this time next year they would be married.

And each morning of this summer was a prelude to the evening's tenderness. Giles and Jonnie spent almost every evening together. They sat in wicker chairs on Giles' piazza behind the leafy screen of Dutchman's pipe, or they went places with Alma and Hetty: to the movie theatre, where they saw *The Perils of Pauline* and Charlie Chaplin, or up and down the Connecticut River on cruise boats, or to band concerts in the parks. Sometimes Alma and Hetty insisted they go out alone. "Are you sure?" Jonnie said, dismayed, pleased. Seeing this, the sisters were glad. Their pleasures were simple and amplified by other people's happiness. They sat on their own piazza in the evening, knitting, crocheting; along the street, elms marked the night's rising with soft stirrings, and from the eaves of sheds came the throaty chirr of pigeons. Sometimes their mother joined them, and they murmured fondly about a future in which they imagined Christmas dinner or Easter Sunday with Jonnie and Giles' fat-cheeked children.

August 4, 1914—President Wilson issued Proclamation of Neutrality. A great relief to Mother, who worries terribly about Daniel should the U.S. become involved.

August 10, 1914—Jonnie to dinner. Mother back in Hartford. She and Father seem to brighten up when Jonnie comes.

Kate snatches her feet from the stove. She examines her toes. A faint scorched smell rises from the wool, reminding her of her childhood when her mother ironed sheets, pillowcases, linen napkins. Those lingering vestiges of Victorian strictures are like leaves tossed on still water, she thinks. Some sink, others turn decorously. Ironing sheets, wearing corsets. She imagines Roselawn Street when Jonnie came to dinner. The dining-room windows were open; a bumblebee batted the screen. The canvas awning lifted and shucked down; a warm breeze entered the room, stirring the pink-flowered cambric curtains and carrying the smell of sun-decayed roses. The mahogany table glittered with crystal and silver. Sitting across from Jonnie, Giles watched as she unfolded a linen napkin so heavily starched it lay on her lap like cardboard. Father's sciatica had worsened, and so Lilian and Mrs. Heaney had returned from Shepton. Cora, the day servant, was accustomed to the house being half-empty in summer, and her hands trembled when she held the serving dish for Father. Jonnie darted a sympathetic glance; Cora repressed a smile, raising her hand to cover her harelip. Giles saw that, although Jonnie sat decorously, looking at the array of silverware that flanked her plate, she was not still. She was like the air, the curtains, the crumpled peonies in a bowl whose petals detached in utter silence. Perception, intuition, emotion quivered in the lines beside her mouth, made her fingertips rise and touch down, sent her eyes flashing. She was like a wildflower in a bouquet of dahlias. She leaned forward and listened to his parents' questions. They asked about Boston, about her studio and classes and teachers. She held her fist to her chin, forefinger pressing her lip; she heard their bewilderment, she told Giles later, although at this moment he worried that she sensed disapproval. She told them about the married couple in the Grundmann Studios who kept a garter snake in a washbasin and the woman in Studio Three who wrote short stories and hung the pages on a clothesline strung across her room. She told them of the Benevolent Society ladies who formed a students' club and who provided tea, every afternoon, in an annex of Emmanuel Church. She told of fetes, musical evenings, student exhibitions. She spoke with enthusiasm, looking openly from Lilian to Charles, and Giles saw their dawning fascination and affection.

August 30, 1914—Baker family came to dinner. Pleasant evening.

And so, Kate thinks, the two families, improbably, met and blended. After a family dinner at Roselawn Street, for example, Giles' sister, Katherine, elegant in linen and pearls, might have sat next to sad-eyed, patient Alma, whose crown of braids accentuated her sincerity. Nonetheless, they found common ground. They spoke of education, of women's suffrage and the war in Europe. Mrs. Thomas and Mrs. Baker were cordial, if nervous, and discussed rhubarb. Each had transplanted a favourite plant to a new site. Giles heard the words "well-rotted horse manure." The fathers sat side by side on the sofa and discussed fishing and football. Both were graduates of Yale University. Richard, Katherine's wealthy young husband, seemed most at ease with Hetty, for both were shy. Giles and Jonnie, like gardeners, were pleased with these combinations. Their love for one another, like rain, melted differences, eased the families into friendship.

September 10, 1914
Grundmann Studios

My darling Giles,
  Here I am, back in Boston, but I'm not yet really here, since the visit to Shepton occupies so much of my mind. I can see it all so vividly that today I tried to paint a picture from memory.

It is of your mother standing in the back door. She's dressed as she was the afternoon of our arrival. A loose cream-coloured frock, and her hair is loose as well. I've never seen her so "soft." Your father stands just behind her (a mere blotch of paleness against the amber interior.) He, too, seemed a different person in the country. Less "proper" in those old flannel trousers. Beside them, in the picture, is a suggestion of the gardening tools on the glassed-in porch. Rakes, bushel baskets and a glint of steel shovels. Over them, the house is so enormous, with all the angles of its roofs and its windows holding the burn of September light. At your mother's feet I painted the bright fall flowers—nasturtiums, chrysanthemums, marigolds—and at her left, the wall of the ell—soft grey shadows under each clapboard. I hope it will capture my sense of the dreamlike splendour of your mother's home. I caught a glimpse, you know, of the child she'd been there. She showed me her father's flute and held it solemnly, like a little girl. Were you there when she handed me her mother's Bible? I could have wept for the tenderness with which she opened the cover and showed me her mother's handwriting . . .

Kate reads this letter twice, fascinated. Yet she feels disturbed, as well. They have no notion of what will come next. She does not exist, even in their imaginations. *The dreamlike splendour.* Her memory feels jostled, pressed, as if by people insisting on room when she herself feels there is none to spare. They will, however, enter. They force their way in. *The bright fall flowers. I could have wept.* And Kate remembers the anguished feeling of her dream. *I should have gone into those rooms when I had the chance.* These, now, are the rooms that when she was a child she had no desire to enter.

She listens to the dry rattle of wind-flung snow against windowpanes. She pulls another letter from an envelope, unfolds it.

September 18, 1914
Roselawn Street

Dear Jonnie,

I am glad to hear that you are settling in so well for your final year in Boston. You asked about the Civil War. Yes, it is remarkable that Mother remembers it. She was born in 1860, so she was four years old when her brother went to the front. She told me this morning (at breakfast, when I asked her to refresh my memory on this story) that indeed she remembers seeing her mother go past, holding a candle. Every night that Henry was at war, Delia (Mother's mother) went to his room and knelt by his bed to pray for his safety. That is why I told you to listen for benign ghosts . . .

Kate imagines Jonnie's visit to Shepton. She might have worn a white ankle-length skirt, a yellow chiffon blouse. In one hand she held a black straw hat with a yellow scarf wrapped round the brim. She followed Giles up the stairs, sliding her hand along the glossy banister like a leaf drifting on water. Giles had told her it was polished only by boys' trousers. At the top of the stairs, Giles crossed the hall and went into a bedroom. "We're putting you in Mother's room," he said. "This was her room when she was a little girl, and then it was Katherine's when we came in the summer." Jonnie stood in the doorway. The ceiling was so low she could touch it if she stood on tiptoe. Autumn light slanted in buttery sheets, collected like dust on the rounded knobs of the four-poster bed, on the rim of the washbasin, on the piecrust glass of the lamp. The room smelled musty, like a chest filled with unused linens. Jonnie stepped to the bed, ran her hand over the quilt. Some of the patches were missing, revealing brown batting. She set her hat on a pillow, lifted the edge of the pillowcase. The initials D.E.G. were embroidered on the hem. "Who was that, Giles?" "My grandmother," he said. "Don't worry if you hear footsteps in the night. It might be her." She stood holding the pillowcase and gazed at him: here in the grooved and worn textures of his family's past he stood, a solid young lawyer, his hair, like the bedposts, dusted with light. She sat on the bed. On the washstand was a white porcelain basin; on a shelf underneath, a china pitcher filled with water, a pink-striped towel draped over it to repel flies. In a corner, three steps went up to a door with an iron thumb-latch handle. "Those go to the attic," Giles said. He sat on the bed next to her. She leaned against him, rested her head on his shoulder. Wind sent the maples rustling. He picked up her hand, and she turned her palm so their fingers slid together. They listened to the grandfather clock. *Tick,* tock. *Tick,* tock.

Kate opens the little diary. July, August. Here. September. Just after Jonnie left for Boston. How could he bear it? How could he bear their parting?

> *September 7, 1914*—Jonnie left for Boston today. Saw her
> off on the train. I went directly to the office, thinking
> that work would console me. After work I stopped by her
> house, but did not stay long. Hetty and Alma glad to see
> me, but seemed as lost as I felt. Their house very quiet,
> and ours as well, for both Father and Mother are at
> Shepton and Cora leaves directly after the dishes are
> washed up. I wrote Jonnie a long letter. Propped before
> me as I write now is the self-portrait she painted. One day
> she will hold our son or daughter in her lap. I miss her so.

And the rest of that visit to Shepton. They might have imagined how one day they would bring their children. To visit the grandparents. Oh, that first night in the blessed country. After supper, Giles took her to see the grape arbour.

Cricket-song chimed in the air. They could smell the sweetness of dried leaves and woodsmoke. The sun had set, but birds still flashed in its last rays. The grape arbour was almost finished. Round cedar posts ran in two curving parallel lines, connected with lattice. The grapes were not yet planted. Jonnie put both hands on the splintery posts. Below, soft light flickered behind the windows of the house, which had neither electricity nor indoor plumbing. Down in the house, Giles' parents read in the parlour by the light of kerosene lamps. Mrs. Heaney was in her little bedroom that would one day be Hetty's kitchen. "It's so quiet," Jonnie whispered. She was a city girl. Over beyond the hayfield a horse and wagon passed the Catholic church. They could hear a brisk thudding, the occasional chink of colliding horseshoes. A cow bawled from a hill pasture. Up and down the village street, rectangles of lamplight stroked the dusk. The air carried the cold of damp shadows, and Jonnie put her hand in her pocket and felt the wrinkly skin of a windfall apple. Apples, stone walls, grapes, ghost-ridden halls—these things made Giles' world. "One day it will be covered with leaves, dripping with purple grapes," Giles said, testing the lattice. "A leafy glade. For children to play under," she murmured. The shadow of the lattice merged with the black grass. She stood on tiptoe. He put his hands on her waist. She moved her lips against his ear, smelled his neck, felt his soft hair against her eyelids. "Giles, Giles . . ." He said nothing, but sighed and slid his arms up, gathered her as she tipped her head.

October 12, 1914—Today I received a package from J. She sent me the skull of a mouse she found in a cupboard. A fragile thing. She painted me a picture of "mouse heaven," which I added to all the other paintings now adorning the wall in front of my desk.

Kate turns the pages of the diary. Her young grandfather wrote in a slanted scrawl, used blue ink.

November 2, 1914—Father, Mother and I shut up Shepton. Gave the keys to Mr. Holmes, uprooted and hung geraniums, turned the compost, etc, etc. Father depressed by the war news and the onset of grey days. J. writes that she is showing two paintings in a national juried exhibition. *Boston Harbour* and *Girls by a Window*. I am so proud of her.

November 16, 1914—Busy day at the office. I was compelled to meet with Judge Cramer, who was more reasonable than I expected. Grey, hard weather. Ground frozen solid. Wondering if I mulched the new roses at Shepton thoroughly enough. No letter from J. for three days and then a largish parcel. A painting of Shepton done from a sketch she made from the west bedroom. I can look at it now and smell the good air and imagine us sitting on the piazza, looking down over the valley. Mother told me that Uncle Fred used to imagine that exact view to keep himself from falling asleep on his horse when he was on cattle drives in Oklahoma.

November 30, 1914—Jonnie came home for Thanksgiving. Light snow when we met her at the train. As usual, she seemed to fly off the steps. She is in fine form. She loves her teachers, Messrs. Tarbell and Benson, who praise her work and keep her up to the mark. I spent every evening of the holiday around the piano at the Baker home.

December 8, 1914—Bought merestones to set around the disputed property. Today I went to look at a house brought to my attention by Howard Canfield. Brick,

more-or-less new, built 1905. Quiet street with trees.
I made an appt. to see it, since I must ascertain whether
there is a room suitable for J's studio. Father's arthritic
knee badly swollen. Wet weather.

December 12, 1914—House is certainly suitable. Upstairs
bedroom could be converted, would need a north skylight. Mother and Father surprised that I am looking at a
house. They would like us to move in here. I think Jonnie
would need something more like what she is used to.

December 18, 1914—Visited with Alma and Hetty over the
weekend. They make me very welcome. Showed me a
notebook of pressed flowers Jonnie made when she was a
girl. Hetty found it in a drawer. Also a lock of her baby
hair. They are as much in awe of J's talent as I am. Jonnie
is self-exacting and the least impressed with her accom-
plishments. Letter from her received today describing an
Arabian Night's Festival put on by the Boston Art
Students' Association. She said I would not have recognized her in veils and satin slippers.

December 22, 1914—Jonnie due home tomorrow. I bought
her a coral scarf pin and a silk scarf to pin it on. Will spend
Christmas Eve at the Bakers' and Christmas Day here.

January 2, 1915—I start the New Year writing here. Not
an auspicious year with the terrible slaughter in Europe,
but in the small sphere of our family such a joyful time.
Mother and Father happier than I have seen them in
years. Wish I had taken the time to write here during the
holiday. Mother and Father have taken to J. Mother gave
her a necklace of jet stars that had belonged to her own

mother. Father read poetry after dinner in the library—in French. Skating in the park—Jonnie fell frequently. Bonfires, cocoa. Dr. Baker already treats me like a treasured son. Hetty like a little sparrow, pecking comfortably. Brings us tea, gazes at us devotedly. I won't see J. again until Easter. She liked the house, and I will begin negotiations next week. I hold a small photograph of her in my hand. Her eyes look into mine with such merry love.

January 12, 1915—Letter from Jonnie with scrawled handwriting. Says she is tired, with a sore throat and racing pulse. I sent her a telegram. Waiting for reply. Mother tells me not to worry. Should I go to the Bakers?

Kate closes the diary and sets it on the kitchen table, far from the dripping candle. She stands, stretches, opens the dark refrigerator. Cheese, a tomato. It is, she thinks, as she spreads mustard on bread, like being in a snow cave, just as Jonnie described her apartment in Boston. Everything—coats on hooks, a pair of scissors, an African violet in a glazed pot—is utterly motionless, like a garden after frost. Glancing out the window into the white-grey light, she sees snow spinning, blown one way and then another, now so thick that she can't see the bushes, then thinning, sweeping back. The wild whirl beyond the windowpanes accentuates the stillness of the room, whose only life is the pulsing light that rims the stove lid and the steam that rises from the kettle.

Kate makes a sandwich and eats standing with her back to the stove, feeling its heat settle between her shoulder blades. She feels dazed by the past. She has become Giles, staring out his own window. *Mother tells me not to worry.*

She puts the rest of her day in order. There will be, after all, only a few more hours of daylight. Deciding to walk to the convenience store and to stop in on Caroline, she pulls on felt-lined boots, shrugs into her heaviest hooded parka. Storms, after all, should be shared, since everyone is equalized, made helpless to the same degree.

She slides sideways out the door. She is instantly assaulted by stinging snowflakes and the hollow boom and creak of wind-lashed trees. She trudges bent-shouldered into the wind, watching her boots, hood pulled low. She is breathless by the time she knocks on Caroline's door.

"God, Kate! You are brave!"

"Or nuts," Kate says, divesting herself of toque, neck-warmer, mitts, kicking off her boots. "Isn't this incredible?"

"Come in, come in," Brian calls. "I can't move."

Their house, too, is lit only by the grey snow-light. She follows Caroline into the living room, where a fire hisses in a small woodstove and Brian sits on the leather couch surrounded by piles of photographs.

"Three years worth," he says, gesturing. He looks up at Kate with a small smile that comes more from eyes than mouth. Caroline lifts the lid of the stove, stirs the coals.

"I *love* this," she says. "Isn't it great knowing that no one is working? Except the poor road crews." Steam spurts from a kettle. Caroline lifts it with a potholder, pours water into a teapot. Her round body is loose and comfortable in tights, Nepalese legwarmers, a gigantic red sweater and a scarf woven several times around her neck.

Kate sinks into the new leather chair. The room is warm, but she can feel how cold hangs in the kitchen, in the stairwell, in the upstairs rooms. Caroline hands her a mug, and Kate cradles it like a ball, fingers spread.

"We've got one year done. Remember that picnic on White's Island? Here, look. Here's you and Tom." Caroline is one of the few people who mentions Tom frequently.

Kate stares at the picture. A couple. Herself as part of a couple. In their minds, she wonders, is she still part of a couple? Do they feel that a great part of her is missing?

"And these, look at the kids."

She sips her tea, watching as Caroline and Brian bend their heads together over a picture, trying to decide which summer it belongs to. They take for granted, she thinks, the fact that they are doing this together.

When she leaves, Caroline comes to the door. She tugs Kate's neck-warmer up to cover her nose. *Just the way Tom would, telling me I look like a bank robber.* Caroline leans out into the wind to wave. Snowflakes star her sandy eyelashes. As Kate walks down the empty street, she glances back at the blue house. It looms in the swirling snow, without definition.

After her walk, Kate stashes her groceries—milk, chicken legs, orange juice—in a cardboard box on the porch. She stokes the fire, drapes her soaking outdoor clothes over a laundry rack and sets it next to the firebox. She lights a kerosene lamp, places it on the kitchen table next to Grampa Giles' diary. Then she takes candles to the living room. She is working on a Bach fugue. She leans forward, peering in the dim light, pencil in her teeth. She plays phrases, then marks fingerings. She wears her wool toque. The stars on its brim dance in the shadowy room as her head bends and tips. Night and day seem not distinct; darkness creeps imperceptibly. When she looks up, the window is no longer grey but a black mirror reflecting a point of candle flame in the heart of a curved room. The wind has not ceased its buffeting. She takes chicken legs and milk from her makeshift refrigerator, cooks supper on the woodstove and leaves her dishes in the sink. She contemplates bringing a sleeping bag into the kitchen and huddling next to the stove, but decides her icy bedroom will be more comfortable than the floor.

The phone rings.

"Hello, Kate?"

"Yes?" She thinks she recognizes the voice.

"It's Gregory."

Ah. He sounds odd. Sleepy, or slurred. Too relaxed.

"Did you lose power?" he asks.

"Yes, it went out in the morning. It's still out. You lost power in Saint John, I assume?"

He becomes voluble. She hears the creak of his chair. It's a wooden office chair on casters with a sprung back. He'd found it at a used furniture store that is a front (he'd told her, smug with knowledge) for a whorehouse. "I went out before the weather started and bought those kerosene lamps I was telling you about." He pauses. "Remember?"

She doesn't, but pretends to. Her phone is on the wall by the side door, exactly where it was when they bought the house, an awkward spot selected in times when phones were seldom used. She leans against the sink and gazes up through the window. Its panes are like galaxies, ice-stars sprinkled on the black glass, drifting over frost-fields. Snow billows past the porch posts. She holds the phone with her shoulder, massages the cold from her hands.

"Bought those lamps," he continues, "stocked up on bread and cold cuts, nice cheese, nice wine, candles. Even got some new wool socks. Oh, this is fine. Just fine." He's pouring wine; she can hear the clink of bottle on glass.

There's a pause. She hears him swallow. Which should she do, Kate wonders, offer information about herself or ask him a question? He leaves the choice up to her and waits with the dulled timing of inebriation. She wonders if his house is freezing cold. *Oh, but he has that little fireplace.* She's glad that he called, glad to hear a voice. And wants, suddenly, to tell him about the letters.

"I actually got quite a bit of reading done today," she says. "The family papers I told you about."

"Ah, yes."

She takes a breath to continue, but he is speaking.

"I spent the day reading, too, " he says. *As if he didn't hear a word I said.* "The most extraordinary thing. I found—"

Kate begins to understand. He uses her as a stepping stone. He touches once, but then leaps ahead, leaving her concerns behind.

A long silence. She hears his chair creak and the rustle of papers.

"Hello?"

"There. Here it is before me. Or rather, here they are. Ummm. The diaries." Pages rustle. "Let's see. 'Went to Fundy Park with the Hardings. Did the Goose River Trail, set up on the point. Four tents. Liam and Jerome put theirs back along the creek, the rest of us faced the bay. Bonfire. Frightened the girls with ghost stories.' Remember the one I told about the wheelbarrow? Man who killed his wife and roamed the streets with the body in a wheelbarrow?" He takes another drink, large enough so she can hear him swallow and sigh. "No, really, I'd forgotten, I was going through a box in my study, well, I haven't had time, you see, been so busy at the paper couldn't get this stuff unpacked, and here were, oh, nine or ten years of diaries, the years leading up—the years we lived in New Brunswick before, well . . ."

Kate closes her eyes. The peace of this day. The storm finally gathering her as once she and Tom had loved to be gathered; storm-stayed, snowbound. When she'd come back from her walk, exhilarated by the weather, cheered by her visit, she'd accepted the way she felt like a rabbit, crouched. Her longings, her fears, her grief had been somewhat assuaged beside the steadfast fire and within the storm's assault.

She thinks how peculiar it is to talk to someone who is drunk. How they appear to be listening, but hear nothing. "Well, as a matter of fact, Gregory, I'm on my way to bed now. It's very cold in my house. Too cold to either sit or stand. I've got to get under a pile of blankets and sleeping bags."

"Ummm. Keep warm, Kate. Socks to bed, that's the thing to do. Socks and long winter underwear and a toque. The nose. The nose freezes, and of course you have to breathe." He takes another swallow, and she realizes he has no intention of hanging up. "I'm thinking of writing about those years. Really, they were so marvellous. Wonder if—if you know, these days, do families still do these things? The survey maps on the floor. Plotting hikes into the wild. Those piles of equipment. Canteens, stuff sacks, frying pans. You know, I felt as if I was actually there all day. Reading about those years, lost in my diaries. Jerome, throwing himself into that icy water. He could do it, he really could. Swim in the bay." His voice is loose, happy. "I could see the marram grass, kids pouring sand from their sneakers, that—oh, one time, let's see if I can find it, a bald eagle came over. Oh yeah, here it is. 'Down the creek at sunrise came a great bird, emerging from the mist. Mist and the smoke of our breakfast fire glowing in the rising sun. It circled over us, sun catching its white head. So close we could hear the swish of air beneath its wings.' Brings it back, doesn't it, Kate?"

Tom had installed a lengthy phone cord when the children were teenagers. Christy would take the receiver and sit on the porch railing in the summer sun. She'd lean against the trellis, a mass of purple clematis, swing her bare feet. Mourning cloak butterflies feasting on the bergamot, just below the railing. Kate trails the cord across the floor, sits in the rocking chair. She does not make herself comfortable but leans forward with her feet apart and her elbows on her knees. She hears his longing, his loneliness. What can she say? She imagines the book he would write. This, he will insist, is how it was. He'll make a place he can go whenever he wants; a world in which he can wander, far from the truth. Who is she, though, to judge someone else's passage through grief? All she longs for, just now, is to be left alone to maintain her own precarious hold on the present.

"What a wonderful find," she says. "I'm happy you were there, Gregory, time travelling. I have to go now, though, really I do." She begins to feel unsure, when she talks to Gregory, who he thinks she is. She is no longer Tom-and-Kate. But she feels oddly null. Blank. Like someone Gregory has invented who will disappoint him if she acts other than as he wishes. "My fire's dying, and it's hellishly cold in this room." Speaking to a drunk. One word after another. *Have to go.* Finally, she manoeuvres him into saying goodbye. He's noticeably slurrier than when he first called.

"Bye, Kate. I'm glad. Glad, you know. That I decided to go see the birds on that memorable Saturday."

She hangs up. She stands listening to the wind, the slash of snow against glass, the tiny ticks and crunches coming from the fire. She wedges logs into the firebox, adjusts the dampers. She fills a hot water bottle from the kettle. She calls the cat. "Here, kitty kitty kitty." He follows her diffidently, his paws tapping. The storm makes his tail twitch; he freezes and stares into dark corners. "Stop that, Mr. Winkles," she says, glancing. She carries a candle. *Tenebrous.* She whispers the word. "Tenebrous, Mr. W. It means dark, murky. There's nothing there!"

The house feels as it did when she and Tom first moved in. The spirits of the former owners lingered: a rusty safety pin on the floor, ribbons in the closet, a prayer thumbtacked to the back of the pantry door, a shoebox filled with ghastly clippings from a Toronto newspaper—

MAN KILLED BY TRAIN

WOMAN LEAPS FROM TENTH STOREY

FAMILY DIES IN CHRISTMAS EVE HOUSE FIRE.

Even, and particularly, smells hovered. Someone had spilled pomade in a bedroom; the floorboards still retained a faint fragrance, making her think of a young man with slicked-back hair adjusting his collar. If a house has soul, it is in its undying smell. This is a disquieting thought, for as she pushes open the door to the bedroom it is not her own family's life she smells on the freezing air, but the era that preceded them: kerosene, stale woodsmoke, countless dinners of boiled turnip and cod, starched shirt fronts, turn-of-the-century dust bearing horse dander and wax, the weary odour of rectitude.

She does, as Gregory suggested, wear socks, a toque and long winter underwear to bed. She pulls the hot water bottle to her belly, curls around it. Feels the weight of blankets and comforter, but is not yet warm. Mr. Winkles makes a nest at her feet. She blows out the candle.

The wind continues, unabated. She thinks of it as animate, a formless creature with its own unfathomable purposes. It's not so much that it attacks the house as that the house is in its way. She hears the wind's disregard. It rampages in the branches, makes a sudden violent buffet at the lower windows, starts a taut singing in the flue. It is everywhere, but not equally. It spins in one place, retreats, makes a long slide, booms over the river, shocks back with a rattle of icy snow.

And Kate clings to her hot water bottle like a life preserver, trying to banish Gregory's voice. She replays the evening in her mind. In this vision, the phone never rings. Instead, she finishes her meal, yawns, stretches. Picks up

Grampa Giles' diary, and stands staring abstractedly, the book held in her palm like a pocket Bible, dreading what she may read next (*sore throat and racing pulse . . . waiting for reply*). Shuffles together the letters she's read, puts them in a folder. Marks it with dates. She looks across the room and there is Tom's picture, and she's amazed to find she can see it as she always has and not as it seemed this morning. But in her mind she can't keep the phone from ringing, and she hears Gregory's voice with its delusional happiness. Her mind replays his portrayal of the past. The eagle flies over their campsite. The little children throw up their arms, waves curl, spume slides down the green water, and in the morning light are coffee, salt wind, campfire, beach peas, the red cliffs. There is, as Gregory tells it, no time. The eagle turns, glances down. The little children throw up their arms. Waves curl.

Well, there were those moments. Moments when they were held and released by what is greater. And Kate, clutching her hot-water bottle, drawing her knees up and feeling the silk of her long underwear, knows that this storm would have produced such a time. Tom curled against her; the cat purring. The house shaking. Temperature still dropping; no sound but the wind. Without power, without volition. They would have done what they could and then been free to sleep, gathered by the storm and their own warmth.

Well. Even without Tom, she had touched this feeling by midafternoon. And been quieted.

Now this morning's fresh wave of grief returns. Eternity. The mind can't grasp it, yet tries, finds wearisome evasions instead. She tries not to be aware of the bed's emptiness, of the longing in Gregory's voice, of the agonizing pain of a child's death. She tries not to pretend that Tom's arms are around her. Then she thinks of Tom, in her vision, when he strode away. He turned and grinned. Kate lets her mind waver and drift so she will see his expression come into focus, and for a fraction of an instant she sees that he's truly happy. She sees that he doesn't want her to follow.

9. Muskrat Trail

COLD-FLUSHED, GREGORY LOOKS GOOD. HIS CHEEKS are red, there are tiny bits of frost on his white-blond eye-lashes. They're cross-country skiing on the river. Prisms spin in the powder snow, and the sky is a hard blue, the light so intense that Kate squints even behind her sunglasses, feeling as if she's in a *National Geographic* photograph of Himalayan explorers on glittering ice fields. Their clothing is brilliant in the flashing light: Gregory's red jacket, black-and-grey wool cap with tasselled ear flaps; her own green jacket and wind-pants; the red markings on their white skis. As they set out from town, the river is wide, with snowmobile tracks running down its centre, but they keep to the edge, skiing over criss-crossing branch shadows. They round a bend and can see across the marsh. The light is like sea light: complex, reflec-tive, brightened by the expanse of whiteness. On a distant hill, low light warms the wood-shingled steeple of the Anglican church, and smoke wavers from unseen chimneys. A bird flies up.

Gregory points with his pole, calls. She skis up beside him.

"Look," he's saying. "Hawk. Could be a rough-legged. Darn, I wish I had my binoculars."

He's boyish, excited. She forgets, seeing him in his city clothes, that he really does know these things. He can read animal tracks. He knows the constellations. She and Tom used to imagine Gregory as a small boy. He would, they decided, have been enthusiastic and pedantic. He would have had a mineral collection (labelled), a microscope, dead snakes in alcohol, scrap books of family trips filled with postcards of mountains and waterfalls; he would have had a shelf of fossils, arrowheads, skulls. What is it about Gregory, she thinks, squinting at the bird that wheels over the willows, that made them imagine him as a less-than-appealing little boy?

He's leaning forward on his poles, squinting. He's not wearing sunglasses; she sees lines fan beside his eyes. He's intent. "Long narrow wings, long tail. Can you see the subterminal band?" He doesn't wait for her to answer. "Ah, look there. See the white at the tail. That's it, then." He grins at her. "Your neck-warmer is frozen solid, Kate."

She feels the frozen wool batting her nose, stiff where her breath has frozen it. She laughs. Standing next to Gregory in the lowering light—their breath smoking, the light becoming richer as it declines, denser shadows creeping out over the riverbed—she doesn't feel like part of a couple, yet he makes her aware of herself. Since she is not sure who he sees, how he imagines her, what he thinks of her, she feels interesting to herself, like a teenager.

"Come on," she says. "We have to keep moving."

"Just a minute, just a minute." Now he lightens his voice, as if he's hiding a surprise from a child. He slides his fanny pack around to the front, unzips it. He takes out a flask, unscrews the cap. "Brandy? Warm you up?" The sun is in his face, the frost on his lashes glitters. He looks into her eyes with an expression she's beginning to recognize. He's convinced himself he's found something.

"No, thanks. Now if you'd offered me hot chocolate . . ."

He shrugs, irritated. He tips the flask rapidly, twice. She makes a kick turn, skis up the river in snow so powdery that her skis disappear beneath the surface. Mouse tracks make a blue necklace down a bank and loop across the river. Branches stand against a sky that begins to flush as darkness gathers beneath bushes, as the hard blue softens towards dusk.

She hears the soft swish of his skis behind her. She's in better shape than Gregory is; she leans into her poles and increases her pace. They'll have to turn back soon, though, and she's regretting this. Sunset draws her, she wants to ski across the marsh into the molten sky, feel the dying light on her face, then turn and come driving back pole after pole in the cold dusk. But they set out well after she'd wanted to. Gregory arrived late and had insisted on opening a bottle of wine. "A robust red." He'd brought smoked Gouda and crackers to go with it. She suggested having it when they came back. He wouldn't hear of it, as if she were denying herself something. She took down two wine glasses from the cupboard, relinquishing her sense of how the afternoon should be. The entire day is, after all, skewed, like a page torn from a diary and stuck back in crooked. For so long, she's done nothing on weekends, and the motionless air of the house begins to seem familiar and necessary, like something she can't do without. Nothing happens, but nothing *will* happen, and this is what she counts on.

In the big house, the winter nights pass, and then the angled February dawn arrives with frost-blind windows, corners that the oil furnace cannot warm, wind, the rattle of branches, frozen soil buried beneath drifts so high they seem like new features of the landscape. Winter has bound her with its buffered crouch. She spends her weekends reading and organizing the letters in the hatboxes. She watches television, listens to the radio. Christy begins to worry about her. "Mum?

Are you lonely? Are you getting depressed? Why don't I come home? Why don't you come over here?" So far, Kate has convinced her that even though she is feeling a bit isolated and sad, it is something she needs to go through, to allow to happen, since she's in the process of learning how to be herself. She tells her daughter this, and it sounds logical, even sensible, but Kate begins to realize it's not true. She is neither allowing nor learning. She is not going through but staying still. It is as though her pain can be kept away only if she remains motionless.

Ever since the night of the storm, when Gregory found his diaries, he seems to believe that Kate—the Kate of his reminiscences—has been and must continue to be part of his life. She is the Kate of his children's childhoods, of his young married life. He phones, reads her pages of his reminiscences, asks her to corroborate. Insists that she must remember. Sometimes she really does. Then their memories meet, their voices relax, they wander together. Canoes drift beneath willow branches; they sit on woven cane seats, lift paddles; the children swim behind the boats in amber river pools. There's rum by starlight. Cows run wild in summer pastures on the Saint John River islands.

He awakens long-lost feelings. Yes, oh yes, once she did find him attractive. Tiny things, never acted upon. At a campfire. His hand, beside hers. The sides of their outflung hands touched. Neither one shifted. Does he remember this, she wonders? He'd been a handsome young man, undeniably: blond, tanned, with his white grin and sandy eyebrows. Watching him scramble up rock faces with his son, Kate had strolled to the cliffs, frankly fascinated, hands clasped behind her neck. Tom and Gregory's wife, Karen, sat together, ignoring the climb. Tom, smoking, was impatient; Karen was frightened, always.

No one, over this winter, seems to need Kate except Gregory. No one imposes on her. She's grieving, she has enough to deal with, they think. His loneliness attracts her. Kate understands his longing, feels its silky desire, its abrasive guilt, the unknotted ends of its love. He grieves for his son, for an unlived life that he can't help imagining. He must, she thinks, know that she feels the same way about Tom. Either one of two Gregorys phones her: the office Gregory is brisk, warm, friendly, remembers to ask her about herself and sometimes listens; the evening Gregory is persistent, expansive and self-pitying, and suggests things they might do together. It was her idea to ski. Early afternoon, she'd thought. Then he would be sure to leave before supper. But he arrived so late. And drank most of a bottle of wine by the time they set out.

A wind stirs, the vague breath of dusk. She sees snow rise as if whisked by an invisible broom. The scud of crystal spins down the river towards them. The crystals are golden, red, carrying the fire of the setting sun. Kate feels the light in her eyelashes, on her cheeks. She can see another bend in the river; beyond it, the trees fall away, the marsh opens. She looks back at Gregory, points with her pole. "Just to there, okay? Then we'll turn back." He raises his hand. He's labouring a bit, she notices.

She passes the last tree. The marsh stretches ahead, blending into blue hills far down the valley. The snow lies in frozen waves the shape of motion, each one bearing a crescent-shaped shadow and glittering in the flush of light. Kate leans on her poles. Sweat rolls down her back even though her toes are numb and her face is stiff with cold. She hears the clatter of Gregory's poles, the steady glide-swish of his skis. All afternoon their talk has been light, inconsequential, yet not evasive. Before they set out, he sipped wine and seemed content to let her bring up topics, which he pursued, equably. They discussed the white-winged crossbill at her feeder; the coyote she's observed, at sunrise, on the riverbank; peculiar tracks—could they be otter?; muskrat burrows with round plunge holes. Since they began skiing, they've scarcely spoken. She feels him coming up next to her. If it were Tom, she would not turn to look at him. She would lean sideways until their shoulders touched. If it were Tom, they would be silenced by the evening's beauty.

She turns to smile at Gregory. "Isn't this lovely?"

His face is a tangle of impulses. His eyes are masked, crafty, they touch hers and spark away. He bangs his hands together. She notices for the first time that he's wearing jeans, without wind-pants. He's fumbling with the zipper of his fanny pack. "My hands are . . ." he mutters. He's wearing gloves, not mittens. He gets out the flask. She feels she should not be watching as he works at the cap, twisting it in his cupped palm. Her mind contracts, the molten marsh is snuffed out. She half-turns, looking back the way they came. There the sky is still pale, but a bird speeding northwards is black and she feels cold rising from the corniced banks.

"Nice," he says. "You and Tom picked a nice place, Kate."

He seldom speaks of Tom. A tone sounds. Twists and snags between them.

"We're going to have to get back quickly." She hears the apology in her voice. Or is it appeasement? "You must be cold. My toes are beginning to freeze."

He doesn't answer. He throws his head back, flips the flask, wipes his mouth with the back of his glove and stares numbly at the marsh. The light fades. The snow seems closer to the sky, knit by falling darkness. Lights appear on the hills: the orange-amber of street lights; the lights of windows made unsteady by stirring branches. He's like a sick bird, suddenly. She thinks of a dying raven they found, one summer, on their picnic table. It sat hunched, its wings tense. Glaucous lids covered its eyes, slid up and down, while consciousness burned and faded.

"Let's go, Gregory." She speaks briskly, as if nothing has changed but the light. "We really have to get going." She pushes off. "It'll be quicker going back in our own tracks," she calls.

She skis, not fast but without pause. They come to a place where the river narrows. The banks rise higher than their heads, and Kate sees a house perched above them on the hillside.

"Good place to swim here," Kate calls. "You can really feel the tide when it's rising." Even this far from the Bay of Fundy, the river feels the tides. The water is deep at this bend, and the current is strong. She stops, panting as much from cold as exertion. Across the snow is a curving animal trail, well-travelled. "Look," she says.

The snow is the colour of lilac; every crystal reflects the sky, every indentation is cupped in blue shadow. He comes up next to her, breathing hard, but he stoops.

"Could it be muskrat?" Kate asks. "Over there in that bank there's a colony. In summer we can see the holes in the mud." *We.*

He points with a stiff gloved finger. "See this curving line? That's the tail. These are the paws on either side. See, back paw steps into front paw. Here, here—" He slides forward towards the bank, stooped.

It happens instantly. The ice gives way where the receding tide leaves a hollow. He shouts, his arms fly up. The ice breaks beneath him, and he falls. He's waist deep in water, lying forward on the ice, clawing. One pole flies from his wrist. His skis are entangled in ice chunks. The black water rises.

Kate snatches up the pole, pushes it towards him. "Grab this. Hold on, I'll get onto the shore."

"Don't you fall in too," he gasps. "Holy Christ, this water is cold." He thrashes with his skis, tries to lift them from the running water.

Kate snaps off her skis, falls onto her belly, slides over the ice. She flounders through snow on the shore, still holding the end of the pole. Gregory throws himself forward onto ice that holds. Kate puts one arm around a tree, digs in her feet. Gregory pulls on the pole and it flies out of her grasp. He heaves himself onto his back, lifts both skis from the water. She crouches on the bank, hauls at the shoulder of his jacket. He worms himself onto the bank.

He sits, panting, shuddering. "Holy shit."

She gathers her skis, his poles. Helps him unfasten his skis. "Up there," she points, too shaken to speak in full sentences. "House. We'll go up through the trees. Not far."

"Holy shit."

"Come on, come on. Up. Get up. Keep moving."

He's dumb, slow. He sits in the snow and stares at his soaked gloves. He seems not to hear her. He frets with his clothing, lifting it from his body, slapping at himself.

"I'm going for help," she says. She begins floundering up the hill towards the lights of the house.

"What? No, I'll—" He gathers his feet under him, stands in the knee-deep snow. She's already halfway up the slope, grabbing the trunks of birch trees, pulling herself up. She glances back, sees him slip, fall forward, arms flinging out. Hears in a terse curse his anger, frustration. She realizes, with a pang, that all of this was her idea. She hadn't wanted to do any of the things he suggested. She would go skiing on the river or nothing. Her choices. Even what they'd talked about before they left. She had drunk the wine begrudgingly; she had continued skiing when he was clearly cold and tired. She had pointed out the muskrat trail in order to make it clear that this was *her* river. Hers and Tom's. Their place. Their marsh, their beauty.

~

He's taking a shower. He left his wet clothes outside the bathroom door. As soon as she heard the water running she went upstairs, gathered them, brought them back down to the dryer.

It's six thirty. The birds in her chest begin to fly at cross-purposes. They mill, sweep in circles. So. Supper? Should she offer him supper? Of course she should. It's pitch dark. Can he drive? He's been drinking brandy ever since they made it up the hill and stumbled into the house above the river. His clothes won't be dry before he's finished his shower. He'll come downstairs wearing her terrycloth bathrobe, socks and no underwear. He'll sit here and want more to drink. Well, there's nothing in the house. Wait. There's his backpack on the floor by the rocking chair. It's open; she sees the neck of a wine bottle. She pinches her lips with one hand, squats by the pack and gingerly widens it, glimpsing what else is there. *Shit.* There's a black canvas overnight bag. Zippered shut, but she sees a toothbrush handle caught in the zipper. A pair of blue cotton boxers. A clean T-shirt, rolled and stuffed into the bottom of the pack. He planned on spending the night.

She walks straight to the telephone. Thinks for a minute. Taps May's number. Speaks in a whisper. "Yes! Well, he's in the shower. You could—you thought I'd invited you for supper. You're eighty, pretend to be doddery. Be obdurate. *Obdurate.* Annoyed that he's—oh, yes, that's good. Absolutely. Perfect. Chicken casserole. But what if he wants to stay too? Okay. As only you can do. Oh God, May. Okay, see you."

She should put a fire on in the wood stove, but she does not want to make the room cozy. Her outdoor clothes lie in a pile by the door. She'd turned to wave at the man who'd driven them home; then struck off her hat, shaken loose her mittens, squatted on one knee to help Gregory untangle the frozen laces of his ski boots. His hands were frozen, he'd begun to shudder. *He'll stay in that shower a long time.* She goes to the door, busies herself picking up her mittens and hat, her coat and neck-warmer. She washes the wine glasses and plates from this afternoon. She wraps the smoked Gouda in cling wrap, starts to put it in Gregory's pack, hesitates, then slides it into her refrigerator. She puts her palms together like a praying child and rubs them up and down. She thinks of the moment on the river when he offered her the brandy flask. *Why can we never speak the truth? No, Gregory.* (She rewrites the moment, sees the sun flushing his face, her own turned towards the cooling eastern sky, where Venus hangs over the village. She sees the expression in his eyes, how he is trying to pick up where he thinks they left off, as if what has happened in the interim has changed nothing.) *No,* she wishes she had said, *I'm sorry. Here with us are Karen and Janie. And Tom's memorial service at the house, at which I stood between my children, gripping their hands. Here with us is Jerome as he sat on that ledge on Mount Baker, carefully arranging his ice axe and crampons, coiling his climbing rope, taking off his mitts and his ice goggles. Here, too, is the horror of how he may have spread his arms and leaned into space. I'm not the Kate of your remembered summers.*

Coffee. Sober him up so he can drive home. Okay, so he'll stay to supper with her and May. But how to get rid of him afterwards? Should she drive him herself? Could call a taxi. She plugs in the kettle, hears the jolt in the pipes as he turns off the shower. The bathroom sink water runs. Why didn't he take up his overnight bag? It probably has a razor in it, toothpaste, a toothbrush. A prophylactic, for God's sake.

Tell him to go fuck himself. She imagines Tom leaning in the door to the living room. She turns to look. She sees the half-dark room with its pile of hatboxes. She pictures him grinning. She goes to the door and leans in the place she sensed him standing. As if she can step into his shape. *Tell him to go fuck himself* . . . She leans her head against the jamb, listening to the unbearable sound of a strange man washing himself in their bathroom.

Gregory is coming down the stairs just as May knocks on the door. He steps into the doorway between kitchen and living room wearing Kate's blue bathrobe, tightly belted. His legs are freckled, furred with blond hair. He wears heavy grey wool socks. He's tried to make himself attractive by slicking back his hair, but it makes him look precious and anxious, like a boy going to his first dance. May opens the door without waiting for Kate. She blunders in, carrying a casserole. Stops at the sight of Gregory and clutches the bowl to her chest.

"Who is this, Kate?" she says, almost shouting.

"Gregory Stiller," Kate shouts. She turns to Gregory. "She's very deaf," she murmurs. "My neighbour."

"Is he coming to supper too?" May says loudly. She sets down the casserole, begins unbuttoning her coat. "I thought we were having a girls' night. Not that we wouldn't be happy to include you, Mr. Stiller. You might not like some of the things we're going to talk about." She turns to Kate, opens her handbag, pulls out a yellow Kodak envelope. "New photos. Of my great-grandchild." She rummages. "And those letters I said I would read to you."

Kate glances at Gregory. He says, irritated, "Tell her why I'm in your bathrobe, for God's sake."

"We had a skiing accident," Kate shouts. "He fell through the ice."

May is still digging in her purse. She pulls out a chair abstractedly, sits. "I know I had those letters." She looks up and sees Gregory still standing in the doorway. "What did you say, Kate? Why is he in your bathrobe?"

Kate has to turn away. She takes coffee from the cupboard, starts the drip. "Skiing," she shouts. "Accident." She takes mugs from the shelf and glances at Gregory. "Your clothes should be ready any minute. I'm so sorry. I completely forgot she was coming."

"Do you have any rum, brandy, whiskey?"

"Sorry, no."

May shuts her purse, hangs it on the back of her chair, throws up her hands. "Can't find them. Did I come on the wrong night, Katie? Of course, that would be like me. I did have it marked on my calendar, you know."

Gregory lifts the bottle of wine from the pack. "Corkscrew?" He doesn't meet her eyes.

He sits in the rocking chair, pulls the bathrobe tightly around his knees. Kate puts the corkscrew and a glass by his side. He drinks, staring through the room's reflection in the window, watching cars crossing the bridge, their lights flickering past its trusses. He says nothing. May carries on about her foolishness with the date, offers to leave, puts her casserole in the oven, says they can have it, but makes no move to put on her coat, actually gets out photographs and shows them to Kate. Kate goes to the laundry room twice, returns the second time with Gregory's clothes. He puts down his glass, takes them without looking at her. He goes upstairs to change.

"He's terribly drunk, Kate," May whispers. "You can't let him drive."

"I don't think he's *terribly* drunk. But you're right, he's probably over the legal limit."

"Who *is* he, by the way?"

"Old friend of mine and Tom's. Just moved back to the province." Kate can barely speak. She presses her hands to her mouth. "This is horrible."

"Look, Kate, you'll have to call a taxi. You can't let him drive. It's not responsible."

"What about his car? He'll have to come back for it."

"Would you rather have him killed? Or have him kill someone else?"

"You're right." Kate gets the phone directory, finds a local taxi company. "But shouldn't I wait and ask him?"

"Just dial, order one to be here when we've finished eating," May says impatiently. May's husband, Kate remembers suddenly, had a drinking problem. May snatches up his wine glass, holds it under running water. Skin is stretched over her nose; it is shiny and curved as a turtle's beak. She takes a dishcloth and wipes the glass, her rings making busy clinks. She has the hearing of a fox. Her lips are pinched. Gregory's footsteps are coming down the stairs, Kate is dialling.

He steps into the room as she bends forward over the phone, giving her address in a low voice.

"What are you doing?" His own voice has gone up, sounds stretched and unfocused. "Did you call a cab? Are you going somewhere, then? You'll have to take it yourself. I'll be—" He stoops, picks up the backpack by its loop. It tips forward, its contents spill out. Kate leans against the counter with her arms folded.

"Fuck." He's on his knees, gathering his bag, his underpants, stuffing them into the pack.

"I ordered a taxi to come at seven, Gregory," Kate says. "After we've finished eating."

"No, no. Don't worry, I won't be staying." He stands, holding the pack.

"Keys, hide them," May mouths at Kate, but Kate ignores her and goes to the coatroom off the kitchen, takes Gregory's red jacket from a hook. She feels in its pockets, withdraws his keys. "Here," she says. He's pushing on the seat of the rocking chair, rises from his knees. "Here," she says, handing him the keys. "Drive carefully. Don't kill anyone."

He straightens, leans back slightly and corrects himself

with one hand against the wall. "What did you say?"

"I said don't kill anyone. When you drive. Since you've been drinking."

"How can you say that to me, Kate?" He stares at her.

She remembers that Gregory blames himself for Jerome's death. "Oh, Gregory. I'm sorry."

"To me, of all people? How can you say that?"

Kate crosses the kitchen, puts her hand out. "Gregory. I'm sorry. However poorly stated, I really did mean, though, that I'm concerned about your driving."

Gregory rips his jacket from her hand. Her arm is pulled forward; he strikes it away. She cradles it against her belly, presses it with her other hand. He stares at her with contempt. He tries to get into his jacket but can't get both arms in the sleeves and so walks out with it halfway on. He turns, reaches back to seize the doorknob. He slams the door so hard that the wine glasses in the cupboard shift and clink, their rims chime.

She walks into the living room as if dazed after a fall.

"Kate?" May pushes back her chair and stands, but does not follow her.

"I didn't mean . . ." Kate's fingers press her mouth. She looks at the overstuffed armchair where she has curled, night after night, listening to music, reading her grandfather's diary. There, in the pool of light cast by the table lamp, is the little palm-sized book. She picks it up, holds it to her heart. Her eyes fill with tears.

10. The Isolation Ward

THAT NIGHT, KATE CAN'T SLEEP. SHE TURNS ON THE bedside lamp and props two pillows against the headboard. She sits, pulls the comforter to her shoulders and then slides her hands back into the warm burrow beneath the covers, wrist over wrist, fingers curled. She listens.

It is a night when cold, like a hunter, stalks. The night's silence is the stillness of crouched prey. The house cracks at immeasurable intervals. The furnace thrums ceaselessly, and to Kate's ear it is not the sound of warmth but of futility. She thinks of the river, how beneath a half moon it will be a pale ribbon binding dark trees. Like a memory, or a vague danger. And the stars. Like bullets, frozen in their trajectory. She, in her bed, within the stretched walls of her house, both prey and target.

On such a night this house should offer comfort. Depth, the lilting dappled tub water, the smell of soap and linens, the promise of daylight in quiescent curtains. She turns her mind from the night beyond her window to the house. The hall, where she's plugged a nightlight into a wainscot outlet. The banisters, gleaming. The way downstairs. And it rises on the treads, the remains of the foolish dance. Gregory. Her home. Violated.

Her mind roils, rage breaks at the crest. He assumes inequality: his power, her frailty; his importance (how he shrugs it off, as if careless of how he is known, well-paid, in demand), her obscurity. He is divorced. She is widowed. There is a difference. No, he does not treat her like a single person, as she was amused to imagine. Rather, he treats her like an aspect of himself that he's frustrated he can't control.

She folds into herself, puts her head on her knees. One bare foot seeks the other, her toes play the harp of bones. *Tom would never . . .* her heart rants into the emptiness . . . *Tom would* never, *no matter how angry, tear a door from my hand and slam it in my face.* The past bends forward or the present snaps backwards and Tom is at her side, and she tells him: *He has no sense of you, no idea who I was when you and I were The Hardings.* She should bend towards him, hear his sigh. The rustle as his arm lifted. Her head on his chest, the gradual release of her hurt as she bent her knee, curled thigh against thigh, slid hand into armpit, breathing Tom's scent. Pithy words. What would he say? Nothing analytical, pitying, empathetic. No. He would slice once, swiftly. And Gregory would be gone.

She breathes into the comforter and is not comforted. Eternity has no sound, no echo, no shape. It exists, but is entirely elusive. Longing for what she has lost is as strong as her desire to cry aloud into the silence, calling Tom. At the same time, a sense of formlessness creeps into her mind. Nothing is bound to anything else, no force compels attachment. This is night's madness, she knows, and yet she cannot withstand or forbid it. It is like slow drowning, swept from shore by muscular currents of unreason.

She remembers how, when Tom was away, she would think to protect herself by imagining his death. The call. Plane crash, car accident, sudden illness. How many wives, she wonders, prefigure the inevitable? It did not seem a dangerous game but a kind of propitiation, or preparation. On the one hand, she confronted fear with imagined strength. On the other, she braced herself for actuality, like an actor rehearsing. Now she is tempted to do the same thing in reverse. What if he were alive? She rolls suddenly onto her side, pulls the covers over her shoulders, stares at the half-open closet door. If this is a night, say, when she is waiting for the car in the driveway. He's been in Halifax opening a show; he called earlier to say he'll be late. And she waits. For the sweep of headlights. The rattle of key. His steps, stealthy. Trying not to waken her.

No, don't do this to yourself. She has forbidden this game, knowing it is like falling to her knees in the midst of a long hike. But tonight she feels the need to repair her sense of the house itself, Gregory having pushed her sideways and kicked away all the bright, assembled memories. *Say,* she continues in her mind, *Christy is just there, on the other side of that wall. And Liam is away at school. Three days ago the van came for the canvasses. Huge. The cliff paintings. He stood here, grumbling. I made him pack his suit. The one he bought in Montreal.* She remembers him telling the salesman, who was Greek, with a swollen knee, how he wanted the suit he'd be buried in. "I'm only going to do this once." How gently the salesman had stroked the fabric. The tender, hurting salesman softened Tom, and the two men patted each other on the back. *I remind him of this day, and he shrugs, admitting nothing, yet I see memory in the curl of his fingers as he lifts the suit in its crackly case. Such is marriage.* Lying on her side, palms pressed together beneath her cheek, her outraged mind is still ranting to Gregory. And she realizes that Gregory is still here, always will be. The kitchen door bears the memory of his contempt. This past evening continues in a loop. Round and round, she hears the shower running, the squeak of rubber mat on the bathtub porcelain, splashing, a violent nose blow. His feet, heavy on the stairs. The slam of the kitchen door. Shouts. A confrontation with the taxi driver, who knocks, demanding payment.

Time, she thinks, staring into the dark, her eyes burning, is like an oxbow. That odd feeling, when you're canoeing. The river loops, you seem to have gone backwards, yet you've been paddling all the while. Just now, she's caught in an oxbow and the river does not stop. She can loop into memory, but time rolls onward. And she realizes that she has wanted nothing in this house to change or to absorb anything new. The air itself, in Kate's eyes, retains Tom's shape. His fingerprints dull the sheen of doorknobs and newel posts. Wool scarves are burred with his scent of tobacco and oils. As long as the armchair is still riddled with burn holes, the drawing notebooks are tipped on the shelf from his careless placement, the frayed ball cap is on the shelf where Kate remembers Tom tossing it on that last morning, after he'd gone out to inspect the roses, then he is close, still part of this epoch of her life. Then she can pretend to forget. Speak to him in her mind and imagine that he hears.

It is madness, these two opposing feelings. This strange man who has blundered into her life sharpens her memory of Tom, hones her longing, reminds her of what she has lost. Tom lounges in the doorways of her mind, grinning. They confer. Her palms feel the silk of Tom's skin. Her mouth twitches with the urge to mouth words that bear their shared history. Her eyes darken with the desire to glance and be known. *Yet. Yet.* Gregory stumbles like a drunken hunter through the delicate crust of her frozen life. His heavy foot displaces Tom. Her house is swollen with his anger, and Tom, in her mind, becomes smaller.

Up. Get up. She throws back the covers. The air is cold; the furnace cannot warm every corner of this large house. *Too big for me. I should sell . . . But what about the garden? Where would I go?* Night thoughts.

She puts on a pair of heavy wool socks and a misshapen wool sweater with frayed elbows and goes down to the kitchen. The light on her phone is blinking. Probably Gregory, whom she'd called shortly after he'd left her house. "Please let me know," she'd said to his answering machine, "when you've arrived home." She picks up the receiver, listens. "I've arrived home," he says. A click.

She opens the cupboard next to the sink. She stands on tiptoe, rummaging. There. In with the almond extract and essence of orange are two miniature bottles of rum, Christmas presents that she'd dropped in her and Tom's red flannel stockings one year. She has not bought hard liquor since Tom's death.

She empties both bottles into a glass, adds orange juice. She sips the drink, winces. She wishes she had a god. Could pray. The stars, the moonlit sky, will not provide what she wants. *What do I want?* She leans against the counter, tips the glass to her lips. She stares at the toes of her socks. Red toes, grey feet. She knit them, years ago, for Tom. *To be known. Me. Separate, with my troubling and mysterious idiosyncrasies, blossomed from my genes. Me. A storied vessel. Minutes of life wedged, jagged-edged, a puzzle construed, cracked varnish of my layers, light, darkness, the blunt scissors, swans, the lost rake, seedlings, snapping turtles, pears, Chopin, fever, childbirth. To be known. To have told as much as possible. To have listened. Soberly, with respect. To the small stories, the great ones. Sideways, upside down, free-floating. This. Is. Me. No one sees. No one will ever know, as he did. Here I drift between past and future. Both inaccessible, both without substance. Here there is substance but no dream. Kitchen, cold. Hard floor. Places, people, time, sunlight, smiles. Consumed with the fire of loss. Falling, drifting.*

She sets down the empty glass. Gathering the sweater close around her neck, she steps into the dark living room and slides her hand over the table until she finds the diary. Going up the stairs, her sock feet make no sound and are slippery on the varnished oak.

She props herself up in bed, opens the diary to the place she's marked with a blue jay's tail feather.

January 12, 1915—Letter from Jonnie with scrawled handwriting. Says she is tired, with a sore throat and racing pulse. I sent her a telegram. Waiting for reply. Mother tells me not to worry. Should I go to the Bakers?

Then there are ten days with nothing written. She turns the empty pages.

January 22, 1915—Service held at the church where we would have been married.

After this, there is blank page after blank page. Twenty-four empty days. Then she reaches a page with handwriting.

February 16, 1915—One month ago today.

She slides her legs out of bed, pulls the heavy socks on again. Goes downstairs and turns on the standing lamp. There, on the floor by the table, its top half-off, is the hatbox where she found the correspondence between Jonnie and Giles. She lifts the box, carries it to the couch. She takes out envelopes whose letters have become fat from having been opened and refolded. She holds them sideways to read their franked dates. No. No. Too early or too late. But here is one. A blue envelope. The return address H. Baker. To Mr. Giles Thomas, 12 Roselawn Street.

February 16, 1915
Hartford, Connecticut

Dear Giles,

We are all as well as possibly can be. My father is a great help to us all, especially Mother. I know you and Jonnie wrote to one another, so I thought perhaps a letter would be a comfort, even though we will see you on Sunday. Father tells us the diphtheria epidemic is spreading. We pray for all the families like ours. We pray for all the other innocent victims, mostly young. I thought to tell you about our bedroom. We gave away her clothes but saved all her special things, some of which we want you to have.
I decided what to put on her desk. I put a framed photograph of Jonnie where the sun will fall on it. And an African violet with such lovely blue petals. I speak to her every night before going to sleep. Father speaks to her in every blessing. It is a comfort, but we are so sad. We speak of you so often and hope you will not become a stranger. Please be sure to come for Sunday dinner. Please give my best wishes to your mother and father, and to your sister, and to your brother when you next write to him.

With fondest regards,
Hetty Baker

Kate steps to her table, where the medical textbook lies under the lamp. She carries it to the couch, bends forward as she flips the pages. They make a dry fluttering in the motion-less room, like a flock of disturbed chickadees.

Diphtheria. Spreads like wildfire in early winter. Schoolchildren become infected by licking the pencils of carriers. Unknowingly, infected dairy workers press the disease into cow's udders with their fingers as they milk. The disease lurks in dust, in unpasteurized milk, on the haze of moisture sprayed from the mouths of coughing carriers. Once sick, the area around the victim's neck swells, causing a "bullneck" appearance. A thick, greyish "pseudo-membrane" forms on the surface of the nostrils and pharynx, and may even extend up into the nose or down into the windpipe and lungs. The kidneys and the nervous system can be affected. Slow, creeping paralysis progresses from palate to eyes, from heart to larynx. Finally the limbs succumb. Heart muscle inflammation (acute myocarditis) weakens the heart, may (mercifully) cause death.

Isolation wards, during epidemics, were filled to capacity with diphtheria patients.

It is two a.m. Kate goes to the hooks in the coatroom, finds a warm vest. She wraps a fleece scarf around her neck, turns the heat up a notch. She plugs in the kettle. She will not be going back to bed. She sends her fingers down through the papers in the box. She's become her own grandfather, longing for something that Jonnie's hands held. At the bottom of the box is a green book, on its cover a gold fairy wreathed in gauze and holding a star-tipped wand. In a child's loopy, tremulous script is a pencilled inscription: To Margaret Baker on her 10th birthday, July 21, 1900, from Hetty and Alma Baker. It is a book of fairy tales. Some of its black-and-white drawings have been hand-painted with watercolours. Here's a plate where a maiden sits in a yellow desert, wearing a pink dress. She leans back on her hands. Around her feet are skulls and bones. Her white veil flutters, and she watches with dismay as a bird flies away. Kate runs her fingers over the drawing, imagining ten-year-old Jonnie, paintbrush poised, anxious to make the right choice.

Perhaps, Kate thinks, her roommate reported Jonnie's illness to the school. Perhaps Jonnie had been taken to the hospital, and word came back that diphtheria was suspected. She imagines how everything in Professor Tarbell's classroom was immediately scrubbed down; how Jonnie's easel, brushes, smock and an apple were set in the courtyard by a gloved workman; how overnight, frost crystals formed on the folds of the smock and the apple froze solid. Perhaps, as soon as she'd been diagnosed with diphtheria, a quarantine sign appeared on the door of her studio. Her roommate and artists in the neighbouring studios moved out. And a Western Union telegram was sent to her parents:

SUSPECT DIPHTHERIA MARGARET BAKER STOP CONTA-GIOUS STOP MASS GENERAL HOSPITAL ISOLATION WARD AS OF 8:28 AM TODAY.

Oh, and Grampa Giles was back in Hartford. Kate pictures him, irresolute, after sending the telegram to Jonnie to which there was no reply. In the gathering dusk, he decided to take a streetcar to the Bakers' house. It was five o'clock, the street lights were lit; along the sidewalks, snow-clad branches of forsythia bushes etched the darkness. Giles knocked on the Bakers' door. No one answered. He let himself in. There was a murmur of voices coming from the kitchen. He stood by the hat rack. His hand lifted to the brim of his fedora, and then his heart made a thick, sickening surge. His mind reeled from the present the way he would throw himself from the path of an oncoming car. He pictured the pieces of his life as they were yesterday, when the sun fell onto the papers on his desk, their snarled problems engaging his mind; when he could sit back, smiling, and imagine Jonnie striding eagerly across Copley Square, cheeks burnished by the winter wind, black hair escaping from a red wool cloche and curling around her face.

He hung his hat on the rack. He walked down the hall and opened the kitchen door. The family stood looking at a telegram that lay on the table. It had arrived only minutes earlier.

Giles started back as if a snake lay on the oilcloth. Dr. Baker picked up the telegram and handed it to him. Hetty lifted her apron, pressed it to her mouth and held it there with both hands, watching him. His eyes took in the words, but his mind wrung them of meaning. He looked up and saw that Mrs. Baker had dropped her glasses to the table, pressed the palms of her hands to her closed eyes.

"Diphtheria?" he said. "I received a letter today. She said she had a sore throat."

"That is usually the first symptom," said Alma.

No one spoke. The coals shifted in the firebox of the kitchen stove.

"Shall we bring her home?" Giles asked.

"I'm afraid, if it is truly diphtheria, that we can't," said Dr. Baker.

"We should go to her, then," said Giles. "I'll go on the next train."

Kate imagines how his hands trembled. She pictures him setting the telegram back on the red diamonds of the oilcloth. His perception of the kitchen changed. The walls seemed to have moved forward; white porcelain knobs gleamed on cupboards varnished the colour of blackstrap molasses. He noticed the calendar on the door to the back stairs, generous squares marking each eventless day, a Saint Bernard holding the handle of a flower-filled basket in its mouth. Light came from odd places, assaulting him; the lip of the coal scuttle, the water tank, a window glass by the sink. He tried to keep his voice from trembling. "Massachusetts General, Isolation Ward." Panic came into the room. Dr. Baker grasped Giles' arm. Hetty's hand flew from her face towards him, quellingly.

"Wait," she said. Her lips trembled and tightened. "I'll pack some things for her. I will come too."

"But, Hetty, it's contag—"

"If you love someone," she said, looking at Giles, "you can't catch their disease. That's the truth. Now you wait, Giles." She began to untie her apron.

In the end, Kate imagines, Giles, Hetty and Mrs. Baker, at ten-thirty that evening, took a cab to the station. Dr. Baker sent a telegram to Hathaway's Hotel in Boston. He and Alma stood in the door, their breath making white clouds on the air. Dr. Baker's head, hatless, was like an onion. Alma clung to his arm, waving. The door to the house stood open. There was a harsh gaslight on the wall behind them, and Giles, leaning forward on his seat before falling back, could see neither the interior of the house nor their faces.

The next morning, in Boston, it was bleak, cold. Portentous clouds carried snow, but none fell. Giles, Hetty and Mrs. Baker were shown to the ward. It was a long, high-ceilinged room, each bed separated by white curtains on rails. The room was lit entirely by light falling from tall windows. There were no sharp shadows; no light danced, glistened or flickered. It was like a pencil drawing or an etching, composed of whites and greys: grey floor, a steel gleam sheening from the curtain rails, grey shadows fluting the white curtains, the cast-iron beds painted with many coats of white enamel and beneath each bed a white porcelain bowl. The nurses wore white, with black triangles on their caps like the wings of penguins. Sounds echoed—coughing, the sticky hiss of occluded breath through diphtheria's pseudo membrane, heel-taps of nurses whose long, aproned skirts and starched caps made them seem unnaturally tall.

Jonnie lay in a bed halfway down the long room. Her hair was pulled back from her face. Her neck was grossly swollen, swathed with damp towels. She lay on her back with her eyes closed, her skin clammy with fever. She held her mouth open as if it were propped with sticks.

Giles, Hetty and Mrs. Baker clustered by a large window at the end of the ward. No, they were told, under no circumstances whatsoever might they enter. Hetty was frantic. "Where is she?" she asked a nurse. "Where is Jonnie Baker?" They were shown where she lay, on the left-hand side. Hetty could not see, so she stood on a chair, steadying herself with one hand on Giles' shoulder. "I see her," she said. Tears glistened on her cheeks, but she was unaware of them. She stared intently. Spoke as if seeing a newborn baby. "I can see her black hair." A nurse bent over Jonnie. The nurse straightened and nodded to the family who clung to the glass. "She knows," Hetty said. "She knows you are here, Giles." Jonnie's hand lifted from the bed. Giles removed his hat so he could press his forehead against the glass. "She's trying to roll her head over," Hetty whispered. Giles could not speak. He put his arm around Mrs. Baker. The nurse half-lifted Jonnie, trying to keep the towels in place. Then they could see Jonnie's face, her despairing eyes that widened, seeking, at last finding Giles.' For the rest of his life, Giles believed she might as well have been speaking, for between them in the ward rose their life as if it had already been lived: the white roses and sweet peas she carried at her wedding, the attic studio, where apples and rooftops ghosted half-finished from canvasses, steam curling from a teapot, babies plump-cheeked beneath wool blankets, Sunday mornings when they lay beneath quilts, arm over chest, cheek on shoulder, murmuring sleepily of their senseless dreams. Her eyes filled with tears. Her lips moved, but he knew they made no sound. He laid his hand against the glass next to his face, fingers bent at the knuckles.

Huddled on the couch, Kate feels rather than hears the winter's silence. It is like a weight, a pressure. Her eyes run over the words of Hetty's letter to Giles. *I thought perhaps a letter would be a comfort . . .* Her grandmother becomes a different person. *I put a framed photograph of Jonnie where the sun will fall on it . . .* Kate sees how her love and her sadness are inseparable and augment one another.

Kate imagines her grandmother, one month after Jonnie's death, sitting in the bedroom she and Jonnie had shared. She sees her putting down her pen and gently folding the letter to Giles. She was sitting on the side of her bed, and the room was cold, even though the radiator hissed and clanked. She wore a wool sweater over her flannel nightgown. Jonnie's bed was neatly made, the bedspread taut over the pillow. Hetty had thought for a long time about what to put on Jonnie's desk. She did not want to leave it empty, and yet she knew she could not bear setting out any of the intimate treasures they'd decided to keep: Jonnie's wooden paintbox or her kidney-shaped palette, choppy with thick daubs of paint, or her books— Rembrandt's drawings, *Gray's Anatomy,* a worn leather volume of Wordsworth. Nor would she be able to bear the sight of her sister's hairbrush, with strands of curly black hair wound round the bristles, or her half-empty bottle of eau de cologne or her mandolin or the coral scarf pin hooked in a peach-coloured silk scarf. All these things they'd gathered into boxes and brought back with them when they returned from Boston, two days after Jonnie's death.

Some diphtheria patients linger for weeks while paralysis creeps from eyes to heart, larynx to limbs. Jonnie was spared this. She died very suddenly of acute myocarditis. On the night that she died, Mrs. Baker, exhausted, had remained at the hotel. Hetty and Giles had gone for a quick supper and returned to the ward at seven o'clock. Even from the window they could see Jonnie's struggle for breath. Two nurses stood by her bed, and then one of the nurses, seeing them, came swiftly down the ward and told them that she was near suffocation, her trachea and nose filled with the grey membrane. Their own throats and chests ached as they watched the bed, where they could no longer see Jonnie, only the nurses and then a doctor. Suddenly the doctor stepped backward. They saw Jonnie's chest lift violently, her arms jerk outwards. Like a breath of wind passing over water, she stirred slowly as she settled, her head falling slack, her hands slowly opening. A nurse reached to pull the curtains and then glanced at the window where Hetty and Giles stood. They stared at the stillness that had been Jonnie. They listened to the sounds of the ward: the rappety-click of the nurses' shoes, a murmur, the clank of radiator pipes, a cough. Hetty turned with a choking cry as if she would run for help, and Giles put out his arms. She collapsed against his chest. He put his cheek on her hair and held her head. She felt his chest begin to shake, a slow lift and then rapid wracking heaves. He clutched her as if he would fall otherwise. They watched through their tears as another nurse came, as the white figures bent like angels around Jonnie, lifting her arms, wiping her face, unwrapping the towels from her neck, their lips moving as they smoothed her beautiful hair.

Hetty could not remember how they found their way back to Hathaway's. Perhaps someone called a cab. She remembered only how all night long she could not stop thinking that she should be at Jonnie's side, helping her. The next days had passed in pieces of time whose linking moments were blank, like the harsh opening and shutting of a lightning-lit land-scape. She and her mother, arm in arm as they approached Jonnie's room in the Grundmann Studios. Giles, removing the quarantine notice on the door and crumpling it into his pocket. Packing Jonnie's possessions. Who provided the boxes? Giles, stooping and carrying the boxes to a waiting cab. Father and Alma, their faces swollen from tears and sleeplessness. Cards and flowers and visitors and food arriving at their house. Giles' family at the funeral, all in a row, black coats, black hats, black feathers, black gloves. Hetty saw their bowed shoulders, how they did not move or look backwards or sideways. Giles glanced up, once. He tipped his head as if escaping the intol-erable strain of keeping it bowed and gazed at the lamb in the stained-glass window. Then he bent his head again, and she saw his hands slide over his face.

After the funeral, they spent their evenings sitting at the kitchen table, reading sympathy cards and answering them. Two weeks after Jonnie's death, Dr. Baker kindly laid his hand on his wife's shoulder and said they should sort through Jonnie's things now and give her clothes to the poor. They did this one evening when Hetty and Alma had returned from teaching. They sat on the beds in what was now Hetty's room, passing Jonnie's dresses and blouses from hand to hand. They spoke in sad, soft voices, as if a child slept whom they did not want to waken. They murmured of the times she had worn such a hat or stood in a summer wind while this scarf billowed. Piece by piece they accepted Jonnie's death, made piles of limp clothing gleaned of memory. They could not give away her possessions, the things she had loved and used. These they sep-arated into a box. The box sat in a corner of the bedroom.

Dr. Baker said a special prayer every night before dinner. "Jonnie, we love you. We pray and know that you are at home with our Lord. We pray and know that you are at peace." Hetty was comforted by the sound of her sister's name, spoken so sweetly by her small, quiet father. She bowed her head and gripped her hands together on her lap under the table. The steamy fragrance of beef stew rose from her plate. As her father's voice soothed her heart and reminded her of God's plan, she made herself picture her bedroom. Brown wallpaper, the gaslight making veils of shadow in the upper corners. Jonnie's bed, smooth, untouched. The box, tied with twine. It was like her own heart, a place suddenly unfamiliar, in which she must live the rest of her life.

She sat, now, on the side of her bed. She'd decided, as she told Giles in the letter, what to put on the desk: an African violet with dusk-blue petals next to a framed photograph of Jonnie. She gathered a quilt around her shoulders and gazed yearningly at the photograph. Frost crystals stood on the inside of the windowpane.

"It's so cold, Jonnie," she whispered. Her nose prickled, her heart began to thud. Tears sprang from her eyes. She did not wipe them from her cheeks but whispered more steadily, as if not wanting Jonnie to know she was crying. "Giles comes every weekend. We talk about you. I tell him you're happy." She smiled. Her eyebrows rose and formed a small tent of sorrow and love. "You are, aren't you? Sometimes we talked about heaven. You said you wanted a kitten when you got there. I told Giles you have a kitty now." She fell silent. The window was like a block of ice. She turned, slid between her sheets, huddled under the covers. She did believe that Jonnie was in heaven. She did believe that somewhere, in sunshine and warmth, Jonnie twitched a string for a kitten, laughing. Every night she mentally sketched Jonnie's new world, gave it roses and ivy-shrouded piazzas, imagined Jonnie meeting Giles' little sister, Ellen, and how they walked together through tossing waist-deep grass. Without this picture that she made—drawing the lines over and over, night after night, until the picture became blurred and indistinct—Hetty could not let Jonnie go.

Kate sits on the couch, hugging the book of fairy stories to her chest. The letter from her grandmother to her grandfather lies open on her lap. She stirs, emerges from her mental journey. She sets down the book and picks up the letter. *I thought perhaps a letter would be a comfort . . .* She hears her granny's gentle voice, and it, too, has changed.

11. Broken Glass

THE NEXT MORNING, SUNDAY, KATE OPENS THE SINK TAP and waits for lead-tainted water to clear from the pipes; trained by Tom, who, irritatingly, always checked to see if she'd run the water before filling the kettle.

On the table are May's yellow Kodak folders. Kate's mouth twitches. Oh God. "Why is he in your bathrobe?" She sighs, holds the kettle to the water. Gregory. His hard eyes. "How can you say that to me?" *I didn't mean it that way.* Then she sees the two miniature rum bottles and remembers that Jonnie is gone.

She lifts the stove lid. She kept a fire going until three a.m. Coals still pulse within a bed of ash. She builds the fire up with more paper than kindling since there are coals; slides open all the dampers. The house is so cold. Icy draughts seep beneath doors, breathe from loose window casings, filter through cracks in old plaster. Another day begins, Kate thinks, taking eggs from the refrigerator. They are all the same, the days. Heavy as unleavened bread, without the yeast of anticipation. She doesn't know where to put her mind.

The phone rings. It's her sister, Ruth. Kate cradles the receiver between ear and shoulder, making coffee while

Ruth talks about her two sons. Then it is Kate's turn.

"I went skiing yesterday with a man who fell through the ice."

"Oh my Lord, Kate!"

"No, no, he was fine."

"Hypothermia?"

"No, I got him into a shower pretty fast. He's an old friend of mine and Tom's. Gregory Stiller."

"What were you thinking of, Kate, skiing on the river if it was possible to break through?"

This is why, Kate thinks, it is tiresome to tell Ruth anything. Still, she tries. "Then I couldn't sleep last night, and I read more of the letters from the hatbox. Did you know that Grampa Giles was going to marry Granny's sister and that she died of diphtheria?"

"Was it around 1915? That was a terrible time, for both flu and diphtheria. Diphtheria was hideously contagious."

"But did you know that, Ruth? That Grampa Giles was engaged to Granny's sister?"

Ruth is silent for an instant, as if reacting to Kate's intensity rather than the question itself. "I think so . . ." she says, vaguely.

A fluttering roar comes from the vicinity of the ceiling. Kate freezes. Ruth is exclaiming as she slams down the receiver.

Chimney fire.

She leaps to the stove, shoots the dampers shut. The roar intensifies. She runs outside in her socks, squints into the sunlight that glances and shatters from icicles. Flames. Flames and dark smoke erupting from the chimney.

"Oh God," she hears herself saying as she runs to the phone. It's like someone else speaking. "Oh God." She dials 911. Then she's standing by the kitchen stove. *Throw water on it. Do not throw water on it. Take out the burning logs. No. Make sure the dampers are shut tight.* She's left the kitchen door open. Icy air pours in and meets the heat that pulses from the stovepipe. *The closets.* She runs upstairs, imagines sparks coming through chinks in the chimney. Her heart pounds; she tastes blood. She rips open the door to Christy's closet, where bits of dry mortar crumble from the flue. She puts her hands on the bricks. They are warm. She can hear the throbbing beat, like wings. She pounds up the stairs to the attic. Dead flies on the floor. Coat hangers, the blind light of ice-bound windows. What can she do, what did she expect? The familiar feeling of utter helplessness. She lays her palms against the chimney, hears the hungry roar just beyond. *Please. Please.* Begging, pleading. *Oh God.*

She hears the fire siren. Runs back downstairs, clinging to the banister, socks slipping. They are in her kitchen, men she knows from town. They're uncoiling hose on the lawn, running with ladders. She's pulling on boots, struggling into a coat, her hands shaking, finding mittens, hat. She's on the lawn, hands to her face. She's standing under the apple tree. Canvas hose, sliding along the shovelled stone path. Boots, seeking purchase in snow. Men standing in the garden, stabbing a ladder through a rose bush, looking up. A siren wails once, then the tones cut, trail down the air. Silence, resonating.

Kate goes into the street, stands beneath the snowy poplars. She senses a gathering crowd, doors slamming, neighbours emerging from houses. Two women stand close on either side of her; one puts her arm across Kate's shoulders and hugs, quickly. The quiet morning is shattered, patchy with sound and colour, the smell of coats, diesel fumes, smoke. Men, running. Shouts. The women ask her how it happened, and she hears herself answer, distractedly telling them that she left a fire in the stove. "It was so cold last night," one says, understandingly. Another emergency vehicle arrives. "No one's inside the house," she says to one of the two men who jumps out. A young man from Liam's class. So solicitous. He invites her into the vehicle, hands her a cup of coffee with a plastic lid. The women help her into the cab as though she is injured. Through the windshield, shuddering, she watches men climb onto her roof as if this house is no longer her concern. Making her feel that she may be responsible, may not have been careful enough, may not have cared when she had the chance. The way she felt when the EMTs burst into the kitchen after Tom's death. Her life—in other people's hands.

They want to return to their interrupted Sunday mornings. Family, church, dinner. It is, after all, a volunteer fire department. The chief lingers, politely. No, he raises his hand, no coffee or tea, thanks. Sorry for the mess, he says, although they did their best, threw plastic on the kitchen floor. He's spare, preoccupied. His worried eyes skirt Kate's; he's uncomfortable being alone with a woman. One hand on the doorknob. Before you use the stove again, he says, get the chimney cleaned. She stands in the doorway, watches him pause on the path to bend forward over a match. Then he straightens, the cigarette returns him to his own life, and he walks rapidly to the idling fire truck. Plume of white exhaust. Another man in the cab speaks into a radio phone. The chief swings up, the men confer, glance at the house, seem surprised to see Kate, who waves.

She picks up the broom. Puts it down. She takes out mop and pail, finds the floor detergent. She runs the water, turns it off. She stands with her hands at her temples, fingers clawed. She paces into the living room, back into the kitchen. She's still wearing coat and boots. The house is cold. It smells of snowy air, creosote, cold smoke, men's jackets. The table is shoved back against the porch window. The rocking chair is tipped sideways, its cushion on the floor. On the black and red tiles, piles of snow turn to slush. The cellar door stands open; the chief took her down, showed her where water and creosote leaked from the thimble, made a stygian puddle. The dank odour rises from the stairwell. Snow and mud track up the stairs, into the bedroom, into the closet. Some of Christy's clothes were tossed on the bed so the men could check the walls. Black paint peels from the stovepipe. She takes the phone book from a drawer. Jack deGroot, chimney cleaning. Her hands shake. She's reading words and registering nothing. She tosses the book onto the kitchen counter.

She goes into the living room and stands in a patch of sunlight. It falls on a picture of Tom that stands on the table. *Why didn't you tell me? Before you died? Why didn't you tell me to clean the chimney? Why didn't you leave a list? If you were going to leave. You were going to leave me, so why didn't you just let me know these things? Things you didn't do, didn't finish, never bothered to tell me. The hose. The outside hose, last winter. Freezing, draining back into the cellar. For Christ's sake. Fuses. You could have gotten someone to organize those panels. It is insane. I mean, for God's sake, how did you deal with that all those years? Why didn't you complain, why didn't you do something about it? The electrician. He gave me a look. Did your husband know where all these fuses connect to? Oh! Those brushes on poles. In the rafters of the garage. That's right, you cleaned the chimneys yourself. For years. But then you stopped doing it. I didn't notice, but you damn well knew you should have dealt with it. But, no, you couldn't be bothered to call someone else to do it. So just leave me with flues filled with creosote. Leave me with all the crap from your dealers, your adoring public, the media, the buyers. Can you even begin to imagine the paperwork you have caused me to have to deal with? Not to mention the hours and hours of silence I have to listen to. It's frightening, numbing. I wait to hear you, and you make no sound. You have left. You have left.*

She picks up the picture. She hurls it to the floor. The glass shatters.

She falls back onto the couch. She can't weep. Her chest is dry. She feels the heat of her own breath, as if it will scorch her lungs. She leans forward, fists against her forehead.

Flowers. Delivered to the door. The smell of death. "With our sympathy." "To Kate, on your loss of a beloved husband." "In your sorrow, may there be peace." Tom's death began with the flowers. Until then, she did not know he was gone. He was Tom. He was somewhere. But flowers came flooding in, meant to fill an absence. Alstroemeria and baby's breath, white carnations, shasta daisies. Then food. Liam and Christy. Their faces shocked, smiles stretched past their grieving eyes. Carrying casseroles to the freezer in the cellar, cakes to the dining-room table. The hesitant, appalled faces at the door. Food, flowers, cards, visits. Filling the silence. The first night. She did not even attempt to sleep in their bed. She sat on the couch in a sleeping bag. Christy came halfway down the stairs. Went back, got pillow and blankets, curled next to her. They did not talk of Tom. They cried, laughed. Woke at three with all the covers gone, ate chocolate cake, made herbal tea. Christy read out loud Kate's favourite parts of *The Lord of the Rings*. They speculated about hobbits, their voices thick with restrained tears.

There was no ceremony. The man at the funeral home had queried her gently. Was she sure? It was not what Tom would have wanted, but what about her? We have no church, she explained, feeling for the first time that she had no reasonable defence against the unspoken pity that this statement pro-voked. Tom, she said, was an atheist. What about you? he'd asked. *Me?* she'd thought, rage blanketing her mind. *This is about* us. Now she wonders what could have more effectively assuaged her grief. For Tom's death seems unfinished. Does he roam here, a disconsolate ghost? What if she had allowed a church funeral? A familiar ritual, elements combined with a certain formality. Like Tom's paintings. Passionate confusion wrestled into a form whose beauty is derived from the ordering of material. As she might have ordered human voice, music, procession, meditation. Instead, people came to the house and roamed randomly through the rooms, holding a plate in one hand, a wine glass in the other. Some asked to say a few words. Couples bent over a guestbook by the door, hovered, inscribing their names slowly as if thinking, instead, of all they wished to say. No one seemed to know when to leave, and as they stepped out the door were both relieved and hesitant. Had they celebrated Tom's life? Rather, Kate thinks, they were barely able to acknowledge his death.

In Kate's clenched fists is the desire to find Tom. If he were buried somewhere, she would dig. She would tear at the soil, press earth to her face. She wishes she had made a gravestone. He had always told her he wished to be cast to the wind over the sea. But you cannot hold the wind in your hands.

Kate sits on the couch. Puddles form around the soles of her unlaced felt-lined boots. She has not moved since she threw Tom's picture to the floor.

The phone rings, and she does not answer.

How far she is, she thinks, from that feeling she had when she and Gregory set out yesterday. When she felt interesting to herself, like a teenager. What an illusion it is, she sees now. She is not yet a whole, single person. She sees the world as Tom's lover. She lives in this house as Tom's wife. She thinks as his partner. Yet everything about her has changed. She moves differently, with less conviction. She lacks resolution.

She is grave, reserved. She hoards her tenderness, her fears, her dreams, her intuitions, her wonder. She's still in the habit of saving it all for Tom. For when he comes home.

The machine answers, cuts off the ringing phone. In the silence, she hears thwarted possibility. Was it Caroline? May? Liam, calling from Ireland?

She should get up. She should sweep up the glass, restore the kitchen, mop the stairs, clean the puddle in the cellar, but she can't summon the energy to move. She is tired of picking up pieces.

12. Elizabeth Park

On Wednesdays Kate has piano students from noon until early evening. It's dark when she sees the last student to the door. The little girl is reluctant to leave. She hugs her piano books to her chest. She's small for her age, chubby. Her shyness leaves her when she sits at Kate's piano bench. Then her back straightens, her fingers are confident.

It's early March, and the cold has relented. The air smells, for the first time, of the river.

There is a car waiting in the street, beyond the pergola.

"There's your mother, Casey," Kate says, standing in the doorway, holding it open. She waves at the car.

Still the little girl lingers. "I'll work on 'Peasant Dance' for next time." The house must seem enormous to her, Kate realizes. Enormous and mysterious. Each time she arrives, the little girl is too shy to stare, but peeks up the stairs, peers into the dining room, skirts delicately past the pile of hatboxes and doesn't ask what's in them. Tonight, darkness crept upon them as they sat together at the piano in the living room. A horizontal bulb isolated the music; within the pool of light cast by a standing lamp, Kate and the child were luminous, their skin peach-coloured, a flash from Kate's wedding ring as she touched the score, the eggplant purple of Casey's fleece, while the rest of the room fell gradually into undifferentiated shadow. Here at her lessons, Kate thinks, smiling, as the child finally steps out the door, Casey's future quivers before her. Kate's house is her treasure box, the repository of her hopes. Life unfolds from this point, boundless, infinite.

Kate closes the door, turns on the kitchen lights. She pushes up her sleeves, rummages in the refrigerator. She peels the tawny paper skin from an onion, folds one leg beneath her on a chair as she slices the onion on a cutting board. The juice is colourless, potent. She wipes her eyes with the back of her sleeve, remembering how she'd walk down the village street to her own piano lessons with Mr. Bradac, how she'd hug her music to her chest just as Casey does, still too innocent to conceal the things she loved most.

Granny and Grampa Giles were her best audience. They listened, enraptured, as if nothing gave them more pleasure than to listen to Kate play, applauding each piece without a shade of criticism. In early fall, before her grandparents went back to their winter house in the city, she walked down to Shepton after supper. She crossed the cushioned grass of the terraced lawn. Her sneakers crept silently along the boards of the porch. She made shutters with her hands, pressed her face to the tall windows. They sat in the parlour with the air of people whose consciences are at rest. They waited for night, like the grasses of the field, like the settling birds. There they were, Grampa Giles in the shapeless brown armchair, reading the *Hartford Courant,* Granny knitting with her head tipped slightly sideways and her eyebrows raised in their sweet, sad expression. What did she do with all those baby booties made of the finest white wool? Kate asked her mother, who told her that Granny knit to keep arthritis from crippling her hands and gave the booties, oh, to some charity. The little spinet stood against a wall, its stool wound all the way up, a tiny braided rug on its saucer-shaped seat. The room was warmed by the last rays of the sun that burnished the hayfield, and she could see how her grandparents seemed not to be alone but in the presence of the ancestors whose portraits hung along the north wall, staring with frozen expressions: the woman who held the chain of a gold locket between finger and thumb, looking up coyly as if sharing a secret with the painter; the man with troubled eyes, one hand positioned on a stiff collar; the elderly gentleman—judicious, patriarchal—whose hand was laid loosely against a long beard. Light glowed in the paintings' black oil, exposed crackled lines, warmed the ivory faces. Granny and Grampa Giles seemed comfortable in their presence, accustomed to their eternal vigilance. Kate, peering in the window, noticed how her grandparents seemed different here; they were quiet, passive, obedient, as if life at Shepton was prescribed, like saying the Lord's Prayer or brushing one's teeth.

Kate rapped on the window, causing the delicious moment between their startled gestures and sudden discovery of her blindered face. Granny limped to the door, caught her in a hug. Grampa Giles folded his paper, laid his head back against his chair and closed his eyes, smiling before she even began to play. If there was a false start, they didn't notice. "Wait, wait. I'm going to begin again." Ten years old, like Casey. She remembers the feeling of the future's allure when it balanced on the edge of the present and she had no sense of time's cost.

She pours olive oil into a cast-iron pan, scoops up the chopped onions with both hands. *Why am I constantly remembering them?* She steps over her boots to open the porch door for Mr. Winkles, spoons cat food from a can into his dish. It's not only the hatboxes, she thinks. Not only the letters, the smell of Shepton in her living room. She stoops, sets down the cat's dish, bunches her fingers and draws them over the ridged fur between his ears. She lives alone now, and her mind doesn't know where else to go. It's dangerous to go forward; painful to remember her life with Tom. Her grandparents, and Shepton, have always been her treasure box, her place of unfolding. Like Gregory's camping trips, she thinks, suddenly.

As she eats, she listens to the CBC news. When she's finished, she calls May and talks to her while she washes the dishes. "It's my Wednesday. All afternoon. Mostly children, but I have a few adults before school lets out. How about you? Did you get outside?"

May has taken up cross-country skiing. She skis on the town's maintained trail that starts by the bridge and winds along next to the river. She seems to Kate to have reached a point of stasis. She is never sick, never injured, never tired. Her body seems so dry and tough that it is no longer vulnerable. Her mind seems correspondingly impervious. Kate hangs up the phone, drains the sink, drapes the dishcloth over the faucet. She remembers how on the day of the chimney fire, after she swept up the glass from Tom's picture, she'd been daunted by the job of cleaning the rest of the mess. She'd phoned May, who immediately came over to help. Together they mopped the floors, swept the creosote puddle into a snow shovel, carried the table back into the middle of the room. "Don't you have a bright tablecloth, Kate? I'm going to buy you some flowers from the grocery store. For heaven's sake, they only cost eight ninety-five. You should treat yourself. I do. I even buy myself roses. Go call Christy. Of course you should call Christy. How often do you save a man from drowning and have a chimney fire within twenty-four hours?"

In the days that followed, May and Kate phoned each other most evenings, and now it's become a ritual. Kate feels herself yielding to May's occasional astute queries. Some feelings she no longer hoards. She makes herself take stock of the bright moments of her life, knowing May will insist that there are such times. She told her, tonight, about Casey in the doorway. "She didn't seem to want to go home. I was so touched."

"Well, of course, Kate! The children love you."

And Kate realizes that there is a small place within herself where something has remained unchanged, steady. Like walking through dark woods and realizing that eyes readjust; the path is pale, but can be followed.

She strays into the living room, surveys the pile of boxes. She has made a general inventory of their contents, enough to assure herself that only three boxes have material relating to her grandparents. Everything she's read so far is sorted, bound with elastic bands, each bundle marked with a note: "1904, receipts from butcher, fishmonger, general groceries"; or "1913–15, Margaret Baker, to and from Giles Thomas." Browsing through the boxes, her nightly habit, helps postpone something else she feels she should be doing, a formless demand that makes her anxious, like an exam whose date looms and for which she's unprepared.

She sits cross-legged on the floor, leaning against the couch. She yawns. It takes energy to turn from student to student, each one bringing her their progress like a gift that she must criticize. Mr. Winkles strolls through the door, tail raised. He curls on the couch behind Kate, purrs into her ear. She reaches back, scratches his head absently. She opens her grandfather's diary, begins to read with the odd sense of exclusion that accompanies travelling in an ongoing present that is not her own.

February 18, 1915—Did not go to Parson's Theatre with
Mother and Father. Don't know how they can endure music.

February 22, 1915—Deep, continuing cold. Looked at
sympathy cards with Hetty and Alma.

February 28, 1915—Mrs. Baker sick. A cold, not influenza. The girls made chicken soup. Helped Dr. Baker with frozen pipes. Father worried about the new apples and roses we planted last summer at Shepton. Mother ex. busy.

March 1, 1915—Mrs. Baker's birthday. I was pleased to be invited and went directly there from the office. Every celebration accentuates Jonnie's absence.

March 7, 1915—Holding the mouse skull in my hand. Poor sleep. Dreams of Jonnie that I wake from terr. distressed. Can't take down paintings yet, can barely stand to look at them. Worried about F. and M. Father depressed, knee swollen. M. seems down, concerned about Father. Days without sunshine.

At the time of Jonnie's death, many letters and telegrams must have passed between Giles and his parents while he was still in Boston, so that by the time he returned home the first shock had passed and there was nothing left but the funeral. Kate imagines how Giles' father—stooped, pale, haggard— met Giles at the door, wearing his despair over Jonnie's loss so clearly that there was no need for them to do more than shake hands. Arm in arm, they slowly climbed the varnished oak staircase. There was his mother, standing on the carpet in the upstairs hall. She stepped forward swiftly and put her arms around Giles. She held him fractionally longer than usual. She looked at him but did not trust herself to speak. At that moment, Giles remembered Lilian's anguished cry at the moment of Ellen's death, and he looked away from his mother, grieved that his own life had brought these black wings back into her heart. They went to the upstairs parlour. Giles and Lilian drank tea, and Charles sipped whiskey and soda. They talked steadily of the train trip from Boston and the weather that had accompanied it, of the funeral arrangements, of flowers and music, of the Bakers. Lilian sat very straight and spoke severely. She was like a person led to the banks of a pond to see the place where, years before, her child had drowned. A tacit understanding resolved during this conversation. Giles' grief would be respected but not commented upon. They would not knock on his closed door.

Kate studies a large studio photograph of Lilian, who by this time had grown stout. She wears a dress with folds over the bust and a wide satin sash at the waist. Around her neck is a heavy necklace. She wears a brooch and (Kate imagines) large hats, fur tippets. Her face is neither serene nor anxious, and she carries her mouth in a slight smile, her eyes fixed in a calm, attentive expression. No doubt she seldom laughed, nor did anyone ever see her cry. She moved slowly, as befitted her stately figure, and was obdurately reasonable, lived by a fixed schedule. Every morning she was at her desk by eight o'clock, answering letters, making lists, arranging her day's schedule of board meetings and teas in a leather-bound book that Kate lifts from the hatbox. She used black ink; her handwriting was firm and clear.

Tuesday, March 17—Order tassel hooks from Brown, Thompson. Call Gillette Bros. re sewing machine. 2:00 p.m. Orphan's Asylum mtg. Cloved ham, cottage pudding.

Wedged in the pages is what must be (for there are words obscured with spirals and X's) the draft of a sympathy letter to Dr. and Mrs. Baker.

Roselawn Street, Hartford

My dear Doctor and Mrs. Baker, Alma and Hetty,

I cannot begin to express my sympathy at this tragic loss of your daughter. I can only tell you of how in our own family we grieve not only for you, but for this terrible loss in our own lives. Your daughter, Jonnie, brought immeasurable happiness into our home. She cheered and livened our table with her amusing stories, her sympathetic portraits of the quaint characters she met in Boston, and with her joyful spirit. It has been a great privilege to have known a young woman who, in her brief years, seemed to have gathered such a deep repository of life's treasures. She made my husband laugh and smile as he has not done for some time. We will always love her as a member of our family, the daughter-in-law she would have been. I know that however many loving thoughts travel your way, you will feel your loss forever. I cannot begin to think of what to say that will lighten the dreadful grief you are suffering, but please know that our deepest sympathy and thoughts dwell with you now and that we hope your faith in God's Kingdom will soothe your sorrow.

Lilian would have sat upright, her pen scratching. She'd have breathed deeply through her nose, her lips tightening, as she folded the letter; paused before sealing it into its envelope. Maybe she reopened the letter and ran her eyes over the words. A spasm crossed her face, and then she refolded it as if in a trance. She sat at her desk with her head forward on her fingers and her eyes closed. Was there a glistening of tears, did she draw her fingers slowly over her cheekbones before straightening her back and shuffling the letter into a pile of others? Later that day, she told Giles she had sent a letter to the Bakers. It did not occur to her to tell him what she had written, and he did not presume to ask.

March 8, 1915—Feel I can't talk about Jonnie any more.
I believe it brings back M. and F.'s memories of the loss of
Ellen.

March 9, 1915—Dream of Jonnie every night. Don't want
to wake up in the morning. Last night, for the first time,
she was not in the dream, but I was trying to find her.

There they are, Lilian, Charles and Giles, eating their
supper in the March twilight, discussing the Shepton windmill. Some of its slats were rotting and its wooden tank
needed repair. Lilian told Charles and Giles that she
planned to have all the piazza rocking chairs repainted.
"What do you think of green? Perhaps a daffodil yellow
would be nice," she mused, setting knife and fork to her
roast beef. Giles had dreamed of Jonnie the night before,
and the dream recurred all day, clouding his thoughts, darkening his heart. In the dream, he'd been looking for her at
Shepton. He'd gone into all the rooms, calling. He'd
climbed the windmill, thinking she might be clinging there,
gazing over the valley. Now, sitting at the table in suit and
tie, he sliced a Brussels sprout and considered how it was
like a tiny cabbage, its leaves folded, fluted, pressed. Father,
he thought, was as doggedly gloomy as ever; but Mother
had changed since Jonnie's death. Every word she spoke
announced that everything that had always existed—the
piazza chairs, the orphanage, the Lady's Auxiliary—would
not be affected by Jonnie's death, that all her energy was
absorbed in clutching the pieces of her life around her like
a quilt, shrouding herself from feeling.

March 10, 1915—Pouring rain. Talk with Father. Told me
of his first wife, Lucy Smith. How he never got over her

death, hopes I will not repeat his life. Felt better for having talked, even with our usual circumspection.

Kate has asked her father to describe his grandparents' house on Roselawn Street, and she pictures, as she reads this entry, the library, darkened by mahogany furniture, maroon drapes half-drawn across a window seat, a Persian carpet. She imagines that a coal fire burned in the Franklin stove, although the cold snap was over and outside the world was in teeming motion. Giles caught a glimpse of their reflection in a large gilt-framed mirror: a young man and an old man sitting in the grey light amidst book-lined walls, potted ferns, a marble table crowded with crystal candy dishes, silver boxes, white freesia. Charles sat with his shoulders slumped forward, his leg propped on a footstool. A cherrywood cane leaned against the seat of his armchair. His moustache weighted both mouth and cheeks, pulled them downwards.

Giles leaned forward to stir the coals with a poker. The stove doors clanked on their hinges as he pushed them partway shut. Charles looked at the *New York Times* tossed on the marble table, repositioned it with his fingertips.

"I don't believe I ever told you," he said abruptly, "about my first wife." He stared at the stove's flickering isinglass. One eye was stubbornly dogmatic, the other fearful. His fingers caressed the polished knob of his cane. "Lucy Smith. She died of yellow fever in New Orleans. She was twenty-four years old."

It was Mrs. Heaney's afternoon off, and Mother had gone downtown. The rain's drumming made the house seem hollow, like an empty biscuit tin.

Charles passed his hand over his face. "I have missed her. I have missed her." He became agitated, picked up the newspaper. His face was drawn, his lips trembled. He seemed not to know what to say next, although he was filled with the desire to speak. "I never . . . quite . . ." His eyes filled with tears. "And then, you know . . . your little sister." He passed his fingers across his eyes, dashed away tears. Giles leaned his head against the back of his wing chair, looked out the window. The wisteria leaves were brown, sodden. "I would wish, Giles, that you would not repeat my . . ." he made a motion with his hand as if smoothing sand " . . . my *frozen* life." Giles lifted his hand protestingly, but his father raised his own. "Frozen, inside. No other way to describe it. I've been uncharitable with affection. Not that I don't care deeply for you and Katherine and Daniel. And for Lilian." His mouth tightened as if with sudden pain. "I seem to have become a solitary man, Giles. Unable to feel joy, or hope. And now I see your life repeating mine." Neither Charles nor Lilian had spoken Jonnie's name since the funeral. "Your mother kept me going. I never felt quite the same after Lucy's death. Something never came quite right again. I don't know if your mother realized it. But, then, I suppose . . ." He folded the newspaper lengthwise and ran finger and thumb along the crease, making it knife-sharp. He stared at the stove, seeking words. He sighed. "Well . . ." He set the newspaper on the marble table, aligned it with the tips of his fingers. "She was a beautiful girl, Jonnie Baker. She was . . ."

He pinched two fingers beneath his nose, stroked his moustache. He shook his head. Giles sat forward, put his forehead in his hands and stared at the carpet.

Together, they listened to the rain. Felt themselves ease, and sadden.

April 5, 1915—Went to New York for business meeting at
Phoenix National Bank. Lunch with Cousin Otto.
Travelled back on train with Dr. Baker, who also had
business in N.Y.

April 20, 1915—Helped Dr. Baker construct cold frames.

May 6, 1915—Phone call from Howard Canfield re that house J. and I were going to buy. Apparently he hadn't heard of her death, was profusely apologetic. Knocked the pins out from under me.

May 8, 1915—Father heading for another depression. Indecisive, spent all day drawing plan after plan of the Shepton garden. Burned them all.

Kate lets the diary fall to her lap. The cat thrusts one paw forward and rests it on Kate's shoulder. She reaches back absently, makes flexing motions with her fingers; the cat rolls his face against them. She runs one finger up and down the worn leather cover of the diary and imagines the Bakers' house as her father has described it to her. When he went there, as a child, no one fussed about how he dressed, if his fingernails were clean, whether he was eating between meals. His Baker grandmother, he'd told her, was very much like Kate's granny: the kind of grandmother who offered you sweet things—love and cookies. There were no maids, no cook. No gardener.

After Jonnie's death, Kate thinks, there would have been obvious reasons for Giles to go there. He and his parents must have made a formal visit after the funeral. Later, he might have gone over to help carry the boxes of Jonnie's possessions upstairs. He was invited to come read the pile of sympathy cards that had come from a great number of Dr. Baker's parishioners and students as well as Jonnie's friends, teachers and fellow students in Boston. Then Dr. Baker phoned him at the office and asked if he would be so kind as to help him with a problem he was having with his water pipes. "I'm afraid I'm no good with this kind of thing, Giles," he said. The next week was Mrs. Baker's birthday, and it would not, Alma wrote him in a polite little note, be much of an occasion unless Giles were there. Not a week went by when Giles was not at the Bakers' house. He was never made to feel like a loose end that would eventually fray and become unattached by virtue of its lack of purpose. His connection to the family was strengthened by mutual need. Without Giles, the family could not accomplish the task of finding a home for Jonnie's spirit, since a part of her arrived with him; and for his part, her spirit lilted in the Baker house—in the cookie jar her child's fingers had lifted, the enormous embroidered cushion with gold tassels and red flowers she'd curled against, the sound of her father's voice, the warped twist of her mother's fingers. At the Bakers,' the dead were not guarded in the heart's silence but were spoken of frequently, with seemly emotion. "Oh, look! How Jonnie would have loved to see this," Hetty might exclaim, seeing a vanguard of red-winged blackbirds arrive and settle in the leafless branches of the elms. Jonnie's paintings were in every room of the house—the rose beds of Elizabeth Park brightened the dark parlour and next to the kitchen door was a painting of the same door standing open onto sunlit sparrows and delphiniums, painted with the ardour of home-sickness.

During the first weeks after Jonnie's death, Giles and the Bakers felt that their daily lives were unconnected to anyone else's; they felt remote, numb, and unwilling to accept the forward passage of time. Jonnie seemed so close they could speak of little else. They reminisced about Christmas: how Jonnie had made stuffing with the chestnuts she'd brought from the Quincy Market; how they'd walked home from the midnight service and sat in the kitchen sipping mulled cider freckled with cinnamon. They laughed about the day they went skating and tried to start a bonfire without paper—Giles had whittled a dead stick into feathers and Jonnie and Hetty had tented their mittens against the breeze, all to no avail. At such moments, it seemed as if Jonnie were still in Boston. Only when their laughter died did they hear the profound silence that had become her shape. The space between their memories grew wider as they realized that after every story their voices fell into a silence increasingly complete, until it became a place where one ceased to listen, knowing there would be nothing to hear. Incrementally, Jonnie faded, like mist absorbed by the bald vibrancy of day. In April, when the forsythia buds were pointy as brand-new brushes dipped in yellow paint, Hetty realized that her mind no longer tipped northeast towards Boston, and that she'd lost the habit of worrying about her sister. A room in her mind, once populated, was empty. Now the winter became a season that had passed and so the first of the gaps separating them from Jonnie's continuum occurred. Hetty also realized that soon the day would come when they would not go to the station to meet her, and would not make her favourite welcome-home meal of chicken and dumplings. Summer would burst regardless, and lilacs would bloom, their scent mingling with the Hartford summer smells of watered streets, sun-baked wood shingles and roses. The world had wavered in February, but now nothing paused: wind made corduroy ripples over the park's ponds, fuzzy-headed cygnets were born, daffodils bloomed in the bright air and children trotted over the greening grass on flat-soled shoes, their hands holding pinwheels or reaching for the summer's first butterflies. The number of people for whom Jonnie's absence could not be soothed by these things dwindled.

May 16, 1915—Went to Elizabeth Park with Hetty and Alma.

June 7, 1915—Continuing warm, walked in the park with Hetty and Alma. Cygnets trailing after mother swans. Fed the carp.

June 20, 1915—At Shepton every weekend. Roses in bloom, new apple trees thriving. New ritual, the Bakers insist I have every Wednesday supper with them.

June 23, 1915—Day our wedding would have been. Went to park with Hetty and Alma. Read out loud, as usual. Hetty brought poems by young poet, Robert Frost. I liked them very much.

Kate imagines how, on the morning of June 23, 1915, Alma and Hetty might have packed a wicker hamper with ham sandwiches, lemonade and gingerbread. They met Giles on the trolley, travelled together to the park. Alma wore her usual crown of braids. She had abandoned all restraint regarding food and was steadily growing into the stout body (for Kate remembers her) she would maintain for the rest of her life. Hetty wore a small straw hat and an ankle-length white cotton dress that was too large for her. Boarding the trolley, she carried the hamper in one hand, lifted the skirt with the other. She saw Giles, and a smile loosened her worried expression. It was a perfect day, the light so clear that shadows were razor-sharp and made everything—trees, fire hydrants, women's hats—seem weightless, dustless. Ribbons fluttered, striped shop awnings were brazen, as if brand new—purple and blue, green and white—and people passing beneath their cool shadows flickered like minnows, re-emerged in sunlight. Hetty sat next to Giles in the trolley and knew they would not speak of the fact that this would have been his wedding day. She could not stop her thoughts, however, and turned her face from him.

At this moment they would have been in a frenzy of preparations. A loose piece of lace, perhaps, in Jonnie's dress, Alma's needle diving and picking; Hetty wreathing orange blossoms into the netting of the bridal veil; Mother laying tissue between the lace-trimmed shifts, packing them into her honeymoon suitcase. And there, in Hetty's mind, was her sister, extravagant in all her moods, one minute wildly excited, the next standing in dazzled serenity.

They stepped off the trolley and walked down the dirt paths of the park. Elizabeth Park was like a sanctuary; adults did not hurry once past its high, wrought-iron gates. Women carried coloured umbrellas against the sun; men wore high-collared shirts, straw boaters and linen jackets. A creak of oarlocks came from the pond, where young men raised their elbows as they pulled varnished oars and girls in gauze-trimmed hats trailed their fingers in duckweed. From the farthest corner of the park came the crack of ball against bat, cheers rising like a handful of dust.

"How are your parents, Giles?" Alma asked. Her voice was comfortable, throaty. Already there were dark patches of sweat beneath her arms.

"Father is not well," Giles answered. His steps were slow. Alma and Hetty adjusted their pace. "His knee is paining him, and he is more depressed. We wonder how long he will be able to continue going to the office. Mother is terribly worried about him." What he did not say, the young women guessed. His own loss was an imposition in the family's current circumstances. He could not speak of Jonnie in his own home; even with Alma and Hetty, now, he spoke her name less and less. It was one thing, after her loss, to reminisce about the happy times just past. But they could not speak of the joy they would have been expecting. Giles tried to resume his habit of cheerfulness, but his grief seemed to grow rather than diminish, and as if this were a failing on his part, he tried to hide it.

They settled in the shade of a copse just beyond the gazebo where Jonnie and Giles had first met. They had formed the custom of reading out loud, since there was little of their own truth they wished to discuss. They spread a tartan blanket. Hetty sat with her legs folded sideways, hands in her lap. Alma sat with her legs straight out in front of her and read from *Pride and Prejudice*. Then it was Giles' turn. He was reading *Dombey and Son*. His voice quivered with nascent sternness, and Hetty, gripping her hands tightly together and lowering her head slightly, chancing a glance at him, thought that this was how he must sound in court. Sun slanted across his cheek and the side of his head, making his hair colourless and shiny.

He closed the book. "Your turn, Hetty," he said. He looked up and caught Hetty's eyes with his own. She was surprised, but like a child did not look away. Rather, her expression became sweet, and she smiled. She reached into her handbag, brought out a thin book of poems by the young Vermont poet. She remained sitting just as she was, with her legs folded sideways, her feet resting wherever they first lay, ankles crossed. She did not seek comfort but seemed always at rest, her body easy within the loose fabric of her dress. She read in a voice so soft that Giles leaned towards her and watched her lips. She noticed this but continued to read, even as out of the corner of her eye she saw the light-cupped 'American Pillar' roses on the gazebo, the criss-crossed shadows thrown by its lattice, the speckled light on the tartan blanket. As her mouth gently spoke the poet's words—"I know that winter death has never tried/ The earth but it has failed"—she was not absorbing their meaning but remembering how, when Jonnie died, Giles clasped her in his arms and wept into her hair.

September 21, 1915—I took apples to the Bakers. Had a
talk with Dr. Baker in his study.

Kate bends forward over her grandfather's diary. She runs
her fingers over the words. *Had a talk with Dr. Baker in his
study.* She knows, now, what he did not when he wrote them.
She sees the blossoming of his life, its fruit-hung branches and
gnarled roots. Dr. Baker, Kate thinks, would have known how
words can be like seeds. How people can be like soil.

13. A Windfall Apple

A COLD WIND BLOWS FROM THE SOUTH. KATE HEARS the chickadees' spring song when she puts out the bird seed. She notices how the river snow is becoming granular, crystals shimmering as the sun warms them. Over the north hills, the sky is pearled with a softer light, and in the shadow of the spruce trees, sparrows peck at cones that appear as the snow melts.

Three weeks have passed since the day she went skiing with Gregory. She has not seen him since, although he has phoned several times and seems not to remember his behaviour.

She sits in the rocking chair by the window. Earlier, Caroline phoned. "I had a terrible sleep," Caroline told her. "Hot flashes. They've started." Then Kate phoned May, arranging a walk for later in the day. She has just put down the phone from a call to her parents. And now she feels irresolute. Perhaps because she knows it's March break. Working in the library, she'd been aware of the impending holiday. There was a sense of release; time shifted so that space took on new dimensions, like a flock of birds suddenly rising. Children ran to the glass doors, forgetting to whisper. Parents told her which ski resort they'd chosen this year—in Maine instead of

Quebec, or vice versa. "No," she said to people who asked if she was going anywhere. "I'll be staying here." Christy asked her to visit over the weekend. She has a new part-time job. "You should come, Mum," Christy had urged on the phone. "I love this job. I'll serve you a cappuccino with chocolate shavings and cinnamon."

Perhaps, because other people are on holiday, her own time feels leaden, her breast's birds remain caged and restless. She's sitting in the rocking chair wearing one of Tom's sweaters. She could not give away clothes she knew she would wear. She doesn't have to roll up the grey wool sleeves; their arms were the same length, just as their feet were the same size. There on the kitchen table are the gardening catalogues that arrived this week. There are five or six, and more to come. Tom loved them. This would have been a day when they stayed in the kitchen all morning, heedless of chaos, like Christmas. The floor would be littered with catalogue wrappers and the table would be buried beneath notebooks, plates of half-eaten cinnamon toast, Tom's ashtray, catalogues tabbed with yellow Post-its. Cigarette smoke would have spiralled with the tea steam, coiled blue and lazy in the sunlight. They would have kept the fire crackling. And their garden would shift its shape, like clouds in a spring sky. *Peonies—oh, Tom, we have to have a "Pink Hawaiian Coral". A new bed? Okay, then, move the lilies. You're right, those day lilies definitely need dividing. Look at these Japanese iris. "Mt. Fuji" (Hoku-botan), God, these "Snow Queens." Let's add to the historic iris bed. Yeah, going down. Look on the map. Down this bank, where there's partial shade. Wind a stone path through it. Mound up the soil there, see?*

Lately the garden has become her overriding fear. It's worse this year than last. Last year, closer to Tom's death, she had no reason to expect anything of herself. It was enough to plant the vegetables, keep the flower beds more or less weeded. She imagines what will happen this summer, how this will be the year when her neglect begins to show. Some precious plants will vanish, become root-bound or be overtaken by invasive neighbours. The bergamot will become sparse. Mallow will appear like dandelions, violets will smother the coral bells, the undivided chives will sprawl, too spindly to support their purple flowers. The foxglove and rose campion seedlings she didn't dig up in the fall will invade every bed. Low-lying branches of the black currant will have layered, and new shoots will appear far from the mother bush. Without Tom, it will take her a full weekend just to prune the roses. It's not the labour she dreads. It's what has to come first: dreaming, desiring, aspiring.

She holds her mug with both hands, lifts the scalding tea to her lips. The wind rises; she hears the hollow, careless roaring in the brittle branches. It's a scouring wind, less restless than persistent. It's the first sign of spring, coming, as always, long before the last snow. It lifts the lid of hope, or change, prepares the earth for light. Kate is ready neither for the clear, benign sunshine nor for the soil's thaw, is not ready to relinquish winter's exonerating darkness, in which she has no expectations, has had to make no choices, has needed to do nothing of an evening except read her grandfather's diary and letters addressed to other people.

The phone rings. The phone has become like her mailbox. She's aware of an irrational certainty that any call will bring bad news, any letter will be filled with inexplicable excoriation. Her voice is sharp. "Yes, hello?"

"Oh, Kate. I didn't quite recognize your voice. This is Gregory. What a lovely, gorgeous day, isn't it?"

For days after his visit she had imagined his face when he reached back to rip the door from her hand, slamming it on her rather than allowing himself to be shut out. She remembered the scathing contempt in his voice and the shock of his hand striking her arm, relived the moment when she collapsed on the couch and May put her arms around her, stroked her hair like a mother. He's called three or four times, since, asking her to do something with him, and every time she has been polite but vague, and has managed to avoid making any plans.

"I wanted to tell you that I've finally begun writing a story based on my diaries. Well, you know, I'm calling it a story to trick myself into thinking it's some little thing, but I want it to be fairly long. Because, after all, there's a lot to tell. There's all the political stuff from those years—you remember, the nuclear power stuff, the budworm spray protests, the disarmament marches. And then, you know, the texture. There were still so many of those glorious weathered farmhouses not yet collapsed. And the wind came straight off the water. It smelled like the sea in every room of the house . . ."

Well, he is after all a journalist; he *does* write, Kate thinks, irrationally annoyed by his lyrical tone. As he may have been annoyed with her, she thinks suddenly, ashamed of herself, when they were on his rooftop porch and she described the refinery in poetic terms.

" . . . especially when we lived in that house down on the coast. Foxglove, everywhere. Someone seeded them years ago, and they ran wild. Remember how the girls put the caps on their fingers? Then there was that raft we built from those broken packing crates that washed up. Remember? Took it out on the outgoing tide—foolish thing to do I suppose. Quite a rush, I remember. And, of course, there are those things that happened at the park. Time—remember this?—when we couldn't get to Wolf Point because the road crew blew up the covered bridge by mistake. They were trying to protect it by blasting away the overhanging cliff. How are you?"

"Just fine." Her tone is neutral. Not great, she implies, but I won't bother you about it.

"What are you doing today?"

"Oh, I'm—I'm going to—I've been invited to do something with friends."

"Tonight, are you busy tonight? You see, I was hoping we could get together. I want to read you some of these parts that you might remember. Over a bottle of wine we might, you know, extract some more things I either didn't write in my diaries or have forgotten."

Frustration rises like a rogue wave. Or is it fear? How can she maintain this dance of pity and avoidance? "Actually, I'm—I *am* busy tonight."

He is silent. "What? I mean, what . . . Oh, I see."

She says nothing. Her heart begins to hammer.

"What you are trying to say," he says, suddenly sour, "is that you would really rather not spend time with me. Is that it?" His voice softens. "What's wrong, Kate? Couldn't we both do with a little friendship? You're lonely. I haven't had time to make any friends. We are, after all, old friends, Kate. Very old friends."

"I didn't think it went very well last time we were together. I'm in a somewhat fragile state. I don't see many people."

"Oh, but you're spending the day with friends."

There is another silence. Kate stares at the catalogues on the kitchen table. It should be so easy to end this. Her heart beats in thick surges. She looks at the door to the living room, where Tom is not standing. Why does this man continue to call her when contempt leaps out at the slightest provocation?

"Anyway, what do you mean it didn't go very well? This is the first time I've heard about this. Did I offend you? Was I less than civil?"

"Apparently you don't remember what happened after your shower."

"I most certainly do. That woman arrived. As I recall, I left because she offered to feed us some mouldy casserole."

And you brought your underwear, your overnight bag. Planned to get into my pants, as Tom would have said. But perhaps, she thinks, she's wrong about this. Perhaps he keeps an overnight kit in his backpack in case his car breaks down. Maybe he didn't even remember it was there. Maybe she should not have invited May over. How could she imagine he would be sexually attracted to her? She feels heat flaming her cheeks. Perhaps his anger was justified.

"Your drinking, Gregory. You got very angry with me. You ripped the door from my hand. Slammed it in my face."

He says nothing. She imagines him staring out his study window, his nose pinched with irritation. Being with another man after thirty years of marriage, she thinks, is like finding yourself in a small sailboat in bad weather, cross-currents running beneath your keel, line squalls putting the gunwales under, waves seething over submerged rocks. No land in sight.

"All right," he says. "Maybe . . . Did I have some whiskey to warm up afterwards? Didn't you give me whiskey when we got to the house?"

"No."

"I—" She hears a crash. Something has fallen in the background. "Shit. Just a second."

She slumps onto the edge of a chair, her legs poised to jump up. Phone in her fist. Pulls a catalogue towards her. The morning, passing. His voice is suddenly loud in her ear. "Sorry, whole stack of notebooks and diaries fell over. Had them arranged by year." His tone makes Kate feel she should apologize for having caused this disruption. "So, what were you saying? I was rude? I drank too much? Point taken. I apologize. Although anyone who falls into a river in February might be expected to need a stiff drink afterwards." Ah, so he does remember, then, that she had no alcohol in the house, or none to offer him anyway. Inhospitable, judgmental, unable to appreciate a man's suffering and the consolation he might need. What did she expect, for God's sake?

"What did you expect, for God's sake, Kate?" he says. "A man is frozen half to death! Look, I have to go." She's keeping him from sorting out his mess of diaries, rectifying his pile of chaotic years. "You have a nice day with your friends."

Only last fall this man was a stranger in a canvas hat, sitting on a log. Now their relationship has reached a point of such intimacy that he can ridicule her.

"My husband was an ugly drunk, Kate," says May. They're walking on the river path. May has wound a plaid scarf around her face, so her words are muffled. Their eyes stream with tears. The wind tosses the willows on the interval islands. They hear the whine of tires, the rattle of loose planks, as Saturday traffic rumbles across the bridge. They've just walked through the dank shadows beneath its buttresses. Now they come round a bend and are confronted with the frozen marsh, where light glints in hillocks of yellow grasses, makes diamonds in clumps of meadowsweet, sleeks the red branches of Siberian dogwood.

"Won't it be nice to see the geese coming back?" May continues. "I love to see the geese. Hear their honking. Don't you, Kate?" She fixes Kate with her goose-like eyes. Round, frank. She wears a black wool hat, Peruvian, with a woven band of southern colours around the rim: turquoise, burgundy red, gold.

"What do you mean, May? Ugly?"

"I mean he was mean. Just mean, when he was drunk. You had to look out for him." She states this matter-of-factly, as if, although inexcusable, it is nonetheless normal. "Oh, everyone knew it. You had to keep out of Percy's way when he began to drink."

"Wasn't it hard for you?"

May darts her a glance over her scarf. Often, Kate thinks, she seems insulted until you know her better and realize that she's merely surprised you've bothered to state what seems to her obvious. "Well, of course, Kate! It was perfectly terrible. He insulted our friends, he said unforgivable things. But people had to forgive him, you see, because he couldn't remember afterwards. So they thought, oh well, Percy never meant to say those things. But they knew, of course. They came out of his mind and lay there in the open for everyone to see. That was the mortification."

"*In vino veritas*." So the place, Kate thinks, where Gregory retreats is where he encounters truth. But then doesn't remember afterwards. "He keeps calling me," Kate adds. She wears nylon wind-pants over her jeans. They crackle in the wind. Her cheeks are red, and her short-cropped hair, flattened by her toque, spikes around her face like grey straw. She doesn't look at May, but lengthens her stride. "He called this morning. He made me feel guilty that I didn't have any hard liquor to offer him. When the poor man was frozen half to death."

May laughs. "I'd classify him as an ugly drunk, Kate. I see all the signs. Don't have anything more to do with him. Hang up when he calls." She leans forward slightly, makes Kate meet her eyes. "I mean it, Kate. Just hang up. You don't need to put up with that kind of behaviour."

"I couldn't do that," Kate says.

"You feel sorry for him, don't you? Oh, I know. That's what they'll do. You'll be like a fish on a line. Don't I know."

Kate glances at May, realizes that she doesn't know Gregory, or remember his children, their faces flushed by fire-light; never saw Gregory as a young father, down on one knee, tying the lace of Jerome's small sneaker. There is reason, Kate thinks, for forgiveness. For tolerance.

"It's complicated, May," Kate says. "I'm a link to the happy part of his past. That's okay. I understand that. I understand why he loves to remember those years. But he doesn't seem able to see that I'm someone else now. I'm not twenty-eight years old, the mother of young children. I'm . . ."

May pulls her scarf up over her nose, wraps her arms around herself. Across the marsh, the willows fling forward, settle back.

"I'm . . ." She lifts her hands. *Afraid. He seems to forget that I, too, am bruised, raw.*

"I know, Kate," says May. "I know. Look at this now. Isn't this gorgeous?"

They stop at the end of a point, stand side by side looking out over the marshlands that spread from the river. Like a hunting fox, the wind makes scurrying pounces, sends snow scarfing up, leaves it to filter down, glistening. Here and there are open pockets of dark blue water; wind makes black ripples race forward. Hills rise on either side, cup the sky. The sun picks out white farmhouses, glints on steel-roofed barns.

Kate puts her hands in her pockets, closes her eyes and turns her face to the sun. *What a thing it is to lose your best friend.* After she said goodbye to Gregory this morning, she'd hung up the phone and then stood in the broad sunlight, staring at the picture of Tom, which she'd reframed. Longing. *Oh, he must hear, he must hear. I must tell him. Tom. Tom. What am I going to do?* She had picked up the photograph, pressed it to her chest, arms crossed over it, her hands spread and fingers clutching her shoulders. She sat in the rocking chair, bent forward over the photograph. Tears fell on the backs of her hands. Her longing to speak to him was an ache in her jawbones. She realized she could not sit in this room, with its seed catalogues, knowing he was not going to come down the stairs.

"Katie?" May is patting her upper arm. "Are you in there?"

Kate feels grief making her heart tender and swollen, as if it can't contain all that it holds.

"When am I going to stop weeping?" Kate says. Her mouth warps. She looks down and sees how May is examining her, worried, her eyes narrowed. "I held Tom's picture this morning. I sat in the rocking chair, hugging a piece of glass."

"The photograph you smashed?"

"Yes."

May slides her arm through Kate's. "You know, it wasn't him you hated when you tried to destroy that picture," she says. She pats Kate's hand. "You'll always miss him, you know. That's a fact." She speaks simply. Her blue eyes are pale as sunbleached cottage curtains. "One day . . ." she says, and sighs. How many years has it been since her husband died? Twenty? She's looking out over the marsh. Her brisk matter-of-factness is gone. Kate sees her private face, stripped of emotion. "One day, Katie, you'll forgive him for leaving."

You have to stop this . . .

After supper that evening, Kate stands in the doorway to the living room. The house is silent. The sky is stained with remnants of light.

Stop this right now . . .

She has just come down from the unheated attic, where their family's past lies in darkness. Her flashlight had skipped along shelves, scanned an open toy chest, touched garbage bags filled with clothing. There was her son Liam's lion puppet lying on its back, its golden paws spread in an eternal embrace, its glassy eyes shining. Children's books, warped by damp. *Goodnight Moon. Pat the Bunny.* A broken easel, made by Tom before he'd acquired any carpentry skills. Their first backpacking tent in a blue stuff sack. Christy had called and asked her if she could find a physiology book from her first-year course and send it to her by courier. "It's in the attic, Mum. I'm sorry to make you go up there, but I really need it." There are very few things here anyone will ever need, Kate had thought, kneeling to turn over books in a cardboard box, yet nothing she can bear to throw away.

Standing, now, looking into the living room, she makes herself listen to the silence. The wind died sometime after she returned from her walk with May. Then the temperature plunged. Spring light, winter cold. There is no single cruellest month in the Maritimes, but surely March is in the running.

"'I heard a fly buzz when I died,'" she whispers, Emily Dickinson's solitude comforting her like music. "'The stillness round my form/ Was like the stillness in the air/ Between the heaves of storm.'"

Would it be better, she wonders, if she had gone up there and found empty space? No remains? Nothing to sweep her into another time, no puppet with the power to make her pause, transfixed, remembering another light, a larger sky, beneath which the house seemed smaller, this house in whose scantily furnished rooms she remembers the echoing rap of children's feet and the smell of the spinach soufflé she once made?

Kate lifts Christy's book to her nose. Its slick cover dampens in the warmer air. She sets it on a table, wipes her hands on her jeans. She herself is between the heaves of storm. One minute she wishes the house were gone and everything in it. What would she do? Where would she go? And with whom? She toys with this vision until its glamour dissipates. All right. Then she imagines grandchildren, sees them sitting on the porch beneath the clematis. "That's just where your mother loved to sit." Or playing beneath the apple tree. Or taking the canoe down to the creek. But she can't help it. Tom is always there. He's lifting one end of the canoe, stopping to wait with a patience he never had with his own son. "That's the way," he says encouragingly. He and his grandson go down the path. The ferns are waist-high.

She sits in her armchair. Yes, it's hers now. It was the first piece of furniture they ever bought. Its upholstered flowers are riddled with small brown-rimmed holes. *I should have been able to make him stop. He wouldn't try gum or the patch. I should have found another, more persuasive doctor.* She lays her arm over the back of the chair, draws up one leg so she's looking out the window. She can still see the boles of trees standing against the river, which, like the sky, gleams faintly, bears the last tender light. The lawn is a gulf of blackness, but the porch floor and the railings are still touched by light, or are themselves luminous, seem stubbornly separate. She hears the silence, feels cold on her ankles. She should turn up the furnace, light the rooms, put on music. But she's lingering like the light, as if once she dispels cold, darkness and silence, her grief will be less gone than changed and some irrevocable shift will take place that she is not sure she would welcome.

Mr. Winkles pads into the room, and she pats her thigh automatically without taking her eyes from the window. The cat jumps into her lap, turns and turns, finally settles and begins a subtle working of his claws. She feels memory tap at her heart, begging entrance. She resists, as if admonishing herself for returning to a book she's already read many times. But there it waits, and she yearns for long ago, when time had no place in her consciousness. She rests her cheek on her arm, floats into a child's endless summer.

It was midmorning. The earth was still damp in shaded places, and she squatted beneath Shepton's kitchen windows, mashing barberries between rocks. Beneath her fingernails were orange-yellow seeds, on her blouse flecks of red skin. Insects made a rhythmic chiggering, like the sound of the earth's heart. Her rocks made a small satisfying snicking as they banged together. A robin's song spilled down from the sighing leaves and spread into the quiet air like a question.

There was Granny's face, dim behind the screen. "Dearie, is that you?" she called. She was holding a spoon, beckoning. Kate scrambled to her feet. Now she was in the kitchen and Granny was digging the sharp-edged spoon into a honeycomb. She wore her strawberry-print apron. Kate sat on the daybed beneath the windows. Sunlight lay across the white paint of the kitchen table. Here, in Granny's kitchen, there was sunlight, the smell of the gas stove, sugar expanding on the dimpled skin of red strawberries, white flour on the rolling pin's green wooden handles. The rest of the house was cool and deep. Its rooms never changed and so were restful, as if they waited patiently for people who Kate did not know. She had no sense of time, and yet the house was filled with it. They could hear the grandfather clock ticking. The honeysuckle was blooming; Grampa Giles was working in the vegetable garden. Granny pushed the spoon into the honeycomb. The beeswax hexagons crumpled, buckled. "Can I, can I?" Kate scrambled from the daybed. Crump, crump, and the golden honey welled up. She lifted the spoon and watched as, within the thick stream of honey, sunlight and the wallpaper ribboned and fell, ribboned and fell.

There was the sound of Grampa Giles' boots on the stone walk; the creak and tap of the screen door. Here he was in the kitchen, wearing his khaki shirt and pants, his hair the colour of corn silk. In his hands was a Hartford bronzehead lettuce. He pulled out a kitchen chair. A breeze came through the screen, brought the smell of fresh-cut grass. Grampa Giles was serious, but the corners of his mouth tipped up. He was in love with Granny; his eyes softened whenever he looked at her.

She flew like a swallow, bringing him things. Coffee, now. The steam curled.

Grampa Giles broke off a leaf of lettuce and cradled it in his cupped palm. He filled it with a tablespoon of white sugar, rolled it up and handed it to Kate. The lettuce was soft and warm around the crunchy sugar. Granny lifted a brimming spoonful of honey, slid it into Kate's mouth. Granny loved cream and sugar. She shook little hills of white sugar onto grapefruit, poured heavy cream over hot applesauce. Down the street at her own house, Kate's mother read books on nutrition and made her daughters eat Special K cereal with brewer's yeast and rose hips.

Kate swung her legs, sitting at the table next to her grandfather. She licked the back of the spoon. They were talking to each other, her grandparents. About the garden. His voice was like the muttering of faraway thunder. A comfortable grumble, ponderous and exact. Granny's voice was soft and responsive. She was like the congregation, reading back to the minister. She never sounded uncertain because she didn't question anything. Nor did Grampa Giles. This was the way the world was. The beans were growing. Soon the rain would come. They used solid, peaceful words: bees, spade, basket, strainer, rake, tarp, mulch.

Grampa Giles finished his coffee. Clink and rattle, cup in saucer. He smiled and got up. He was a lawyer, but Kate thought of him as a gardener. He smelled like leaves and apples. She knew this from when she sat in his lap. Sometimes Granny sat in his lap. She perched quietly, with her feet dangling, and Grampa Giles put his arm around her as if she were made of eggshells and he must neither crush her nor let her fall.

Kate, curled in the armchair, doesn't want to disturb the cat, who will jump down if she straightens her legs. She reaches up carefully and turns on the table lamp. The lingering light over the river, the just-visible porch railings, vanish behind the room's reflection on the black panes. There, just where she left it, is Grampa Giles' diary. She picks it up, wondering what words she may find, scattered like glossy apple seeds that she may sow in her mind, that may yield the truth of her grand-parents' love.

She seeks the last entry she read:

September 21, 1915—I took apples to the Bakers. Had a
talk with Dr. Baker in his study.

That quiet little man. Dr. Baker. Kate's granny's father. She'd asked her own father, this morning on the phone, what he remembered about this grandfather. "I remember a September morning when I was quite a little boy," he'd said, readily, and Kate imagined rich light slanting through the maples. "We sat in the sun, leaning against one of the Shepton barns. He was smoking a corncob pipe, and he made smoke rings for me." And it had occurred to Kate that her father must be very much like Dr. Baker. Granny's father. How gentle he must have been, how patient. A minister, in those years, must have attended so many deathbeds. Seen so much sorrow. What, she wonders, did he say to Giles on September twenty-first?

It was early evening, Kate imagines, closing the diary over her finger, and the Bakers' house smelled of the apples Giles continually brought from Shepton, where he'd spent the pre-ceding two weekends raking leaves and harvesting the orchard. Bushel baskets of Baldwins and Winesaps stood against the dark varnish of the hall's wainscot. The apples were luminous, held tiny silver mirrors of light. Their sharp, earthy scent followed Giles up the stairs, making him feel that he'd brought something essential of his own into this house. Dr. Baker had invited Giles up to his study while the women washed the supper dishes.

In the study, Dr. Baker motioned Giles towards a carved wooden chair with padded leather upholstery. (That chair had stood in Granny's winter-house parlour. Kate and her cousins took turns perching in it. "Now *I'm* the queen.") The small man stood on the threadbare carpet, tamping tobacco into his corncob pipe. He held a match to it, made small sipping sounds. The sun was low. It accentuated odd parts of the room and left others in shadow, making the study intimate, containing mysteries, like faces at a bonfire. Pipe smoke hung on the air. Dr. Baker settled himself across from Giles, worked his shoulders into a comfortable position. Neither man spoke, and Giles, not wanting to interrupt Dr. Baker's meditative pleasure, pushed himself back in his chair and let his eyes roam the room. Around the ceiling was a narrow strip of brown wallpaper with gold stripes; the walls were lined with wooden packing crates set end on end, filled with books. Between Giles and Dr. Baker was a round table covered with a fringed cloth. It was strewn with books, newspapers, a tobacco tin and a cast-iron bank in the shape of an elephant, which held a dime in its slotted trunk.

Dr. Baker sipped at his pipe, glanced at Giles. He pointed the stem of his pipe at the bank. "Twist its tail and the dime goes into the slot." He leaned forward and demonstrated. "Jonnie gave that to me. Christmas of 1914. She found it in Boston." He looked at Giles, pulled at his pipe. "How are you bearing this, Giles?" he added.

Giles was expecting this question. He would answer it honestly, since he himself spent his days querying people, seeking points of view, evaluating conflicting evidence. For a moment he was silent; his eyes pondered a place neither close nor far. "I carry on," he said, finally. "I simply carry on. I can't look too far ahead. I can't look back. I don't really know where to look."

Dr. Baker nodded. He watched a swirl of smoke rise into the dusk-reddened light. "You're afraid to imagine anything. You're afraid to build a life."

"Yes, I suppose that's it. Well, I'm working hard."

Dr. Baker pointed his pipe at Giles. "That's different. That's like driving a horse into the ground. Imagination is hope. Hope is the food and drink of life. Lose it and you wither away like an unwatered plant."

"My father—" said Giles, and stopped. He never discussed his family. Dr. Baker closed his eyes briefly and bowed his head to indicate both his awareness of this and his assurance of confidentiality. "Father," Giles continued, "has no hope."

"Why do you say that, Giles?"

"He worries about himself. He's lost interest in everything. I look at him at breakfast and see him wondering why he bothered to get dressed."

"It's a terrible thing," said Dr. Baker. He slid back in his chair and crossed his legs at the ankles. His feet were suspended above the floor, but he seemed not to notice. He pulled on his pipe, sighed. "It's how you describe yourself, though. Do you see that? You don't look ahead, you don't look back. No past, no future. That is a place of impenetrable dark- ness. It is a place without love."

Neither man spoke. They heard voices, the clatter of dishes, quick, light steps in the downstairs hall.

In his study, Dr. Baker spoke as he did not in company, where he was invariably silent. Giles had grown to expect this of him. The man was like a mushroom, softly luminous in deep shadow. Dr. Baker ran a hand over his bald head, let it linger at the rim of sandy grey hair, his fingers brushing it idly. A line of tobacco lay in a fold of his vest. He let his head rest against the back of his chair and said, "Jonnie gave you a gift that you must not waste. She taught you to love her and to love yourself. That is the gift of Our Father. Once learned, it never dies. You will always love her, Giles."

Giles' eyes filled with tears. One hand rose and fell against the chair's cracked leather armrest.

"That is your past. Look back at it. Rejoice in it. Weep for Jonnie's passing, but do not let love pass. Without memory, there is no future." He leaned forward and took up his Bible. "Here, in John," he said, "Christ speaks to his disciples. There are a few things here that I would share with you: 'Whither I go, you cannot come, so now I say unto you. A new commandment . . . that ye love one another; as I have loved you, that ye also love one another.'" He turned back a page. "Or here. 'He that walketh in darkness knoweth not whither he goeth.'" He read through the bottom of his glasses. "'I am come a light into the world, that whosoever believeth on me should not abide in darkness.'"

He set the book back on the table. "'Whither I go, you cannot come.'" He drew on his pipe and let the smoke come wavering from his mouth. It lay on the room's air, seeking its way. Giles watched it spread, thin and vanish. It was the first time, he realized, that he had heard Jonnie spoken of as someone now inhabiting a time not their own, a place unknown to them.

"It is a great loss," said Dr. Baker. "An inexplicable and bewildering loss. We will never get over it, Giles. We will grieve for her all our lives. We will grieve, and we will wonder. For all events, there are reasons. One day we may understand. Or perhaps not. But for now, what is left is our love for her." He glanced at Giles keenly. "'As I have loved you, that ye also love another.' If you send your love into the grave with Jonnie, you will be as good to anyone, or yourself, as a windfall apple rotting in the grass." He looked at the ceiling with a smile touching his lips. "Return love when it comes to you, and your heart will be eased."

Giles looked at the little man, feeling as if Dr. Baker had spread grief out before him like a map, shown him its territory and the road leading home.

Kate's eyes focus on the purring cat in her lap as this vision of Giles and Dr. Baker slowly fades. She smiles.

For Giles had not, after all, married Jonnie, and his life with her remained, forever, an untarnished dream. Nor had his love for her had the chance to run deep, transmute itself, become absorbed by many roots: habit, kindness, forbearance, anger, passion, patience, sympathy, jealousy. Still, at her death, love possessed him, like a skill, like an art. He waited, his heart ripe as a pear, his skin tender. Dr. Baker would have known that Giles' trust in life's essential goodness, already broken by Ellen's death, had been tested once again by Jonnie's. And temporarily lost. But not his faith in love, which lay intact. Dr. Baker would have seen Hetty's eyes resting on Giles; would have known that faith, for young people, is like a shattered bone that can reknit, given time.

And me? I have given too much of myself to Tom. We grew together, and with his loss went an entire language that only he and I could speak: the language of aesthetics, of touch, of play, of memory.

Yet.

She strokes the cat, scratches his chin. She hears the oil furnace come on with a leaping thrum.

No. I can't imagine another husband. But a lightness touches her heart. It is like a searing flame, a sudden eagerness. *I may reknit. I may see myself as different, but whole. Someday.*

Part Four

14. Black Ice

"THOSE ARE WEIRD SKATES." A TEN-YEAR-OLD GIRL SITS just far enough away from Kate not to seem intrusive, tugs at the furred ankle of her white figure skate. She's the grandchild of old friends of Kate and Tom's. Many families have gathered at the launch site just below the green bridge. The launch site is a small town park: a few picnic tables, a parking lot and metal trash cans painted green. It's at the end of the street that passes Caroline's house. The pavement slopes down the riverbank so that cars pulling boat trailers can back them into the water. The sky is less steely than milky, an absence of colour brightened by the hidden sun. Kate sits on her long coat; cold air seeps like water through the toe of her wool sock as she angles her foot into a stiff skate. She tugs her laces, grins at the child.

"They're river skates. They're made for distance and speed. See how long the blades are? But they're not as good as yours for turning."

"Hi, Kate!" Caroline and Brian are walking down from their house, laced skates slung over their shoulders. Other people arrive in cars. Children sprint back and forth between river and parking lot, needing extra socks or mittens, abandoning sunglasses, putting water bottles in backpacks.

"Hi!" Kate waves.

It's too cold to stand and talk. Everyone bends busily to their laces. People perch on the picnic tables, on logs that surround a firepit, on folded blankets. The first people to get on their skates strike out onto the ice, sketch a few stumbling steps before catching the sudden freedom, the long thrust. Kate hears the vigorous metallic slicing of blades across ice. Last week it rained for a day, and then the temperature plummeted. A layer of perfect black ice smoothes the river's corrugated surface, where winter's history lies in striations of frozen snow, rutted tire tracks, broken branches, fissures, windblown soil.

Kate tugs the laces of her second skate. The skaters have disappeared into the trees on the interval island. She hears their whoops. The island, at freeze-up, lay underwater, and now the trees are ice-gripped, like cattails.

"Ready?" she says to the girl. She stands, wobbly, wraps a black-and-red scarf around her neck and mouth. She tightens the belt of her long coat, which she always wears for skating, enjoying its skirted swirl, remembering how Tom told her she looked like a raven, gliding.

She loses the child as soon as she steps onto the ice. There are many children; they want only each other, they scream and chase, staggering, heedless, arms outflung. The adults are calling to one another: "Marvellous . . . look, oh look . . ." And it is marvellous, Kate realizes, the instant she slides into the trees; it is an odd, dreamlike sensation to be skating through a forest. Men and women in bright jackets and toques scatter like a handful of berries, gliding through a motionless world of black ice and grey trees. Ice rings the trees in thick collars that pull away from the bark, leaving dark gaps. The ice sags between each tree; Kate swoops and rises as if skating on frozen waves. She loops between the maples, thinking how, in summer, it is their green crowns she sees from her porch, brooding under thunderclouds, welcoming morning with their sun-sparked leaves. Cows graze on the silky bottomland grass, and she can see the white tufts of their tails flashing, switching away deerflies; at dusk, the heifers cluster in the sandy shallows at the island's end, heads lowered to the water like so many eggs. It might have been right here, Kate thinks, as she nears the end of the island, that she and Tom picked fiddleheads. She stops, hooks her arm around a tree. In this space, memories are as layered as the ice. Time, epochs, build upon one another until they become a single entity, like Tom's beloved cliffs. Kate closes her eyes, listens to the shouts and whoops, the rhythmic scrape of skate blades. Here, by this tree, at this moment, are fiddleheads, grooved stems snapping between her fingers. Here is sunlight through the nylon walls of a tent. Here is Tom in the stern of a canoe, here she reaches out with the blade of her paddle, making a necklace of drops on the still water. Here, now, she leans, panting, in the unearthly frozen forest, a young widow filled with life.

The ice slopes at the end of the trees, and she leans forward, skates down, is spun onto the broad, tree-lined river. A friend's husband catapults from the trees, trips and slides past her on his belly, laughing. She braces, hauls him to his feet. Together, they brush down his coat. They push off, but he soon outstrips her, and she does not mind, but falls into the rhythm of long, pushing glides. The group plans to go down the river until the children tire, or time runs out. Then they will return to the launch site, arriving back at sundown, when they'll make a bonfire in the pit.

So they spread out and skate. They call back and forth, share their delight, but no one talks.

The ice is so smooth that Kate coasts occasionally, arms crossed over her chest, one leg braced forward. Beneath the diffuse clouds, the bare-branched trees do not scratch the sky, needle-sharp, but are grey as the breast feathers of mourning doves.

Grey. Like Granny's wedding. For she knows, now, that Hetty married Giles two years after Jonnie's death. January, a grey day. Hetty wore a grey suit and a small, wool hat with feathers tucked round the brim. Giles' parents did not attend. They had rushed to Key West immediately after Christmas. Charles' health had gone downhill so suddenly that his doctors thought he should be taken to the heat. "I'm so sorry, Giles," Lilian had said, but with such distraction that Giles had immediately begun discussing train schedules, thinking that these details would ground her. Father, Giles told Hetty, had never been the same since Ellen died. "The poor man," Hetty said, sorrowfully. Nor had Lilian, but this did not need to be stated. Hetty and Giles saw them off at the station. Lilian thought to kiss Hetty on the cheek. "Next time I see you, you will be married," she said. Nothing more, and her face was drawn, she could not manage a smile. A nurse accompanied them.

Grey, their wedding, Kate thinks, smiling. *My sweet grandparents. They would not have minded.* The Bakers were there. And Giles' sister. Some cousins. Giles lifted Hetty's hand to place the wedding band on her finger. Not a person in the church could refrain from imagining Jonnie. Least of all, Hetty. She gazed into Giles' eyes and saw his love for her sister. Love, as Dr. Baker had promised, bred love. Giles slid the ring on her finger, she slid a ring on his. She raised her arms to him. He gathered her gently, placed his lips on hers. No cheek was without tears. Hetty and Giles folded their love for Jonnie between them like a flower that their gentleness would never crush.

They went to Shepton for their honeymoon. Hetty had visited the house only once, for a weekend in September, just after they'd announced their engagement. This time, they stayed for a week, in mid-January. Giles had arranged for someone to open up the house. For several days before their arrival, fires had been kept burning. Warmth pulled frost from plaster, made the armchairs and couches, like thawing soil, effuse the smell of old fabric and damp padding. Upstairs, all the bedroom doors were kept shut except the door to the southeast bedroom, the room with the sleigh bed in which Lilian had been born. Even though a fire had been burning for days in its fireplace, frost sparkled from the plaster ceiling and the smell of smoke lay on the chill air. The bed was made with aired sheets; kindling and split logs were laid in readiness across the andirons.

Hetty and Giles had taken the train directly from the reception at the Bakers' house, so Hetty was still in her grey bride's suit, bundled in a long wool coat with an Astrakhan collar, her face dwarfed by a matching hat. Her cheeks were pinkened by the cold air. It was snowing when they arrived, small flakes falling diffidently from a sky fisted with blizzard. The driver of a hired car helped carry their suitcases to the door of the glassed-in porch. Hetty waited while Giles paid, noticing how snowflakes starred the pale grass. Giles scraped the key in the lock, pushed open the door. The kitchen was warm, smelled of apples and mice. The fire hissed and snapped. They stood, for a moment, absorbing the quiet and the ways in which the house was alive. Giles put his arm around Hetty's shoulders; she leaned her head against him. They noticed the asynchronous ticking of clocks. They heard the flick of snowflakes against the windowpanes. On the gate-legged table was a loaf of molasses bread wrapped in a dish-cloth, a basket of brown eggs, butter in waxed paper and a honeycomb on a white dish. "Mrs. Pearl," Giles said. Hetty stepped forward, placed her hand on the loaf. It was still warm. "Oh," she said. They stood, forgetting to remove their coats, moved by the kindness of neighbours.

They carried their suitcases upstairs. Giles lit the fire in the bedroom, set up a fire screen. Already, light was fading from the sky, and firelight saved the room from the equalizing darkness. Objects came to sudden prominence: the silhouettes of Giles' great-grandparents, caught in a frame of shadow over the mantelpiece; a ladderback chair in the far corner, on whose post Hetty hung her hat. She could barely see herself in the spotted mirror, but she peered at her reflection, smoothed the hair at her temples. And then they went down into the great, dark house to make supper.

Giles showed Hetty the china cupboard, where, years later, their grandchildren would play store. He held a candle while Hetty selected two white dinner plates with gold-lustre rims. On the woodstove, she set canned peas to boil and cooked corned-beef hash in a cast-iron frying pan. She sliced the molasses bread, spread the pieces with butter. They ate without self-consciousness since they'd eaten together at the Bakers' house for so many years. They spoke of the wedding. How happy Dr. Baker seemed afterwards, at the reception, when he'd insisted on carrying plates of strudel to the young couple. How lovely Alma looked in her blue dress. As they ate, the wind rose, and they could hear the cracking rush of maple branches. Giles told her stories of the house. His mother, he said, remembered her older brothers repeating stories told by their grandmother, who, as a young bride, had come to this house when it was brand new, in 1797. Her brothers had fought in the Revolutionary War. These walls, he said, had heard tales of Valley Forge. Her niddy noddy and spinning wheels, he told Hetty, were still in the attic.

Later they sat by the fireplace. Giles pulled a wing chair close, laid a blanket in it. Hetty sat with a shade of dignity, smiling, aware that on this night she could allow herself to be treated like a queen. Giles, seeing this, pulled the blanket over her shoulders and fussed it around her neck. She waited, gazing at the flames, while he went to the kitchen for a mug of cocoa. He placed it in her hands; she clutched it, warming her fingers. Cold hung in the darkness, just beyond the circle of heat. Soon they would go to bed and be physically joined.

They sat for a while, sipping their cocoa and watching the flames. It was the first summer, they began, in soft voices. After her death. When they spent so much time reading in the park.

"It was you," Giles said, smiling. "Remember?" Her eyebrows peaked, worried. He reached over and smoothed them. "You reached over and touched my cheek. Alma was reading. I don't think she noticed."

"Well," Hetty replied. Looking shyly at her husband. "You were so sad."

His own eyebrows slanted low over sombre eyes. His lips softened. "And you," he said, "were so small. I put my arm over your shoulder." He glanced up and saw her watching this moment in the flames.

Kate watches the ice as it comes towards her and passes back, the way this same river will slide, on a sultry summer's day, beneath the prow of her canoe. It's like skating over the night sky; white bubbles swirl in the ice, delineating its depth, drifting and motionless as constellations, galaxies, planets. She pushes, side to side—*scrape, scrape*—and is herself drifting within the imagined moment of her grandparents' lives. A few nights ago, she read: "Went to Shepton for our honeymoon. Mr. P. opened up the house. Very cold, but we kept fires going and were comfortable for a week."

And their love becomes a layer of this day. She summons it from the past, and it is present in the frozen reeds, it rises with the flock of snow buntings that sheers skyward like white fireworks as the first skaters round a bend. She's smiling, slightly, as she watches her skates come forward, forward, as she hears the dragging scrape of blade, sees the white furrows she cuts into the black ice. Their love is such a relief. So brave and simple. Kate herself feels healed from Jonnie's loss. She wishes to tell someone: "Did you know that my grandfather—" But the joyful news, she realizes, is more than eighty years old.

She rounds the bend. Behind the clouds, the sun is lowering and the shadows grow cold. People collect, skate in small circles, pat their hands together.

"Isn't this fantastic, Kate?" It's Mary, her boss at the library. Other women join them, women she's known for years, with whom she'd have mingled easily if Tom were over there, laughing with the men. Yet Kate senses that these women are truly glad to see her. They're no longer afraid to speak of their shared past. They no longer shy from the presence of Tom's absence, are not intimidated by Kate's grief. Or is it she herself, she wonders, moving her skates backwards and forwards to stand in place, rubbing her cheeks with her mittened hands, who is less spiky, who has thawed? The women bump into one another, lose their balance. She feels soft bodies, is gripped by mitten-thickened hand bones, sees eyes brightened with cold. A child careens into the group. Arms fly down, scoop the child from falling. Someone calls to the men, reporting a decision seemingly made without discussion: "We think it's time to turn back." Kate finds herself regretting the sudden dispersal as the group turns upriver. Space, once again, spreads between them, but now, skating homewards, everyone skates with ease, chatting, laughing, calling to one another, sharing gobbets of news like tossing a baseball.

The river curves beside the marsh where straw-coloured grasses sweep forward, bent and unmoving as a frozen quilt under clouds suffused by the sunset they obscure. Kate skates steadily—*scrape, scrape*—beneath them. The muscles of her inner thighs feel the unaccustomed stretching. The ice grows blacker as the light fades.

And she is thinking, now, of how there had barely been time for Hetty and Giles to enjoy being a married couple, since seven months after their wedding, Giles' father died. He was sixty-two years old. After the funeral, they accompanied Lilian on a trip to the White Mountains. Was it at one of the grand New Hampshire hotels, in the late summer of 1917, in thin mountain air that smelled of pine trees and cold moss, that Lilian proposed the annex? Did they hesitate, Kate wonders? Did they discuss the idea in the privacy of their hotel bedroom? Hetty would have seen how Giles was torn between his mother's desires and his own imagined future, which centered around Hetty's comfort. "I don't mind," she imagines Hetty saying, with true lack of regret. "I'll have my own kitchen." For Lilian proposed building an addition on to the back of her Hartford house. Perhaps they saw it as a temporary measure, and knew it would be a help to her until she recovered from the shock of Charles' loss. But there they lived, every fall, winter and spring, until the day of Lilian's death. There they brought up their three boys. There Hetty found her place in a home of proud presence and hidden grief.

As Kate skates, Granny and Grampa Giles accompany her. They're about an arm's length away—*I could reach out and touch them.* She's felt this all winter. Sometimes it is Ellen whose presence she feels; frequently, it is Jonnie. They jostle Tom, and he appears less often, always at odd or disturbed moments: he comes when she feels herself insufficient, as if he's her reserve strength, or at times when parts of her mind seem missing, as if they've atrophied in marriage. Her grandparents now accompany her the way a known, living person can be called to mind: as essence, the shape of intention. They are no longer the parings of a child's self, benign shapes that curve round her in vivid scrapings of memory: red shoes, fishing creels, blue smoke from frying trout. Now they gaze at each other, or at Lilian, or at their growing boys, and Kate sees that she is not the centre of their world. She sees how Jonnie weaves through their lives like a breeze that slides feathers, stirs curtains. They speak her name, and after so many years of recounting remembered joy, its sound brightens their eyes.

After Charles died, Lilian waited for a month before visiting Shepton. "It was," she wrote to Giles on a plain one-penny postcard, "my saddest coming." Giles' heart would have ached for her. He knew how the house itself softened her; how she dreamed of its verandas cooled by watery, lilting shadows, of its rooms filled with the peaceful must of old furniture; how it was still the place of the first twelve years of her life, before she was sent to boarding school, when she and her brothers and parents had only to walk across the lawn, on Christmas Eve, to reach the lamp-lit church. All his life, his mother had gone to the country house seeking sanctuary. It was a place of refuge; its silvery cricket-song and the foot-worn grooves of its tilted floors nullified pain. He absorbed this in the child's way, as an aspect of his mother intrinsic as the sound of her voice, never not known, never first heard.

Sanctuary, Kate thinks. What is it? She has been seeking it herself.

She skates up close to the bank, cutting off a large bend in the river, and notices how the motionless grasses gather light from the hidden sunset. She envisions the photograph of

Lilian standing commandingly on the Shepton lawn, wearing a string of pearls so long it swings like a noose and a bucket-shaped hat whose brim obscures her eyes. Was she a spoiled child? Treated like a princess by four older brothers? The bank rises to Kate's left, its grasses pale against the sky, and Kate, skating into a breath of dank air emanating from the frozen soil, thinks of the receipt she found for her great-grandmother's wedding dress. Twenty yards of white silk, nine-and-a-half yards of lace, satin-heeled slippers, four yards of illusion, pearls, elbow-length gloves. An extravagant dress for her wedding to Charles, who had already had one wed-ding—to Lucy Smith—when Lilian was only seventeen. Charles, Kate thinks, was in fact Lilian's brother's brother-in-law, and so he was already part of the family when his first wife died. Lilian was young, sympathetic and available in his time of grief. Yet. Was it an unbalanced love? Did she bury feelings of being second-best? Perhaps, Kate thinks, when Ellen died, husband and wife encountered doors never opened, which, at first need of admittance, remained shut.

Kate glides, watching the ice. She can no longer see the white, fluting bubbles. The banks loom, featureless. Branches arch overhead as the river narrows; they are black, meshed. *Grief, too, is an expression of love.* Grief is tender, wild, aban-doned, frightening. Hold it forth in your arms, and others will embrace it. As the Baker family held their grief for Jonnie, passing her tenderly, one to the other. *Here is Jonnie, here is Jonnie.* But when Ellen died, Charles and Lilian were broken. Charles withdrew from his family in deepening gloom; he sickened, and died young. In Lilian's heart, the eight-year-old girl sang an endless, yearning song, incomprehensible and heartbreaking as the words she'd babbled on her deathbed. Of what use was it, this tragic cry that twisted Lilian's heart? Ellen's loss, Kate realizes—feeling, now, as if she is flying, since darkness has crept from the roots of bushes and in her black coat she feels disembodied, the ice glides past her feet as if it is the river that is moving rather than her—Ellen's unshared voice shaped the rest of Lilian's life.

Kate remembers the picture window over the horsehair couch, where she and her cousin knelt to watch Granny, outside, kneeling on a rubber pad wearing cotton gloves and shaking the soil from chickweed with a determined set-mouthed vigour that surprised the children, who thought their Granny could not be unkind. The family seemed embarrassed by this enormous single-paned window. Kate realizes now that it was Lilian's window. That it was Lilian who added the dining room and the master bedroom to the west side of the house, who converted bedrooms to bathrooms and put in plumbing, taking the extraordinary step of making changes to her beloved Shepton just so that her children, Daniel, Giles and Katherine, would have no excuse not to stay with her every summer. After Charles' death, she seldom passed a night under a roof that did not also shelter one of her children. Did she think to protect them, or hope that they would protect her? She bid people to her will; commanded workmen, servants, her own children; continuously readjusted her grasp of the slippery illusion of control. It must have been she, too, who returned the decor to the way it had been between 1860 and 1872, when her parents' Victorian sensibilities buried, like an Oriental bazaar, the simple Puritan belongings of the previous generation. "I found Father's flute—only imagine, someone put it in the back of the games closet. Willie's pipe! The pressed-flower album I left behind when I went to school. The dearest little red shoes; I am wearing them in an early photograph. Lace antimacassars, only slightly browned. I had Mrs. P. lay them out in the sun. Mother's epergne, packed away in the attic. The samovar I remember so well. Found, on the same day, Great-uncle John's diary of his European trip and Fred's labelled mineral collection." And Kate sees that the house was an expression of Lilian's desire to return to a time when she felt safe, enfolded, unbroken. She must have ferreted in the attic over and over again, bringing down abandoned treasures—mah-jong sets, a cracked leather quiver filled with arrows, quilted baby shoes—comforting herself with the creation of a place that seemed familiar, and fostering the illusion that she might exist, within its walls, as the person she had been in the days before both her child and her grief were buried.

She imagines the glossy, expressionless eyes of a snowshoe hare, crouched within its nest of grasses and leaves. Its hiding place, should one find it empty, would be the precise shape of a hare. Lilian made of Shepton such a womb-like place, a burrow, a mould of her own shape, fashioned from the past.

They return to the launch site just as the black branches and ragged meadowsweet fold into darkness. People fetch old blankets, folding chairs and food from cars. The fire is lit; flames worm without sound through crumpled paper, then leap to make a fiery skeleton of dry spruce boughs. Kate sits on a blanket with another blanket wrapped around her shoulders. She takes off her skates, massages her insteps before pulling on felt-lined boots. The fire sears her face. She runs her hands over her cheeks and up through her hair, which the fire makes dry and hot. She smiles, holds her palms to the flames. She feels the peaceful weight of her body, the pleasure of simple sitting. Caroline approaches, holding two bottles of cold beer in mittened hands.

"Thanks, Caroline. Wasn't that a great workout?"

"I can feel it," Caroline says. "Can I share?"

Kate wriggles sideways. Caroline squats, bulky in snow-pants, then sits, grunting. They laugh. She snuggles close so both their bottoms fit on the blanket. Their arms and shoulders touch; Kate feels Caroline's arm rise as she tips her beer. How long it has been, she thinks, since she has been held. Cradled, treasured. Their eyes meet; they smile as they raise bottles to lips. Neither woman speaks, enjoying the sharpness of carbonation on their tongues, the pulsing heat against their cheeks.

"Oh, how lovely," Caroline says.

"Skating made me think," Kate says. "Like any repetitive act—mowing the lawn, folding clothes. Your mind floats loose. You make discoveries."

Caroline looks intently at Kate. Her face is so close that Kate can see carrot-coloured hairs on her cheeks. "What did you think about?"

Kate has talked about Tom with Caroline, but not about grief. She feels the wet beer bottle through her mittens. She takes a swallow and stares at the place just between wood and flame where there's a leaping blue pulse.

"I thought," she says, "about how you can make a house into a hiding place."

Caroline nods, half-smiles. She turns her face to the fire, repressing comment.

"I have to learn how to accept what has happened to me," Kate continues. "Not just acknowledge it. Not be able to say, 'I'm a widow.' But learn *how* to accept it."

Her words are like notes, offered hesitatingly, from a contemplated work. Caroline recognizes this, astutely asks no questions. "It's good," she says. "It's good when you begin to see these things. Look at you!" she adds, teasing.

"What?"

"You've almost finished your beer."

Kate has been swallowing avidly, as if the beer is mountain water.

"Brian! Kate needs another beer."

Brian. Teasing, smiling, flipping a cap. He brings her a beer, then settles a chunk of wood close on her other side and sits on it, whittling alder branches with his jackknife, handing them to children. He passes one to Caroline, one to Kate.

Later in the evening, her cheeks are sticky with hot marshmallow, and she sings with everyone else, "'And we'll all go together, to pluck wild mountain thyme . . . '"

She stands in the dark kitchen. She's unwound her scarf, slid loose the top button of her coat. Her skates hang over her shoulder, the laces tied together. Her left hand, like a foot resting in a stirrup, is tucked between one skate's sole and its blade. The familiar space seems larger. Its sounds are more distinct and come from peculiar places; there are close, dense smells. *This is my home.* Her mind speaks carefully. The house doesn't feel empty. Rather, it hums and ticks, it makes small, friendly rustlings, it reminds her of the mushrooms she sautéed in butter, of the geraniums she watered, of the books she has not yet read that sit in the darkness and of how, momentarily, she will stand naked, hot water drumming her scalp and enveloping her in a long, sliding tunnel of warmth, while her mind lilts back to the icebound forest and the black-ice journey that she and her friends will relive forever.

She unbuttons her long black coat. Her scarf hangs on either side of the thick, folded turtleneck of a wool sweater. Her face is animated, cheeks reddened by cold and exercise. She takes off her mittens, drops the skates, heels off her boots. She walks into the living room. Light from the street lamp makes it a place of angles and reflections without depth. *As I've been.* She pulls the chain of a standing lamp. Shadows leap into the corners.

She feels as if she's been gone for a long time. Here is her life, waiting for her. In the half-darkness, her projects are like suggestions, beginnings, dreams. The desk. Letters bundled with coloured elastic bands. A novel, tented beside the couch. The smell of the hatboxes, a spicy, inky essence so much a part of the house that she has to separate it, consciously, like picking burrs from a horse's mane. Around her in the night-shaped quiet, tipping on the ticks and sighs of a windless dark, are all the things Tom does not know about. She's leaning into a new history, one that starts on the morning Tom slumped forward over the kitchen table.

She walks back into the kitchen, unwrapping her scarf, tucking her mittens into the pockets of her coat.

But Tom *is* here, she thinks, sliding her coat over a hanger. *He's in my thinking, the way I see the folds and furrows of this coat; he's in the firm tenderness of my fingertips and in the way I shape my vowels. He's in the cushions of the rocking chair, the worn legs of the table. He's gone, and he's here. He's within the shape of my life, however it may crimp or broaden. He's the complex light in my eyes, its sadness, its delight. Tell me your Tom, I need to say to my friends.*

She plugs in the teakettle and sits in the rocking chair. She is thinking of how she will describe this day to May, to her parents, to Christy and Liam. *My God, I'm smiling.*

And she realizes that today she did not curl in her armchair as if, should she wait long enough, changing nothing, pulling the past around her like a cloak, Tom might return.

15. Sally's Café

THE HOUSE IS WARM AND PEACEFUL.

Kate is in the dining room, planting seeds. Through the south-facing windows, she can see Tom's studio buried in drifts, its windows white with frost. The perennial beds are snow-covered, the stone steps are only a shadowed indentation. Last night's fluffy snow falls from the roof in glistening, sun-shot prisms. Wind rattles the lily stalks that poke through the icy crust and whips the new snow skyward in twisting spindrifts.

Years ago, she and Tom installed heavy glass shelves across the dining-room windows. By March, the shelves were filled with seed flats. Dinner guests stood on tiptoe to read the white plastic markers tipped into the black soil. In Kate's neat, rounded printing were the Latin names: *Gaillardia aristata, Heuchera sanguinea, Digitalis purpurea.* Blanket flower, Kate would explain, patiently. Coral bells, foxglove.

Today, she's planting red cabbage, tomatoes and broccoli. That's all. But last year, she thinks, she'd planted nothing. The month of March had almost passed before she realized that she'd forgotten. Shocked, she'd opened a seed catalogue. She'd turned the pages, seeing pictures of glistening red tomatoes, of children embracing pumpkins, of massed beds of poppies and pansies. She remembered how she turned the pages faster and faster. The catalogue, like everything in her life, seemed bright, slick and artificial. Filled with arch promise. Calculated to lure, and delude. Instead, last year, she bought all her plants at the local greenhouse. As she'd lifted packs of zinnias and marigolds, she could see their flowers, smell their bruised astringency. She did not have to imagine the cheery yellow blossoms with petals like tiny mouse ears.

Her ability to imagine anything in the future is mostly absent, at best diminished. It's like a sense that's been damaged. One end of the table is covered with newspaper. She manoeuvres a kitchen spoon into a plastic bag of potting soil, tips it into a seed flat. She and Tom had covered this entire table with plastic. Tom would bring up from the cellar buckets of peaty soil that they'd prepared in the fall. Kate would follow, carrying white plastic trays filled with fibre packs, markers, indelible pens. They kept their own saved seeds in marked envelopes. They brought these from a desk drawer as eagerly as they ferreted out the Christmas decorations or the Easter eggs or the children's birthday presents.

Nothing, she thinks, running the spoon's back over the soil, nothing to do with the garden had ever had the deadening weight of necessity, what might feel like hard work if one felt compelled rather than inspired to dig, lift, hoe, tug, sweat. Planting seeds in March, year after year, Tom and Kate had worked within the impetus of vision. It was not arch promise but an ache of beauty. As their fingers dropped the dry seeds, they imagined day lilies, peach-pink, cupping dusty yellow like a handful of sunlight; spires of blue delphinium rising from red bergamot; the translucent bells of white campanula nodding beside rose petals neither pink nor white but suffused with both, like sunrise.

She hears the hollow rush of wind, a dry flicking as snow collides with the window. Mr. Winkles' paws pad heavily—*ga-thump, ga-thump*—as he comes down the stairs. She makes a furrow in the soil with the edge of a wooden coffee stirrer, tears open the paper packet, shakes round seeds into her hand. They are a rich, peaty brown, the colour of bog water. They roll into a crease in her palm, make a necklace. She tries to recover the feeling that once pervaded seed-planting days: a sense of unfolding, of renewal, as she and Tom contemplated seeds so dry they would grind like peppercorns under a shoe and envisioned each one as a cabbage or a pink geranium or a vine on the sweet-pea trellis. Now she picks the seeds from her palm, one by one, sprinkles them along the furrow, watches them settle into place. *Maybe when the soil is broken by green shoots, I will feel. Something. Gladness would be okay. Or even surprise.* For she is aware, as she tamps down the soil with the backs of her knuckles and eases warm water into the seeded soil, that she's hooking onto the past, making herself repeat patterns that grew, spontaneously, from the rich soil of her married life. Last year at this time, grief was like physical pain: it was both her support and her struggle, pinioning her on the bedrock of self. It absolved her from the need for bearings, direction, grounding. Now it ebbs, drains away. It's like Tom leaving her. Nothing replaces it. She sets a seed tray onto the glass shelf and snugs plastic wrap over it to retain moisture. Maybe this is what it feels like to lose one's faith. To kneel in church and see the once-divine sanctuary as a place of wood and plaster. To listen for God and hear nothing. No one, she thinks, can tell you how to rekindle that fire. No one.

There's a knock on the door. In the quiet house, it is the sound of impatience, of expectation. Kate starts. She takes a deep breath, wipes her hands on her jeans, hurries into the kitchen. She opens the door to the smell of snow, and Gregory.

He's holding flowers wrapped in clear cellophane sprinkled with blue, red and green dots. The bouquet is tied around the stems with a froth of the crinkly ribbon that comes alive beneath a scissor blade. He holds the flowers cradled in one arm, like a baby. He grins. His blue eyes slant into hers; she reads hesitation, hope.

"I came to apologize." The wind scuds along the porch floor, harries snow over the red-painted boards.

"Come in," Kate says. He steps in. She hears the cellophane crackling, and when she turns from securing the door, she sees daffodils shining from green tissue paper.

She opens her mouth, about to protest.

"No, no. I thought about it. I remembered. I slammed that door. I was boorish." He hands her the flowers. She avoids his eyes by burying her nose in them. The faint, earthy essence. Spring.

He's watching her as no one does any more. He's waiting, hoping for forgiveness. And what, she thinks, do I get myself into if I do forgive him? But she is touched.

"I love daffodils," she murmurs. If Tom were here, one of them would begin to talk about heritage daffodils. They'd wait to see which of them would begin. They'd stumble in their enthusiasm, knowing their friends would laugh and indulge their obsession. They'd talk of their latest discovery. Or their newest acquisition. Perhaps even open a gardening book to a marked page—"See? We planted these under the bank." But she says nothing, turns to find a vase.

He begins to unwind his scarf, talking to her back as she holds the vase under the faucet, her hands trembling slightly. She hasn't thanked him. He speaks, she thinks, to make this less apparent.

" . . . down to that restaurant at the corner? It's lunchtime. Could I buy you soup and a sandwich?" He's standing close to the door since she hasn't invited him to remove his boots. One hand holds the tartan scarf, as if he will either pull it from his neck or wrap it back around.

"There," she says, setting the flowers on the kitchen table. May, she thinks, will be pleased. "Oh, how lovely. Thank you so much, Gregory. They're so . . . Well, they're spring. The essence of spring." She doesn't want to talk about Tom in Gregory's presence any more. Is this a betrayal? She's not sure. She looks at him, sees that he seems submissive, ready to be either rejected or accepted. And she is, again, touched. "Yes, sure," she says. "I'd like to have lunch."

They walk to the café, which is on a corner at the far end of Kate's street. They walk side by side, rapidly, as if it is colder than it actually is. The space between them is so tangible that they both look straight ahead and maintain their distance precisely, speaking of the weather. Gregory asks her with a hint of deference if it has been more severe than usual. Kate hears his politeness, realizes he is feigning ignorance. For God's sake, he knows about New Brunswick winters. But she takes it as an apology and agrees that, yes, it has been unusually cold. In the café, they busy themselves unwrapping scarves, loosening sweaters, fluffing toque-flattened hair, settling themselves into the warm, coffee-scented air.

The café is in the old courthouse. Its windows overlook the river, the gas station, the green bridge. The flowered wallpaper is tired. On the floor by the door is a basket of colouring books and broken crayons. The kitchen door stands open, and Kate can see a stout young woman wearing a hairnet. Her upper arms move steadily, her hands are hidden. The place is filled with sunlight; the smell of pea soup thickens the air's texture. They order soup and sandwiches. Coffee arrives in thick white mugs. Gregory tears open a sugar packet, pries at the aluminum tab of a creamer. Kate holds her mug in both hands and squints at the streaked window. She raises her eyebrows, sips. Winces. The coffee is weak and extremely hot. "May I?" She pours in the remainder of his second creamer.

"So," he says, clearing his throat and glancing into her face. "I've been taking a sea kayaking course at the Aquatic Centre. Marvellous course. That's why you haven't heard from me for some time. I've been rather obsessed. Between that, running a newspaper and trying to scramble together my memories . . ."

"Ummm. I can imagine."

He settles back, stretches his legs and stirs his coffee. In the kitchen, the chopping knife stops; there's the intermittent whine of a blender. He's prepared to become comfortable. She notices him glance sideways at the blackboard, squinting to read today's desserts.

"Yes, well, I've always wanted to kayak. Of course, as you know, I've canoed since I was a child. Haven't we all . . ."

"What are you learning? I mean, what is there . . . particularly . . ." She's not really interested, but it seems a neutral topic. Down below the bridge she sees a father pulling a toboggan over the frozen river. Two children sit bolt upright, sausaged into snowsuits. She notes the peculiar insularity of a young family. The father, forging ahead steadily, looks back over his shoulder, his mouth moves. One of the children raises a mittened hand. Sun makes shattered rainbows in the wind-blown snow.

"Oh, all sorts of things." Gregory relaxes, Kate notes, more rapidly than his earlier formality would warrant, making her suspect the extent of his contrition. "Feathering, for example. Now it takes a little technique, but once you get it down it means your blade isn't catching the wind on the backstroke. It's more efficient. Of course, you see these idiots with their paddles upside down, and they don't even know it. If the label is right side up, you know your paddle is in the proper position. Then you need to be aware of paddling 'in the box.'" He straightens his back, fists his hands over the table. "You don't want to lean forward or back, you see. You want to use your whole upper body, use the power of your torso and legs. Then your arms don't get tired. Of course, you yourself, Kate, have very strong arms, but even so you need to paddle for endurance."

She nods. *Oh Lord.* If Tom were here, would they exchange glances, signal to each other their bemused tedium? But Tom is not here, and Kate finds Gregory's pedantic energy oddly appealing.

"Oh, we learned all kinds of things." He's careless with his knowledge, eager to impart it. "Let's see. Well, self-rescue techniques of course. T-rescues, paddle-float rescues. Wet entries. It used to be if you heard the word 'kayak' all you'd think about was rolls—we used to call them 'Eskimo rolls.' Nowadays there's more emphasis on paddling properly. Sweep turns. High and low braces. That sort of thing."

She raises her eyebrows. She senses the sadness in her eyes even as she smiles. *It's my eyebrows; they've become like Granny's. Will it ever leave me, this deep sadness?* She feels an odd twinge of envy as she watches Gregory's freckled face relax with enthusiasm. He leans back as the waitress sets steaming soup in front of him. He unfolds his paper napkin and sets it in his lap, lifts a spoonful of the thick green soup, blows on it.

"Now, I haven't actually purchased anything yet. The plastic boats are everywhere, of course. They're cheaper, more durable, I suppose. But the rigid Kevlar boats are things of beauty. Really. Much faster and lighter."

Bells on the door jangle as customers step in, pulling off gloves and mittens, rubbing cold from their fingers. Kate glances up. The word will be all over town by tonight. "Saw Kate Harding at Sally's with a man." After Tom died, she didn't mind when her friends' husbands called to see if she needed help with firewood, plumbing, snow removal. She felt vulnerable, fragile. It made sense, then. Now she's firm about her self-sufficiency, knows it is respected, yet she still feels vulnerable. Do people perceive widowed women as somehow forlorn, like animals strayed from a pack, or is she being overly sensitive when she imagines how people see her? In any event, she's angry, often. *So fuck 'em,* she hears Tom saying, in his wry voice. And it occurs to her for the first time that she needs to hear her own voice, not his, telling her to be strong.

"Well, Kate. I most certainly haven't forgotten you, even if I haven't been calling. In fact, I came here not only to apologize, but to suggest a plan."

He is smiling at her. He makes her feel, once again, as she felt when they first set out on the river, the day they went skiing. He doesn't see Tom. He doesn't think of her, it seems, as a remnant, a shard of what was once whole. He doesn't choose his words carefully, as she hears her friends doing. He thinks of her simply as Kate. A strand of his own past. Someone he needs.

Kate slides her spoon into her mouth entirely without self-consciousness. She wipes her mouth with her napkin. "Good soup," she says. It warms her; she feels a sudden lift of her spirits. She smiles back at him. "Okay, Gregory. What? Something better than my plan to go river skiing?"

He lifts a hand, dismisses her apology. "I wondered if you would like to go sea kayaking with me. Now, it would be entirely safe. We'd go in a double. Absolutely no worries: you can't even *make* a double go over."

She drops her spoon. Her hands fly sideways, spread forbiddingly, thumbs braced. "Oh, no. I don't think—"

"This is what I thought. We'd put in at St. Martin's. Lots of the guided tours leave from that beach. You know, right there down at the end of that dead-end street. Now, we'd have to go out on an incoming tide. Absolutely safe if you go on the proper tides. I do know my tides, Kate. Paddle around Quaco Head. Where the lighthouse used to be. Well, there's still a lighthouse, but no keeper, no keeper's house the way there used to be. I thought we could head down the coast, have a snack on that gorgeous little beach. Remember the one? The one we hiked in to with the kids? It's not so far down. Then come back. We might see murres, petrels. Maybe mergansers. I'll bring the lunch. Well, it might be tea, depends on the tide. I've found a marvellous little bakery. Portuguese. Simply wonderful sweet bread. We'll be wearing wet suits. Not that we're going to fall in. Just a nice precaution, and besides it will be cold out there."

"When . . . umm. When were you thinking of doing this?"

"Sometime in late April."

"April? Good God, Gregory. The bay would be hellish. I thought you were talking about summer."

"No, no, in a way that would be the fun of it. The adventure. My instructor and his pals go out in the bay all winter. Last weekend, for example. Yes. Absolutely. I'm not kidding. I thought if we went around the time that the rivers are beginning to break up, it would be a way to celebrate . . . new things. Old things. Coming of spring, passing of winter. Old friendship renewed. And perhaps . . ."

For the first time he looks out the window. His fingers are seized with sudden trembling, and he presses them against his lips. Then he makes his hand into a fist and punches his mouth lightly, twice. Clears his throat.

"You see, the bay is where Jerome and I spent most of our good times together. You know, Kate, I did try to stay close to him during his teenage years, but it seemed a futile effort.

Overnight, it seemed, he began to hate me. They say, you know, this is typical of fathers and sons. But this was . . . well . . . of a different magnitude. He resisted anything I wanted him to do: things he was good at, things I knew he'd succeed at. And then, once he'd weaned me from my vision of who he might be, so to speak, he went out west and began to climb mountains."

His chest seems concave. He holds his shoulders high, as if he's about to shrug and has forgotten to drop them. He runs his thumb up and down the handle of his mug. He stares out at the frozen river, at the marsh with its tapestry of red-barked alders, clumps of meadowsweet, cattails.

"I never . . . You see, I never . . . When they found his body, they advised us that it would be difficult for us to see it. They asked if there were any family members nearby to make the identification. Well, there weren't. And in any case, Karen decided immediately to fly out. I . . . didn't go with her. I had many ways to rationalize that decision. Work, deadlines, my desire to leave my memories of Jerome intact. Now I profoundly regret my absence. I've visualized the scene so often: Karen, walking into a sterile room with a police officer at her side. All she could tell me about it was that she kept repeating "Yes, it's him," and that if the officer hadn't put his arm around her she would have fallen. I should have . . . I think of her going back to her hotel room alone. The casket was flown back for the funeral but never opened. And I keep trying to believe he's actually gone. That he really did die. I can't stop talking to him. I explain myself. I try to make him understand me. I beg him to reconsider. I plead with him. I wake up in the night from a recurrent dream that I'm standing beside him on that ledge. I give him back his rope, his sling, his crampons. I put my arm over his shoulders and we . . . go back. We go back together. Down off the mountain."

Kate's eyes fill with tears.

Gregory's mouth widens, not in a smile but a stretch that narrows his eyes as if he's trying to see whether the hawk soaring low over the marsh is a red-tail or a harrier.

"So now I'm finally trying to find a way to say goodbye. Not a ceremony, exactly, but I thought, well, to be honest, Kate . . ." He turns away from the window. He seems to be looking up over the rims of his reading glasses, which he's forgotten he's not wearing. " . . . I think his spirit is at the bay. I thought we could make a fire on the beach, and since you remember him as a child we could, well . . . I don't know. I feel that you're the kind of person who might devise some words, or find a poem to read or even . . . we could even sit there in silence and bid him farewell."

One tear runs down her cheek, and she does not wipe it away. She picks at the window sash, its green paint lifting in platelets like the papery skin of an abandoned turtle shell. She can't separate all the strands that make this fibrous statement bind her. He includes her as an accessory to his guilt, as if in those mornings of bacon and blue smoke she, too, might have foreseen Jerome's tragedy, might have watched for signs, saved him from himself. This ceremony, then, is as much about exoneration as farewell. She, who shared those days of marshmallows and sandy sleeping bags, of gooseflesh bodies and damp towels, can bear witness to Gregory's innocence. Why not, though? He longs for her to remember that he loved his son, that his son loved him. She knows this to be true. There are few people who can help him in this particular way. Tom is gone. Karen is absent. And she understands, as well, what it is to wait for someone to truly die.

There's a stuttering scrape as the waitress pulls a chair to the chalkboard, climbs onto it, erases today's menu. She begins chalking new specials. There are pauses as she searches for different coloured chalks. Clicking taps, screeks.

Kate plucks a sugar packet from the cut-glass bowl and turns it end for end, feeling its contents sift past her fingers like sand in an egg timer. "Gregory," she says. She runs her fingers through her grey bangs. "I won't go in the kayak with you. But what I'd be happy to do is to take the car down that road as far as I can. Then I'll carry the stuff down to the beach. I'll bring the makings of a fire, and food. That way, you can go in a single kayak, and you won't have to pack anything." Does she mean this? To her surprise, she realizes that, yes, she does. It is something to look forward to. She imagines herself on the beach, listening to the gulls, sniffing the April wind that carries the sharp smell of salt water, spruce trees, cold sand. "You could even just go only one way if you wanted. If the weather deteriorated, I'd have a car as near as I could get it, so we could carry the kayak out."

He passes his forefinger over his lips. He nods. Their eyes meet. Amazed, she sees that he is irritated, as he was when she went outside to avoid overhearing his conversation with Janie. *Why, why? Why did this man surface? Why did I agree to even this much?*

"Don't want to go in a kayak with me?" he says, prepared to persuade her.

"No, Gregory, I do not. The idea absolutely terrifies me." I am, she does not say, my children's only parent. I do not take risks.

His irritation passes, and he smiles, relents. His enthusiasm returns. "Well! That will be delightful, then, even without the boat trip."

She smiles, gravely. She reminds herself of Grampa Giles. "Thank you for asking me, Gregory. And I think . . ." She stands, picks her scarf from the back of her chair, winds it around her neck. Gregory comes around and holds the shoulders of her long black wool coat.

"What? You think what?"

She drops her arms into the sleeves. She pulls on her gloves, stretches her fingers. "Oh, about the reason for the trip." She's remembering Jerome. The little boy who had played on that beach, his life stretching before him. "I think the bay will give you your ceremony. The wind and the waves will say what you need to hear."

16. Tulips

IT'S A WATERY MORNING AFTER DAYS OF RAIN. THE weather turned unseasonably warm shortly after the day Kate went to lunch with Gregory, and now, some weeks later, the river has spread far over its banks. The holes of muskrats are drowned; the creek is only a rippling disturbance in a plain of blue water in which the red-budded maples are temporarily stranded.

After breakfast, Kate puts on overalls, rubber boots and a denim jacket. From the porch she can see the glint of water not far below the edge of her lawn. The air is filled with its bright, raw smell, and overhead a flock of Canada geese pursues the northlands in a wavering wedge. The damp air smells of life's starting point and something twists within her, like a twig shedding a load of early-spring snow. This spring, unlike last, she feels her own sources, their raw, disturbing power. *Energy.* In herself, it has returned. There, she thinks as she starts down the steps, pulling on her work gloves, is the stone path. *Funny how it surprises me every year, after being buried under snow for five months.* Like everything else in the garden, it is dishevelled, spattered with shreds of wet leaves and sticks, bordered by clots of dirt and thawing cat shit. But here it is, firm under her feet as she strides with her long-legged walk out to the garden shed.

She trundles out the wheelbarrow, empty save for a hayfork. This first gardening chore of the year feels, as it should, like a celebration. As she pushes the wheelbarrow down the path, she remembers how last year she stood by the lily bed, gloveless, hugging herself, her cold hands tucked into armpits, and in the cold wind became aware of the distance between herself and the house and of the fact that Tom would never again step through its door. She could not bear to uncover the red shoots that came bursting upwards with merciless renewal. Her cheeks had felt chapped from tears. *I have no memory of doing this last year. Perhaps I hired the boy.* She starts beneath the apple tree, next to the path. She stabs the tines of a three-pronged fork into a thatch of straw that is still partially frozen, and it comes up in a slice, like a block of Shredded Wheat. *Will I ever again lose this particular sense of delight, of discovery?* This year, she does not feel the bitterness of reproach, cannot blame these shoots for their irrepressible life. They have come so far in darkness, they emerge from the womb of frozen straw in an embryonic slither, featureless and succulent, flame red, purple, yellow, speared, whorled, flat. Daffodils and tulips, narcissus, crocuses, scilla. She kneels, puts her nose to the soil. With her fingertips, she gently disengages frozen straw from a clump of columbine, whose nubbed centre is frilled with lacy fronds. She uncovers the limp scissor blades of iris, the papery-skinned brown rhizomes of maidenhair fern.

She pushes the straw-filled wheelbarrow across the lumpy, partially-frozen soil and upends it on the compost pile. Wind, rushing like the sound of freshets, tosses the spring-supple branches. Coming back, she sees the sloping lawn with its quilting of snow-pressed leaves, the mulched flower beds, the stone steps with their cracked terra cotta planters. She drops the wheelbarrow's handles and stands with her hands at her sides. She senses a clarity within herself. What is it? She listens to the wind, and decides that it is the absence of the grinding effort of replacing what *is* with what *was*. She's not doing it any more. She's not looking at the house and imagining Tom standing in the half-open door or Christy's hand waving from an upstairs window. She has lost her sense of obligation to retrieve such images. Instead, she is herself, Kate Harding, standing in the garden, while the recent past—last week, last month—quivers across her brain like leaf-broken light: skating; the bonfire; Grampa Giles' diary; talking to her parents on the phone; the boy who'd stood at the library desk and asked if she'd ever heard of someone called Hitler; Christy's invitation to visit Newfoundland together this summer, motivating her to buy maps, investigate ferry schedules.

Every blade of grass, piece of straw, slab of stone is so precise that she feels disoriented, as if she has suddenly awakened. The light is sleek, knife-like, disinterring frost, prying ice from gutters, glaring on the brown needles of the Christmas wreath on the compost heap and the weathered wood of clothespins. This must have been what Sunny Hill felt like to Granny when they arrived at the house on the first weekend of spring, Kate thinks, taking the hay fork from the wheelbarrow and beginning another bed. *Not* Shepton, she reminds herself, but Sunny Hill. She has to rearrange her vision of the past. Giles and Hetty spent most of the summers of their life at Sunny Hill, the house that Kate and her cousins had always thought of as their uncle's place.

August 20, 1921—Signed deed for Burdick house. Will take possession in two weeks. Mother pleased. Hetty v. excited.

In the summer of 1921, when Kate's father, Sam, was a newborn baby and his brothers were aged two and four, the house across the shared driveway from Shepton came up for sale. Hetty, Kate imagines, held the baby in her arms as she and the little boys followed Giles over flagstones deep-set into the scorched August grass. Giles opened the kitchen door, the little boys pressed against his legs. The house was cool and empty, smelled of kerosene and soil. Kate tries to imagine Granny *excited*. It would evidence itself not in speech but in hasty movements, a nervous patting of her buttons, lips folded inwards and clasped by her teeth. Her eyes did not dart, glance and dance, as Jonnie's would have, but were bright with earnest hope. The day they bought Sunny Hill was possibly as important a day to her as those of her marriage to Giles or the births of her sons. For it was their first house, and meant that they could spend their summers living as Lilian's neighbours rather than as her guests.

Kate rolls the wheelbarrow, sets it on the first broad stone step. She slides the fork under the hay, lifts gently. As she works her way up the east side of the steps, she thinks of what her father told her on the phone last night. Over the winter she has called her parents frequently to tell them what she discovers in the letters, in receipts or in Grampa Giles' diaries. They know the broad outlines of Hetty and Giles' story, but are fascinated by Kate's findings. She is in the odd position of telling her father about his own parents. He ponders her questions, enjoys how he can bridge the gaps in Kate's knowledge. Last night, he told her of his childhood summers and described Sunny Hill, plucking details from his memory profuse and plump as raspberries, dropping them into the pail of Kate's mind.

Like Shepton, Sunny Hill was an eighteenth-century house with low-ceilinged rooms and no electricity. Behind it was a sunken garden overrun with sweet-brier roses. From its front rooms, the family could look down over the village street to the sun-washed facades of houses on the other side, beyond whose wood-shingled roofs were the blue ridges of distant hills. The kitchen held no more and no less than all the things Hetty loved: clear light, birdsong, the fresh smell of soil, evidence of children, her tools. In the deep drawers and the shelves beneath the counter were her metal applesauce cone and wooden masher, mixing bowls, a wooden rolling pin, cheesecloth, clothespins, loose-weave dish towels; by the back door, on a table protected by a piece of carpet, was a wicker basket containing her trowel, cotton gloves, crumpled seed packets. The room's wooden floor had neither carpet nor linoleum. The cupboards were painted white; the walls were decorated with a child's watercolour of a girl in a straw hat holding a daisy and a Traveller's Insurance Company calendar with a Currier and Ives etching of trotting horses. Beneath the calendar was a small table on which Giles kept a pad of legal paper and a pencil. He kept a list of things he must do when he returned the following weekend, for he spent Monday through Friday in Hartford. Check the calcium carbide hopper, pick raspberries, weed the vegetable garden, pick twigs from the lawn, repair the barn stairs, fix the stove, check the early apples, the Melbas and the Grimes Goldens.

"On a summer's morning in the late 1920s," Kate's father told her, "we might have been hunting for eggs in the Sunny Hill henhouse or playing in the Shepton barns. Grandmother's cook probably had a fire on in the big range in the Shepton kitchen. There was a maid over there with huge bosoms. Once, we hid in the lilac bushes, and my brother shot her with a stick-arrow . . ."

As he spoke, Kate imagined Hetty in her kitchen on a day that promised to be a scorcher. The back door was open, as it had been all night, and through the screen Hetty could hear the domestic heat-croon of hens as they pecked or settled in their yard out beyond the jungle of overgrown forsythia. She stooped to touch a match to the round wick of the kerosene stove. The wick flared, and she adjusted it. A bubble of air broke the surface of the kerosene in the glass jar at the side of the stove. The stove needed continual repairs, but she did not worry because Giles always fixed it when he returned. She carried the kettle to the sink. The tap sighed; windmill-pumped water sputtered and then resolved into a trickle. She opened the cupboard, took down a drum-shaped box of oatmeal. She wore a cotton dress worn thin by repeated washings, manglings, sun bleachings and wind dryings. She loved being in their own home in the country, where it didn't matter what she wore. Giles would go straight to their bedroom as soon as he arrived on Friday afternoons and change his suit and tie for khaki work pants and a cotton shirt whose sleeves he rolled, slowly and with pleasure, to the elbow.

She set a saucepan of water on the stove, shook oatmeal into it. The kitchen was striped with short bands of light that fell from two doors leading into the sun-flooded front rooms. A square table in the middle of the room was set with a thin blue-and-white checked cloth, willowware bowls, mismatched spoons, glasses of pulp-flecked orange juice. She could hear children's voices. Holding one hand under a wooden spoon, water-darkened and steaming, she went to the south window and peered out through the buckled screen. Giles would be pleased to see what a good job Mr. Fitts had done on the lawn. Such a dear little bit of a man, Hetty thought fondly, with his wizened arm. Every Thursday morning before sunrise he pushed his lawnmower the entire length of Main Street, past the library, the cenotaph, the general store and the church. People surfaced from sleep to the eggbeater whirr of its blades.

Before lunchtime he had mowed all of Lilian's lawns and their own. She saw a boy burst from behind the barn, run up past Shepton's woodshed. "Ready or not, here I . . ." Was it Sam's voice? The three boys so close in age all sounded the same. Sam, the baby. Alex, Oliver. Hetty saw smoke stuttering from Shepton's kitchen chimney. The small-paned windows of the kitchen ell were opened against the heat of the wood stove. Shepton, from her perspective, was massive and aloof, its roofs half-hidden beneath the old maples, its north-facing windows black and stippled with reflections. The piazza, with its elegant Italianate columns, was prepared for afternoon guests, set with card tables and wicker chairs.

She opened the screen door and stepped out onto the path. She cupped her hands around her mouth and called the boys in a flute-like singsong. Then she pressed her fingers against her mouth, and her eyebrows lifted. She would not want Lilian to hear her calling the boys, for Lilian would think they should not have been out rampaging before breakfast. "Coming!" she heard, the voice barely audible. She went back inside. The oatmeal was done, and she set it on the side of the stove. She set a bowl of blackberry jam, a hinge-lidded glass jar of applesauce, a plate of butter and a dented silver pitcher of cream on the table. She poured herself a small cup of coffee and sat on a low chair, both feet on the floor. She held the saucer of her cup, the side of her hand braced against her favourite strawberry-print apron. This time of waiting for the children might be the one time all day when Hetty sat still, although this did not occur to her. The kitchen smelled of kerosene and oatmeal, of the molasses stickiness of cupboard shelf paper, of new-mown grass faintly tinged with the sour scent of the chicken pen. The birds, subdued already by the pressing heat, made chipping noises like dripping faucets from their cool refuges beneath bushes and under eaves.

And Kate imagines Hetty lifting the coffee to her lips, thinking how the day will be a scorcher, and hearing the boys' voices, the skittery scrape of a stick being dragged along stones. The boys burst into the kitchen carrying a dead snake. "It was lying on the driveway. Can we preserve it in a jar?" The boys smelled of dusty soil. "My," said Hetty. "You have old brown leaves in your hair. You must have been under the barn." She sent them to wash their hands, laid the snake on the windowsill, straightening it like a strand of putty. The boys sat at the table, folded their hands while Hetty spoke the prayer. The sun lay over the table, lifting, in its lazy warmth, the murmuring of robins, the rising buzz of cicadas. Its heat prickled her scalp. Her hands lay loosely on either side of her bowl as she watched her boys.

"Shepton," Kate's father told her, "was a very different kind of place from Sunny Hill. Lilian gave dinner parties; wealthy people came out to visit from Hartford, arriving in chauffeured cars. It was a formal place, with maids and fingerbowls. Grandmother made us recite Latin declensions and checked our fingernails." Once, he told Kate, she gave his next-oldest brother a manicure set for his birthday. They bargained for it later, wheedling, all the boys longing for the tiny, useful cuticle scissors. They never went to that house to play, as Kate and her cousins had, but sat at the dining table on Sundays, after church, in pressed knickerbockers and short ties, or else went in late autumn to help their father close the place up for the winter. Dank, silent, lit only by the grey light of a rainy October day, devoid of their grandmother's presence, the house did not seem like anyone's home but like a place waiting for its people to return. They might be any of the dead-eyed men, women and children who stared from daguerreotypes or oil paintings—men who wore frilly neck-pieces or white stockings with buckled shoes, grim-mouthed women in bonnets, boys in uniforms, affronted or earnest children perched on straight-backed chairs or clutching the necks of wooden rocking horses. The pictures stood on bureaus and sideboards, hung over mantelpieces and head-boards, lined the staircase, were stacked in cardboard boxes. They were all dead, but the house seemed to be theirs, filled with their belongings. "No," Kate's father said. "We didn't play with things. It was like a museum. Our father told us not to touch anything, Grandmother didn't want things disturbed."

Kate is now at the mulch pile. She dumps the wet straw, leaves the wheelbarrow upside down, its wheel slowly spinning. She walks up the stone stairs and sits on the top step, unbuttoning her jacket. She props her elbows on her knees, slides her fingers into her hair. Behind her, the woven willow-sapling fence shines in the glancing light. Her hazel eyes watch the reflection of cirrus clouds that surge across the window-panes of her house. *My God, what a size this house is for one person.* Two waves of her mind crest at the same time. One despairs. The other counsels patience. They absorb each other. There is no resolution. She doesn't know what she is going to do, ultimately. She vacillates. Should she sell this place, buy a bungalow? Move into an apartment? Move to Halifax to be closer to Christy? She observes herself observing herself. This, she realizes, is a step forward. She is not truly imagining a future, but her mind, like the spring shoots, begins to stir, seeking light.

Meanwhile, her grandfather's dry voice runs in her head. He is getting older. He worries, patiently. He and Granny are gradually growing into the people Kate remembers. She ponders the information that fell from his diary as she read it last night:

June 12, 1933—Mother wandering in her mind. I drove
the Franklin from Hartford. Mother desirous of Shepton's
cooler air.

June 14, 1933—Called Dr. T. Hetty and I went over and
sat with Mother. Very confused, much talk about Ellen.
She asked for yellow tulips and thought Father was coming.

In the fall of 1933, when the older boys had gone to the
Chicago World's Fair with their aunt and uncle, Lilian died.
Mother died at ten o'clock this morning. He does not say any
more than this, but Kate, who returned compulsively to the
diary after saying goodbye to her parents last night, imagines,
now, how it must have been. How the maples burned in their
flamboyant dissolution, and in the orchard, crickets feasted on
windfalls. How the air was hazy, stone walls were half-buried
beneath drifts of maple leaves, the dusty purple Concord
grapes had begun to split, the Shepton barns were filled with
bushel baskets of early apples. Lilian lay in the mahogany
scroll end French bedstead in which she had been born. For
months, she had been wandering in her mind through the
years when her children, and the century, were young. She
ordered curtains for the Roselawn dining room, she murmured of awnings and russet calf oxfords, she asked Giles to
specify fringed damask and informed him that Mrs. Heaney
required a new ice cream mould. Hetty passed a wet cloth over
Lilian's brow, made gentle shushing sounds. Lilian stared at
the ceiling and imagined Hetty to be her seamstress. She spoke
in a hoarse undertone, describing clothes for Ellen: dresses,
coats, hats, nightgowns. She spoke particularly of eyelet lace
on the cuffs of puffed sleeves. The past bent, or rather Lilian
travelled towards it, as her life described a circle. The little girl
she had not spoken of for twenty-seven years came towards

her, gradually, as from a great distance. "Hello, darling," she said tenderly to Sam. Should he pretend to be Ellen? He glanced at Giles or Hetty, who in turn gazed anxiously at Lilian. It didn't matter. She closed her eyes; her hand fell on her breast. The big house was quiet. Only Lilian's cook remained. Like the summer season, the house came to a slow ripening, its momentum halted. Its windows stood open. It gathered the scent of goldenrod and wild asters. The clocks ticked in a space of warm wind and footsteps. Spoons clinked on trays. Hetty and Giles conferred downstairs, and Sam was told to play quietly, on his own side of the driveway. Lilian, within her burrow, travelled steadily backwards, passing Ellen in time, speaking to her own mother of doves and kittens, of writing paper (pink, please), until her face smoothed and she became quiet, as if reaching the safe place, here, in this bed, where she had started.

For the next twelve years, Giles' sister, Katherine, who inherited the house, came to Shepton in July, while Giles and Hetty and their boys continued to spend their summers at Sunny Hill. Then the boys finished high school and went to college. The war began. All three boys enlisted, all were overseas at the same time. All three miraculously returned.

Katherine died in 1945, childless, widowed. Shepton passed on to Giles, and then the big house across the driveway from Sunny Hill sat shuttered, no longer used by anyone. Shadowed by maple trees, biding its time through the seasons, it was empty of people but filled with their history. Shallow closets stuffed with clothes so old they'd become costumes, their hooks rusty, their stitches brown. All the antiquated tools—looms, butter churns, flatirons, washboards—that drifted, like floating detritus, up into the attic. Photograph albums, croquet sets, wicker baby carriages, leghorn hats. Agricultural journals, leather-bound cameras, feather dusters. Letters. The *voices* of letters. (*I did remember to tell Ann to sprinkle some black pepper on the flannels. You do not know how much I wish you were here to help us eat cherries.*) Family heartaches, fears, hopes. Beneath the leaf-drifted angles of the roof lay a family's history, layer upon layer, piled haphazardly like the board games beneath the stairs, the slipping piles of letters in the attic, the scratchy woollen blankets in the cupboards.

Kate feels the cold stone of the step penetrating her gardening overalls as she props her elbows on her knees and sits gazing at her house. She thinks of her own attic. How there is nothing she can bear to throw away. She realizes that Katherine's death put Hetty and Giles in exactly the same place of irresolution that she finds herself in at this moment. She swivels on the step to stare up at Tom's studio. When was the last time she went in there? She feels, again, the cresting of two waves in her mind. An impulse to open up Tom's studio rises bravely and encounters the fear of what she may feel when she does. She gets to her feet, pauses and then walks across the vegetable garden, where the brick path is tipped on as-yet unthawed ice spears and a few abandoned cabbages still stand on their stalks, shrivelled as shrunken heads. She reaches under the eaves for the key and unlocks the door.

Nothing has moved since last time she was here; it's chill as an ice cave, and the redolence of oil paints still possesses the air. There's a loft at one end. Once, it was filled with finished canvasses, but his dealer came and took them all. Light falls from three skylights in the north-sloping ceiling. Beneath the skylights is an empty easel. Tom's absence is signified by the neatness of his work table: his brushes stand in glass jars pushed against the wall; next to them an orderly row of square cans—linseed oil, mineral spirits. A deep drawer is partway open, and Kate can see the glint of paint tubes. A window faces west, over the creek. There's his desk, its pigeonholes filled with stones, rusty iron spikes and hinges, odd bits of wood. On its top, a horse skull. There's his old office chair with its brass rollers. She pulls back the chair, sits in it. She grips the edge of the desk with her fingertips, rolls the chair forward, reaches with both arms as if she will embrace the desk, and lays her cheek on its scratched wood. Her fingers touch a wooden elephant. Liam, when he was five years old, picked it out for Tom. It's crudely carved, with deep ridges indicating rough skin. She touches the tusks, remembers Liam's little fingers roaming the tiny animal. It was, she remembers, for Tom's birthday.

She sits up, rolls the chair around to face the open door. It frames the pearly sky, where wind-blown clouds stretch and dissolve. Earthy air teases the room's cold like a fox snuffling a mouse hole.

There were so many places like this at Shepton. Rooms, closets, attics, lofts, sheds: places whose dusty air held the smell of decay, jumbled with things kept because once-loved hands had held them. Places filled with things whose only function was as reminders of vanished lives. Places filled with things that should connect you with the dead, but did not.

Or did they? Do they? Kate holds the wooden elephant in her lap. Oddly, Tom's spirit seems to be less in this room than it is elsewhere. She felt him more strongly on the river, when she remembered canoeing over the submerged island. He rises in unexpected places, untriggered by his possessions. *This elephant should be on my desk. Tom's things should be given to young artists, their history described as they are handed over. The horse skull should be set beneath a tree, deep in the woods—I will go visit it and see how moss creeps into its eye sockets.*

She feels an impulse to do these things immediately. Gather the paint brushes, the elephant, the skull. Empty the room. Sweep it. Shout at the past. *Leave me. Leave me.*

She wrestles the window open. The sound of wind and birdsong is so vibrant now, it seems as if it's always been part of the room, running along the paint-spattered plywood floor, dancing on dusty shelves. She goes to the door; a moonflower vine hangs across the opening, and she gathers it in both hands, tugging gently, disengaging the dead vines from the trellis. She stands, half-out, half-in, hands filled with crunchy vines, and examines the studio. It's big enough to be made into a studio apartment. Or a guest cottage. *Bed and breakfast?* Her mind glances, sheers off this thought, returns. *People would enjoy my gardens . . . homemade muffins, tea . . . served up here . . . a double bed? Paint the floor green? Imagine lying here, on vacation, listening to the river, the birds. Gazing out this door at tomatoes ripening, Mr. Winkles in the zinnias.* She dismisses this idea, decides she won't do much more for now than gather everything of Tom's and take it down to the house. Dust and mop. Open these windows on warm days, let the air eddy through like cleansing breath. Come and sit here occasionally. Wait to see what's going to happen next between these walls, within this air. Wonder who else might someday stand with her and watch the osprey, talons spread, making a precise descent into the treetop nest where the beaks of clamouring babies are hidden behind sticks.

She goes out, leaving the door and window wide open. She sits again on the uppermost stone step. It's almost warm. She shoves her denim jacket up so her forearms can feel the air. She'll have to call the boy next week, see if she can engage him again this summer. His first task will be to remove these planters that are now held together only by the frost in their frozen soil. Next week they'll be lying in shards. She looks down at her grey wood-shingled house with its red trim. Her eyes skip past it to the shine of the river through the trees. She sees herself, bent over the pool of light on Tom's table, studying the medical encyclopedia; or curled in the soft chair, holding her grandfather's diary to her heart; or clutching a letter in her hand and weeping for Jonnie. Winter's thread thins, severs. And now she has suddenly woken to the sleek light of the present, and her vision is set within a larger context. *It's as if I have a larger landscape inside myself within which my life finds its place.* The past is reconfigured. She has not lost her own version of it, but rather it is augmented. She remembers the dream of last fall, when one side of Shepton was part of time's continuum and the other was dry as an abandoned wasp's nest. How bereft she'd felt when she woke. Was the dark, crumbling side of the house the shape of longing? The colour of nostalgia? The crumbling texture of hidden grief?

She goes back down the stone steps, pushes the wheelbarrow through the opening in the tall lilac hedge. She'll uncover what they've always called "the secret garden." It's a small plot of land that came with the house. Once, it held a horse barn. Kate and Tom never did anything to it except encourage the spread of forget-me-nots and plant heritage tulip bulbs every fall. In May it's a sea of blue supporting a flotilla of tulips with their fleshy, sun-trapping petals: pink, apricot, yellow, ivory. There's a bench, a bird bath. Through the branches of the lilacs she can glimpse the street going up the hill, but hardly anyone passes. Sun spins down and then radiates back. Kate rattles her wheelbarrow into this quiet, windless place, where she can hear an early robin's liquid *cheerio cheer-up.* She takes off her jacket, begins lifting mulch.

The tulip names drift into her mind as the stocky red leaves emerge, shaped like pony's ears: 'Demeter,' 'Van der Neer,' 'Peach Blossom.' Oh, the little 'Ducs.' And 'Preludium,' 'Prince of Austria,' 'Kiezerskroon.' *If I don't empty Tom's studio, I'll be coveting his soul, hoarding his spirit. And then it will turn pale and shrivel, as these tulips would, were*

I not to uncover them. Yet to what lengths, she wonders, should she take this idea of emptying, disarranging? Does it mean that Christy's children, should she have any, will have no musty treasures to discover, no crisp and faded flowers pressed between the pages of mildewed books to crumble, deliciously, within their fingers? How can she stretch loose from the shape of her life as it was and at the same time preserve the shell she's shed?

Somehow, she thinks, kneeling to tease with her fingertips a fat shoot from a maple leaf collar, it has something to do with not thinking of the past as refuge. For it was when she truly understood that she would never again be held within the circle of Tom's arms that she began to long for Shepton. *Do we all dream of places unbound by beginnings and endings, drifting in childhood's eternal present, where nothing, it seems, will ever change?* Yet how natural it would have seemed to her as a child that such a world could exist, when Shepton's clocks had not stopped ticking, its closets not been emptied, its wallpaper not been changed for a hundred and fifty years. Her father had told her the house felt as lifeless as a museum to his generation. But he and his brothers had not known Shepton as the Kingdom of Heaven: a place that floated in its sea of maples, its floorboards creaking in apple-sweet winds, its clocks ticking steady as the heartbeats of the grandparents whose love made no corner of the place, except the beehives and the windmill, inaccessible or dangerous. For Kate's father, it was merely a house fraught with the necessity of untouchable preservation and inhabited by a woman in hiding.

Kate leans and gathers a nearly rootless scrap of chickweed. *Oh Tom. If you could see these tulips.* She leans on her fork, feeling the sun between her shoulder blades. *Where is he? Where are they all, the vanished people?* The forget-me-nots are still a tangle of last year's stems, their new growth not apparent, but the area is alive with furled red tulip shoots, freed from the insulating darkness and thrusting towards light. She lifts another forkful of straw. *Never mind all that I've learned about my grandparents' lives. The place as I remember it was my own truth. That is how it was to me; that is truly how I knew it. Here inside me it will always be.* She hasn't yet decided whether she will perpetuate or destroy her own closets of memory-laden objects, but she feels a shift inside herself, as if she's come to terms with longing and feels how it has ripened into a feeling closer to love than loss.

17. Quaco Head

THEY ARRIVE AT THE BEACH LATER THAN PLANNED, BUT Gregory says it won't matter, the tide is still dead-high and has only just started to turn. Kate climbs out of the car. She walks over the asphalt and in two steps is standing on the slippery stones of the beach. Just to her right, so close she feels as if she's standing in its yard, is a house whose white, wind-scoured clapboards gleam with a harsh brilliance. Like the light-polished beach rocks, the house seems an element of the sea's indifference. It has no garden, only a wind-twisted lilac bush. A Canadian flag snaps on a white pole; spotless window glass reflects the sky. The bay is encircled with cliffs. Far away, indistinct as dream or myth, is the scrawl of Nova Scotia.

They carry Gregory's gear down to the waterline. On the empty beach it makes a bright jumble, like toys in a sandbox. Yellow kayak, red paddle, blue life jacket, plastic water bottle, pump. Several shiny new Drybags. Gregory is anxious to be off. Every wave hisses up less far than the previous one; within ten minutes, there's a scalloped trail of foam-spittled seaweed that the waves no longer reach. Gregory winces in his neoprene booties; he flails like an eccentric ballerina, trying to pull his spray skirt up over the layers that he described to Kate, on the drive, with satisfaction: black wet suit ("sleeveless top and legs, I got the farmer-John style for freedom of movement"), layers of polyester and fleece, a yellow Gore-Tex paddling jacket with rubberized neck and cuffs. Kate squats with her hands between her knees. Wind snatches the hood of her windbreaker, presses it against her head. There's not another soul on the beach on this Saturday morning. It's only late April. The sun is deceiving—the wind carries the season's truth. It has strengthened, blows steadily onshore.

"Gregory," she calls. "I don't like this wind."

He flaps a hand dismissively. Gregory, who lived by the bay all those years ago. Not to worry, he knows wind, he knows tides. "Kate, could you help?"

She secures his water bottle and pump beneath the kayak's deck lines, shoves gear into the front hatch. Gregory snaps the buckles of his lifejacket, draws the straps tight. He works his brandy flask into its pocket. Kate straightens, steps back. For the first time, he reminds her of Tom, who, in his twenties, canoed on whitewater rivers. Gregory's toque covers his eyebrows, and she wants to adjust it for him, even gently. He's looking down, patting himself, checking. His anxiety is balanced by excitement, and Kate respects this masculine ritual, its preoccupied self-absorption, the dawning and necessary aloneness of self-induced peril.

He grins, then. "Okay! I'm ready."

She grins back. "Okay!"

The wind, as she predicted, says all that they might, or might not; it casts away particulars and prises from them an odd exhilaration that comes from the sea's heave and sigh, from the earth's turning and the moon's pull.

"Damn this!" The wind is so strong he shouts. He's trying to work the spray skirt around the cowling. The back snaps loose just as he secures the front. Kate helps. At the last minute, she pulls his toque up over his eyebrows, gives his head a quick pat. Finally he's shut in, one with his boat, buoyant as a water beetle. She shoves the kayak; he begins to paddle as soon as the bow enters the water. She feels the sudden lightness as the boat is water-borne, and then he's gone, bobbing, falling, digging the water with his paddle, instantly small beneath the sky.

She stands on the beach and watches until the rhythmic rise and fall of bow and stern is no longer apparent, until he's a moving speck on the sea's surface, his movement only discernibly human because of its unwavering purpose, its persistence.

The road down the coast to the little beach has deteriorated. The ruts are so deep she doesn't dare drive in them but wrenches the wheel violently, attempting to drive on the verge and the ridge between the ruts. Sometimes the car slides off, drops into the muddy troughs. She floors the accelerator, races through brown puddles whose depth she can't gauge. *No, this is far enough.* Best quit before she's stuck. She turns off the engine. Fortunately, everything they'll need is in a backpack. The Portuguese bread, smoked Gouda, salami, apples. A Thermos of coffee. Mustard. Smoked herring. Newspaper and matches to start a fire. She even packed two pairs of heavy wool socks and mittens. *He'll be cold.*

She trudges down the road. She's managed to drive in fairly far; she can hear the hollow wash of surf to her left. The air is icy, damp, smells of moss and the wet bark of fir trees, of snow that lingers in hollows, of the faint astringency of salt air. Old man's beard threads the tips of dead spruce. Buds are still furled tight; spring comes later by the coast, she thinks, than it does in the river valley. Just then, belying her observation, she steps into a patch of granular snow and sees snow fleas freckling the surface like animate pepper. She hears the call of a white-throated sparrow: *weet, sweet, Canada, Canada, Cana*—. Wind whisks up the phrase's ending, folds it into the rising roar as branches twist and groan, needles slither against one another. The track doubles back, cuts down between steep banks. Now she's walking in a stream bed; water trickles steadily, and she steps carefully from rock to rock. At the bottom, the walls fall away and the ground is firm underfoot. As she walks forward, she feels a familiar sense of her own diminishment beneath the sea-sky. Ahead of her is the shingle where they once put their tents. To her right, a river emerges from a deep cut in the steep hills. The hills tower over the valley, their dark bulk dwarfing the little cove. Spruce trees on the ridges bend in the wind, slash the sky.

Down by the beach are a few firepits filled with charred driftwood and beer cans, circled by ATV tracks. Black sand and seaweed-shaggy rocks are exposed by the dropping tide. The beach is a slope of round, egg-smooth rocks rising into the shingle, in whose gravelly soil grows a winter tapestry: yellow grasses with sleek, dried awns; red-barked rugosa roses with shrivelled hips; the lavender-grey remnants of beach peas. Cliffs jut into the sea, curving round the north end of the cove, and there's a massive free-standing rock with a keyhole opening that she and Tom once paddled through in a canoe.

There's no sign of Gregory. Kate shifts her pack on her shoulders, looks at the sky. Clouds have been chased up the bay by a vigorous southwest wind. It's noticeably colder.

She remembers a sheltered place where they camped when there was wind. It's behind an outcropping of rock and faces the hills rather than the sea. The kids would complain. "Well, put your tents anywhere," one of the parents would say: she, or Tom, or Gregory, or Karen. All night the grownups would hear the gun-crack snapping of taut nylon coming from the kids' exposed site. Oh, but they'd come back here, Kate thinks, squatting with an armload of driftwood, as soon as they smelled supper. Sausages in a frying pan. Potatoes breaking up in boiling water, the sticky steam. And shadows leapt on the rock, sparks streamed into the black sky, vanishing like shooting stars, and the pound and hiss of surf made them . . . what? She crumples balls of paper, wedges them into the triangle she's made of driftwood smooth as bone. Made them feel as if they had a single mind between them, four adults, four children; as if they'd become part of the same body with its beating heart, its wordless simplicity. *I'll tell him.* She shields a match, strikes it, touches the paper. *I'll tell him I do remember. I'll tell him I remember Jerome, when he was very small, sitting in his dad's lap with his little feet side by side, sticking straight up. I'll tell him I remember how Jerome would streak down to the water before any of the other kids, plunge straight in.*

She glances at her watch. Twelve-thirty. She rummages in the pack, gets out the Thermos of coffee. She sits on a chunk of porous, square-sided timber and pokes the fire with a stick. Sips scalding coffee. *So. What else shall we say? In memorial.* She is fortunate, she realizes now, to have held Tom, in the kitchen, long after he was dead. Liam and Christy did not see him until his body had been taken to the funeral parlour. They had a private viewing; she insisted the children see him when his spirit, she felt, had not quite abandoned its shell. Liam drew from his pocket a small man he'd carved, lifted one of Tom's inert hands, slipped the little man beneath his palm. Christy tucked a piece of paper folded to the size of a matchbook into his pocket. Kate observed these acts with amazement. In the presence of Tom's body, they had not cried but were overwhelmed, silenced. As, Kate thinks suddenly, they were once held, here, by the voice of the sea; stilled by a vast presence. But afterwards, when death became less a presence than an emptiness, then the weeping began, and the grief, like an incurable disease. So here, now, Gregory tries to experience the overwhelming truth of his son's death.

One o'clock. Kate stands, walks down over the slippery seaweed, the draining ocean floor. One-fifteen. A spattering rain begins. She pulls her hood over her head, stands at the sea's edge with her hands tucked beneath her arms.

Two o'clock. Maybe he turned back. Maybe he's waiting furiously, back at the beach. No, he'd go up to that restaurant. Have a beer. What if she leaves and he comes, though? What if he had to pull in to some cove on the way down? What if the kayak sprang a leak and he figured out some way to repair it and he's just set off again and ten minutes later he'll paddle around the point to find her gone? Well, then, he'll have to wait. He'll have the fire; she'll build it up, try to be sure there'll be coals. No, wait, he wouldn't do that. He'd see the fire and know she'd been here, realize she'd started back. He'd leave the kayak and start walking. Her fingers are freezing cold. Then she imagines what *his* hands must feel like. Yes, but not if he's happily having a beer, waiting for her. Which is the most likely scenario. *Okay,* she tells herself. *Put on those mittens you brought for him. Eat. I'm worried. I'm . . . No, eat! Get out a slab of bread and cheese, eat as you go.*

By the time she reaches the car, it's almost three. It's become the worst kind of April day, a flat, grey light equalizing trees, sky, the green station wagon, mud. The cold rain, wind-flung, is sharp as the points of icicles. *No, you will not get stuck; don't think it or you will.* Her neck aches, twisted, her arm clings to the passenger seat. The car slides down into the ruts; she accelerates, turns the wheel sharply, senses her mistake, jerks it back in time to avoid a tree. *God. There's a turning place, might be soft, soggy moss. Risk it. Okay. Forward now.*

She reaches the paved road and drives as fast as she dares back along the coast. The road is set too far back from the cliffs to see the ocean, although she glances frequently in its direction. She joins the main road, speeds past the gas station, the church, the fire hall, down the village street, past the tiny post office, Pearson's Groceries with its stamped-tin ceiling, the special care home. There's the turn. The dead-end street. *Stop at the restaurant at the corner and see if he's there? No, quick, go to the beach.* She stops the car where they parked hours earlier.

There's no kayak.

She calls 911 from the restaurant. It's a fishing community. Two men at the bar listen intently, hands frozen on their glasses. One waitress sets down a tray, the other stops halfway through the swinging door to the kitchen. A white-haired woman lays her knife and fork on her plate, slides her hand over her mouth. Kate's words violate the smell of French fries and coffee, the slices of lemon meringue pie in a cooler, the steamy windows. Voices supply her with answers. "Beach Street." "Fundy Family Restaurant."

Five minutes later, she's sitting in the front seat of an RCMP cruiser. The officer shuts her door, comes around and settles himself behind the wheel.

"My name is Corporal Merrick." He removes his hat, sets it between the seats. He has a high forehead, a short grey moustache. He holds her gaze. His eyes are blue. They're steady, neither cold nor unkind, but trained.

The engine is idling; the windshield wipers are on intermittent. He checks his watch, angles a clipboard on the console, writes the date and time on a statement pad. There's a gold crest on the shoulder of his blue jacket, which is zipped halfway down—she can see the vest that makes him bulky, unapproachable. Broad yellow stripe on his pants. Pistol in gleaming black-leather holster. A bunch of keys glints like coins. Shotgun on a rack over his head. The back seat seems like another room, separated by bulletproof glass. There's an apple-shaped air freshener hanging from the glove compartment. It turns in the hot air rising from the floor.

"Your name?"

"Kate Harding."

"His?"

"Gregory Stiller."

"Husband?"

"No, no, just a friend. Old acquaintance."

"Okay. Tell me the situation."

She describes their plan, Gregory's departure. Tells the officer how long they expected the trip to take, how long she waited at the beach. Her decision to come back to see if Gregory might have returned and been waiting for her at the restaurant.

He remains silent throughout her explanation, takes notes. Then he nods. "Does he have any medical conditions? Heart problems? Diabetes? Is he on any medication?"

"I don't know. I don't think so. I don't really know him very well."

"Did he have any emergency supplies? Food? Water?"

"He had water. No food. Oh. He had a flask of brandy."

He looks up sharply. "Was it full?"

"Yes."

"Is he a heavy drinker?"

"Ah, well. Relatively. Yes."

"Is he likely to drink when he's out there?"

"Possibly."

"Was he wearing a PFD? Can he swim?"

"Yes, he had a new lifejacket. He can swim."

"How old is he?"

"About fifty-five. He's not in great shape."

"How well does he know the area?"

"Years ago he lived up the coast, up by Alma. He knew that area. I don't think he knows this stretch of coast particularly well. I'm sure he's never been out around the point in a boat."

"Is he an experienced kayaker?"

"No. He just took a course this winter. It's a rented boat."

He asks for a full description of the boat. What Gregory's wearing. "Does he have any kind of distress signal? VHF radio? Cell phone? Flares?"

"I—no, I don't think so."

"Is he likely to panic?"

Her heart begins to pound heavily. She takes a deep breath. She tries to picture Gregory as they knew him, she and Tom. "Oh God. My husband could answer that question. He knew Gregory. I'm sorry, I just wish—no, I don't know. Well, yes. Yes, I think he would panic."

"What can you tell me about his mental state?"

She takes another deep breath. Corporal Merrick lays his hand flat on the pad. The pen stands between two fingers, does not tremble. He studies her, and she feels that she is not Kate any more, but a suspect.

"How specific should I—I mean, I don't know where to start."

He intervenes rapidly. "Marital problems?"

"He's divorced. His ex-wife lives in Ontario."

"Suicidal?"

"His son committed suicide out west. Today was, in his mind, a sort of pilgrimage. He thought he might sense his son's spirit here. In the bay. Years ago our families, mine and his, were close. Years ago. We used to camp down at the little beach. We were going to meet at that little beach to . . ."

It sounds improbable. Pagan. Ludicrous. She presses her hands over her eyes.

He's reaching for his mike. The car fills with other voices. He stares out the rain-blurred windshield as he speaks. "Search and Rescue. Fundy Coast. Single kayak left St. Martin's at eleven o'clock headed towards Quaco Light. Man, fifty-five."

There's sand on her hiking boots. She smells of woodsmoke. Her skin is stretched and salty, the way it always feels after a day at the beach. Mr. Winkles was in the kitchen when she left. "Don't you want to go out?" she'd asked him. No, he didn't, and since she'd expected to be back by late afternoon she left him. She looks out her window. Just there, at the end of the street, is the beach.

He must have put into a cove. If he's neither here nor at the other end, it is the only answer. She never should have dialled 911. He's sitting on some wet sand, waiting for the tide to be low enough so he can walk on down the coast, scramble over the slippery bladderwrack until he arrives at the beach.

Now Corporal Merrick is talking into a cell phone. The radio emits voices. She imagines them as black fish flickering somewhere over her head.

"Don't you think—" she says.

"Hold on just a minute," he says into the phone.

"He must have put into a cove. It occurs to me that he's just waiting for the tide to be low enough so he can walk out."

It's not a smile, but a brief change in the set of his lips. He's seeing not her, but her fear. He'll know how to deal with it. He nods briefly, raises his finger to her. He finishes his conversation.

"Where's your car?"

She points.

"Get anything you want from it, all right? I'm going to take you to the fire hall. We'll be setting up a rescue coordinating centre. Let's hope you're right about that cove."

Stepping out of the cruiser, she crouches involuntarily. The rain has strengthened; it's mixed with salt spray. She hauls open her car door. Somewhere, a flag is clanking against a pole. She hears the boom of the foghorn off Quaco Point. How could they be so wrong about the weather, those forecasters? She's breathless when she gets back in next to the officer.

They turn out of the parking lot. He tells her what has been set in motion. Coast Guard. Search and Rescue. Helicopter on its way from Fredericton. RCMP Zodiac beating its way over Reversing Falls, coming up the coast from Saint John. Local fishermen contacted, boats going out immediately. Victim Services organization setting up in a room over the fire station. They'll bring blankets, coffee, doughnuts, sandwiches. She'll be fine there. Someone will be with her at all times. He'll be her main contact person. Call him Wayne. She feels a shift in his attitude, sees how he's begun to reassure her. About herself, her own comfort. The fact that she will be cared for. In the face of certain tragedy.

There's a person crossing the street, walking sideways to the rain in an attempt to shield a parcel. There's the Anglican church, chalk pink, with its wind-stunted maples. Wrought-iron railings, rain glistening as it worms down the spiralled rungs.

Among the coldest waters in the world. The tide was going out. The wind rising. Wind opposed to current. She wants to ask the corporal what it must have been like at the point, but can't open her mouth around the words.

It's a large room used for meetings. There's a faded photograph of the queen at one end. There are washrooms, a coat rack, stacks of metal-legged chairs with blue-fabric seats. Tile floor. Acoustic-tile ceiling. The building is on the slope of a hill. At the top of the hill is a playground where the helicopter lands. At this end of the bay, a salt marsh separates the village from a curving line of sand. As long as the light lasts, Kate can stand by the windows and see the sea, a silver band gleaming beneath the dark sky.

She phones May, asks her to feed Mr. Winkles. She leaves a message on Christy's answering machine: "Hi, sweetie. Don't worry if you don't find me at home. I'm down in St. Martin's. Gregory may have had an accident in his kayak. I'm waiting here with the police. They're out searching for him. I'm absolutely fine, don't worry. I'll call as soon as—I can. Love you." She writes down the names of people who should be contacted if the worst should happen; all she can think of is the newspaper and Gregory's daughter, Jane.

Night falls. Now, besides Gregory, his rescuers are also at risk. Women bring fish chowder, white rolls, butter, coleslaw. Kate eats with a round plastic spoon. Pepper floats on the buttery milk. A portable radio monitors the search-and-rescue frequency. It sits on a table next to the coffee machine. The room remains brightly lit.

At midnight, Kate sees the revolving lights of several cruisers parked out front. The boats and helicopter are searching down the coast now, towards Saint John. Gear from lost boats has been known to wash as far down the bay as Grand Manan. Women whose men are out all night have come in to confer with the police officers, listen to the radio. Everyone operates from the same premise—hope becomes energy. Some of the women come and sit beside her. They speak the long-evolved language of women waiting at the doors of despair. This, they tell her, is Evelyn's chowder. She is the best chowder-maker in town. They went out after her husband. In 1984. He was found—cold, adrift, perfectly fine. They rise, pat her arms. Someone hands her a napkin wrapped around a doughnut. She can feel the sugar through the paper, like sand. *Thanks.*

No one knows at this point what is real. They'll net either tragedy or joy. They can't let themselves imagine either outcome.

Kate sits on the floor, makes a pillow with her pack, curls on her side and pulls a blanket over herself. She stares at boots, table legs, listens to the static-blurred voices. "Pretty rough seas. No sign of anything out around the rocks here." "No sign." "Circling Roger's Head. No sign of anything." Black sleep. White acoustic tiles. She wipes sleep-drool from the corner of her mouth. She should sit. Should attend. It's Gregory's nightmare. She's inside it. No future without a known past. No present without an imagined future. So he drinks. And makes up a past. And takes her with him. She should have said no. She should have told him it was stupid, foolish, crazy. She should have taken the flask from his hand.

Corporal Merrick is squatting by her side. It's early morning. His hand is on her shoulder. She sits up abruptly. The room smells of coffee. The radio is silent. Someone is leaving the room. She senses their gentleness.

"He's been found, Kate."

"Where?" It's obvious. What he's telling her.

"Wedged in between some rocks. Not far down the coast from the little beach. Kayak washed up farther down."

She says nothing. He's still squatting, half-kneeling. His arm rests on his bent leg, his hand hangs loose. The pistol. The bunch of keys. Same bulky vest, neat collar. Blue eyes, now assessing and kind. "He must have flipped off the point. There's a terrible current there, and the boys tell me there were standing waves six feet high. He didn't have a chance."

Gregory is dead.

"I'm afraid you're going to have to identify the body. I'll come with you."

"Yes," she says. My God. There's the backpack. With the kippered herrings. And the Portuguese bread that Gregory bought in Saint John yesterday morning. She stands. Corporal Merrick steadies her. She feels his solid arm under her hand. She's dizzy.

"Sit," he says. He pours her a cup of coffee. "Take your time," he adds, and goes to the window. He stands with his hands clasped behind his back, looking out at the bay.

The sun is rising over the cliffs. Wavelets ripple over the glistening mud flats exposed by low tide. There's no wind. The roofs of the town absorb the morning light—asphalt shingles glitter, steel roofs are bright as laundered sheets. No one, yet, has come to retrieve the coffee pot, the radio, the blankets, the chowder-stained bowls. Kate thinks of last night's women and hopes they are in bed, curled close to their men. Sun warms her cheek. She sips the strong, sour coffee. Where is he? He'll be wearing the brand-new paddling jacket. Sand in his blond eyelashes. Bruises, white skin. His most intimate privacy, exposed. She stands abruptly. "Okay, let's go." She hears her own curtness. Better to see what is real rather than the horror she imagines.

18. Dovetail Joints

IS THERE ANYONE IN THIS TOWN, KATE THINKS, WHO MAY doesn't know, any committee she hasn't served on, any challenge she hasn't met?

Two weeks after Gregory's death, May and Kate are at a - fund-raising flea market in the old train station. It's a long room whose windows overlook the tracks. Trains no longer stop, but still pound past, whistles blowing. Cub scouts sell ice cream cones on the station's veranda, although after the hot days of the first of the month, the weather has reverted to normal April temperatures. It's cool, windy. The lawns are greening, daffodils shoot up close to foundations, but the tree buds have remained prudently closed, and wind chases last winter's sand along side streets.

"Oh, for heaven's sake, Kate. Look at this! Now, don't you wish you had grandchildren?" May plucks a red corduroy jumper from a table.

"Look! Here, this matches." Kate holds up a T-shirt with strawberries on the collar.

The woman behind the table laughs at their excitement. "A dollar fifty."

"Let's see if we can find a sun hat. They have to wear sun hats these days, you know. I put my children in sun hats, but it was like wearing hats to church. You just did it—you weren't worried about skin cancer. Didn't know a thing about it."

They move to another table. People at flea markets, Kate thinks, are like chickens. They stop, peck, and are easily distracted, lured by a formless lust. For the first time in months, she wants to buy something for herself. Anything. A surprising treasure. Something to put on her kitchen table that will be a touchstone, reminding her of the power of this simple belief: that surprises can be concealed within the ordinary.

Boxes of vinyl records. Hinged Mason jars filled with marbles. Hockey cards. Old books. Teacups commemorating Charles and Di's wedding, some anniversary of the queen and Prince Philip. Baskets of mismatched cutlery. Hand-knit socks. A plastic darning egg.

"Isn't this fun?" May's eyes glance past the egg; her mind is on something else even as she asks the question.

"Actually, yes, this is wonderful. I love this. This is the first time I've ever come. I've always avoided flea markets. Tom hated them. He said if we ever came to one, we should be sitting behind a table getting rid of our own junk, not accumulating more."

"Well, of course. Everyone thinks that. But you just never know what you might find. And better yet, who you might meet."

People stop Kate in the street to express their sympathy for the ordeal she's been through. No one is intimidated by her loss as they were after Tom's death. Papers, both provincial and national, have reported the incident widely. "Well-known Publisher Dies in Boating Accident." Kate is named as a friend, her peripheral relationship to the deceased has been made clear. People want to tell Kate of the raging currents they've witnessed off Quaco Light. They want to describe disasters they've heard of or experienced—the man whose body was never found although the rangers scoured the beaches for three months; nights spent on rocky outcroppings when people were cut off by tides; the teenagers licked from slippery rocks by a single rogue wave; the couple killed when a cliff path crumbled beneath their feet. Hypothermia. Hurricanes. The transport truck that rolled in the hold of the Grand Manan ferry. Pleasure boats lost in fog and run down by tankers in the shipping lanes. Everyone talks about the water's icy temperature. How many minutes a person might live, once in its grip. *Ten minutes*. It's as if Gregory's act has confirmed both desire and dread. No one swims in the bay. Sailing boats are rarely seen. It is a place whose treachery is legendary, whose wild beauty is beloved. The bay is embraced and avoided, like a person who cannot be entirely known.

A wooden box. Dovetail joints. Kate picks it up, slowly swings the top back on its hinges. Inside, crunchy shreds of linen cling to one side. The box is stained as if it once held ink pens. She closes the box, runs her finger over the keyhole.

"I'm afraid there's no key." A ruddy-faced gentleman in his seventies. He wears a red sweater vest, a plaid necktie.

"I won't want a key," she says. Seven dollars. She reaches for her small leather bag, slung over her shoulder. Hands him a five-dollar bill and a two-dollar coin. "I'm not going to keep anything in it."

"No?" He's disappointed.

"No. It's enough. Just by itself."

He smiles, comprehending. He runs his finger over the wood. "Well, yes, it's a nice little box. It's been around. Many owners. Like me!"

Kate smiles at the man. She feels gentler these days, as if diffused by shock. Gregory's body was taken to a funeral parlour in Saint John. Then his ashes sent on to Ontario, where his remaining family held a funeral. Gregory's mother, his brother and his sister. Their families. His daughter, Jane, accompanied by her mother. A few family friends. Janie told Kate about it over the phone. They have spoken several times. Early next month she'll be down to pack up Gregory's belongings. Kate has invited her to stay while she does this.

Who will grieve for Gregory? Kate wonders. Well, Janie, of course. And his elderly mother. A daughter and a mother. Neither of whom Gregory communicated with.

Kate does not feel leaden, as she did after Tom died; her indecisiveness has changed character. She's feels, rather, a peculiar fragility, like thistledown, seed fluff, anything poised and about to become disengaged, liable to winds, unable to control its destiny. She feels light-filled, weightless, unstable. She is on the verge of tears most of the time. She's fraught, excited. She feels about life as she feels about this box. There it was, the box—the treasure she sensed she would find, quiet and plain amidst the jumble. "I'm so sorry. It must have been awful for you," she hears as she scans library cards in the computer and hands people their books, as she pushes her cart in the aisles of the supermarket or stands waiting in the post office queue. "Yes," she says. "It was terrible." Then they tell her their own stories. Dare to ask her what happened. Put a hand on her upper arm. "We didn't know you knew him," they say.

May was waiting at her house when she returned that morning. Kate was too tired to drive safely, and so Corporal Merrick drove her in his car while another officer followed, driving Kate's car. They came up the stone path with her, carrying her pack. May stood in the door. She took Kate's pack, ran a tub, made her a drink of hot water, lemons, honey and rum, filled a hot water bottle and put it in Kate's bed. When Kate woke, late that afternoon, the house smelled of roast chicken and potatoes. They drank some wine. May, with dextrous questions, helped Kate retrieve one detail after another. *Let's set it down right now. This is the plain truth.*

It would take too much energy to tell the man that this is what she's going to keep in the wooden box. Open it and see that there's nothing there. The past is known, but gone.

She pushes the door open. Nothing has changed since she went out this morning. Sometimes Tom would have a fit of domesticity. She'd come back from a walk to find the kitchen sink scoured; the surface of the wood stove gleaming from vegetable oil, rubbed on with waxed paper; the black and red floor tiles swept and mopped. A sense of renewal and peace. And no sign of Tom. He did it for his own pleasure. His short, strong hands scrubbed a sink as methodically as he sanded wood or sketched vague shapes on canvas. He stopped to smooth or squint. Reached with a finger, stroked a surface. He loved texture, the cast of shadow, the light's bend.

The tablecloth is puckered with candle wax. Crumbs from this morning's toast are gathered along a fold. Noon light has no mystery. It will take Kate's energy (a fire in the stove, whisking away the tablecloth, music on the radio, steam rising from the kettle) to make the room less dreary. She walks to the rocking chair by the window. She hasn't removed her windbreaker. She sits, one hand resting on the wooden box in her lap, the other clutching the chair's broad wooden arm. On a table next to her is a book: *How Green Was My Valley.* She stares at the cover, a photograph of a Welsh village. Stone roofs, stone walls, green pastures, white sheep. The valley that was green, beloved, poisoned by slag heaps.

She feels as if she holds a phrase of poetry balanced in her mind. She clings to it, repeats it over and over so she'll be able to tell Tom. She needs to tell him. About Gregory. About her friends May and Caroline. About Christy, her lovely young self, her generous spirit. Liam. How shocked he was to hear her story. How angry he was with Gregory for presuming to take his mother into danger. About the wooden box she's holding in her lap. No matter what she does, a part of herself is drawing Tom's attention to it. Gathering, plucking, collecting; like picking berries or daisies. Love. She stares at the brown, woody remains of the scarlet runner bean vines that twine the porch trellis. *That was love. This, now, is love. I feel like a teenager. Longing. For my beloved. To see myself in someone's gladness.*

The way the world appears to a person is governed by one's mind. Children see, in wallpaper, leering faces, tigers or mad mouths. Shadows are animate. Observant clocks seem to tick prophecies. Here she sits beneath the same walls, in the same chair. Nothing has changed for thirty years. There's the same pane of glass, scratched with someone's initials. There's the hill, rising beyond the river. The ceiling has always been precisely this high, and her babies lay in baskets on these same tiles. But the room is continuously recast, seen through her mind's filter. Today the house seems different. It seems cluttered, dingy, filled with unnecessary objects. Gregory's death has set a new barrier between this moment and the time that has past. He's reeled her forward into yet another changed present, just as she was getting accustomed to the last one.

She closes her eyes, listens to the April wind. It's eager, boisterous, like a colt in a pasture. It changes course, one minute moaning in the flue and the next prying at the porch, making the trellis scratch and bang. This change in her perception of the house is a change in her perception of herself. She's thinking about Corporal Merrick. His steady eyes, his patient bulk as he looked down at her while she slept. Her old friends the Healeys, who walked up her path carrying an azalea in a clay pot. May, bustling in her kitchen. Her co-workers at the library. People she and Tom had known for years: phone calls, cards, the expressions of wondering sympathy that have touched her for the last two weeks, gently, without obligation, like falling petals. There are two feelings inside her. They're not in opposition, but rather in juxtaposition, like a hard seed and warm soil. Her longing for Tom fills her chest, an actual ache. It's obdurate, dark, swollen. But there's a drift, a sigh. Pulling back through the pebbles of her longing is a sense of urgency, a call to attention. It sets her off-keel. She lists, listening. She feels a peculiar emotion. It feels like yielding. It feels like the desire to sleep, or weep, or sing. She feels as if she's awakened from the long silence that's possessed her since Tom's death. He's gone. He's gone. The box is empty.

What will she do this summer when friends call and ask her to picnics with their families? She will find no solace in solitude, as she did until Gregory's accident. Tears stand in her eyes, make the wind-lashed trees beyond the window stretch and thicken. She was the only one of all of Gregory's small circle to see his body. There, in front of the fire hall. In an ambulance. Constable Merrick drew back the sheet. Someone had crossed Gregory's arms over his chest. His hands were white, puckered. Curled like claws. She'd wanted to press them between hers, straighten the fingers. "All right?" the constable said, holding his respectful pose, the sheet held gently. "It's him?" She'd nodded, struck, for some reason, by a memory of the glimpse she'd had of Gregory's bathroom. The maroon towels, the Japanese brush painting. The sink into which he clipped his fingernails, the mirror where he watched himself smooth his cheeks with his fingers after shaving. Now Kate's pity is far deeper than the reason she agreed to go with him in the first place.

She imagines the small yellow kayak rising over a wave, vanishing into a trough, flipping. He bobs up, buoyed by his life jacket. He flails, trying to swim in his cumbersome layers. How long does he drift, feeling the numbness creeping upward, unable to move his hands or arms or lift his head? Does he call, look for the nearest rocks, make futile efforts to steer his inert body towards them? How long is it before his mind tells him what is going to happen? Is there grace or terror? Does he enter darkness or light?

She leans forward, puts her face in her hands. In her silent house, she listens to the sound of the wind. She hears the thundering boom. Then a diminishing sigh, branches feathering into stillness. In the lull, a robin spirals its spring song into the calm.

Part Five

19. Barberry Pie

"NIGHT, MOM. NIGHT, DAD. SLEEP WELL."

Kate sets down the phone and stands in the kitchen, listening to the sounds of a May night. Even though the air carries the evening damp, she leaves windows propped open with glass jars. The kitchen door stands open; through its screen she can see how the porch railings hold the last of the day's light. The light is both present and remote, sinking into darkness like the swallows who shear over the darkening river. The night air smells of cold earth and spruce needles, rides like a current over softer air that still carries the day's warmth, its smell of sun-crumbled soil and wild cherry blossoms. It lifts papers on Kate's table, makes the cords of overhead lights sway and tick. She hears the dispassionate throb of peepers, the clank of halyards against the mast of a sailboat moored in the river beyond the trees. Trees loom over the lawn, becoming shadows, presences. Night begins, like a new world shaking itself awake.

She is absorbing what her father told her, just now, about how her grandparents died. Granny outlived Grampa Giles and ended her days in a convalescent home. Frail as a winter robin, she sat in a wheelchair with her hands folded in her lap, gazing out the window. It was not the rectangle of grass or strips of stiff autumn annuals that Hetty loved, but the sky. Clouds, the ungovernable and shifting shapes. She sat for hours with her hands in her lap, peacefully watching the towering crucibles of light. On the walls of her room were drawings the grandchildren had brought. She'd caught her lower lip, exclaiming over each one as if she'd never seen anything so special. A tall, red tower-like house. *Oh my, see all the stars!* And the tallest spiky tree. And many cats. *But they don't eat birds, Granny.* Rena was her special nurse, who adored her. Her breath smelled of wintergreen, her dark, freckled hands were slow-moving and warm. She loved to brush Granny's hair. "Fine as a spider's web," she said in her voice that made ordinary words into song. She made a loose night-time braid, a daytime bun as tidy as a dinner roll. Rena and Hetty were sitting side by side when Hetty felt icy cold start at her feet and creep up her legs. She gathered a blanket from her lap. "Rena?" Hetty said. "What is it, Mrs. Thomas?" Hetty held the blanket towards her, lifted it. "Wouldn't you like to have this? It's so cold." Then her eyes widened, and she slumped forward into Rena's arms.

Granny and blankets. When Grampa Giles lay zipped into an oxygen tent after his heart attack, she sat by his side knitting a white wool blanket. It was merino wool, and the blanket was perfectly plain, a garter stitch. Her fingers looped the soft wool, her needles clicked. Reaching the end of a row, she smoothed the growing expanse over her knees with her twisted fingers. She sat tidily, ankles together, and welcomed everyone into the hospital room as if she were in her own home. On the bedside table was a framed photograph of the entire family. Giles lay motionless in a morphine-induced sleep. Occasionally he would groan, or his eyes would fly open in sudden pain. The room was on the tenth floor; its window overlooked the weeping willows and butter-yellow forsythia of a park. April light quivered across the blue walls. Hetty's sons bent over her with concerned faces and then turned to stare at the oxygen tent. Nothing was left of Hetty and Giles' life but their love for one another. The room was dense with it, it stirred like pollen, it thickened sound, the light swirled slowly as if caught in honey. This honed love shone from Hetty like a nimbus. She loved the people who cared for Giles. She loved her children; she loved the baby with eyelashes like fly's legs who would sleep beneath this blanket. She loved the thought of the family gathered around the table on any sunny Sunday, last week or years hence, steam rising from the roast and sun glancing on the carving knife. All day, as her children visited, their faces shocked and distressed, as the lights came on in hospital hallways, as the smell of supper came from jingling trolleys, Hetty sat knitting. That night the nurse unzipped the oxygen tent and motioned to her. Giles was awake. His eyes were open and calm. Hetty bent forward. He smiled his sober smile that hovered at the corners of his mouth. It was the middle of the night, and Hetty had come to help him, and so he began to say something to make her smile. Her eyes lightened; she leaned to hear. His eyes closed as if he had suddenly dropped to sleep. Like the shadow of a hawk passing over the sun, an expression of surprise touched his face and then swept past, leaving peace.

Kate stands in the kitchen, where the diminishment of light makes tables, cabinets, lamps, plates seem part of the night-call of birds, the quiet stirring of leaves. Certain objects—the chrome handles of the wood stove, the stainless steel kettle—shine, as they will long after other things have been absorbed by darkness. She stands with her arms folded across her chest, imagining Granny looping death into love, knitting its approach into her gift for an unborn baby, catching it in the blanket she offers her companion. That day of Giles' death, as she waited for the moment she'd known would come ever since the day she'd laid her hand on his cheek, had she drifted within her image of heaven, in whose shining grasses so many beloved people now walked? *He'll wait for you. Love doesn't die.* Had she heard Dr. Baker's voice, which she came to think of as the sound of God? Kate remembers Granny saying, as simply as telling her the weather forecast, "Remember, dearie. We'll always be together."

Kate goes upstairs and searches the back of her closet until she finds her knitting basket. In it is a crumpled sock pattern and balls of two-ply wool, heather blue and dark grey. She carries the basket down to the kitchen. The river is a sheet of blackened copper shadowed with steel blue bands. The peepers rise, subside, their pulse as rhythmic as wind-borne rain. *How do you cast on? Oh yes.* Absorbed, she bends forward. One loop, slip it over, extend the yarn with a finger. Granny taught her to knit. Patiently, as if rediscovering the mechanics of what she did without thought, she would unravel Kate's ungainly stitches, stopping at the flawed place where there was a purl instead of a knit. Or a gap. She'd always go back. It surprised Kate, for Granny was never critical. Never corrected her grammar. Never refused her a third helping or shushed her at table. Yet in this matter of knitting, where one knot supported the next, she unravelled perfect stitches to reach the place where the continuity was broken. One quiet, small stitch she'd make, and then she'd pass her warped fingers, twisted by arthritis, over the wool. "There now," she'd say peacefully. She'd hand the needles back to Kate, who sat cross-legged, with her tomboy's hands arranged into the dancer's arrested gesture, scooping with her little finger the yarn that unrolled seemingly endlessly from the bulky ball. She made one small awkward loop. And then another.

Now Kate switches on a light. She sits in the rocking chair, with one leg folded beneath her. It's been over a month now since the accident. People phone her, aware that this is no longer a time to leave her alone. Caroline brings bath salts and forced daffodils in a flowerpot. May steers Kate towards spring and new plans. They speak of the returning mergansers, the flocks of Canada geese, the bank swallows scooping insects from the river's surface, the yellow-rumped warblers. Of muskrats, owls and fiddleheads. May shows Kate her yoga stretches, urges her to join a coalition to preserve the marsh. Kate feels, as she begins a sock for Liam, how May's blue eyes watch her, even now, as if her concern drifts in the room along with the darkness that settles like blown sand.

She makes one loop, and then another. Connected, Kate thinks. Knit two, purl one. She lays a piece of blue yarn against the small cuff of dark grey. Considers. *Yes, blend the colours.* She breaks off the grey yarn, begins with blue. *Connected. Like these colours.* Maybe, she thinks, what we call happiness, contentment, is when all the separate parts of a world are connected. Strawberry pie and a child who died in 1906. Green grapes and a spinning wheel. Dead people and living people. Surging together like water droplets making a river, like rivers making a sea, like clouds carrying rain. Last summer, seeking the place she ought to be, the house had felt like a collection of objects, devoid of spirit. *Yet now,* she realizes, laying down the knitting and listening to the peepers, *I'm being gathered.* She feels a stab of fear, sensing this. *Tom. Tom. Life takes me on; I'm travelling away from you. You spin like a windblown feather.* Kate puts a hand to her mouth. The room quivers, floats on a bed of thick tears. Or is it she who floats? She lifts the sock and feels in her own hands an ancient gesture of faith. Of patience. Small loops. Linking her both to past and future. She considers how some things fall away.

Some concerns. Gregory's death connected her to his daughter, Janie. Janie and Christy now phone each other. Soon they will come here, to this place where they remember childhood. *I open my hands and release the scratched plans, the drafts of my future.* Gregory is like the breeze that disperses the foxglove seeds. Friendship blooms from death. Kate feels threads looping her to the moment. *Where is Tom?* It is a thought that has never left her since the moment of his death, and yet it is like a seed whose roots snake and grasp, whose shell breaks from the pressure of life. Not in his studio. Not in this house. Not in his paintings. *He's here, only as long as I allow myself to feel the relationship between the canoe and the swing, the birds and the rocking chair.*

And she thinks, suddenly, of how on just such a peeper-rung evening she spent a night alone, without her sister, at Shepton. In the dusk, the head and footboards of the sleigh bed curved like black waves. She heard Granny come up the stairs on her lame leg. *Step* step, *step* step. She came into the room and pulled the heavy cotton sheet and a thin quilt up to Kate's chin. The bed linens smelled of lavender and dried rose petals. Feather quills pricked through the pillowcase. Kate gazed sleepily at Granny, who laid her palms together and whispered a prayer. After Granny tiptoed away, Kate watched dusk gather light from the room like fingers sweeping through cobwebs. She listened to the grandfather clock ticking so slowly that there seemed to be a hesitation at the end of each swing. *Tick.* Tock. *Tick.* Tock. Would it continue? She lay flat on her back, small in the massive bed, with the folded sheet just under her chin, and did not feel as if she were in a strange room but that the night-rustle of the trees, the ticking of the clock, the village houses in the darkness and the musty smell of chests and quilts and ancient woollens grew from her like wings, took her floating into sleep.

Now, in a Canadian spring, Kate leans into the circle of light, sliding stitches down a steel needle, and imagines the same evening from Hetty's perspective. How, after she'd put her granddaughter to bed, Hetty went down the stairs, gripping the smooth banister that was as wide as her spread hand. Summer dusk gathered the house. Floors gleamed with remnants of light. The rooms were motionless. Hetty could see everything—couches, armchairs, the portraits on the wall—but their forms were softened, there was a silvery sheen along their contours. It was as if the house itself was in the process of falling asleep, while outside the night awakened. Through the open windows came the dark syncopation of cicadas, tree frogs, crickets. She crossed the parlour. Through the long windows, she could see Giles sitting in a wicker chair on the porch. She pushed open the screen door. He sat with one leg bent, ankle resting on knee. The porch columns were still pale in the dusky light. Trees and bushes were darker darknesses. She held the arms of a rocking chair, thrust one foot forward and lowered herself carefully. He reached over and patted her arm. "Katie's tucked in?" "Fast asleep," Hetty said fondly, not doubting for an instant that this was the case. She pushed with her foot. Her chair made a rubbling sound as the rockers, no longer evenly curved, rolled forward, settled back. They did not discuss politics nor ponder the future, but sat absorbing the day's end on Giles' mother's porch, now theirs. Giles was sixty-five years old. Hetty turned seventy in May. She folded her hands. They'd sit here until nine-thirty, when they'd begin to feel drowsy. She rocked, gazing across the lawn, where fireflies blinked on and off, moved invisibly, reappeared. At the end of the porch was a trellis covered with a froth of York and Lancaster roses. They were mottled, pink and white. Their scent was frailer now than it was in the heat of noon, when the roses opened so fully that their petals detached and made a shawl over the grass that Katie scooped into a berry box.

They heard a fox barking. It made a high yipping, sharper and clearer than a dog's. "Up in the hayfield," Giles said, as Hetty stopped rocking and cupped her ear. They rented out the big field; the first cutting had been made, and the grass was knee-high again. "That was a good pie," Giles said, comfortably, in his rumbly voice. Hetty's voice was whispery—people leaned forward to hear her. "Katie helped me make it," she said. Well, she didn't really, come to think of it, Hetty amended in her mind. But *some*times she does. So she might as well say she did. No, today Katie was doing something outside the window. Digging, or banging with rocks. Hetty had looked out the window, and her eyes had travelled across the driveway to Sunny Hill. She had named the house in an outburst of contentment. "Sunshine" was her word for elements of happiness: the solid bodies of children, their fat fingers wandering over pictures of rabbits in vests; cold apples, the beading of their burst cells when sliced; fingertips in lard and flour; creaky floorboards over which she might pass the straw of a broom and then stand watching sunlight or listening to the sound of her sons' voices or the rumbling crump of summer thunder. This morning, Hetty had gazed over at her beloved Sunny Hill and then called to Katie through the screen. Oh, *that's* what she was doing: mashing barberries. Making barberry and dirt pie. She'd seen her granddaughter scramble up. *Granddaughters,* after never having had a little girl. She bought them dresses for Christmas, red ones with lace and satin buttons. Most of all, though, she loved to feed them. Floury dumplings in chicken gravy. Chocolate pie with whipped cream. Mashed potatoes with enormous chunks of butter. So when Giles had told her, six years ago, that he'd been thinking they themselves would have to move over into

Shepton since none of their sons seemed to want the place, she'd sat quietly, thinking about cooking. She could not work in the big Shepton kitchen, where she felt as lost as she had on the day they'd moved into the house on Roselawn Street. She couldn't be shadowed by the spirits of cooks and maids. One room, at least, must be entirely theirs, the shape of themselves they had discovered in Sunny Hill's brambly backyard and overgrown fields. So she had asked Giles for a small kitchen.

And, oh, she did love that little room, she'd thought this morning, turning from the window after calling Katie, wiping her hands on her apron and sliding one hand with pleasure over the stove's sleek surface. Once it had been the cook's bedroom. Now, all around the walls were new wooden cabinets painted grey, countertops, a gas stove, a gleaming sink, a refrigerator. Under the windows that overlooked the barberry bushes was a low couch where Giles could lie comfortably when he came in for a midmorning coffee, his head propped on a large pillow with a flower-print covering. It was safe, cozy, a place where no one could ever be far from anyone else. Children's legs swung as they sat on the chairs of a small table pushed against a wall. Giles, on the couch, was three steps away.

She'd heard Katie open the door of the glassed-in porch; Giles would be coming, too, and she had hurried to fill a saucepan with water, scratch a match, hold its flame to the dependable hiss of gas. Katie and Giles had come in, then they'd all sat for a while. Katie, with sugar on her face. Giles, lying on the couch with fingers intertwined behind his propped head, looking so pleased with his granddaughter's pleasure. Honey from his hives, lettuce from his garden. Hetty had observed his pleasure and thought how Shepton was truly his own home, perhaps more so than Sunny Hill had been. Hadn't he shown Jonnie his grape arbour, so very long ago?

He'd given her a sketch of it, which she'd painted in water-colours. Hetty had found it, recently, pressed between the black pages of a photograph album. Lavish bunches of purple grapes spilled from pointillistic leaves, just what, in fact, it had become. He'd built the stone wall beneath the maples, dug gardens, pruned pear and apple trees, shot woodchucks from his bedroom window, harvested hay in the upper field. Unlike his own sons, he'd spent his childhood summers sleeping on Shepton's rope-mattress beds; he'd drifted off to sleep breathing Shepton's particular spice.

Hetty had poured herself coffee, sat at the kitchen table. Her hip had begun to ache; she had shooting pains in her fingers from arthritis. "Let me help you," Katie had said. What was it? Oh, yes, Hetty had been fumbling at the hairnet that she tucked round her bun. Her fingertips were stiff, and the hairnet was fine as sewing thread. Her granddaughters loved to watch when she let her hair down at night. She let them brush it. Sometimes Giles brushed it, so tenderly, as if it must be coaxed through the bristles lest it separate like unspun wool. Katie's little fingers had tiptoed through her hair, poked the net back in place, made her sleepy.

After Giles had gone back to the garden and Katie had slipped away somewhere, she had assembled her strawberry pie, flattened the crust with the back of a fork and slid it into the oven. The house, at midmorning on this July day, had been filled with the breath of summer borne by cool breezes that danced in through all the doors and windows, came brushing over the sea of myrtle and the stone terrace, rose from the cool soil beneath syringa and honeysuckle. She had untied her apron. This house was cooler than Sunny Hill. She'd walked down the hall into the front parlour, her heels clicking on the wood floor. The large rooms amplified the sound of rustling leaves and the ticking of the clocks. She'd heard the scrape of a door upstairs. Katie, going up into the attic. She'd sat on the edge of the parlour couch with her hands laid loosely in her lap, one cradling the other. She was facing the portrait of Lilian's mother, Delia. The room had smelled of a summer's morning—roses, cut grass, sun-warmed leaves—and, at the same time, of the mustiness of age. She had looked at the things in this room, which she would never feel were hers. Plum-coloured Persian carpets. An ebony clock, an epergne of chalk-ware fruit, a pair of French porcelain dogs. Victorian lace antimacassars. A long mirror, holding in its tarnished glass a reflection of the horsehair couch and a series of hand-coloured prints of Versailles. The bookshelf was filled with brown books whose leather spines were flaky as old bark. On a side table, like an ornament, was a satin pincushion pierced with black-headed pins; next to it lay a pair of swan-shaped scissors. In the umbrella stand were feather dusters, bone-handled walking sticks, parasols. On the pianoforte was music that Lilian had once sung, the flute that had belonged to her father.

Hetty wondered what war had done to her boys, since when they returned, they wanted houses with empty rooms. They hinted, when offered Shepton either as a year-round home or for a summer place, that the place felt more like a burden than a treasure. Their eyes skimmed sideways whenever the subject was raised. *The sweet boys.* They didn't want to disappoint their parents. So Hetty and Giles packed up their dear, simple Sunny Hill. It had been so easy to dismantle; it took only a few days to move out of the place they'd spent summers in for thirty years. Hetty had brought the contents of her Sunny Hill kitchen over to Shepton in two or three cardboard cartons. All she needed was down the hall in the new kitchen, or in a few bushel baskets in the glassed-in porch, or in the drawers of a bureau in the downstairs bedroom. They'd left behind all the Sunny Hill furniture since they were not displacing anything. "Mother would want . . . Mother loved . . ." Giles reminded his family in his reasonable, courtroom voice. He said that Lilian had wanted Shepton kept just as she had left it. So they had hardly moved a thing. They picked up the continuum of Lilian's desires like the train of her skirt.

It was all familiar to Hetty, not only their obedience to Lilian's behests, but the way in which a wife accepted her husband's decisions. She remembered helping her own mother take down curtains, roll teacups and china plates in newspaper and scrub empty kitchen drawers with baking soda as the family followed Dr. Baker from parish to parish. For Hetty's part, she did not harbour regrets. Sunny Hill hung in her mind like the bedroom she'd shared with Jonnie; like her own mother's kitchen with its dark cupboards and potted geraniums; like the annex at Roselawn Street with its view over Lilian's formal gardens. She remembered places only as settings for the people who had sat in their chairs, drunk from their teacups. She remembered not the texture of rooms but the texture of family. These feelings were so vivid that sometimes she forgot who was dead and referred to them in the present tense. When you were seventy years old, life bent up around you like a vine, people hung like bright blossoms. She didn't bother about sequence, just as she no longer cared about things. She'd forgotten where Jonnie's mandolin was, or her wooden paintbox. But on this hot morning in her husband's family homestead, as she sat gazing at Delia's portrait, she had heard the sound of her sister's voice and imagined her face lifting with delight. What could she be looking at? A pear in the soft light of a rainy day. Sheen of light on black leather boots. Jonnie's hands would lift, she would insist that they share her wonder. Then Hetty had smelled the sweet burnt-sugar smell of strawberry pie. She'd felt the floating bliss of sudden happiness. She'd gotten to her feet and hurried back down the hall to the kitchen. The cicadas were beginning their noonday searing buzz, rising to a peak of intensity, then abruptly ceasing before beginning all over again.

Kate puts down the spiky triangle of needles and wool, stands, stretches and goes to the door. She breathes deeply of the sharp spring air. It's dark now; she can't see the river or the sky, only blackness stirring with the fluid press of life. Children, she's thinking, don't ask or think about the past. For children, the past is yesterday, and anything farther back—a few weeks, a month—seems unreal, wedged at an odd angle in the brain, like a dream. She closes the door, pulls the cord of an overhead light, plugs in the tea kettle. She opens Granny's tea caddy and scoops two teaspoons of fragrant, crunchy leaves into a teapot. She stands holding the handle of the kettle as its water begins to stir. She is staring at her reflection in the window over the sink, but doesn't see it. She's absorbing the fact that her grandparents never wanted to live at Shepton and only stayed there for a few years, maybe ten. Yet it was the span of her childhood, and for all of Kate's life, until now, Shepton has been the shape of her grandparents' life and of her own child's world: dense, generous, perfect as the heart of a lily.

The kettle begins an agitated whistling. She fills the teapot, sets it on a table next to the rocking chair. She pours a bit of milk into a stoneware mug, chipped at the rim, and returns to her chair and knitting, waiting for the tea to steep. *Odd.* She doesn't have to worry about the abrasive ring of the telephone. Gregory is not going to call. All winter, he's spiked her, the way a cat works at a mouse hidden beneath a couch. Prising, making small effective jabs. His attention both irritated and quickened her, but now his absence changes the texture of her life.

What a strange thing memory is, Kate thinks, as she pours the tea, watching light twist in the amber ribbon. It seems that there are two kinds of memory. There are pictures that stand alone, disconnected, like torn scraps from a larger picture. *Tom in the funeral parlour. My feet, when I was three or four, stepping up the wide stones. The blades of the windmill, turning.* But there's another kind of memory, the stories that run within her like the river and feel close, as if time is a circle and she can loop around it and slide into events that haven't yet ended. And they are like sequences of music, each with its own distinct quality. There's the sequence just past, a band of time that begins with the sight of Gregory at Mary's Point, the day she went to watch the sandpipers, and ends with his dead body. It bulks, this memory, like a piece of driftwood. She will have to step over it to return to an earlier time, when she was alone, freshly acquainted with grief. Now she feels herself spinning forward into a new sequence in which she feels loose, liable to tears or laughter, disintegrating in an easy way that feels more like opening than falling apart.

She picks up her knitting, begins again. *Knit two, purl one.* She enters the ongoing stream of the past. Tom comes into the kitchen smelling of oils and varnish, black hair grey-flecked. He washes his hands in the sink, talking agitatedly. *But even as I imagine this, he's gone and I'm in my quiet house, knowing he will never return.*

Soon she'll roll forward into yet another epoch that will eventually run through her mind and will have a different quality from this one. Like light. Endlessly shading the day, tempering its moods. Say, for example, when Christy and Jane come. In a few weeks. How good, she thinks, that they've been in touch again. Christy called Jane when she heard of Gregory's death. They've agreed to meet at Kate's and go together to pack up Gregory's belongings. Nothing, Kate thinks, is permanent except change. Life is like the garden, growing with its own blind vigour. The red Maltese cross that's always stood behind the veronica disappears, while a bed of foxglove shoots up beneath the apple tree.

She remembers herself, last summer, just before autumn. Hunting through her books, reading Isak Dinesen. "Here I am," Dinesen wrote, "where I ought to be." And when Dinesen arrived at that place, Kate remembers, she felt a "lightness of heart." *Where ought I to be?* Life flickers past like light on a wall. But can't there be one shape that stays the same? Something you can count on? Like a boat, strong-sided. Whose curved sides you grip, whose ribs cradle you. That you can ride through the changing light.

20. Summer Wind

KATE WAKES. THERE'S NO SINGLE MOMENT. FIRST there's birdsong and sunshine. Cool air that smells of white lilacs, touching her face. The window, wide open. Then the dark stab that slides into her heart every morning, like a weight anchoring a loose sheet of paper. Tom. Not in bed next to her. Her mind skips beyond these first perceptions. The girls. Left a few days ago. Kate rolls onto her side, grasps the tissuey curtains of sleep, seeks the dream from which she's awakened. *Shepton. It has been closed for months. We're all there, a family reunion. The aunts and uncles are very old. We troop through the dark, grey, dusty rooms. Nothing has changed; the place has been waiting for us. One of the aunts cradles a baby in her arms. It glows like a freshly laid egg. Colour begins to return to the rooms as we walk through them. The entire family is eager; we stumble against one another, pressing from room to room. In the dream, I think: It's okay to keep this house in storage merely so we can return and walk through its rooms. This is something that everyone needs. It is a feeling we all share, all humans, the need for such a place.* She opens her eyes. Mr. Winkles stalks across the hall, stands on the threshold of her bedroom with shining whiskers. He meows, aggrieved. She pats the blanket;

he jumps up. Kate slides into a sitting position against the headboard, draws up her knees. There are her jeans, on the braided rug. Her leather clogs, kicked sideways. T-shirt, draped over the wicker laundry basket. She leans over and buries her face in the cat's fur, smiling, remembering her trip to Grand Manan with Christy and Jane, how she and the girls sat around a campfire beneath a starry sky spiked by the tips of spruce trees, while from far below, in the gulf of darkness, came the explosive, gentle breath of whales.

Every window in the house is wide open. She throws back the blanket, pulls on jeans and an oversized sweatshirt, scuffs into clogs, runs fingers through her hair. Mr. Winkles precedes her down the stairs. The kitchen is flooded with sunlight. She flips the switch of the coffee maker and goes onto the porch.

There are dew-blackened clots of cut grass on the lawn. The leaves of the riverside trees ripple, tossing sunlight. She can see that someone is putting up the sail of a boat; there's a rattling, a sudden crack of wind in canvas. The sail appears, bunched, travels upwards, resolves into a triangle. It flaps, snaps, the ropes slap. She hears the shearing cry of an osprey: *kyew kyew kyew.* The sound trails like a plume of smoke, marking the speed of its flight. She hears the sound of tires on the bridge. Voices on the boat. She goes back into the kitchen, pours coffee, returns to the porch and sits in the rocking chair that used to be Tom's. Or they called it Tom's. Like sleeping on a certain side of the bed. He liked to be on the left-hand side of the wicker table in case he needed to sketch or scribble. She glances at the thermometer. It's already twenty in the shade.

Behind her, the house is still animated by Christy and Jane's visit. Things are disarranged. Jane stripped her bed, stuffed her sheets into a pillowcase; Christy made hers, loosely. Shells and rocks are strewn across the kitchen table. A gannet feather is propped on the windowsill. The girls picked wildflowers along the river path, put them in a Mason jar: daisies, red clover, vetch, buttercups.

The house seems larger in summer. Storms brood and darken the face of the river, warm winds snatch curtains, over-turn vases. Wind blows through the house, crickets hop over thresholds, rose petals fall from bouquets, sheets are sun-baked. She and Tom used to eat every meal outside. Breakfast, here. Barefoot. Lunch on the stone steps. Wind caressing skin, beer, a wedge of lime. So begins another summer, Kate thinks. And her energy seems separate from herself, something that has arrived like an unexpected or unbidden gift. She feels an unfocused restlessness, heralding change.

She stands. Steam rises from her coffee. She walks back into the kitchen and leans in the doorway of the living room. She's decided to donate most of the contents of the hatboxes to the American Antiquarian Society. Someone else will finally read, collate and preserve the repository of family letters that do, indeed, date back to the 1700s. She has lifted tiny black notebooks, deeds, legal documents and bundles of letters from box after box, and realized, dismayed, that they represent a genealogical tangle she is unwilling to unravel. She phoned her sister and her parents, informing them of this decision. No one minds. Last week she spoke to a curator at the society; they would be more than pleased, he said, to assess the collection. In two days, she's driving down to Massachusetts. Before Jane and Christy came, she removed all the papers having to do with her grandparents: Jonnie and Giles' letters, the diaries, anything relating to Hetty, the Bakers, Ellen, Charles and Lilian. These she carefully arranged in labelled bundles that she tied with string. The papers fit into two hatboxes, which she slid under her bed. She emptied the other papers into sturdy liquor store cartons, taped them shut for the trip back to New England. She carried the empty hatboxes up to the attic and stacked them beside a window, where dust and river light would fall on them.

She leans her temple against the door. Sun angles across her shoulder blades. She feels an unfamiliar geometry within herself: a square feeling, trim-sided and strong as the cardboard boxes. Some things, she thinks, should be kept. And others should not. One night during Christy's visit, they sat on the living-room floor, and she showed her daughter the diaries, the letters. Christy sat cross-legged, holding the diaries in her tanned, capable hands. "My great-grandfather? The one who lived in the big house you're always telling me about? His fiancée died? Oh, the poor man. How do you think the sister felt? Being his second choice?" And Kate began to tell her the story. These letters will live under her bed since they are connected to her own memory. She can recall the colour of her grandfather's eyes and the sound of his voice. She will tell Christy and Liam, who, when their children become curious, will pass the story on to them. And so these stories can be kept with this house that is disarranged by summer winds and by her own changing needs. Her house, she thinks, is Liam and Christy's Shepton. *Someday I'll say to them that they may do with it what they will. My God. I've decided to stay.*

She goes into the kitchen, breaks two eggs into a bowl, drops a sliver of butter into a frying pan. Puts one hand on a loaf of bakery bread and slices with a serrated knife. The baby, she's thinking. In the dream. What does it represent?

She carries a plate of scrambled eggs onto the porch. The boat's sail is taut; it leans into the wind and slides silently past the treetops. Kate thinks about the dream. The baby was luminous, gentled her aunt's tired face, gave her radiance. The baby, Kate muses, must represent memory. For memory, like a newborn child, confers eternity. *The act of remembering, untainted by longing, takes us to the place of an eternal present*

where everything is always beginning. It's my life with Tom. It's
Shepton. It's my past that I'm bearing, precious as any newborn
creature, into my future.

She pushes her plate aside, leans her elbows on the wicker
table. Remembers how Shepton, after her grandparents'
deaths, became like a boat abandoned at a mooring. No one
came except Kate's father, who prowled around it occasionally, sniffing out its leaks, its loosening storm windows, its hanging gutters. He made cursory repairs, devised stop-gaps. In
autumn, it drifted, obscured in mist, rising from its stone
walls, flanked by leaf-shrouded lawns, a house waiting for its
people. Nothing was touched. Kate, age twelve, walked on the
porch, made blinders with her hands, peering in the long windows. Two layers of glass made the interior seem inaccessible,
another world, like looking through water into a tidal pool. There
was the sideboard, the horsehair couch, the dining table.
There was Grampa Giles' misshapen brown chair. There was
the hearth broom, leaning by the fireplace. There were the
marriage portraits of Lilian's parents: Delia, her mother, who
held a long chain with one little finger raised, and Henry, her
father, the man with troubled eyes who rested a long-fingered
white hand on his starched shirt front as if quieting a racing
heart. They stared into eternity, their painted eyes wise and sad
as the eyes of horses. The sun struck points of light from the
crystal candlesticks. A porcelain bowl on the sideboard held no
fruit. Kate saw its dust and remembered filling it with pears
and grapes; she'd taken them out, put them in again. Fussing,
child-important. Making it beautiful to show Granny.

Shepton's gardens went wild. Climbing roses, unpruned,
grew top-heavy and fell from trellises. Trellises rotted around
nails, slipped sideways. In the perennial beds, primroses were
crowded by dandelions; the columbine vanished and was
replaced by great clumps of daisies. Vestiges of Korean

chrysanthemums straggled through goldenrod. Wild mint and forget-me-not spread into the lawn. Poison ivy grew up the posts of the grape arbour, snaked round the wrist-thick grape vines. The strawberries vanished, overtaken by clover. Flocks of cedar waxwings stripped the raspberry canes of their berries. On the terraced lawn beneath the sugar maples, the grass turned to moss. In October the lawns were calf-deep in warm leaves, and Kate and her friends buried themselves beneath gigantic leaf piles. November wind whisked and spun the leaves into drifts that settled around the foundations of the house, lay in soggy piles against the barns, gathered along the stone wall. Apple trees in the orchard crouched like ancient spiders, their branches grey, twiggy, arthritic. Dead branches lay in the wispy red-top grass. Deer roamed unhindered, feasting on drops. The summer-house roof began to rot under an accumulation of leathery leaves. The chicken-wire fence around the tennis court sagged and fell; the court was pocked with the prints of horse hooves.

Still, the house was ready for occupancy. Chests were filled with sheets and quilts. The beds were made. There was pink soap on the sinks. Facecloths hung from hooks. The attic was just as she and her cousins had left it the summer before Grampa Giles died: the spinning wheels, stopped where they'd spun down, the humped lids of chests left open. Mice, scuttling. Browsing. Making nests from hand-spun woollens or the edges of leghorn hats, nibbling the flourished signatures of parchment envelopes. Kate thought the place was waiting for her to grow up.

Then, six years later, it was a day of wind and bright April sunshine. Kate was eighteen, and had come from college on the bus. She slipped into the house while her parents and aunts and uncles were lingering outside, leaning on the warm hoods of their cars beneath the pine trees. There was almost no sound inside the house. The pendulum of the grandfather clock hung still. With no furnace rumbling, no refrigerator humming, no clocks ticking, the house was like a shed or a barn, a hollow place that amplified the throaty wind. She heard the sap-limber branches of the maple trees bounce, wind-seized. Red-tasselled buds were like tiny brushes, stroking the sky. Their shadows danced across the plaster walls. She went into the living room. She wanted to place it in her mind's eye. The portraits. The ebony clock. The hearth broom, its wooden handle touching blackened brick. Always here, the swan scissors. Just here. And the pincushion. She might see these things again, but never in this configuration as familiar as her own body. She went into the front hall and started up the stairs, running her hand over the broad, smooth banister. She stepped over the worn threshold of the southeast bedroom door and sat on the mahogany sleigh bed. Sun wavered across the floorboards, was broken by the seamed fractures in a small stone hearth. Kate slipped sideways, drew her legs up on the patchwork quilt, buried her face in the feather-bristled pillows. There it was, Kate thought. The troubling smell. It had always troubled her. It was the smell of obligation, loss, remembrance, love. It was the smell of fore-shadowed pain, of time that no one could arrest. On and on, the generations had breathed the same intensifying scent of sweetness and sorrow. In a rocking horse were the vanished children; in lace and crinoline, the vanished young women. In top hats and collars and leather boots were the vanished young men. In a flute were tender fingers. In jam jars and rolling pins were vanished feasts and fleeting, bountiful summers. Here in this house was the evidence of love. For they saved everything, Kate thought, face buried in the prickly feather pillow. They could not bear to part with anything a loved person's fingers had touched.

Kate heard the voices of her parents, aunts and uncles. Now they were in the downstairs back kitchen, stamping their feet. They were going to walk through Shepton room by room, deciding who should have what, what should be given to museums, what, if anything, should be sold. They were remarkably equable, Kate thought. It was Granny's legacy of sweetness coming through. And Grampa Giles' sense of justice. "Take what you want," her uncle Oliver had said to her, easily. "Take anything you want. We'll take it away if we don't think you should have it." She thought of Uncle Oliver, the surgeon, wearing fairy wings at a family charade party, pretending to be a butterfly and making swimming motions with his hands, staring owlishly from behind rimless spectacles.

She could hear that they'd reached the living room. She went down the narrow hall. She stepped into the men's bathroom, opened the door to the attic and went quietly up the steep stairs. Plaster dust made the treads gritty. It was cold. There were dead flies on the floor. The tossing branches, seen through the dusty windows, seemed a long way away. She sat on the floor with her arms around her legs and listened to the attic's silence, magnified by the remote roar of wind. She'd made a collection of Granny's things as soon as she came into the house. Down by the back door was a cardboard box filled with Granny's rolling pin, her bulb trowel, her potato masher, her applesauce cone and wooden pestle. A little paring knife and a grey metal cracker tin. But when she'd looked into the box, she'd realized that Granny was not there. It was just a collection of things. Like this house. A collection of things that once disarranged loses its magic. Kate thought of how her grandparents adored her, as only grandparents can. What was left of them? She'd thought it was this house, with its barns, its hayfields and gardens, the maple trees and beds of myrtle, the wide stone steps. A place where every object bore a story:

the dresses in the attic, the carriages in the barns, the stereop-ticons, the feathered hats. A place echoing with the sound of church bells, the ticking of the grandfather clock. But they're not here, Kate told herself. Granny and Grampa Giles are not *in* these things. They're not *in* this house. It's just a house. It's just an arrangement of things. She laid her cheek on her knees, clasped her legs in their bell-bottom jeans. She summoned a long memory, gathered it into her heart. *Remember.* The way this place was.

Kate carries her breakfast dishes to the kitchen and washes up. She scribbles a list: laundry, get U.S. cash, find passport.

She's given herself a two-week break before the start-up of her summer piano students. She goes into the living room. There, on the table. The pile of new music. Her heart races, slightly, a frisson of nerves edged with excitement. She's begun to say yes. "Yes, I'd like to do that . . ." She's agreed to be the accompanist for a twenty-voice choral group in Saint John. She shuffles through the music, carries a score to the piano. She begins playing "Dies Irae" from Mozart's *Requiem.* The notes fill the empty house, travel out the open windows, lilt on the warm summer air.

When she's finished playing, she goes outside and sits on the wooden bench beneath the apple tree. She's expecting May. She can smell the damp soil, cooled by the dense bed of violets, spotted-leaved lungwort, white-veined hostas. A breeze ripples the river. She feels sun on her face, and smiles. *This is the place where the garden began.*

Acknowledgments

Thanks to the institutions that helped with finances and facilities: The Canada Council for the Arts, for its assistance from Grants for Professional Writers Creative Writing Program; The Banff Centre for the Arts and the dedicated staff at the Leighton Artist's Colony, Banff, Alberta; Kings Landing Historical Settlement, Kings Landing, New Brunswick; the American Antiquarian Society, Worcester, Massachusetts; the Oliver Ellsworth Homestead, "Elmwood," Windsor, Connecticut.

Thanks to those who answered odd questions: Forest Ranger Jack Mackay, RCMP Corporal Wayne Foran, RCMP Constable Alan Kincaide, RCMP Constable Jacques Cloutier, Dr. Suleiman Khedheri, Dr. Rolf Sers, Dr. Phyllis Sers, Dr. David McMillan, Tracey Dean, Ed Eustace, Cheryl Diotte, Art Goold, Mark Connell, Mitchell Long, Kevin McCaig, Bob Osborne, Tyrrell Pearson, Kathy Hooper, Mark Woolsey.

Thanks to Grant and Kate Kerr, for Gregory's house; and to Taco Pica, for the perfect setting.

Thanks to early supporters of the concept and readers of the drafts: Molly Peacock, Mary Wood, Peg and Pat Powning, Cathic Davis, Mark and Beverly Davis.

Acknowledgments

Thanks to my family, especially Roger Davis and Frannie Hassinger Everhart, for tape recordings and written memories.

Thanks, with deepest gratitude, to Jim and Janet Robertson, for their years of transcribing the family papers, for their book *All Our Yesterdays,* for generous loans of materials and transcriptions, for astute reading of the manuscript, for friendship and encouragement.

Thanks to those who have inspired me: in memoriam to Judy Maddocks, and most especially to Anne MacNeil, whose courage, generosity and positive energy have helped so many.

Thanks, beyond words, to my agent Jackie Kaiser, whose encouragement, unwavering belief, keen vision and warm friendship carried me through the long process of finding this novel.

Thanks to the marvellous team at Knopf Canada—especially Scott Richardson, freelancer Sue Sumeraj, and Scott Sellers—and to my editor, Diane Martin, whose enthusiasm, wise guidance and careful touch has shaped, honed and immeasurably enriched this book.

Thank you, Jake, Sara and granddaughters Maeve and Bridget—my own dear family—for your love and respect.

Thanks to my parents, Wendell and Alison Davis, for reading many of the drafts, and for letting me rummage in the treasure chests of your memories as well as in the dusty boxes of your barn. To my father, for entrusting me with your parents' most tender truths; to my mother, for proofreading the final draft, and for being the first to realize the hatboxes' potential. For your enthusiasm, excitement and faith, my deepest gratitude and love. This book would not have been possible without you.

And to my husband, Peter, whose imagined absence as I lived in Kate's mind made me treasure our companionship more deeply—thank you for your ideas and insights, your attentive listening and careful proofreading, and your steadfast love.

BETH POWNING is the author of *Seeds of Another Summer: Finding the Spirit of Home in Nature* and *Shadow Child: An Apprenticeship in Love and Loss*. She lives in Sussex, New Brunswick, with her husband, the artist Peter Powning.

A NOTE ABOUT THE TYPE

The body of *The Hatbox Letters* has been set in Adobe Garamond. Designed for the Adobe Corporation by Robert Slimbach, the fonts are based on types first cut by Claude Garamond (c.1480-1561). Garamond is believed to have followed classic Venetian type models, although he did introduce a number of important differences. Garamond gave his characters a sense of movement and elegance that ultimately won him an international reputation and the patronage of Frances I of France.